Praise for
Elinor Lipman's
ISABEL'S BED

"Lipman has a remarkable ear for the way certain women talk. . . . Her voice is natural and spontaneous and her observations have the authenticity of everyday life. . . . *ISABEL'S BED* is a very funny story."

—Diane White, *The Boston Globe*

"Lipman's colorful characters come alive. . . . her writing seems both spare and rich. . . . *ISABEL'S BED* is a story that moves. And Lipman's characters invite you right along. The book feels like going on a long car ride with a friend who regales you the entire way with funny stories about her childhood, lovers, and friends you have in common. . . . funny and ultimately touching."

—Maureen Conlan, *Cincinnati Post*

"This confection of a novel will amuse you, touch your heart, and leave you gasping with surprise and pleasure. . . . When every startling, balmy bit of plot has been successfully tucked into place, your only regret will be that there is no more."

—J.C. Martin, *The Arizona Daily Star*

"Lipman's insights into life and people are extraordinary. . . . This is storytelling that is imaginative and genuinely funny, but at the same time you feel a kinship with each and every character. . . . Lipman has the gift of making the reader feel good."

—Milton Bass, *The Berkshire Eagle*

A LITERARY GUILD SELECTION

Also by Elinor Lipman

The Way Men Act
Then She Found Me
Into Love and Out Again

Isabel's Bed

A Novel

Elinor Lipman

POCKET BOOKS

New York   London   Toronto   Sydney   Tokyo   Singapore

"The Next Poem" copyright © 1991 by Dana Gioia. Reprinted from *The Gods of Winter* with the permission of Graywolf Press, Saint Paul, Minnesota.

POCKET BOOKS, a division of Simon & Schuster Inc.
1230 Avenue of the Americas, New York, NY 10020

ISBN: 0-671-88161-2

First Pocket Books paperback printing August 1996

10 9 8 7 6 5 4 3 2 1

POCKET and colophon are registered trademarks of Simon & Schuster Inc.

Front cover illustration by Pol Turgeon

Printed in the U.S.A.

*This book is dedicated to my
first editor, Stacy Schiff—enduring reader
and remarkable friend.*

ACKNOWLEDGMENTS

I have been unusually blessed in the editorial department, as anyone who knows Jane Rosenman will attest. I am grateful also for the talents of Donna Lynne Ng of Pocket Editorial and Adam Rothberg of Pocket Publicity, a special pal who works on my books as if they were his own. Special thanks to my agent, Lizzie Grossman, who, among her other contributions, slipped me the ghostwriting idea.

My thanks to James C. Orenstein, Assistant District Attorney for Hampden County, Massachusetts, for his writerly eye and ear; Annick Porter, interior designer to the fictionally rich and budgetless; Christopher N. Otis, M.D., Director of Surgical Pathology at Baystate Medical Center; Chuck Stern, who is both an artist and a doughnut maker's son; and Steven Palat, bagel maven. I would also like to thank the audience at Bennington College which heard part of this story on the evening of July 8, 1993, and sent me home to finish it; and, once again, Arthur Edelstein, who taught me how to write in a workshop that bears no resemblance to Harriet's. None of this Truro tale would be possible without my two anchors, Bob and Ben Austin. My thanks and love.

How much better it seems now
than when it is finally written.

—Dana Gioia,
    "The Next Poem"

1

YOUR LIFE WILL BE YOUR OWN

 WINTER BEFORE LAST, a tea-leaf reader at a psychic fair looked into my cup and said she saw me living in a house with many beds and a big-mouth blonde. At the time it meant nothing to me. I was sharing a one-bedroom apartment in Manhattan with a balding, malcontent boyfriend of twelve years, who said we'd get married if I conceived his child or when he felt like it. Since I was looking for literary prophecies—that I'd write a best-seller or at least find an agent—and because my tea-leaf reader wore, in a room full of gauzy peasantwear, a knock-off Chanel suit, I moved on to another booth.

Six weeks later, Kenny took me out to dinner at an expensive chef-owned restaurant and told me he was ambivalent about us. I said what I'd been saving for such an occasion—that we were common-law spouses by now and he'd better get over his ambivalence.

"I met someone," he replied.

There went twelve years: my youth. In three months, he was married.

So at forty-one, feeling like eighty, I was looking for something—a job, a friend, a hiding place where I could live out my days—when I overheard a stranger on the subway confide to her seatmate, "There are no guarantees in this world, but chances are that people who take out ads in the *New York Review of Books* aren't idiots or crooks." I bought my first issue and read the personals for laughs, circling one or two that didn't ask for "pretty" or "vivacious" before my eyes wandered into "Share." And there it was, my answer, my job, my tea-leaf destiny:

Book in progress? While you're at it, why not share my Cape retreat? Gourmet kitchen, beach rights, wild blueberries. Considering lap pool. Roomy and peaceful: your life will be your own. Write me about your spectacular self. Room and board negotiable in exchange for services. Include writing sample. Box 8152.

"Harriet Mahoney," I heard between the lines, "your troubles are over. Box 8152 will cure everything that's been wrong with your life." I could see myself, a better me, at this Cape retreat: at my typewriter, sharing thoughts and kitchen privileges with a kindred soul, baking wild blueberries into muffins.

In the past, I would have signed up for a course on pouring my heart into a cover letter, but I figured even prophecies had expiring deadlines. I had to write the letter of my life, threading my frayed self through the eye of the employment needle into the Yes pile; to find the silver lining in the fact that I'd spent my thirties unofficially engaged to a spoiled child; to put a good face on my B.A. in English from a defunct women's college, my two unpublished novels, and a string of secretarial jobs where I had learned to clear the paper path in all makes of copying machines.

So I wrote that for twelve years I had successfully shared quarters with a challenging roommate, that I was intelligent, considerate, and neat. I sent a laser-printed chapter from my first novel, *American Apology,* along with its best rejection letter ("competently written, at times even affecting") and a short story that my writing group insisted *The New Yorker* should have taken.

Although dozens of people applied, people with Ph.D.s and hardcover contracts, it was my letter that Isabel Krug liked best. "I didn't want any big shots," she told me later. "No prima donnas. You sounded normal."

She liked the "secretary" part. She wanted someone to ghostwrite her story, and she figured if it were a simple matter of channeling her voice through someone else's fingertips, why not a blunt set that typed 105 words a minute?

Over the phone she asked without apology how old I was, if I'd been in jail, if I had AIDS or the HIV virus, if I'd be squeamish about male visitors, and if I drove a stick.

It wasn't a tone I could stand forever, but it was offering what I needed. Assuming I had beat out the others on the strength of my prose and my suddenly spectacular self, I accepted ecstatically. Without meeting Isabel Krug. Without asking who else lived in this Cape retreat. Without asking what her story was.

2
WORK IN PROGRESS

 KENNY HAD SAID he was sorry about the apartment but, God, this *thing,* this awesome, unqualified, brave new love was so huge that he needed all his closet and floor space. How soon, in other words, could I move out?

I dug in, slept on the sofa, snapped his head off with every word of relocation counseling. He produced the lease to remind me that my name was nowhere on it.

I said, "You can't evict me. I work for eleven lawyers."

He said, "Please don't make me change the locks."

To save face, I set a date and collected cartons. I demanded he reimburse me for everything we had purchased jointly, down to cleaning fluids, spices, potting soil, and bottles on which we'd paid deposits.

"What about going home?" Kenny tried. "That might give you some time and distance."

I said no. Not at my age; not to my parents, who'd take me in, all right, but in the spirit of weary pet owners collecting their repeat-offender dog from the pound.

"There's a trend," he said. "I wouldn't hesitate to live with my parents if circumstances dictated it."

"What about my work?"

"It's a job. You could get another one closer to them."

"I meant my writing. My new novel."

"Oh, that," he said.

I couldn't go home to my parents' house because I was secretly writing about them. After years of crafting stories about love between quiet people, the kind of love that small English movies celebrated, I had written a high-concept story about how my parents married each other twice. The night I read it, my classmates applauded. One person said, "Brava!" Someone else said she could see Eli Wallach playing the father.

"So what do we do with it?" asked our workshop leader.

"Send it out?" I asked.

"Eventually. Read me the last sentence again."

I did, fingering the beads around my neck the way I'd seen women authors at readings do: "Arthur set down the tray gently so the apple-scented tea wouldn't overwhelm its vessel, and, with ineffable sadness, departed Charlotte's lightless room."

I didn't look up, but heard the purrs of approval from the backs of the other writers' throats.

"Can you see it?" our leader asked. "In italics? A prologue? And then we turn the page to chapter one"—he had mimed this with a graceful turn of his wrist—"and read about Charlotte's and Arthur's lives leading up to this moment. How about that?"

I heard more approving murmurs all around me. I couldn't imagine writing one page past these six about my parents; couldn't imagine why people liked them more than Cecily Biggins or Maisie Trumbull or Emma Liversidge of my shopkeeper trilogy. But what a night! I jotted their comments in my margins for later savoring: "Has your usual clarity and optimism." "Best thing you've done." "The dishwasher scene is great!"

And this, unless I was dreaming: "Shimmers with potential."

Kenny owned A Decent Bagel, Inc., and considered himself a writer since he had composed the slogan "Baking the best bagels in TriBeCa." He used to evaluate my stories late in the creative process after they had been rejected by several magazines. "It's not terrible," he'd say—he who made bagels, not out of love but out of market research.

I tried to show him how a person can be constructive and positive in his criticism at the same time he's finding fault.

"But what if it stinks?"

"Where does it stink?" I cried. "Show me the lines that stink."

"'Jelly-bean toes,'" Kenny read. "Wouldn't that make the baby deformed? And here—why is the mother scrambling

7

egg substitutes? Why not real eggs? You don't give any reason."

It wasn't only what he said but how he said it: no delicacy, no credit for the good parts, no gradual approach to the bad. I said, gathering my pages to me, "Some people really liked this story."

"Sure," he sniffed. "And when it's their turn, you'll say nice things back."

"You can always find something nice to say, even in the worst stuff."

"But isn't it kinder in the long run to say, 'This really stinks. You'll never be a writer, so why don't you give up?' "

I'd say, "That's not our job. Sometimes a person writes for other reasons, personal reasons, and doesn't need outside validation."

"So why go to a workshop? Why not just write in the privacy of your bedroom and keep it to yourself?"

"Because," I said.

"Wouldn't you want to know if you had no talent?"

He didn't get it. I said yes, okay; I'd want to know.

Somewhere along the course of this downward spiral, he met Amy, a customer. Twenty-six years old. It started with a sesame bagel every day on her way to her job leasing lofts to artist-entrepreneurs. One macho morning Kenny said, "The usual, doll?" Reportedly, Amy had flushed with pleasure at being recognized as a regular and said yes. Soon he asked where she worked and why she never catered her staff meetings with A Decent Bagel's bagels.

"You do that?" she breathed.

He gave her a business card. "We supply trays, napkins, cutlery, nova or lox, capers. . . . Everything but the holes."

He laughed as if it weren't the stalest joke in his bagel repertoire.

"What does she look like?" I asked.

"Harriet," he said. "You're not hearing me. I didn't fall in love with Amy right away."

"When?"

"It took months. Months of seeing her every morning. Then she started coming in for lunch when I expanded the menu. We talked. She liked me."

"But who made the first move?"

"She asked me if I'd sit down at her booth. I heard myself saying, 'Can I see you some time? In the evening?' She said yes like this—'*Yessss,*' with this hiss of relief, almost like she'd been waiting and praying for me to ask."

I asked how long afterward they had slept together.

"I promised myself I wouldn't get into specifics or say anything hurtful. It isn't necessary. Just know that we've practiced scrupulously safe sex from the beginning."

All I could say was, "What about me?"

He looked puzzled—what *about* me?

"I have nothing," I said.

"I'm forty-two years old," said Kenny. "I thought you'd understand."

3
MOVING DAY

 ISABEL KRUG'S RETREAT, win-
ner of two national awards for
its team of architects, was the
most despised house in Truro. It was more Malibu than Cape
Cod, the only thing in sight not covered with weathered gray,
or soon-to-be-weathered, cedar shingles. The nerve, it said;
the sheer size and cost of me: cement cylinders painted white,
big ones and small ones, as if client Krug had said to an L.A.
architect, "Make me feel as if I'm living inside a toppled
pyramid of canned goods."

I saw it for the first time on a Friday in February when I

arrived with all of my belongings. I had accepted the job, if that's what it was, and agreed to stay a year minimum to help her write The Isabel Krug Story. My clothes, books, electric typewriter, and manila files were in my rental car; my mail was being forwarded. As I left the New York apartment, painters and floor refinishers were arriving to refeather Kenny's love nest to Amy's hypoallergenic specifications.

Isabel had mailed me instructions in aqua ink on scalloped stationery: "Rent a car if you don't have one. I'll reimburse you. I'll have my man drive it back to Hyannis. That's where the nearest car rental place is. The house is the big white cement one on the left with no windows facing the street (my neighbors hate it) don't block the driveway." I had analyzed her writing style and thought: short, choppy sentences; that's why she needs me; it's good that she knows this about herself.

The map led me by icy salt marshes toward water and sand, past an empty parking lot for Corn Hill Beach and up a narrow blacktop road to the highest stretch overlooking the bay, fully expecting my trip to end at the ugliest house ever built atop a dune.

"Oh, God," I said aloud as I pulled into the gravel driveway. I didn't hate it. It was huge and stark; the windows were flat caps of glass topping each cylinder in a twenty-first-century-lighthouse way.

I loved it. I thought of Diane Keaton's house in *Sleeper*. I imagined the rain hitting the glass ceilings and me writing my best prose ever to that sound. If there was landscaping at all, it was in the way the sand drifted against the foundation and the beach grass whipped in the wind. There were no silly green lawns or window boxes, no rail fences planted with beach plums. I'd take pictures and send them to my parents, to the

11

writing group, maybe even to Kenny. I'd write, "Here is my new dwelling. I sleep in the tower marked with an X. The work is fulfilling. The ocean is my backyard."

She yelled, "It's open."

There was no doorknob on the curved steel door. "The Jetsons," I thought. Then I noticed hinges to my right. I pushed with my shoulder and the door opened. My first interior view reminded me of movie locations and Sunday supplements: glass wherever there was ocean, blond wood wherever there was floor, spiral staircases wherever ceiling disappeared into cylinders.

And inspecting me from an immensely long, flesh-colored satin couch, a telephone receiver to her ear, was the mistress of the house.

"Harriet Mahoney?" she said.

I nodded and stepped forward. She was bigger than I had expected, and younger, maybe my age; not old enough to be my boss or own this house or have a dowager's name like Isabel. Her vanilla-blonde hair was pulled back tightly and knotted at her neck in the style of the perfectly featured who don't visit hairdressers or own hot rollers. Her pink face, I guessed, had lately become more round than oval. Her eyes were large and light amber; later I would learn that for dress-up they became swimming-pool blue or broccoli green. She was wearing iridescent black leggings and a tunic in a shiny, nubby fabric that made my mother's voice pronounce "shantung" inside my head. She raised a hand to stop me and mouthed that she'd be right off. I backed up and stood by the door; I focused on her large earrings, which were in the tree-ornament family, while she watched me back.

"That's what I have an agent for," she snapped into the phone.

I could feel her evaluating my mail-order baggy sweater over my one-size-fits-all denim skirt above my navy blue opaque knee-highs and penny loafers—which five hours ago seemed a perfectly reasonable outfit to wear on moving day on Cape Cod in winter. Her gaze traveled up to my graying hair which, until that moment, I had believed lent me character and substance.

"I really have to go," she said.

I waited for a signal—a smile, anything—that would have made me feel less like the meter reader and more like a professional who had arrived at the appointed hour on the appointed day. Suddenly, Isabel Krug rolled her eyes and wagged her head back and forth, mocking the rhythm of her caller's speech. I smiled. She pointed behind me, jabbing the air.

My stuff? I mouthed.

She nodded vigorously, pointed then beckoned: *Go get it and bring it in.*

She was standing in the doorway when I came back with the first load, two suitcases and a sleeping bag. "Did you think you wouldn't get a bed?" she asked, kicking the bag with her silver-sandaled, pink-nailed foot, her voice teasing, a notch friendlier than its telephone version.

I smiled weakly. Why the hell *had* I brought my old bedroll from Camp Win-Jo-Bar?

"You look like a good egg," she said.

I said I was a good egg. The sleeping bag was for . . . who knows? I had always brought my sleeping bag to the Cape. And besides, I was moving in. These were my belongings.

"What were you doing on the Cape?"

"Vacationing. But ages ago. With my family."

"Where?"

"My mother says it was Dennis or Dennisport."

"That sounds right," said Isabel. "Are they still alive?"

I said yes, living in Brookline, Mass. Retired. She asked what they were retired from.

"Mahoney's Donuts." I didn't tell her everyone's favorite Freudian fact about me—that on top of doughnuts, my old boyfriend made bagels. I raised my suitcase-laden fists: where to?

"You choose," she said.

I followed her down a hallway, past the curved white glossy plaster of the interior wall, up a semi-circle of stairs to what she was calling "one possibility."

"It's sweet, isn't it?" she asked.

Instantly I said, "I'll take it." It was the inside of a cylinder, pale gray walls, pale gray carpeting that looked like thick velvet, and a gray-tinted glass dome for a ceiling. The bed, bureau, and night table were the color of driftwood. The bedclothes were a festival of natural fibers—cotton, wool, silk, mohair—all flavors of the same pale gray. The bathroom was another cylinder, tiled in metallic silver-gray from floor to ceiling, the floor in aquamarine. Everything else was gleaming stainless steel: toilet, a second toilet-like fixture, a pedestal sink, a fan-shaped bathtub, towel bars.

I doubled back to the bedroom and stared at the generous bed, at its piped linens and pillow shams, its duvet, its extraneous throw pillows that were smocked and edged like a handmade trousseau. I said, "I can't imagine I could like the other possibility more than this."

ISABEL'S BED

"It's bigger," said Isabel, "and it has *the* most outrageous
bathroom. C'mon."

She led me out the door, back down the steps, past my
humble baggage to an opposite wing.

"Were you ever married?" she asked over her shoulder. "Or
are you now? I forgot what you told me."

"Neither."

"Are you gay?"

"No," I said. "I just ended a twelve-year relationship. With
a man."

"Whose idea was that?"

"His," I said.

She paused for a few seconds, cursing softly as if in solidarity, then continued down the hall to a creamy-red door. As
soon as she opened it I said again, before I could stop myself,
"I'll take it." The walls looked like petrified sand, like indoor
dunes. The bed was built on a platform of raisin-colored
wood; raisin-colored leather formed a fitted quilt. The carpeting was raisin-colored velvet. The art on my dune walls was
signed and numbered. Sliding glass doors led to a private deck,
a private hammock, and what felt, by this point, to be a private
ocean. She led me into an adjoining half-glass pyramid. "You
get used to showering in front of glass, unless you worry about
every pervert with binoculars," she said. The floor was
sand-colored stone, and there was a drain in the middle. I got
it: This was the bathroom, all of which was a shower. You
stood there naked and turned on these wall jets and there you
had it. The sink and toilet seemed to be carved from boulders.
*(Dear Group, I arise at first light with the sound of the ocean in my
suite. It's made of indigenous materials so I feel as if I have invited
the sand inside. As the great orb rises, I take my coffee out to*

15

my private deck and stare at this glorious panorama before I actually commit words to paper. I wish all of you could see it, and could have a setting like this in which to write. With fond regards to all, Harriet M.)

"Like it?" asked Isabel.

I nodded, too awed to say what was already worrying me: How would I ever leave a room like this and what would I go back to?

"Good. It's yours." She opened and shut a few empty drawers, slid a mirrored door back and forth, then put her hands on her hips. "Now what?"

"Is it too soon to unpack?"

"It's yours," she repeated. "Move in. Take it over. Throw your clothes on the floor. Is this everything, these two bags and the junk in the foyer?"

I said, "This is everything, pretty much," neglecting to say I used to co-own a good deal more, but had divested.

"If you need something, ask me," said Isabel. "I have more shit than I could wear in a lifetime."

I said thanks, but that probably wouldn't be necessary. I reminded her about the rental car: She had said in her letter that "her man" would drive it back to Hyannis.

"Oh," she said. "Did I?"

"Do you have a butler?"

"A handyman/driver," she said. "Pete."

"How will he get back from Hyannis if he drives my car there?"

She laughed, put her arm around my shoulder like best friends heading outside for recess, and cried, "How the hell do I know?"

* * *

"Good Portuguese fishing stock," Isabel announced as she introduced me to Pete DaSilva the handyman, embarrassing us both on the spot. "It's a great combination, don't you think: olive skin, white teeth, big brown eyes—plus he never sulks." I didn't think so: Pete was not handsome. He saved me from agreeing or disagreeing by telling her to cut the crap. He welcomed me to Truro. How did I like it so far?

I said, "The house is amazing. I never dreamed I'd live in a house like this."

He smiled and said, "You'll grow into it."

Isabel said matter-of-factly, "So far I like her. She's very thoughtful. She's worried you'll get stranded in Hyannis."

"No problem," said Pete. "My cousin's following me in his cah."

"Everyone on the Cape is his cousin," Isabel murmured.

"Why do you think every guy I bring here is my friggin' cousin?"

"Because they all look alike and all have the same name!"

Pete slid his baseball cap down to his nose and back again and exhaled slowly. He took my keys and asked if we needed anything else in the big city.

Isabel squinted at some Roman numerals inlaid above the fireplace. "What time does the Anne Klein outlet stay open till?"

"She just got here," said Pete. "She's not gonna feel like traipsin' back to Hyannis."

Isabel asked hopefully, "You like outlets?"

I nodded, wanting to be the perfect employee-companion.

"She needs stuff. She only filled two suitcases."

Pete said, "Why don't you go next week once Harriet gets settled. She can drive you."

"Or sooner than that," I said.

"Want anything else while I'm out?" asked Pete.

"Like what?"

"You set for suppah? Want me to pick something up?"

"Thanks, anyway, but I can't think of a thing," Isabel said convincingly, as if she operated in an ordered universe where shopping preceded eating.

We drank wine, very good red wine, as soon as I hung up my coat and put my toothbrush into its new sandstone holder. We sat on the satin sofa where I had first seen her. It was dark outside; someone other than Isabel had drawn the drapes and made a fire.

"I can't believe you've never heard of me," she said, but pleased, as if charmed by a rare moment of obscurity. "Don't you read the newspapers? Didn't you wonder why I was writing a book?"

I said, "Everyone I know wants to write a book."

"Guy VanVleet?" she tried again. "That doesn't mean anything either?"

I repeated the name.

"Shot dead in his bed?"

Be cool, I thought: We're talking about a murder; I'm going to collaborate with a murderess; I'm going to be the *housemate* of a murderess. I asked hoarsely if this crime were known outside this room or whether we'd be breaking the story.

"It was front-page headlines everywhere—Wife Kills Millionaire Husband. Every variation on that you've ever heard."

"You?" I asked. "You're the wife?"

"I was there," she said, "but I didn't kill him. I was an innocent bystander."

I said I didn't understand. What was she doing there exactly?

Her eyes told me I had disappointed her. She said, "Guess."

"Committing adultery?" I asked delicately.

"What else?" she replied.

Pete, she told me, had been part of the crew that built the house. "We liked him and he designed his own job—handyman, watchman, driver. Whatever needed to be done indoors or out. When the house was finished last year, he stayed."

"And it's worked out?"

"Are you kidding? He can do anything. Even stuff he hasn't done before, he figures out. Plus everybody trusts him so I get built-in community relations." She lowered her voice to confide that the house was considered among the locals to be "way out"; that sometimes they cracked jokes to Pete about how's life in the Hamptons.

"Maybe because it's original," I said, "and they're used to a certain Cape Cod look."

"You can say that again: If it doesn't have shutters and a trellis over the door, they think it's in bad taste."

I looked around the stone, glass, and white room and back to Isabel. "How could anyone not think this is beautiful?"

"You'd be amazed what people like. I was amazed every day."

I didn't examine that. I assumed she was telling me about life as a rich woman, as a hostess, a shopper, a giver of gifts and a patron of the arts.

"You do a lot of entertaining?" I asked.

"None," said Isabel. "It's too much trouble. Besides, who would come?"

19

I told her I hadn't been one for entertaining either, but of course I'd never had the room. "Any other employees?" I asked. "A cook, maybe? Someone who keeps house?"

"Pete's mother used to clean for me—she's a cleaning genius, but she went back to school—way the hell up in Bridgewater, so she cut back to once a week. I don't need a cook because I don't eat. Not in any meaningful way."

"Oh," I said, wondering, if that were true, why she looked so ruddy and well-fed. It was at least seven o'clock and food had not been mentioned.

"*You* can. You can cook your little heart out. I have this drop-dead kitchen that my architects insisted on for resale value. It's got the best view in the house."

"Do you eat an evening meal?" I asked.

She shrugged. "Occasionally for social convenience. Otherwise, cereal, Lean Cuisine. Yogurt. Tuna fish. My feeling is, what's the point? It's fuel. Why waste time shopping and cooking when life is so short?"

I said I wasn't a great cook, but I did enjoy my meals. Would my regular observation of mealtime undermine her personal philosophy?

"Regular—meaning three a day?"

I nodded, unsure.

Isabel smiled a brilliant smile—a smile that put a whisk in my hand, and a knife and a fork in hers; a smile that asked, When do we eat?

4

"In Wrong Place at Wrong Time"

 I HAD A recurring dream in my childhood: I'd walk into my bedroom closet to the small attic door inside, open it—something I was afraid to do when awake—and find a hidden suite of rooms, sunny and beautiful, which made our small house something of a magical duplex.

Isabel's kitchen had a similar effect on me. I had missed it on my trips between the car and my new room, had thought about it briefly when the wine appeared, and had assumed there must be an efficient, prize-winning galley around one of these bends.

I was wrong about that. I had missed it because I had failed to look up while I waited for Isabel to get off the phone, up into the skylight that made her foyer an atrium. There was the suggestion of a black and white kitchen, which looked from below like a balcony café at an upscale mall.

I could see even at night that the upper level was its own world: the harlequin kitchen in gleaming black and marbled white, the master suite with its two penthouse lofts, the dim glow of Provincetown up the coast, and a deck designed by a student of the tides.

Isabel's room was a shrine to herself, or at least to the story she wanted me to tell. Newspaper clippings floated magically on its curved mauve-woolen walls. There was no desk or work table. Her bed, covered in sheared sheepskin the color of eggplant and littered with celebrity biographies, appeared to be her office. I approached the most crowded wall to read the particulars. **"VanVleet Friends Say Dead Man, Wife 'Perfect Couple'"**; **"Nan to Cops: 'I Lost My Mind.'"**

"Who's Nan?" I asked.

"The wife."

I moved slowly from clipping to clipping (The *Star*, The Arizona *Republic*, The New Orleans *Times Picayune*, The Detroit *News*, The Sacramento *Bee*, The Akron *Beacon Journal*) until I found one (The Trenton *Times*) that mentioned her in a headline. **" 'In Wrong Place at Wrong Time,' says Isabel."**

"Wow," I said. She was following on my heels, gauging my reaction to each headline. "Wow what?" she asked eagerly.

"Your name . . ."

"You know how it works: When someone dies in your bed—or you're in their bed as the case may be—it's news.

You become infotainment. Remember Alexandra Isles, von Bulow's girlfriend? She wasn't even involved with the case, and it still made her career."

"You were in bed with"—I checked a caption—"Guy VanVleet when his wife shot him?"

"Through the heart."

"Were you hurt?"

Isabel shook her head as if to say, Regrettably not. "Have you ever been shot, or did you ever hear a gun go off at close range?"

I said I hadn't—

She touched my arm. "I swear to God, I *thought* I was being shot—the noise was unbelievable. Horrible." She shuddered happily.

"But you didn't actually get injured?"

"Not physically."

"Did his wife just happen upon you, or was it premeditated?"

"That," said Isabel, "was the crux of the case. She claimed that she came home and found her loving, faithful husband in bed with a voluptuous younger woman and she freaked out."

"Is that true?"

"She barged in on us—she was supposed to be at a parents' weekend at Colby—aiming her big revolver at us, swearing like a marine. Guy jumped out of bed like a schmuck and she shot him at close range."

"What about you?"

"I could've been killed, believe me."

"Was she shooting at you?"

"She might as well have! The bullet went right through him and out the other side and, luckily, into the grass cloth. I

23

didn't find that out till later but she could've killed us both with one bullet." Isabel fell to a crouch then jumped up, lunging at me. I screamed, which made her smile as if she liked my contribution to the reenactment. She went on, with me the stand-in for Mrs. VanVleet, "I ripped the gun out of her hand, ran into the bathroom—remember I'm stark naked—hid the gun, came back out, dialed nine-one-one."

Stark naked, I thought, in front of a complete stranger; accomplishing all that without clothes and without apparent embarrassment. I couldn't move on without asking, "Did you get dressed at some point?"

"I think so. I must've grabbed a robe—I remember seersucker. When the cops showed up, she *was* a zombie. But that was after the fact. And guess who they took to the station for questioning?"

"You?"

"Me. The victim of circumstances. The only eyewitness. Nan, on the other hand, the murderess, got a sedative and a team of cops to stand outside her door all night."

"Where was this?" I asked.

"Where *was* this?" She stared for a long few seconds. "It depresses me how fast this stuff fades from the public's memory."

I said that was understandable; there were so many of these incidents competing for the reader's attention.

"Still, I'm counting on people staying interested long enough to buy my book." She stared at a clipping, frowning. "One of the problems is it never got a name, like 'The Wood-Chip Murder' or 'Long Island Lolita.' Greenwich has no sense of humor."

"Is that where you lived at the time?"

"He lived there. He sneaked me in for the weekend since his wife was allegedly in Maine."

"Were you in love with him?" I asked.

Isabel raised her index finger into the air. "That," she said, "is a very insightful question. Not that I can answer it. But I'm relieved, frankly. It shows that you can get right to the heart of things."

She flipped the light switch, as if our work were finished. I decided my question had been such a success that I'd let it resonate over the corn chowder and get the answer another time.

"You're a genius," said Isabel. "It's a talent, creating something out of nothing. It must come from the same part of your brain as making up stories."

I dodged the compliment. "This is cafeteria corn chowder. The real thing needs bacon and potatoes."

"You make up a list and I'll send Pete to the A & P when he gets back."

"Tonight?"

"Aren't supermarkets open at night?"

"Tomorrow morning's fine."

"No, unh-uh. This is a guy who used to spend seven or eight days out on a boat, night and day, rain or shine. That's why he was such a find—anything I ask him to do is easier than what he was used to." She was stirring the pot of chowder with enthusiasm, like a child assigned a grown-up task. "His father died at sea, a typhoon or something. If that hadn't happened, Pete would be on the boat this minute. You don't change careers, you don't even go off and have an identity crisis when you're a second-generation Portuguese-

American fisherman. Not unless your father dies and takes the boat with him."

"Is that what happened?"

Isabel shrugged. "It was before I moved to Truro."

"Does Pete talk about it?"

"His boss told me, the builder."

"Does he live in?"

"Most nights," said Isabel.

I must have looked as if I was straining for nonchalance, because she said, "Don't give me that look. I know better than to bed my handyman." She grinned. "Even though I'd have to be dead not to have thought about it."

"I wasn't thinking that."

"C'mon. You're a writer. You're supposed to look into people's souls, aren't you?"

"Sometimes."

We carried our orange sponge-painted bowls to the shiny black half-moon bar that served as a kitchen table, overlooking the atrium. Once we were settled Isabel said "Your novel? The one you sent me a chapter of?"

"An American Apology."

"Whatever. How come nobody published it?"

I explained that it was impossible to get editors to read stuff not submitted by an agent.

"I have an agent," she said. "A big one."

I asked how she found an agent before there was a manuscript. Isabel put her spoon down. "The days I testified at Nan's trial? They carried it on Court TV, live, in every time zone."

"So agents came to you?"

"Dozens. I had my pick."

"What other writers does he represent?"

"Writers! This is not Stephen King's agent; this is a Hollywood agent with an unlisted telephone. He represents celebrities on the theory that someday they'll write their memoirs and people will line up around the block to get them autographed."

"Wow," I said.

"Name someone on a *People* magazine cover," she commanded.

"Jane Pauley."

"I mean someone sleazy. Think of divorce and litigation."

"Donald Trump."

"Exactly. *And* Burt Reynolds. *And* Bess Myerson. *And*—get this—Fergie's American boyfriend."

"Does this agent do fiction, too?" I asked.

"Fiction? Like the stuff you write?"

I said maybe I could talk to him some time, that maybe if our book did well, he'd take me on as a client.

Isabel wiped her bowl clean with a piece of the Portuguese bread I'd found in the freezer. "Lemme ask you—what're you working on?"

"A new novel."

"What's it about?"

"My parents."

She made a face. "What *about* them?"

I told her more or less the premise, that my parents had been divorced but remarried each other after my stepmother died. Then, instead of making my father just Arthur Mahoney, the doughnut maker, I had reimagined him into Arthur Mazel, a retired cantor. "A Room in the Cantor's House" was my working title.

"And you think people want to read about a cantor?"

I said I thought it would add texture to the story. "Besides, my mother was Jewish—"

"And Jews buy books," said Isabel. "Not the worst idea you ever had."

"I have two themes," I began, but Isabel interrupted. "Let's have coffee and you'll read to me. I've got instant hot water at the sink."

I explained my policy against reading from early drafts, based on my negative experience with my ex-fiancé, the bad critic.

"What about just the beginning? You could read me the first couple of pages and I could tell you if it grabbed me."

I said no, I couldn't possibly.

"C'mon," she wheedled. "I'm sure it's great stuff."

I paraphrased and summarized over instant coffee: "The novel opens with Frances Mazel's funeral in a beautiful stained glass temple. Everyone's there, including the widowed cantor, his stepsons Troy and Brent (I wanted to get across that Frances was the kind of shallow woman who gave her sons movie star names), also the cantor's daughter from his first marriage and Charlotte, the cantor's still-devoted first wife. The cantor sits between his stepsons; his daughter sits slightly apart. Everybody's crying, even though Frances was generally disliked by the entire congregation. Troy rises to speak. He says—and this I pretty much stole from his actual words—that he knew his mother always seemed to be more *Vogue* than *Good Housekeeping*, more fur coat than bathrobe, more coq au vin than chicken soup, but that her heart was gigantic, that her clothes went to charity, that no two boys on earth were loved as much as he and his brother had been. More crying—he's very handsome and looks a lot like Frances, who was tall and angular, but on a man it's flattering. The stepdaughter is feeling ambivalent, which is symbolized by the seating plan, becauses she's never really gotten over her parents' divorce. Then the rabbi announces that following interment at Temple Bat Yam cemetery, friends and family are invited back to the Mazel house. Wife number one, Charlotte, who's a little uncomfortable attending the funeral of a sworn enemy and adulterer, decides not to go to the cemetery because it might be in bad taste, since everyone there knows she hated Frances.

"I skip two lines, and the next thing you see is Charlotte walking up the path to a front door. (She volunteered to put out the pastries and plug in the coffee). She enters the front foyer: Her overall impression is blue, blue, blue, her least favorite wall color. (*Her* house is predominantly yellow, so the colors are metaphors for the two women). Straight ahead, there's a staircase with a blue Bokhara runner.

"It's the last detail she takes in before the feet, then knees, then torsos of two men come down the stairs: two punks smiling, swearing, looking pleased with themselves. The punks see Charlotte and yell, 'Shit!' Both jump the banister and run. As an afterthought, one of the punks backtracks, swings his pillowcase at her head, and knocks her out. That's where I end the first chapter."

"So far, so good," said Isabel.

"Next the mourners arrive home. The stepsons enter the front door ahead of Arthur and spot what they think is

Charlotte's dead body. When the cantor sees her crumpled on the floor he falls to his knees, sobbing. One of the stepsons says, 'Get off her, she's breathing.' The cantor snaps out of it. Now he's worried about me. He keeps saying, 'The boys called an ambulance. She's not dead, honey. She's going to be fine.' Then the EMTs arrive and take her to Brigham and Women's Hospital—"

"She lives?" asked Isabel.

"She lives. But that's as far as I've gone."

"This really happened?"

"I changed some stuff—names, the cantor motif."

"Your mother got whacked with a pillowcase while everyone was at the cemetery?"

"It had a VCR in it."

"And then they get back together?"

"Yes, eventually." The cantor feels responsible for Charlotte, I went on, and insists she recuperate at his house. Pretty soon he realizes he doesn't want her to leave. He hadn't ever stopped loving her; it was just that he got seduced by Frances and was too nice a guy to turn her down.

"What about with Charlotte? Did the cantor bring the meals to her bedroom himself?"

I said yes—three a day plus her medications.

"This could be good," said Isabel. "I'd put her in negligees, slinkier and slinkier ones until he can't stand it anymore."

I said I'd have to check with my parents first and see how faithful they wanted me to be to their story.

Isabel dropped her voice to a confiding whisper. "Do you think it's good? I mean, really good. Like a best-seller?"

I said I didn't know; my writing group thought it was the

best thing I'd done. I, on the other hand, would settle for its getting published.

Isabel looked thoughtful. My theme? I wondered. My characters? My metaphors? My prospects? Then she smiled broadly.

"What?" I prompted.

"I guess I'm your writing group now," she said.

5
THIS IS GOING TO BE GREAT

 I WOKE UP to the sound of a foghorn droning, and smiled to myself as soon as it registered—foghorn, fog, ships at sea. I was Shirley Temple sharing a lighthouse with Captain January, adapting myself to ocean business. I tried to go back to sleep, but was too enthralled with my luxurious setting to do anything but lie in bed and think. This house, this job, this new woman in my life, part friend, part employer, part celebrity. And Kenny, even: there was less tenderness around the edges of that bruise than there was a day ago.

I am pulling back my percale sheets, I said to myself. I am sinking my toes into a velvet rug that cost more than my college tuition. I am walking past sliding glass doors through which I see the land mass of Cape Cod curve around and become Provincetown; past a desk built by a cabinetmaker whose work is sold at the Museum of Modern Art's gift shop—a desk where I'll write a book which will say "with Harriet Mahoney" on the jacket.

I imagined my next postcard, an understated one to my parents, confirming that I was alive, but not in a house they'd want to visit too soon: "The drive took five hours and change. Stopped twice. I have my own furnished room and full bath. Weather has been cold and overcast with high winds, but the house is warm."

Like toast, I thought. Like a buttery apricot Danish. I showered in the bright sunshine of my glass bathroom, wondering if I'd lose the urge to install drapes. Outside, below the soapy, nude me, I saw scruffy low bushes covering the ground—the wild blueberries I'd later discover—which I told myself would not accommodate walkers, joggers, or peeping Toms. Still, I was happy to see I could produce a curtain of steam between me and Truro after stepping under the hot water.

Pete had packed the black glass refrigerator with a fortune in groceries. He had shopped like a fraternity on the eve of the Super Bowl: pretzels, potato chips, corn chips, salsa, nuts, three colors of Cracker Barrel cheese, crackers, hot dogs, ground beef, cold cuts, bread, rolls, beer, tomato juice, cranberry juice, Clamato juice, ice cream, milk, Coke, and one jar of every condiment advertised on television. I didn't see him around, nor could I hear any other signs of life in the house. I would soon learn that Isabel slept until someone else made the coffee, at which point she'd sweep into the kitchen wearing a caftan, lipstick, bracelets, gold lamé booties, and the smile of a gracious house guest.

"I told him to get a little bit of everything for starters."

I jumped, but recovered and said, "Good morning."

"He can always go back. Just make a list of what's missing." She sniffed the air happily. "Thank God you're not a tea drinker." She walked over to the coffee maker and watched it drip.

"He bought half and half, if you take that," I said.

"I do, very light." There was a moment's standoff. I smiled and returned to my refrigerator inventory, saying in effect, "I'll write and meal-plan and even cook in exchange for room and board, but I expect you to pour your own coffee."

It didn't temper her enthusiasm. "I see my life changing before my eyes: morning coffee, drip. Coffee breaks, drip, drip. Decaf after dinner, drip, drip, drip—"

"Did you know you have a cappuccino machine?" I asked.

"I do?"

"It's in a box in one of the cupboards. I found it when I was looking for placemats."

"Must've been a housewarming gift," she said.

"Do you mind if we use it?"

"Mind!" Isabel yelled. *"Mind?* Cappuccino in my own kitchen? I didn't know I'd experience such a thing in my lifetime!" She sat down at the shiny black bar and cupped both hands around her faux-marble mug. "This is going to be great," she said. "I thought I needed a ghostwriter, but maybe what I need is a mother." She took a sip and asked, "Any thoughts on breakfast?"

"What do you like?"

"Toast and marmalade? The drawer at the end of the island is a bread box."

I sawed some slices off a new round loaf of yellow Portuguese bread, and put them into the space-age white toaster oven. While I waited, I worried silently. After a minute Isabel said, "Something I said didn't sit right with you."

I considered, *I don't mind cooking casual meals, but my understanding of my contractual responsibilities is . . .*

Or, *There'll be mornings and some nights when I just won't feel like . . .* Finally I just repeated, "You said you need a mother?"

"I use the term loosely. My own mother slept until noon and never made anyone's breakfast."

I pictured servants and a beautiful young mother lighting tapered candles in a taffeta strapless gown, like one I'd seen Jackie Kennedy wear in a photo of her Georgetown years.

"Will you be telling me about your family and your childhood?" I asked.

Isabel said, "Of course. Every second of it."

"Want to start now? I can get my tape recorder."

"Sure." She turned my wrist to see the time. "I'll have my toast—the marmalade is in a white crockery thing—then give me ten minutes to run the bath."

"Just ten minutes?"

"I meant, get your notebook and meet me in my bathroom. I'll talk while I soak."

"We can wait until you finish."

She looked me up and down, and I sensed she had isolated just the character flaw she was probing for. "You're not uptight about nudity, are you?" she asked.

I said no, certainly not.

"Good. I do some of my best thinking in the tub."

I said fine, ten minutes. We'd eat, clear the dishes, and meet in her bathroom.

"Leave the the dishes. Costas will clean up."

"Costa? Is that Pete's mother?"

"Costas."

"I'm sorry," I said reflexively. "I thought it could have been short for some female Portuguese name."

"Costas is Greek, a Greek man's name. Not everybody in this house is Portuguese."

"Costas," I repeated. I pictured another Pete—dark-haired, dark-eyed, hardworking, helpful, another young fisherman taken in by Isabel when his ship went down.

There weren't even bubbles in the bath to obscure her private parts from me, her acquaintance of less than twenty-four hours. It was not the lolling soak of Calgon commercials: this was Isabel soaping her wash cloth and scrubbing her armpits and crotch in a manner I hadn't done in front of Kenny after a decade of intimacy. I sat on a wrought iron stool at the foot of the black marble steps, which led to her elevated, sunken tub. She talked and soaked, talked and scrubbed, then talked and rinsed, while I tried to be as casual about her nudity as she was, and while many Isabels bounced off the mirrored walls.

And there was no getting around her breasts, especially in the context of Isabel as tabloid paramour, as the woman Guy VanVleet died for. They were big. Enormous. They drooped from their own weight below the bath water, then surfaced on display, areolas the size of coasters. I wanted to ask if they were real, but decided that no certified plastic surgeon would have built these. Ordinarily I'd feel sorry for a woman with water-balloon breasts, knowing the burdens they imposed, but I could see that Isabel prized them and regarded them as my first research project, as if seeing them would help me write between the lines.

I said, "Do we want to start with your life and proceed chronologically, or do we start with the night Guy was shot."

" 'The Night Guy Was Shot,' " Isabel repeated. "Write that down. I like that." I made a note on my first blank page.

"Are you writing in shorthand?"

"Not lists you may be reading," I said.

"Good thinking."

"How are we going to approach it?" I asked again.

Isabel turned on the crystal faucet and ran more water into the black tub. "Approach what?" she asked, sinking deeper and closing her eyes.

"The narrative."

"I've been talking into tapes for months. You play them back and take it all down and that's where we get a book."

When I didn't answer, she said, "Don't get nervous. I know I'm no writer. I only meant, first you'll listen to the tapes, then you'll ask me questions to fill in the blanks. Then you'll make it into a book. I'll give you all the newspaper clippings I have and when you're done, we'll get started."

"Are you going to be the only source?"

She sat up a little straighter and said, "I don't understand your question."

"What if I want to interview some of the principals?"

"Like who?"

"Mrs. VanVleet?"

"Fat chance."

"You don't think she'd cooperate?"

"Why should she? As a favor to me, or as a good citizen?"

"Do you know where she is?"

"Pomfret, Connecticut. A cushy sanitarium for the rich and criminally insane."

"Wouldn't you cooperate if someone were writing a serious piece of journalism on the case?"

"Not with me, I wouldn't! She hates my guts."

I asked what Nan's sentence was.

"No sentence! She was found not guilty by reason of temporary insanity, which is what you plead if you'd rather be in a mental hospital than a prison. She's there until the shrinks give her a clean bill of health." She stood up and extended her hand, meaning *towel*.

"I'd love to talk to her," I said.

"It's my book. It's about me. Nan VanVleet can write her own book."

"Just for background? You want people to think it's balanced."

"I've got two years of clippings *plus* the transcripts, plus videotapes of my testimony. Examination, cross-examination, the works."

"Do you have her testimony on tape, too?"

She looked perplexed: *What am I, a documentary filmmaker?*

I didn't want to argue with my large, naked boss. I said I was going to find a nice sunny spot in my room and read as much as I could by Monday.

Isabel neither endorsed this plan nor objected to it, but I sensed a hesitation. "Is that okay with you?" I prompted.

"Fine. Pete Xeroxed about a million pages."

"I read pretty fast."

Still, she was quieter than she'd been all morning. I asked if talking about the case opened the old wounds. I mean, it wasn't all that long ago. Post-traumatic stress disorder and the like.

She shrugged: nah.

So I said I'd be breaking for meals, naturally. How many would we be for dinner?

Her face brightened and the brisk toweling resumed. "Just the three of us," she said.

6

ON THE RECORD

"VanVleet's mistress" was the favorite handle for Isabel in the tabloids. "Alleged companion," "alleged intimate partner" or "alleged girl-friend" was as far as the respectable papers went, while the grown VanVleet children could only spit out "that Krug woman," which half the reporters heard as "crude." Although Greenwich police withheld her name, a Greenwich *Time* reporter came up with "Isabelle Kroog" on her first call to Nan VanVleet's distraught doubles partner.

Friends and neighbors attested in one voice to the

VanVleets' fidelity. A woman who didn't want to be identified told the Stamford *Advocate,* "I'd see them walking out of the house holding hands like newlyweds. They weren't faking it—you can't fake that kind of devotion. How many people still hold hands after twenty-five years of marriage, especially when they don't know they're being watched?"

("1. How did he feel about his wife?" I wrote on my list of questions. "2. Did he confide in you about his marriage? 3. Was he still physically intimate with Mrs. VV?")

A coffee shop owner told a *New York Post* reporter that VanVleet "brought that woman here a bunch of times. I remembered her because of her, can I say this?—chest? Can you say that?—and because of her hair—blonde, very light, pulled back straight off her face. Classy. We're not what you'd call a toney hangout, and maybe he thought he wouldn't run into his Wall Street buddies here. He always paid cash and stuck around after they finished eating, which nobody minded because he always left a fifty percent tip. Hamburg plate or turkey club, nothing fancy. Did I think they were *lovers?* Let me put it this way—she didn't look like nobody's wife, especially his."

Nan VanVleet, on the other hand, looked in her photos like every fifty-year-old Republican wife at the Greenwich Country Club: chin-length page boy hair dyed a Tricia-Nixon yellow, a velvet head band, a two-piece print dress over a wide torso and skinny legs.

The VanVleet children dealt with having a jailed mom and a dead, philandering dad by blaming everything on Isabel. Perry, the eldest at twenty-four, was a soap-opera actor whose role had swelled from high school walk-on to malt-shop sidekick to prom date of the teen ingenue. "We're hiring our

own private investigator," he would murmur instead of "no
comment" as he ran past reporters. The older daughter always
shrugged past the press, then whirled around to cry, "My
father never cheated on my mother! That woman had some
sexual power over him, which can happen when that type
throws herself at a basically decent, red-blooded man. ("Ask
I.K. who started it," I wrote in my notebook.) The younger
daughter, though never quoted, began to date a son of Colleen
Dewhurst.

Photos showed Perry, Sara, and Heidi VanVleet, aged
twenty-four, twenty-one and nineteen, huddled with their
maternal grandparents at the funeral; huddled later with their
own lawyer; huddled under one umbrella as they entered the
Greenwich Police Station, and eventually huddled behind
their mother at the trial.

Always there was the same two-year-old file photo of Isabel:
in a spangled evening gown, all cleavage, leaning over a
paralyzed New York City Police officer at a gala ball for the
victims of violent crime.

The last photo taken of Guy VanVleet alive was dated from
New Year's Eve 1991 in Palm Beach. Wearing a plaid,
short-sleeved shirt, his left arm circled Nan's shoulder, the
hand cupping a lighted cigarette. His mouth was open in
what appeared to be a wisecrack—maybe the guy with the
camera had suggested the arm around the wife. Both held
tropical-looking drinks in goblets. The photo made me
readjust my view of Guy VanVleet from distinguished dead
man to generic pot-bellied husband. Even in my limited life I
had seen that smirk on a thousand Guy VanVleets.

The early newspaper reports (April 4–6) didn't place Isabel
in Guy's bed at the time of the shooting, and didn't name Nan

as the chief suspect. The widow was alternately reported to be under sedation, in seclusion with her children, or being questioned by Greenwich detectives. Finally, to appease the neighbors who assumed there was a crazed killer at large, Deputy Chief Edward P. Lennon spoke into a bouquet of microphones at the police station three days after the murder: As of six-thirty P.M. that night, Mrs. Nancy McKenny VanVleet of 1010 Round Hill Road, Greenwich, had been arrested for the murder in the first degree of her husband, Guy Henrie VanVleet.

There was no gasp of surprise recorded from the audience.

Deputy Chief Lennon, reading from a prepared statement, mumbled that there was an eyewitness, whose identity could not be disclosed.

"An Isabel Krug of New York, New York?" reporters asked calmly, in unison.

"No comment," said the officer.

"K-R-U-G," a front-row reporter offered to her brothers and sisters of the press.

"Eyewitness, huh?" said one reporter. "Do we assume the obvious, Ned?"

"Prostitute? Hooker? Call girl? Escort service?" they demanded.

"The witness has no criminal record," he answered, "and appears to be a legitimate businessperson."

The Associated Press found her first.

"Nan was arrested?" Isabel was quoted as saying. "I have no comment on that, except to say it's about time."

The reporter asked if she and the victim were engaged in sexual intercourse at the time of the alleged assault.

"Alleged assault?" Isabel threw back at him. "Is that what they're calling it?"

"Were you making love to Guy VanVleet when his wife walked in?"

"I think I'm supposed to do this through my lawyer," Isabel said.

He must have countered with, "Oh, come on, it's public record. Your being there is not in dispute. Besides, you're not being indicted for anything."

"Let me put it this way," she said—reportedly "in a sardonic tone"—"Guy was in bed, naked, and I wasn't exactly from the Visiting Nurses Association."

Asked how she knew the victim, Isabel replied, "We were business acquaintances."

The story continued: "Krug stated that she was a consultant to 'many New York businesspeople.' When pressed to describe the nature of her consulting work, Krug hesitated, then stated she was 'a personal shopper.' This reporter asked for clarification. Krug repeated that her lawyer should be called. When the question was rephrased to elicit a definition of 'personal shopper' Krug answered, 'I shop for men and women who need someone with empathetic taste who can tackle the job for them. The average married career person with a spouse, a secretary, two children, and one living parent purchases a minimum of forty-two gifts per year, and that's not counting miscellaneous house-warming, wedding, and baby gifts, and what I call self-shopping.'

"Asked if she had been hired as a 'personal shopper' to Guy VanVleet, Krug replied, 'No comment.' She refused comment again when asked how long she had known the victim, and what she had purchased on his behalf. A concern listed as

'You Shouldn't Have!' under 'Personal Shoppers' in the Manhattan Yellow Pages matched Krug's home phone number.

"Krug refused to say whether she was married or single, again referring the reporter to her attorney. A neighbor at her upper East Side apartment building estimated Krug's age to be 'late thirties' and confirmed that Krug was separated from Costas Dimantopoulos, a self-employed painting contractor. Greenwich police will not confirm whether they have questioned Dimantopoulos."

Costas?

I dug into the carton with a new commitment, but all I could find about this startling development was one unsatisfying paragraph—that Costas Dimantopoulos had fallen from a scaffolding on the March 31st before the shooting while painting a church ceiling in Teaneck, New Jersey, and had been rushed to Holy Name Hospital with collapsed vertebrae. Greenwich police had questioned him at his bedside. Thereafter, no newspaper reported on his recovery or ran his picture—being hospitalized and immobile at the time of the murder made him a nonstory, apparently. He was reduced to a single sentence at the end of Isabel features, typically, "Krug is separated from her husband, painter Costas Dimantopoulos, who couldn't be reached for comment."

Their relationship might not have interested the police or the press, but it was the first thing I needed to find out from Isabel. I was furious with myself for having failed to ask the hard follow-up questions. Or any question at all. The worst reporter at the Greenwich police briefing would have jumped on Isabel the first time Costas's name came up at breakfast.

I knew what my problem was. I was raised to be nice, to

clear the table, to remember birthdays, to smile at customers. I had to change, to be Mike Wallace demanding full disclosure instead of Harriet Mahoney cooking meals.

For the sake of our book, I'd force myself to bend the golden rule of house guests—she who asks rude questions doesn't get invited back.

7
I HOPE YOU'LL BE
HAPPY HERE

 I WANTED TO walk on the
beach and focus my strained
eyes on things far out to sea,
but I wasn't sure how to do so: Did I put on my coat and leave?
Did I stick a note on the refrigerator, or yell, "I'm going for a
walk, be back in a half hour"? I could have slipped quietly out
my private exit, but I first made a dutiful tour of the public
rooms to see if Isabel was paying attention. Her door was
closed and the house was quiet. I put a ham sandwich in a
Baggie, heated a cup of breakfast coffee in the microwave, and
followed the brambly path to the dune steps.

It wasn't a straight descent. Topography dictated the course of the steps—right, left, a turn, a landing, more steps, a more acute angle, as if promising that no grain of sand would be disturbed for something as frivolous as human access to a beach. Because I clutched the railing with one mittened hand, held my coffee mug in the other, and watched my feet on the icy, slatted steps, I didn't notice the man sitting on the beach until he yelled, "Hey!"

In New York I didn't necessarily speak when spoken to, but this was a private beach below exclusive mansions, and the man was waving and hailing me in a neighborly voice. Besides, his Adirondack chair, his binoculars, and his tucked-in Hudson Bay blanket made him look as if he'd been torn from an L.L. Bean catalogue. I negotiated the final half-flight of stairs and walked toward him.

"You are . . . ?" he asked, when I reached his chair.

"I work for Isabel Krug," I said, pointing to the top of the stairs. It was my first view of the house from the beach below, and I felt a thrill of pride in my association.

"The hired writer," he said.

I nodded.

"I'm Costas Dimantopoulos."

Not Costas. Not Isabel's Zorba of a paperhanger husband, not the burly, mustachioed character I had fashioned from every Greek villain who skulked around Hayley Mills in *The Moon-Spinners*. This was a gaunt, elegant man with the droopy features and bassett-hound eyes of a retired French president. His dark hair was sparse with long wisps blowing every which way across a bald crown.

We shook hands. I said, still staring, "I'm Harriet Mahoney."

"Interesting," he said.

What was interesting? Me? My name? My taking food from the house?

"Do you know who I am?" he asked.

"Isabel's husband?"

"Did she tell you that?"

"She told me you lived here. I was reading newspaper clippings all morning and that's when I found out who you were, officially."

"Officially?"

"Was I correct?"

"Miss Mahoney—you didn't hear 'husband' from Isabel's lips, because she doesn't consider us married. We do not enjoy marital relations, to use a euphemism and, in a court of law, that happens to be the test." He turned away, raising his binoculars and pointing them out to the bay.

For a person like me with no talent for small talk, it was one of those interminable moments: alone on the beach with a dour stranger who's just said something sexual and unanswerable.

"Any boats out there?" I asked.

"Lobster traps."

"Yours?"

"I don't know whose."

"Do you like lobster?" I asked ineptly.

He didn't answer right away. Without lowering the binoculars from his eyes he said, "I'm sorry for having said that the first time we meet—about the marriage. I wanted to hear the sound of my own voice. Please excuse me."

"No problem."

"Would you like to sit down?"

I said no thanks. I was taking a walk before it got dark—before I have to start your dinner, I thought.

"Winter's the best time on the beach. Summer is over-rated."

"Too many tourists?"

"I *own* this beach in the off-season," he said, smiling for the first time. "No one gets by without giving me the password."

I couldn't tell if he was pulling my leg, if his engaging me in conversation was the same thing as detaining me at his border. I said after a few moments, "It must break up the boredom—people coming along for you to talk to."

"Do you think I'm bored because I stopped you to talk? Is that an unusual thing to do where you come from? I'm never bored with an ocean at my door."

I looked above us at the house—all glass facing the beach—and wondered which window on which level was his. He followed my gaze to the top of the dune. "Do you like your quarters?" he asked.

I said I did—who wouldn't? Very conducive to work.

"Where did you live before this?"

"In Manhattan."

"Where in Manhattan?" he asked with a touch of impatience.

"Murray Hill. Thirty-fourth and Third."

"Did you live by yourself?"

I told him I had had a roommate, but that had changed.

"So this is more than a relocation?"

"He met someone," I heard myself saying. "He asked me to move out before this came up."

"How long were you together?" he asked.

"Twelve years."

"As man and wife?"

In a court of law, yes. "We never married," I said.

He shook his head sadly.

I said, "I wanted to come. I could have had a number of jobs in the city, and I could have written this book long distance—lots of collaborators live in different cities—but I welcomed the move. I grew up in Massachusetts and used to come to the Cape as a child."

"To Truro?"

I said no. It was my first time in Truro; in fact, the first time I'd been outside since my arrival.

He said formally, "I hope you'll be happy here. You must be talented to write books."

I murmured something affirmative, then thanked him and said I was going to start my walk. Finish my coffee. If he'd excuse me.

He pointed with a long arm and a bony finger. "Great Hollow is this way. And the other direction is Corn Hill. No one will bother you in this neighborhood."

"I walked everywhere in New York," I said. "I was careful but I didn't let it rule my life."

"Would you like company on your walk?"

I must have look dismayed because he said immediately, "No, I won't. I think you'd prefer to walk alone."

"Either way."

He removed the blanket and got to his feet. He was tall, slightly stooped but broad-shouldered. "I'll go up to the house. I don't want to become a fixture, or I'll look like one of those old men—*bored* old men—whose nurses put them out for an airing."

I asked if anyone else was around this time of year to notice. The houses looked dark and I had not heard a single car.

"One or two diehards. Especially weekends. You'll see lights on in the evening."

I started up the beach toward Great Hollow, and walked

51

several hundred yards before taking the ham sandwich out of my pocket. When I turned back to check on Costas, he hadn't moved from his chair, except to rearrange the blanket over his knees and to fix his binoculars on me.

I made meat loaf for dinner with tomato sauce and roasted potatoes suggested by countless Greek diner menus. Isabel, in khaki-green velour lounging pajamas, chipped away at the potatoes with a peeler. I could have done the job twice as fast, but she seemed to be enjoying what was clearly the novelty of helping, and I was glad to have time alone with her before Costas joined us.

I told her I had read most of the clippings and had found out some facts, two things in particular, which surprised me: that she was a personal shopper and that this Costas person was her husband.

"We live in the same house," she said primly, "a very large house, in case you haven't noticed, which does *not* make him my husband."

"Are you divorced?"

"We don't need a divorce. We have an understanding."

I hoped she would expand on it, but she didn't. Finally I said, "Could you tell me what that understanding is?"

She took a few more swipes at a potato, all polished fingernails and all thumbs. "Simple. Weekdays, we avoid each other. He takes his meals in his room. He pays the bills. We have dinner Saturday night and Sunday afternoon. If I see other men, it's in secret and/or out of state. We live under the same roof until he dies."

She disappeared after her wide-eyed lesson in preparing potatoes for roasting ("That's it? That's all you have to do?

Who taught you this?") and reappeared in a red satin V-necked blouse tucked into gray flannel pleated trousers and black suede high heels. I excused myself, assigning her to watch the temperature rise on the meat thermometer, which she did with gusto.

In my room, I changed into my black stirrup pants and a busy Peruvian sweater which hit well below my thighs. I polished my silver earrings with toothpaste—the dangly Mexican ones I thought said "writer"—and brushed my tangled hair outward from the roots as I bent from the waist. The coarse gray hairs were taking over; the wild-woman results had to be tamed back inside my only hair accessory—a puckered doughnut of tapestry-covered elastic.

I put on blusher and lipstick. *Winter Rose.* It sounded to me like the Cape in February, like beach plums crawling up rail fences. Another sign that I was meant to come to this place.

Costas did not comport himself like a man who would die any time soon. He had dressed for dinner in a black wool sports jacket with flecks of white in the weave, a black cashmere turtleneck, and black wool trousers. He carved the meat loaf, praised its texture, and deftly arranged two overlapping slices on each plate as if it were rare prime rib. He drank the Bordeaux with much swirling and sniffing, likening its finish to various berries. He smiled and asked me questions about myself. He was the courtly, indoor twin to the gruff, enigmatic Costas of the beach, part headwaiter and part talk-show host.

To me, anyway.

He and Isabel, on the other hand, were waging war. He couldn't respond to anything she said without snarling. He would ask me a respectful question—How has your work been received by the publishing world? Where have your stories appeared? We would chat pleasantly about my encouraging rejection letters and near-acceptances. Then Isabel, apparently thinking his kind questions signaled a cease-fire, would jump in with a follow-up for me, triggering another assault: "You ask her if she studied writing in college? You don't know that about a person you hire to write a book for you?"

There was no use mediating with earnest answers about the shortcomings of my résumé or Isabel's exemplary hiring practices. I let it go. I didn't want to answer a seemingly gracious question, then see his lip curl as soon as Isabel chimed in. There wasn't much room to maneuver, conversationally or physically, with the three of us at the small lacquered half-moon table, our knees touching. I brought up the cold weather; asked if they got a real spring here in Truro.

"We'll get some warm days in April," said Costas.

"He should know," murmured Isabel.

"Why do you say that?" he demanded.

"Because you're a big piece of driftwood! A human log! You sit on the beach ten hours a day thinking about the weather."

"Is that what you think—that a person who sits on the beach thinks about weather? Or does he think about his life and the world?"

"You don't do anything else!"

Costas turned to me. "To her it's black or white: 'He always does this. He never does that.' She's not interested in careful observation—something you should understand if you're telling her story. She's not interested in whatever else I may spend my day doing."

"And she's not interested in being your shrink," Isabel threw back.

"She's a writer! She's interested in everything, and she has to be observant."

"*Are* you?" Isabel asked me.

I said I *thought* I was, but there was always room—

"Tell me what you've observed about your new mistress."

"Leave her alone," said Isabel.

Here's my chance to take her side, I thought. "She's very nice," I began. "And interesting. I like her taste. She seems to be a self-made woman. Very hospitable—"

"Do you think she's beautiful?" he asked. "Do you think men find her kind of beauty exciting?"

"I'm sure they do," I said.

Suddenly he was smoothing the front of her blouse, sliding his palm down one breast and cupping it for a few seconds. Isabel didn't flinch and didn't slap him away. "Wouldn't you think that some men would find parts of her grotesque?"

"Don't be so European. You're upsetting her," said Isabel.

He took his hand away, and began refilling our wine glasses. "I've known her since she was a girl—"

Isabel said, "Twenty."

"And when she was twenty, I was in my forties, which made me somewhat glamorous." He broke off a piece of bread and shook it at me. "Not old. Older. Worldly. Experienced."

The whole time I was thinking, *a house painter?* A guy in paint-spattered overalls came along and swept Isabel off her feet?

"How did you meet?" I asked as brightly as I could.

"The same way everybody meets," said Isabel. "He

watched me from across a room all evening and he finally walked over and said, 'Who *are* you?'"

"Was it a party?" I asked.

"A wedding."

"And did you get together that night?"

Costas said, "Not that night."

"We talked briefly in the receiving line and we danced one dance together," Isabel informed me. "He had no business coming on to a twenty-year-old kid."

I asked whose wedding it was. Both were silent. I said, "You don't know whose wedding you met at?"

Costas said, "Of course we know. I also know the date, the band, and half the guest list."

I asked again whose wedding it was.

"His," said Isabel. "Mine," said Costas.

It was June 1973, they told me. The bride, a rich Philadelphia girl who'd come to New York to pursue a well-bred, Grace Kelly–kind of acting career, was pregnant. Costas did not love her, and didn't fake it for the sake of the guests.

Isabel couldn't remember who she came with—maybe one of the acquaintances Costas invited by telephone a week beforehand. Except for the civil ceremony and the receiving line, there were no rituals observed, no first dance, no cake cutting; nothing that required the new Mr. and Mrs. Dimantopoulos to act happy. Costas table-hopped and paid little attention to the bride, a pale, thin redhead in an ivory mini-skirted silk suit and matching pillbox hat. Prenuptially, they had agreed to stay married for one year, then get divorced without an argument.

With his relatives either back in Greece or boycotting the non-Greek-Orthodox ceremony, he was free to fool around with his friends. He danced with their dates and led increasingly drunken lines of the *sirtaki*. After watching her for a long time, he asked Isabel to dance a slow dance. He said, "I'm Costas Dimantopoulos. I don't think we've met."

"You're the groom," she said. "Everyone knows who you are, and we're all appalled at how you're treating the bride."

"Why? They wanted this, not me."

"You could at least be nice to her at your wedding," said Isabel. "She looks miserable."

"We married to make our child legitimate," he said. "It's a business arrangement, not an American love story."

"Your wife married for love," said Isabel. "I don't even know her and I can tell you that. And if she slept with you, that's even more proof. Girls like her only sleep with men they're in love with."

Costas liked the sound of this; clearly this woman could imagine love-making for reasons other than love. "I know you're not married, but are you engaged?" he asked.

"No."

"That's good." His hand moved up her back, past the top of her zipper to run one finger across the exposed skin of her scooped neck.

"I have a boyfriend," she said.

"Is he here?"

Isabel shook her head.

"Where can I find you tomorrow?"

She looked around to see who might have heard. "You're going to call me on your honeymoon?"

"Our honeymoon," he whispered.

Isabel didn't answer. After what she hoped was a chilly silence, she said, "I feel sorry for your wife. She'd die if she heard you."

"My wife doesn't care. We agree about these matters."

"I'd never go out with a man who cheated on his wife, because he'd eventually cheat on me, and that's a fact."

"I'd never cheat on you. Ever."

"Men like you are sick," she said. "It's a disease."

"Are you a virgin?" he asked.

He was holding her close, and she pulled back to look him in the eye. "That takes a lot of nerve at your own wedding," she said.

"Ah. The answer I was hoping for—*not* a virgin."

"I am so."

"No, you're not." He pulled her tighter. "Do you think I'd want you to be?"

Isabel said she didn't care and didn't want to dance with him anymore.

"This marriage doesn't change things," he whispered, his lips against her hair. "I'm as free as I ever was. I want to see you and make love to you. And when you think it over, you'll realize that I'm an honorable man to marry the mother of my child."

"Don't you dare call me," said Isabel, their parting words that afternoon.

The redheaded wife, whose name was Margaret, had a redheaded baby, Daphne Deborah, on February 11. She had hoped for a son; she knew a girl would count less in Costas's eyes and make the separation certain. Margaret went directly from the hospital to her parents' house in Bryn Mawr, where the nursery and nanny were waiting for little Dee-Dee.

Costas sent the agreed-upon check every month; he didn't get photos or reports on his child, and didn't ask for them. The divorce was granted on the grounds of abandonment. Two or three years later, Margaret's lawyer sent papers asking for Costas's consent to allow Margaret's fiancé to adopt Daphne Deborah. He couldn't believe it—they wanted him to stop writing checks every month and relinquish all parental responsibility. He signed the papers. Isabel witnessed his signature, and they celebrated with champagne that night.

I finally asked, "Were you a painting contractor when you and she met back then?"

Costas asked, "Who told you that?"

"I read it in the newspaper clippings."

"You know where that came from," Isabel murmured.

"I was a *painter,*" said Costas. "An artist."

"Some stupid neighbor in my apartment building," Isabel continued. "She didn't know us, didn't know what we did, but had seen him coming and going with paint on his clothes, and assumed a big, gruff guy with a foreign-sounding name had to be a house painter."

"She was an idiot!" Costas spit out. He stabbed as many roasted potatoes as could fit on the serving fork, then looked up for takers. I shook my head; Isabel held out her plate.

I asked, "So what do you paint?"

"Huge canvases," said Isabel. "The kind you'd see in the lobbies of office buildings."

"And museums," said Costas.

"Wow," I said. "That's fantastic. Congratulations."

"Do you know what photo realism is?" he asked.

I said sure I knew.

"That's what I did."

59

I said I'd love to see his work. Or maybe I *had!* Which museums was he in?

His mouth twitched. He said bitterly, "I'm in storage now. I've been discredited. My techniques weren't pure enough for them."

"Why is that?" I asked.

Isabel was motioning discreetly: *Don't ask. Serve the rice pudding. I'll tell you later.*

"Fortunately, I have collectors who love my work and don't care if my technique is unorthodox."

Isabel added, "That's another reason why I didn't care if a neighbor said he was a house painter. He was a brand name! Anyone who knew the art world knew Costas Dimantopoulos."

What about the scaffolding? I asked. The accident in New Jersey when he hurt his back? The newspaper account had given me the impression that Costas was painting the ceiling of a church when he fell.

"Another case of sloppy reporting," he said. "I was doing a major installation."

"He always supervised the installation of his bigger works," Isabel offered.

"House painter! Because I had paint on my shoes! It would be as if an ignorant neighbor told a reporter that you were a secretary because she saw you sitting at a typewriter all day."

I murmured that he had made an excellent analogy. Excellent. I, a writer, couldn't have illustrated the point better myself.

8
PETE

TUESDAY MORNING AROUND ten, a white van bearing the orange and purple Federal Express logo pulled up to Isabel's house and delivered a lumpy package, which turned out to be two dozen A Decent Bagel bagels addressed to me "and any other bagel-lovers on the premises." That would be Kenny's idea of cute—that and the basic act of charity, as if a meal on wheels would square things between us. I could picture him at work, brown plastic tongs poised over wire baskets, clucking to his employees, "These are for poor Harriet. I'm sending her a little gift from all of us. Hope she's doing all right."

61

I called the store collect and Kenny accepted. I said, "They're here. Thanks."

"Did you taste them yet?"

I explained that I woke up early because I couldn't wait to get a jump on my extremely compelling work. Breakfast had been hours—

"Could you take a bite and tell me how they traveled?"

I fished out a salt bagel, my favorite. The crystals had melted slightly and blistered the surface, the telltale sign of yesterday's goods. "It's a little hard," I said. "But they'll be fine toasted."

"Damn! They were still warm when I packed them."

I could feel his famous sulk coming on, but it didn't have its usual effect on me. "Look," I said, "it was a nice idea, but it's a little extravagant to send bagels overnight. You should save your money."

"I thought that at first, but then I said, 'Look, if I drove up there and took her out for a bite, even for an inexpensive lunch—twenty-five, thirty bucks—I wouldn't think about it twice.' This way, for the price of a meal, you don't have to eat *goyishe* Massachusetts bagels." He laughed his hollow, cash-register laugh.

"Why would we be having lunch?" I asked.

"I was speaking hypothetically."

"Good."

"You don't sound very happy."

"I don't?"

"You sound a little mad."

"Why would I be mad? Shouldn't I be thrilled to receive two dozen symbols of your life and work?"

He exhaled loudly once, twice. "That's so like you, to throw this back in my face. It was meant to say, 'No hard feelings. I hope we can be friends, and I hope you'll be happy in your new situation.'"

"I am happy," I said.

"Good. That's what I want. I had hoped you could be happy for me as well."

I couldn't help myself. I asked how *was* the marvelous human being and perfect woman Amy?

"Working hard," he said earnestly. "There's a chance she'll be made manager of her office."

"I meant, are things still as wonderful as ever?"

Kenny sighed, the poor misunderstood romantic and bagel philanthropist. "We're good for each other. I'm sorry if that hurts you."

"I'm not hurt! If you hadn't fallen in love with her, I'd still be riding the subway to a dead-end job, never having the time to write. Now I'm in the most beautiful house I've ever seen, let alone lived in. On top of a dune. Overlooking the ocean. I have a leather comforter on my bed, and my own private deck. It's a suite. The kitchen has granite counters and marble tile floors. I'm going to send you pictures as soon as I take some."

He told me to mail them to A Decent Bagel rather than to the apartment. I said I'd do that, but I had to get off; my research beckoned.

"How's your boss?"

"Fine."

"You getting along okay?"

"Why wouldn't we?"

"Just asking—it's hard to live in someone else's house, especially when it's an employer-employee situation, and there's just the two of you."

"Who said there was just the two of us?"

"That's what you told me."

"It's a huge house," I said. "There's an artist named Costas Dimantopoulos—that's a man's name—and a former sea captain, a young sea captain, named Peter. That makes two men and two women. So far, anyway."

When Kenny didn't say anything, I added, "There's a state-of-the-art toaster oven here that'll be great for heating up the bagels. I'll ask Pete to pick up some cream cheese later. We'll have a bagel party."

"As long as you don't microwave them," he said petulantly.

"When did I ever microwave a bagel?"

He didn't answer, but after a few angry breaths said, "I sent you some jalapeño-corns. We're test-marketing them this month along with salsa cream cheese, which I would've sent but I didn't want to get into refrigeration issues with Fed Ex."

"I'll let you know what I think," I said. "Thanks. Gotta run."

"You could blend some yourself if you can get fresh cilantro up there."

"Whatever."

"How's the writing coming?"

"Which writing?"

"The novel."

"It's on the back burner right now, but I'm going to put some time aside every day to work on it, as soon as I establish a routine."

"How's the other work, the new work?"

"Fascinating."

"Oh, yeah? What's it about?"

I said it was confidential, but it had everything a ghostwriter could want: murder, adultery, headlines, marriage, divorce, sex—

"Whose murder?" he asked.

"I'm not at liberty to discuss it with anyone outside my team."

"What was this woman's role, your boss? Was she the victim or the perpetrator?"

I pointed out that she couldn't very well be the victim if she lived to write about it, could she? Guess he'd just have to wait like everyone else until the book came out.

"Can you at least say whether anyone on your team was the murderer?"

"Don't be ridiculous."

"You think every murderer is in jail? People get off on technicalities and go write books about it."

"No comment," I said, just like one of the principals.

The intercom had a button labeled "Pete," which I buzzed lightly, a quick tap so he could ignore my page if atop a ladder or in the critical phase of a Super Glue application. The new me needed cream cheese, but the old me wondered how many items a reasonable person—one who had been unnecessarily buzzed herself for a thousand secretarial tasks—would consider just cause for a grocery run.

"Yup?" he answered immediately.

"It's Harriet," I said. "The new person."

He said dryly, "Thanks for the introduction."

"Where are you?"

"In my room," he said. "Where you buzzed me."

"I didn't know where it buzzed."

"Janitor's quarters. It's where I hang out between jobs."

"Like in my elementary school, in the basement. Where you'd go to find Mr. Doucette when someone threw up."

Pete said, "Right, for the sawdust."

"Maybe we went to the same elementary school," I said. A joke.

"Doubt it. We had Mr. Pavo."

It was the longest conversation I'd ever had through an intercom. All anyone had ever said to me was "Harriet, coffee."

"What can I do for ya?" Pete asked.

"Will you be going into Provincetown today?"

"Sure."

"Could you pick up a few more things at the A&P?"

"No problem. How'd you like the last orda?"

"It was fine."

"Isabel told me to fill up the refrigerator, so I kinda just took one of everything. But you should tell me what you really want."

I said that I did, in fact, have a short list. If that was convenient. Maybe a dozen items, which he could hold off on until I had more—

"Hey," he said. "This is what I do."

When he came upstairs a few minutes later, I was sawing bagels in half and putting them in plastic bags for freezing. He asked where they came from.

I said New York, from a friend who had his own bagel store.

He turned over the Federal Express envelope and read the label. He looked up. "This guy evah hear of sending flowers?"

I remembered that this was a house where everyone but me went straight to the heart of the matter immediately after introductions. Hadn't I resolved to be more direct myself? I said, "It's not like that, believe me. This is just a have-a-nice-life present. Good luck, Harriet."

"Is this what he does?"

"He makes bagels."

"I meant, does he ship bagels as a business, like those fancy English muffins that come U.P.S.?"

I said, "Not as far as I know. This is just Kenny showing off."

"Kenny, huh?" He picked up a bagel and held it in the palm of his hand at eye level.

"He used to be my boyfriend, but we broke up."

"Did you want to break up with him?" he asked quietly.

"I didn't have a choice. He fell in love with someone else." After a moment of reflection I said, "Not that he was ever in love with me."

Pete politely took the knife from me and said, "You're gonna cut your hand open doin' it that way. I can't stand watchin'." He sliced each one with a hard, sure, stroke, top to bottom. He was as good as the guys at A Decent Bagel, who chopped the eat-in orders through butcher's paper. "How long was this guy your boyfriend?" Pete asked.

"Twelve years."

He whistled.

"I met him when I was almost thirty, and I thought *that* was old."

"You're fotty-two?"

"Just about."

"I'm around there," he said. "I'm thirty-six." He waved the knife back and forth as if to say, I'm enjoying this; bring on the rest of those bagels. I emptied the Fed Ex envelope, seeds, crumbs and all, onto the granite countertop and reached for a second bread knife. He slid the cutting board a few inches in my direction.

"You think that's so hard to do?" I asked, brandishing my own knife.

"I cleaned a million fish in my day," said Pete. "I can fillet anything, even stale bagels from New York, New York. . . . Even yellow bagels with green slimy things baked into 'em."

The jalapeño-corns. They had specks of red dotting their surface—cayenne or chili powder, I guessed. I said matter-of-factly, "If you're thirty-six, I'm old enough to be your older sister."

He laughed as if I had said something funny, as if *I* were funny. So I smiled, too.

"It's gonna be nice to have anotha person around here closa to my age," said Pete. "I mean, someone who's not strictly speaking the boss."

I noted that I was still forty-one; wouldn't be forty-two until the end of April.

"My mutha was fotty-one when she had me."

I said I hadn't met her yet.

"She's a hoot," said Pete. "A tough old bird."

"Isabel said she was a cleaning genius."

Pete rolled his eyes. "Isabel thinks everyone's a genius. I'm a handyman genius. My mutha's a cleaning genius. My cousin Joseph is an automotive genius—he fixes her cah. You'll be a genius, too."

I said she'd already called me a genius over my corn chowder, but I was hoping to earn the title on the basis of our professional collaboration.

"How's that comin?" asked Pete. "I know I copied a shit load of newspapah stories for you."

"That's what I've been doing since Saturday. Today I'm starting on the trial transcripts. And then Isabel and I'll sit down with a tape recorder."

"Don't let her work you too hahd. You should have your Satidays and Sundays to yourself."

"Is that what you do, work Monday through Friday?"

"If she needs me Satidays or Sundays, I get time and a hahf, regahdless."

"It's not quite the same."

"Why not?"

"I'm the live-in ghostwriter. I'm on call."

"Fa what?" Writing emergencies? In case Isabel gets a hot idea in the middle of the night?"

"It's a funny deal," I said. "We haven't worked out all the details."

Pete opened his mouth, closed it again, then said carefully, "Let me give you a little advice: You don't have to be her slave. She asks for a lot, but she doesn't mean it. It's disguised as work, but she's really askin' for company."

He was cut off by a loud buzz. Isabel's voice squawked, "Pete? You up there?"

"Yup," he answered calmly, as if he hadn't just been psychoanalyzing her.

"He came up for my shopping list," I offered.

Pete shook his head and drew his mouth into a frown, as if to say, no explanation needed.

"Don't forget the mail," she said.

"Like I evah forget."

"Would you pick me up a movie if you see something good?"

He winked at me. "Sex or violence?"

"Either," she said. "As long as it's gratuitous."

He laughed and so did she. "Ovah 'n out," Pete said.

"Harriet?" she asked sweetly.

"I'm right here."

"How's the reading coming?"

"Good. I'm starting on the transcripts."

"Were you just taking a coffee break?"

I looked at Pete. He shut his eyes and shook his head.

I said into the intercom, slowly, unconvincingly, "We should talk about my work schedule so we both know what's expected." I winced when it was out. Pete made an okay circle with two fingers.

Isabel said, "How about right now! I'm in the tub."

Pete shook his head again.

I said, "I was going to get back to work now. How about over lunch?"

Pete left, nodding, waving the shopping list in a flutter of solidarity.

"Lunch!" said Isabel.

With Pete gone I was free to be apologetic. "Is that okay with you? If we discuss some things?"

I heard splashing—the happy toddler in her bath—then the gulp of the drain.

"Is that okay? Over lunch?"

"Lunch is wonderful! I'm starved!"

The microwave clock said 11:03. In New York, a boss's hunger pangs could be cured with one phone call and a tip.

"You're a genius," she said, "and I'm a genius for finding you."

I released the button and said to the wall, "I wouldn't bet on it."

9
PEEP SHOW

 I WATCHED ISABEL do something I hadn't seen in the twenty-five years since I'd eaten lunch in the cafeteria at Brookline High School: stick potato chips inside a tuna fish sandwich. When she caught me staring, she bit into the bread with added gusto, exaggerating the crunch by baring her right-side molars.

"Ever try it?" she asked, her mouth full.

I took a big Cape Cod sour cream and dill potato chip and slipped it between my tuna salad and bread.

"I like a smidgen of sweet relish in my tuna, if you think of it next time."

I took a bite. Isabel leaned closer across the table and said, "Well?"

"Good."

She smiled, satisfied, and picked up a sandwich half. We ate and sipped our seltzer, lime, and grape Juicy Juice, which I had mixed for her, and which she instantly proclaimed the house nonalcoholic drink. "This business about what we both expect?" Isabel said after a minute, "About your work schedule? Were you getting nervous, like you wouldn't have any time to yourself?"

I was pleasantly surprised; I didn't think—since it followed the word "lunch"—that my agenda had registered. "A little bit," I said. "When you asked me if I was taking a coffee break, I thought, Shouldn't I be?"

Isabel took more chips for her plate, and wedged a pickle spear inside her sandwich. "Look," she began, "you do what you want, when you want to: read, write, cook." She chewed and spoke at the same time. "Right now you're reading the stuff Pete Xeroxed?"

I said I was figuring out a filing system for the clippings, then a labeling system, and then I'd start reading the transcripts.

"Good. I'm still pouring my heart into my tape recorder. One of these days, we'll sit down together and compare notes."

"When do you think you'll finish your dictating?"

"I'm done with the factual and legal parts and now I'm concentrating on the love story."

Hers and Guy's? Guy and Nan's? Costas and Isabel's? I knew I had to be careful here, knew I had to demonstrate my insight, my romantic empathy and my narrative compatibility. I asked, "And how are you approaching that?"

"No holds barred. Because I said to myself, what the hell do I have to lose? I might as well give my readers their money's worth—tell them what made Guy VanVleet risk everything for Isabel Krug."

This was the part I'd been waiting for, the juicy, novelistic details. I said, "Can you give me a for-instance?"

Isabel hunched forward and said, as if testifying into a microphone, "Nan VanVleet stopped having sex with her husband the day after their twenty-fifth anniversary."

"She did?"

She snapped her fingers. "Once after the party, then nothing! Like she had reached some quota and could retire."

I remembered a teary neighbor in the clippings mentioning an anniversary, so I asked Isabel if that hadn't been a fairly recent event. Like right before the murder?

"The December before."

"How long had you been seeing Guy?"

"Oh," she said breezily. "Since the November before."

"Could she have found out about his affair and decided to punish him?"

"Nan didn't know about me! She stopped having sex with Guy because she didn't want to be bothered anymore. I'm the only one alive besides Nan who knows this fact, and she's not about to advertise it. Believe me, this is the kind of detail that people eat up in a book."

I agreed with that and said so: Sex sells. Regrettably. My writing group discussed this phenomenon all the time when analyzing why our most literary stories and deepest poems went unbought.

"Of course sex sells!" said Isabel. "Look at Nancy Reagan: if she had put that stuff about Frank Sinatra and Peter Lawford in her own book instead of letting Kitty Kelley run with it, people would have gobbled it up. *And,* people might have more respect for her now. I like an author who says—whether it's sex or some other scandal—'This is what I did, for whatever reasons. I probably shouldn't have but I can't turn back the clock, and I'm not gonna lie about it. If you don't like it, lump it.'"

"You have to give your readers something more than they got from following the case in the papers," I agreed. "They want the inside story."

"Exactly. It's like you paid your admission to the circus, and now, for a little extra, we're offering a peep show." Isabel mouthed something, then said, "Peep Show. That's good. Write that down."

I said I certainly would, and, with regard to my time being essentially my own, I did intend to write a page or two on my novel every day.

"I love it! We're a writers' colony—a little non-fiction in the morning, a little novel-writing in the afternoon. And why not? There are a lot of hours in the day."

I liked the way this sounded: no formal hours and conditions. What about leaving the house for a walk or an errand, or taking a day off and going to Boston? Did I just do it? Did I give her a certain amount of notice?

Isabel blotted her mouth with her napkin, then said, "When did I give you the impression that you were an indentured servant?"

"You didn't. We just hadn't discussed any ground rules."

"But you're a grown woman sharing my home, and it depresses me that you want to punch a time clock. My philosophy is, you go to sleep, you wake up, you eat, you work, you do what you want, you eat some more, you do your own thing, you invite your friends over, you go to sleep when you want to, with whomever you want"—she checked my face for a reaction—"and somewhere in the course of all that, the work gets done to everyone's satisfaction."

I said, "I'm just trying to be a good collaborator and a good house guest."

"Which is sweet," said Isabel.

I wanted to refute that, to say something assertive, to sound like the chairman of my own grievance committee. I tried, "I know I said I'd be happy to take over the cooking, but what if I can't get meals on the table three times a day?"

Isabel pointed to her plate, empty now except for four crusts. "You mind *this*? Making two sandwiches instead of one?"

"Not the actual work," I said. "Certainly not the work. Maybe the responsibility? Like, if I wanted to eat a bowl of ice cream in bed instead of cooking dinner, would I be derelict in my duties?"

Isabel laughed, a loud hoot, then covered her mouth. "Sorry."

"Does that mean *no*?"

"That meant, I haven't heard the expression 'derelict in my duties' ever come out of an actual person's mouth. And it also meant, if you want ice cream in bed, you eat ice cream in bed."

"You could go out to dinner on those nights."

Isabel walked her plate to the sink and jiggled the movable parts of the coffee maker as if to say, "I know it's in there."

I joined her at the sink, sensing it was time for a lesson. "Use cold water," I began. "See these markings? I fill it up to seven when I'm making it for the two of us. That's about four or five actual cups of coffee. Then you pour it into this well, and make sure the coffee filter doesn't collapse on itself or else the water will miss the grounds."

I stood back and talked her through it. I told her about working in an office: How annoying it was when the person before you left a trickle of coffee in the pot just to avoid putting a new one on to drip. "You got to know who the lazy ones were," I said.

"Didn't you ever say anything?"

"I'd say it to another secretary, but not to a boss."

"Not to a man, you mean?"

I smiled. "Right."

"Well, you can forget that regime. Here, whoever takes the last cup has to leave at least a full cup behind for the next person or else makes a fresh pot. That's a new rule as of this minute."

"Fine with me," I said.

"Look," she said. "It's coming! It's brown!"

When enough had dripped into the pot, I filled our cups. "You can *do* that?" Isabel said in awe. "You can take coffee before it's completely done?"

"Taste it," I said.

She did. I could feel her congratulatory grin coming on, and a pronouncement. I said, "Don't tell me: I'm a genius."

Smiling coolly, she carried both cups to the table. As soon as we were seated she said, "We can order pizza, or get take-out from some places in Wellfleet that do fried clams and scallops. And I know a couple of fish markets that sell ready-made chowder. You don't have to cook every meal."

I asked if she really hated going out.

"I hate going out *alone*."

"What about with friends?"

"You think I have friends here?"

"Costas?" I asked. "Wouldn't he go out with you?"

She raised her eyebrows as if to say, *you have to ask?*

"Why don't you?"

Isabel took a sip of coffee and from the rim of her cup said, "Neither of us drives."

"Why not?"

"Who learned to drive in New York? Did you? I never needed a driver's license before I moved here."

"What about Pete?"

"I'd ask him during the day, certainly—"

"But you feel silly having him drop you off and pick you up at a restaurant?"

"Ex-actly," she breathed.

"Why don't you get a license now?"

"To go out to eat once a month?"

I knew where this was heading, and I let it. A new-found authority was radiating from my driver's license. I said, "Isabel, would you like me to drop you off at a restaurant and pick you up afterward? I could do that occasionally."

"Would you?" she cried. "Like twice a week?"

"What about Costas? He must get a little stir-crazy."

"I'm not ruining my nights out by bringing Costas. No, thank you."

"Maybe it would be more civil in public. Maybe he wouldn't growl at everything you said."

Isabel narrowed her eyes as if watching an imaginary scene over my shoulder—Take One: Costas in a public place. She shook her head. "No way. Not unless you're there."

I confessed that I felt as if I were in the middle of an awkward situation, like a daughter whose quarreling parents speak only through her at the dinner table. "Are you and

Costas currently having a fight," I asked, "or is this the way things always are between you?"

"Both."

"I mean, is it going to get any better?"

"No."

"Because of Guy VanVleet?"

"There's some of that."

"Were you separated at the time like the newspapers said?"

"We've been separated forever."

"Literally?"

She walked over to the coffee pot and absentmindedly poured herself another inch. I could tell she was speech writing in her head. She sat down again. "Costas and I are like a chronic disease to each other. We've figured out a way to live with it. It doesn't kill us, but it doesn't get any better."

"But you got back together—or whatever you call this— after the murder."

She said in a small, tight voice that gave him no credit, "He called me."

"After how long?"

"I forget."

"Months? Years?"

"A year."

"What did he say?"

"Nothing too flattering."

"But he wanted to help?"

"Not out of any sense of compassion! Duty, maybe; Greek male macho duty. He threw money at my lawyers and then said to me, 'I can give you a place to hide.'"

"Here?" I asked.

"Of course here. I was living in a one-bedroom apartment among neighbors who signed a petition saying I was threatening their security or lowering their property values or some such horseshit. . . . All of a sudden, he's there with blueprints for a dream house on the ocean—one million bucks for the lot alone—in a place he tells me is loaded with artists and writers and psychiatrists who mind their own business because they're hiding from their patients. . . . A place *this* far away on the map." She measured an inch of air between her thumb and index finger.

I asked, "Does the money come from his artwork?"

Isabel said yes. Some before he was discredited and some since.

"What happened with that?"

Isabel said, "Major scandal."

"Yeah?"

"You know photo realism—it looks like a photograph but it's a painting? Well, Costas practically invented that, or so he says. But the problem was he was using actual photographs— huge Polaroids—with a little paint thrown on and calling them paintings. Big disgrace. No one stood by him."

"Did you?"

"Are you kidding? I loved it! I reveled in it! I couldn't have dreamed up such a punishment if I had hired a consulting firm to do it. Don't forget—you're seeing him bowed. Can you imagine Costas Dimantopoulos, with this arrogance, this mouth, *before* he was discredited? As a guy who had beaten the odds and was actually getting rich from painting?"

"Good premise for a novel," I said. "You go to bed famous and you wake up disgraced."

"You could do a lot worse than Costas in the villain department."

I said maybe next time, my next novel. Luckily I was all set with this one; my characters were knocking on the door. All I needed was the time to write them. Even if I was a little blocked.

"Why are you blocked? You mean writer's block?"

"A particular chapter I know I have to write, but it's not coming."

"How come?"

"It's sexual," I said.

"Oh yeah? Who's doing it?"

"Charlotte and Arthur."

"That's a tough one—getting between the sheets with your parents. How explicit do you have to get?"

"It's completely up to me."

"I'd go for it. That's what sells books."

"I have to be true to the tone of the rest of the novel," I said. "I can't suddenly have a steamy chapter that's at odds with my personae."

Isabel made a face. "Just do it," she said. "Put your nose to the grindstone. Get their clothes off and let them roll around on the page. It'll get the juices flowing for The Isabel Krug Story."

I said I'd go to my room and try.

"And tonight we go out for dinner?"

"Oh," I said. "I was going to work straight through dinner. Maybe have a bite at my desk." Her face fell.

"Maybe around eight? I could stop then."

Isabel beamed. "I'll ask Pete what's open on a Tuesday night. A place with music? Casual but good food? I've heard him mention a Portuguese restaurant in Provincetown that he and his cousins like. Maybe he'll introduce us to his friends, they'll tell us what's good, and we'll buy them a round of whatever they're drinking."

How nice, I thought, and how truly democratic. How refreshing to see a woman of Isabel's station break bread with the locals.

My writing group recognized that in the 1990s a sex chapter was absolutely necessary. Not gratuitous sex, not pandering to a mass-market readership, but sex of a character-developing nature. "Look," my teacher had said, "you put a normal, lonely man on stage and you send a sexually available woman out to play opposite him, and you damn well better have them kiss by the end of the first act. The audience expects it. They bought their ticket to see that kiss, even if it blows up in the second act."

I knew what he was really saying: You, Harriet, write pretty parlor skits about manners, unlike me, a published writer who dramatizes the underbelly of life, whose characters offend and whose words change people's lives.

One of my classmates, Ferris Porter, an English professor at LaGuardia Community College who wrote mysteries set in the Maritime Provinces, said he wouldn't presume to tell another writer how to take on the task, but that I might consider actions which *suggest* rather than delineate sexual activity: the closing of a door, the shutting off of a light, the ending of a chapter immediately after a pressing together of lips. He himself had found these devices useful. Many of his favorite movies employed similar techniques such as flickering flames in the fireplace or ankle shots of satin nightgowns slipping to the floor.

"Would that work?" I had asked the others.

Becca Friedman, whom I wasn't too crazy about (she dyed her short hair sludge-black and was assumed to be sleeping with the teacher) said, "Why are you afraid to move in close? Are you afraid that Charlotte's goodness is inextricably linked to her virginity?"

I backed down because I wanted to be a good sport. If "A Room in the Cantor's House" needed sex, then I would reach inside myself to find it.

The best advice, I decided in the end, was Ferris Porter's, who—even though he'd had no nibbles from agents or publishers—was a professor and the kind of reader I imagined would buy my book. I sat at my typewriter, experimenting with opening lines:

> ~~Tea would be soothing, Arthur thought from the kitchen upon hearing Charlotte's relentless cough.~~
>
> ~~Charlotte and that endless cough of hers, mused Arthur.~~
>
> ~~"Come in, already," Charlotte declared.~~
>
> ~~"Come in, Arthur," he heard Charlotte murmur.~~
>
> "Who is it?" Arthur heard Charlotte murmur in response to his knock.
>
> "I brought you a nice cup of herbal tea," he replied.
>
> "~~Hold on Just a see~~ One minute," said Charlotte. "I'm giving myself a sponge bath."
>
> Arthur hesitated, but not for long. His reflection in the tea gave him the courage to push open the long-closed door.

So there it was: a sex scene. Arthur would go in and they would do it. Implied rather than delineated. Rendered in such a way that my parents could live with it. I read it once with some hope, a second and third time with increasing distaste.

It stank. *I* stank. My writing group stank. Not one of them had called or written to wish me well. If anyone else had announced she was moving away, I would have thrown a good-luck party, just wine and cake at the break. But apparently no one was deeply affected enough by my departure to organize the phone tree. I'd have baked something myself or brought in bagels if I had sensed a groundswell, but I didn't. For such keen observers of the human condition, you'd think they'd be a little nicer.

10
ON THE TOWN

 IN PROVINCETOWN, OFF-season, in a Portuguese bar serving only kale soup and deep-fried linguiça, there weren't many over-sized blondes wearing raccoon coats, alligator pumps, blue jeans, and a Red Sox cap as an ice-breaker. Heads turned. Isabel swept in like a movie star soaking up atmosphere for an ethnic character role; I followed like an apologetic escort from the chamber of commerce.

We sat down at the only empty table. Isabel maintained the brilliant smile she had arrived with, as if everything in sight was wonderfully pleasing. She took her arms out of her coat

ISABEL'S BED

and draped it over her shoulders. "Oh, miss!" she sang, when a barmaid stared. "I'd like a beer on tap, and my friend Harriet will have . . . ?"

"A bloody Mary."

"What kinda beer?" asked the waitress, who looked like a mean fourteen-year-old boy with a stringy ponytail.

"You decide," said Isabel. "And may we have menus?"

The waitress jerked her thumb over her shoulder. "The food's up on the board."

Undeterred, Isabel squinted happily. The waitress said she'd be back with our drinks.

"Kale soup," Isabel read. "Chourico sub—whatever the hell that is; linguiça omelet, fried squid and chips. Cheeseburger." She raised her eyebrows and said under her breath, *"Quel variété."* I laughed, relieved: It *was* an act.

The waitress returned with a drink in each hand and plunked them down. Isabel thanked her elaborately, then asked if she knew Pete DaSilva. Our friend Pete, on whose rave recommendation we had come.

"How d'you know Pete?"

"He's my neighbor," said Isabel. She kicked me under the table as if I required help catching on. "I understand he's a regular."

"Yeah. D' ya know what ya want?"

"What would you recommend?" Isabel chirped. "What's the specialty of the house?"

"The sub."

"And how do you pronounce its main ingredient?"

"Chorice."

"Is that Portuguese?"

"Yeah. It's spicy sausage."

I noticed men at the bar were turning around for quick

85

glances, as if word was rippling down the stools, "Check out the dames in the back."

"I'll have that," I said. "And a cup of the kale soup."

"We only got one size."

"Fine."

"I haven't had eggs in ages," said Isabel, "so I'm going to try the omelette. Well-done. What comes with that?"

"Fries."

"Good. And could I have a cup of decaf with my meal, if it's brewed decaf. With milk."

"Omelet dry and decaf. Sub and soup. Anything else to drink?"

I said no, not now.

As soon as our waitress disappeared, Isabel said, "Did you ever in your life see such a sullen little shit?"

"I think she thinks we're tourists—"

"That's a reason?"

"Maybe it's an ethnic thing."

"Big deal! I told her I was a friend of Pete's."

I said I wouldn't take it personally; this waitress was probably rude to everybody. It was a neighborhood bar, and in walk two strangers—

"What is this, Birmingham, Alabama, in the 1950s? And we're two old black ladies at the front of the bus?"

I sipped my bloody Mary and let her rail: We weren't tourists. We weren't undesirables. Nobody here read the *Daily News* or the *Post* or kept up with events in Greenwich, Connecticut, so that they might have taken the VanVleets' side against hers.

Our waitress came back with something close to a smile on her face and two glasses of red wine.

"We didn't order wine," I said.

She put the glasses in the middle of the table and struck a pose, one hand on her hip and her eyes on the ceiling. "I'm supposta say, 'Welcome to the Old Anka from two admirahs.'" She looked back toward her audience at the bar and smirked. I knew that look: high school stupid girl, called to her feet by the teacher, plays to her smart-ass friends.

"How lovely!" Isabel exclaimed. She lifted her glass to salute the whole row of potential secret admirers. "Harriet?" she prompted.

I raised my glass an inch off the table.

Thank you, Isabel mouthed to each of the half-dozen men who were paying attention. Thank you, thank you, thank you, thank you, thank you, thank you.

"Jesus," I said under my breath.

"Completely harmless," she muttered without changing her expression or missing a beat.

"They'll think you're inviting them over."

"So?"

"I don't want to meet any of them."

"Aren't you curious which ones did it?"

"Not in the least."

Isabel leaned across the assortment of glasses. "Party pooper."

"So? Did I ever claim to be anything else?"

"You said you liked men."

"As opposed to women! That doesn't mean I like every man at a seedy bar."

"Then you're a snob."

I looked over at the candidates. They had turned back to their own drinks and to the television show, which looked like home videos of real crimes being committed and real police

87

rushing in on the heels of the criminals. "I don't think there's one over twenty-five," I said.

"So? Are we going to marry them?"

"Guys send wine because they're interested in meeting you, and if you don't think it's for sexual purposes, then there's no use discussing it."

She pursed her lips before answering. "How can I say this: I *know*. I'm not offended. I'm available, and so are you, at least on paper. We're sending out signals. And, like it or not, this is the population of available heterosexual men in P-town. The rest are married or gay or even younger than these guys."

The food arrived, looking better than I would have guessed. My sub came with purple cole slaw and a red pickled pepper.

Isabel crooked her finger to our waitress. "What's your name, sweetie?"

"Stephie."

"Stephie, can you tell me which two gentlemen sent the wine over?"

Stephie shrugged.

"Isn't that the point? To establish personal contact?"

"I guess."

"Are they seated together?"

Stephie checked the bar stools. "You could say that."

Isabel unzipped her pocketbook and offered a ten-dollar bill between two fingers. "If you can remember who sent the wine, I'd like to return the favor. Would you have the bartender refill their drinks with my compliments?"

I was beginning to enjoy Isabel's sideshow. Stephie studied the ten as if doing the arithmetic.

"Does that cover it?"

"I guess so."

"And can you say this: 'The ladies are old enough to be your mothers, but they appreciate the gesture.' Also: 'You made their day.'"

"You made their day."

"Excellent. Keep the change."

We watched her confer with two twenty-fivish-year-olds in down vests, no better or worse than the candidates on either side of them. They waved good-naturedly and that was that. I told Isabel she had done the right thing and had done it with panache.

She preened, and stabbed a round of sausage with her fork.

I said, "I think you're very talented in the man department."

"I am. And you know what's better than that?"

My mouth was full of sub, so I opened my eyes wider and shook my head.

She reached across to pat my hand. "I give lessons."

We drove home along 6A, the shore road lined with mostly dark motels and restaurants. Isabel cried out whenever she saw signs of life: "Mexican! . . . Italian! . . . Opening Memorial Day! . . . Doug Dougherty at the piano! . . . Raw bar! . . . Kids Stay Free!"

I asked if she was looking forward to summer, to having more options.

"Now I am," she said happily.

"We should be well into the manuscript by then."

Isabel swiveled her head to look at me. "That's, like, three months away."

"Right."

"Won't we be done by then?"

89

"You're dreaming," I said.

I could see in my peripheral vision that she was smiling and I asked what I had said that was funny.

"Is that the Bloody Mary talking? 'You're dreaming.'"

I smiled back. "Maybe. Or maybe I'm not as worried that you'll send me home if I say something rude."

Isabel snorted. "If I was going to send you home over something, it would have been that 'derelict-in-my-duties' act."

"It wasn't an act," I said. "Unfortunately."

She nodded once and turned back to the motels and cottages out her window. "This guy you lived with?" she said suddenly. "The bagel man? Were you really knocked for a loop when he broke up with you?"

"I shouldn't have been. . . ."

"But you were, weren't you?"

"We'd been together twelve years. I thought I was past the point when I had to worry about every little rough spot."

"How long ago did it happen?"

"A month."

Isabel sucked in her breath. "Just like that?"

I felt tears start in an ache behind my eyes, not for Kenny but for Isabel's kindness—that she who had lost a lover in cold blood could gasp at such a mundane parting. I said, "I didn't see it coming, even though things weren't great. Then he announces he's met someone, and life is wonderful. *She's* wonderful. They're wonderful together—oh, but please don't worry because they're practicing safe sex."

"He said that?"

"He poured his little heart out, every detail—how they met, what kind of bagels she liked—"

Isabel clapped her hand over her mouth, but too late to

smother a giggle. "Sorry," she yelped. "Forgive me. He's such a prick! He confesses so he'll feel better, like you're *interested*. Like you give a fuck how they met and how happy he is."

"I was a little interested."

"Of course you were. But you don't want to hear it with all his flourishes, right? How she makes mad, passionate love to him on the dining room table. And shampoos his hair in the bathtub and massages him with vanilla oil. How he's alive again."

"Something like that."

Isabel shifted in her seat and faced me as much as her seat belt allowed. "I'm not making fun of you," she said. "And I'll only continue insulting him if that makes you feel better."

I was so surprised by her kindness, so unprepared for the contract it implied, that my throat tightened and my thanks were a hoarse whisper.

She turned back to the darkened scenery. "Prince of Whales Motel," she murmured. "Get it? Whales, with an *h*?"

"I get it."

After a while I broke the silence. "I never discussed Kenny with anyone. It happened, and I told people, but no one else ever said, 'What a prick. It wasn't your fault. It would have happened no matter what. You shouldn't blame yourself.'"

"No one? Not even these great friends in your writing group who know everything there is to know?"

"That's different. We don't know about each other's private lives, except when it turns into fiction."

"You don't meet for drinks after class? I thought drinking was part of the process. Like what's his name—the actress's grandfather?—Hemingway. Not even a cup of coffee?"

"I didn't join them."

"There wasn't anyone in that whole bunch you'd call up to find out what the homework was when you were out sick?"

"Ferris Porter," I said. "But that was because he called *me* one time for an assignment, and because he was always kind when my stories were read."

"Married?"

I said I didn't know—his detectives were divorced so I assumed he was, too.

"Does he know your new address?"

I said yes, I had given the whole class a handout announcing my new address and phone number. I'd probably be hearing from them any day.

"I'm sure you will," Isabel murmured. Then, "Where were your parents in all of this?"

"In Brookline."

"I meant, what did they do when he threw you out?"

"They offered me my old room."

"Were they knocked for a loop, too?"

I said, "No, they had predicted it. They never trusted Kenny. My father used to go down to the store when he visited; he liked seeing other people's operations. I know he thought Kenny was a little too familiar with the women customers."

Isabel closed her eyes—my life depressed her, too. We didn't say anything more for the rest of the ride, from 6A to 6 through Truro Center and up Corn Hill. Not until I had made the sharp left into Isabel's driveway did she call out, like a conductor announcing our destination: "Boy, will he be sorry."

It was not quite ten o'clock when Isabel and I said good night in the main foyer. She gave me a quick hug and thanked me for my company. I said I'd see her at breakfast . . . Sleep well.

I followed the curvy fun house walls down the long, private walkway to my room, humming the last tune I'd heard on the car radio. As I got closer, I heard water splashing. My first thought, like everything associated with my tower suite, was rosy and literary: A servant drawing me a bath? A driving March rain outside my own personal Wuthering Heights? A dark and stormy night?

Even with the door to the bathroom open and steam wafting toward me, I didn't assign the noise to anything other than my own human error, to a shower jet I had left open. And what was this white terry cloth robe with a blue Ritz-Carlton crest doing on my bed? For me? A gift from the gracious management of this luxury hotel?

I didn't snap out of my trance until the romantic sound of driving rain stopped suddenly. By itself. And there in the doorway, big and dark, naked and uncircumcised and completely nonplused, was Costas.

I yelped and turned my back on his wet, hairy, unblinking body. I heard the muffled sounds of his feet padding their way to his bathrobe and finally, unapologetically, "I didn't expect you back this early."

Like a parent. Like a guilty boyfriend. Like a worst-case Goldilocks. "Why were you using my shower?" I squeaked.

"Because I designed it," he replied coolly, "and because it's the best one in the house."

"Don't you have one?"

"You can turn around now. I'm decent." He was smiling, tying his belt slowly and carelessly, low over his bulges with no remorse.

"Why didn't you close the door?"

93

"I should have. I apologize."

"There are hooks on the back of the door for robes and towels." *You schmuck. Who parks their bathrobe a room away?*

"I know that. I was afraid it would get wet when I turned the jets on full blast. This is where I've always left it."

"They don't get wet on the hooks."

"Never? In how many showers since you've been here?"

"Many."

"And do you share my regard for this shower?"

I said, "I'm getting used to it."

"The openness, you mean? You were accustomed to showering in enclosed spaces?"

This guy was creepy anyway, but more so talking about my shower habits while he stood next to my bed with his bare feet and long toes digging into my carpet. I returned to the original offense; I lit my candle to sexual harassment. I said, "I think this is a privacy issue, Mr. Dimantopoulos, and I'd like to think my privacy is respected."

Costas smiled. His pelvis shifted with his weight. "I think I'm the one with no secrets left, Harriet."

He was proud of it, of his big parts and his locker-room swagger. I said, "I think you find this funny but I don't."

"Am I never going to be able to use my favorite bathroom again? Even by appointment?"

I asked, more or less, What exactly was the big deal? If he loved it so much, why hadn't he chosen this suite for himself?

He said solemnly, "Because I need northern light."

"For painting?"

"That's right."

"Doesn't it have a shower?"

"Of course."

"But mine is better?"

"My bath is also my darkroom, which seemed like a good idea when we built the house. Now it seems oppressive, like living in one's office."

I gestured all around me: I lived in my office, didn't I? Blissfully?

"But your work doesn't smell like chemicals. In fact, your bathroom smells like some exotic fruit."

He walked over to my desk, which was stacked with clippings, turned on the lamp, and read the piece on top of the pile. After a minute, without turning around he asked, "Do you believe her?"

"Who?"

"Isabel. Do you think everything happened the way the newspapers reported it?"

"As far as I can tell."

"Because she testified under oath and you think people who put their hand on the Bible tell the truth?"

"She was the only eyewitness!"

"Except for the dead man. And the blubbering wife who lost her mind in all of this. Quite conveniently."

I asked what he was trying to say. To imply.

He turned around to face me and said, all innocence, "Not a thing. I'm having fun with you. But I'm done. I can see it shocks you to find the owner of this house in his own bathroom because he innocently misjudged the amount of time it would take his wife to meet a man and seduce him."

"Isabel didn't seduce any man."

He tsk'd theatrically. "No luck tonight? What was this unfortunate choice of dating bars?"

"It was a restaurant, a place Pete recommended, the Old Anchor."

"So it was a tête à tête, just you girls?"

"That's right. I didn't feel like cooking."

"No? When you do it so well?"

I said, "You don't have to make fun of me."

"I'm making conversation. I'm deflecting my embarrassment at being discovered in the nude by a woman who seems horrified at the sight."

I said, "That doesn't mean you have to make nasty remarks about Isabel."

He smiled. "I'm making trouble, that's all."

I could have challenged him with the facts, reminded him that all the physical evidence supported Isabel's testimony: that Isabel and Guy were having, by all accounts, a great time before the missus burst in; that Guy had lipstick kisses up and down his torso in Isabel's long-wearing Ooh-La-La Red; that there was what police called a "marital aid" vibrating under the night table, a movie titled *Dicks and Janes* in the VCR.

What I did say was, "Isabel hired me to tell the personal side of the story, not to rehash the case."

"That's right," he said. "And you are the ideal woman for that job."

He knocked against my shoulder as he walked past me. There was nothing forceful in it, but it felt deliberate, and he didn't excuse himself.

At the door he turned and said, "I'm her husband. Why would I want to change a very satisfactory outcome?"

"I don't know."

"I think you're lying," he said calmly. "You think I'm cruel and even a little dangerous. You see no other purpose in my life except to punish Isabel. Am I wrong about that?"

Because the doorknob was in my hand and because he was already in the hall, I felt safe enough to say, "You do make me a little nervous."

Costas laughed as if I had said something droll and flattering. "Harriet Mahoney," he said, "I like you. I might even miss you when you're gone."

11

HOW WE MET

 OVER BREAKFAST, ISABEL said she had a personal blueprint for me, if I didn't mind her sticking her nose into my love life.

I sipped my coffee and waited, offering no encouragement.

"First," she began, "let me say this: I don't do things in a romantic fashion." She shook her head. "Correction: I do romantic things in a pragmatic fashion."

I said I didn't know that.

"Yes, you do." She widened her eyes, as if prompting the clue that would win the round.

Costas, she meant. I checked the floor below the kitchen

railing and whispered, "He was using my shower when I came in last night."

"Ignore him," she said with a dismissive wave, "unless you don't want to, in which case you have my blessing."

Without saying "ugh" or pronouncing the obvious—that I found him sinister, rude, and repulsive—I murmured something diplomatic about not getting involved with a married man.

"Me neither," said Isabel. "Not anymore."

I got up to pour myself a refill of coffee. When I sat down again I said, "Why not 'anymore'? Because of Mr. VanVleet?"

"And Costas! Don't forget that little wedding-reception romance."

After a polite moment I asked, "Were you really in love with him once?"

"Yeah. For about five minutes twenty years ago." She put down her slice of toast. "Not really five minutes. But that's what it feels like from here."

"What about Mr. VanVleet?" I asked.

"You mean, was I in love with him?"

"Would you still be together if he had lived?"

Isabel said, "I knew we'd get around to this sooner or later."

I jumped in with my privately forged theory, that Guy was going to give it all up—the house, the children, his standing in the community, his heiress wife—for Isabel, and that Nan killed him rather than lose him in a humiliating divorce.

"Harriet," said Isabel, "you are truly from another century."

"You weren't in love with him?"

Isabel wagged her head: maybe.

"Is there an answer?" I asked. "Do you know yourself?"

"Of course I know," she said. "And it's what I'm planning to announce to the world in either the first chapter or the last chapter, depending on which packs the biggest wallop."

I asked when I'd find out.

She squinted at the microwave clock. "Right now."

"A personal shopper is different things to different people," she began in a sing-song appropriate for explaining to six-year-olds how babies are made. "There was nothing out of the ordinary about our first consultation. His secretary—a lou-lou, the type who slammed things around and sulked when she felt put-upon—called me because she was tired of doing his personal errands. I came to his office." Isabel pushed up the sleeves of her caftan and smiled. "He made a very nice first impression—cuff links, English shoes, custom-made shirt—not handsome but pleasant looking in a well-groomed, puffy way, and he was certainly friendly, even eager. I could tell he was pleased to meet me, extremely. And not what you'd call subtle about it. The secretary had told me, 'wife's fiftieth birthday,' and when I got there he said he needed a present for his *sister's* fiftieth birthday. I played along with it—these little flirtations are good for business. 'Tell me about her,' I said. 'Tell me about her likes and dislikes, about her tastes, her hobbies, her collections.'

" 'She likes to play tennis and she likes to garden.'

" 'Indoor or outdoor?'

" 'She likes to force bulbs,' he said, staring at me.

"I asked what else; what she liked to wear, if he had a picture. He opened his wallet and took out an old photo—blonde pageboy, black drape, pearls—had to be her college graduation picture—and handed it to me. I said, 'You and your sister must be close if you carry her picture in your wallet.' He said, 'She's a sweet kid.' *I* knew it was his wife, and *he* knew I knew it was his wife, but I played along with it. I asked how personal a gift he wanted; would she be opening it privately or in front of others?

" 'You're good,' he said.

" 'Dollar range?'

" 'Whatever.' Waved his hand, wedding ring big as life.

"I said that wasn't an answer: ten thousand dollars could be 'whatever' or forty-nine ninety-five could be 'whatever.'

"He said, 'Up to ten thousand?'

"I told him he was a generous brother.

" 'She's a sweet kid,' he repeated.

" 'Jewelry?'

" 'That's what I was thinking.'

" 'Tell me what she has.'

" 'I can tell you what she *wants*,' he said, 'and that's anything in a Tiffany box.'

"I asked where she lived and he said, 'Greenwich.'

" 'A tennis bracelet,' I said, just like that, very decisively. I told him what it was and what it cost. Asked if she wanted diamonds, rubies, sapphires, or emeralds, or, for less, a custom job in tourmaline or garnets. He looked a little sheepish and said he'd better go for the real stuff; were sapphires the blue ones? His sister liked blue.

"I never do this, but I said, 'I don't think you need me. You could take it from here and order the bracelet by phone.'

" 'Oh, no,' he said. 'That wouldn't be fair.'

"I said, 'Sure it would. I'm a busy woman. Unless, of course, you have more gifts on your list.' He said he did, something else for his sister, but from her husband, who was extremely busy himself, and kind of a straight arrow, but who

101

did want something personal for his wife's birthday, if I knew what he meant."

" 'Lingerie?'

"He nodded.

" 'Negligee?'

" 'Or one of those short things that has straps up here and snaps down there.'

" 'A teddy.'

"I asked size and color and he said, 'Large, black.' I wrote everything down and asked him what else. He hesitated, and I knew he was weighing whether he should make his move then or lock me into a second appointment. He asked how he should pay; I told him I had my accounts established: I purchased the items and the stores billed him. He fell over himself complimenting me on my business practices. I said I usually needed a week, but frankly this was a cinch. I could pick up these items immediately and deliver them the next day.

" 'Where?' he said, falling over himself again. 'I'll meet you. You don't have to come all the way down here. I'll be near Tiffany's at lunchtime tomorrow. I could meet you.'

" 'Fine,' I said. 'You tell me where and when.' He named some fancy restaurant—I can't remember which one. I made a face like, 'I'm going to pull a black lace teddy out at The Four Seasons—wherever—to get your okay?' He says, and by this time he's sweating—'Let's make it some place small and quiet.' So next thing I know we have a lunch date for the next day."

"Wait," I interrupted. "I should be taking this down." Isabel said, no need; this would be on a tape: How We Met.

I asked, "So? You said yes? Did you actually meet him for

lunch the next day, and was that the beginning of the affair? Like, immediately?"

Isabel dipped a cold crust of toast into the marmalade jar. "Affair?" She chewed and swallowed. "That's not quite what we were."

I waited, wishing I had a pen and a steno pad regardless.

"Okay. I did the shopping—the bracelet and the teddy— size large, Bergdorf's, nothing scandalous. I met him at this dark bistro kind of place; it was in the basement of a brownstone, no windows. I showed him the bracelet: 'Fine.' All business. Then I opened the box with the teddy— discreetly, on my lap; 'Feel the material,' I said. 'It's an acetate but it feels exactly like silk.' Nothing; he just sat there, paralyzed. Finally he said, 'I can't.'"

Isabel looked at me, all meaningful eye contact, as if we were simultaneously reading poor, dead Guy's mind.

"Why couldn't he?" I asked.

"It was too much for him, too eroticized: me, the teddy, the teddy on my lap."

"Did you realize all this at the time?"

"Yes and no. I wasn't being flirtatious when I asked him to feel the teddy, but when I saw the look on his face, I knew immediately."

"That he was attracted to you?"

"I already *knew* he was attracted to me. This was something else—he wanted to fuck me. On the spot. Till the cows came home."

"So what did you say?"

"You know—what women say in these situations to defuse them. I mentioned his wife, the real birthday girl."

"Was he embarrassed?"

"No! They're never embarrassed. He said, 'I've never lied about being married, but when you walked into my office and you asked whose birthday it was, something happened.'

"I said, 'Look, this is all very flattering but I don't ever see, date, entertain, whatever you want to call it, my clients. It's lousy for business in the long run.'

"He said, 'I've never cheated on my wife. I've never even had a discussion like this with another woman.'"

I asked Isabel if she had believed him.

"You know, I actually did. He was so . . . goofy about it. He was practically melting all over me."

"Did you feel anything?"

Isabel shook her head, frowning.

"Why didn't you just say, 'I'm married'?"

"That wouldn't have stopped him." She thought it over and said, "Which is an attractive quality, if you know what I mean."

"So you weren't really resisting."

She rearranged herself on the kitchen chair, tucking her legs underneath her. She said, "Let me put this in perspective for you: Opportunities present themselves in business and you weigh them. Guy VanVleet said to me, 'Anything. Any time. Any place.' I said, 'I think I've just been insulted.' He said, 'Are you always in love with the men you go out with?' I said, 'Absolutely.' Then, like a dying man he whispered, 'Once. Just one time.' He reached over to my side of the table and took the Tiffany box and said, 'I hope you like it.'"

I blinked and repeated, "He gave you the box, just like that?"

She nodded. "Seven thousand bucks."

"And you slept with him after that lunch?"

"Not that very day. We made a date." She hesitated then asked, "Am I shocking you?"

I said not really; people sleep with other people for all kinds of reasons, and I could see the progression from customer to, well, satisfied customer.

Isabel asked, "Have you ever been anyone's fantasy?"

I said, "I'd be very surprised."

"It's heady stuff." She laughed. "So much for Guy's thinking 'once.' And you know, I got into it. I amazed myself with my kept-woman routine—always at my place, always with teddies and gimmicks; always in the mood. He thought *we* were real life: not Nan in her flannel Lanz nightgown jerking him off with one hand while she flipped through *Town and Country* with the other. I wanted to say, 'Give the woman a break! There's a huge difference between seeing you once a week for a date and living with you for twenty-five years.' "

"Did it change?" I asked. "You know—like in stories, like in a marriage of convenience where it starts off as an arrangement but then the two people fall in love and it evolves into something meaningful and quite beautiful?"

She shook her head. "He was a client, Harriet."

"Always?"

"I enjoyed it, if that's what you're asking. And there was no commerce discussed. From where I sat it was satisfactory sex with tokens of his appreciation sprinkled in. Not money, things: baubles, presents, tickets, gift certificates."

I asked if she enjoyed Guy's company.

"You know, looking back, I actually think I did."

"Where was Costas when all of this was happening?"

"Away. Not bothering me."

"Did Guy know there was a husband in the wings?"

"Of course. And get this: They owned a Costas Dimantopoulos."

It took me a few seconds to understand she meant they owned one of Costas's paintings.

"It was a complete coincidence. And the funny part was, they were just the kind of people Costas used to say bought his paintings—rich, conventional, boring collectors with lots of wall space and a New York decorator. I talked Guy into a second one."

I said it didn't sound to me like Guy was too conventional or too boring.

"He was definitely a kid in a candy store, which was quite appealing. And he was uncomplicated. You always knew what made him happy, and when you gave it to him—that was enough. Even with a wife and three kids in the picture, it was a very straightforward relationship. Kind of a simple, low-maintenance guy—"

"I wouldn't consider all you did low-maintenance."

Isabel lowered her chin and said solemnly, "Be-*lieve* me. It's low maintenance when you can do no wrong."

"Did you ever do it with no strings attached?"

"You mean just for the hell of it?"

I nodded.

"No," said Isabel. "It was still my time, my apartment, my refreshments, my underwear."

"Did anybody else know about your arrangement?"

"No one."

"Nan thought it was a love affair?"

"As far as I know. Which I think was worse for her. Much worse. I think you can deal with your husband paying for sex better than your husband being in love with someone else."

"What about Costas?" I asked. "Did he know?"

"You think Costas analyzes the fine points of my relationships with other men?" She made a face.

"Your lawyer?"

"My lawyer heard what he wanted to hear, which was 'presents.' 'Baubles.' He never blinked."

"Did you have other clients like this?"

"Absolutely not."

"Why not just leave well enough alone? Why announce to the world that you had sex with Guy VanVleet for money?"

"He didn't see it that way. He was a man in love." She tapped her long, squared-off index fingernail on the table top. "I want you to explain it in such a way that people reading The Isabel Krug Story see his gifts as tokens of his affection to a woman of great passion and loyalty." After a silence she said, "Really. He didn't see it. If you asked him why Isabel Krug was sleeping with him once a week, he'd swear on a stack of Bibles that she was doing it for love."

I said softly, "Then he must have died happy."

Her eyes filled with tears. Without her tinted contacts, they were almost ordinary. She said, her voice wobbly, "No he didn't. He was shot in the chest, and he died gasping for breath."

We cleared the table together and to distract her I asked, "What about this personal yet pragmatic blueprint for my love life?"

"Oh, God." She sighed and blew her nose on a paper napkin. "I got sidetracked. It's about what's his name—"

"Kenny."

"No, the other one."

I said there was no other one.

"The guy in the writing group with the funny name."

"Ferris?"

"That's it."

"What about Ferris?"

"There's something there. A little flame I think you could fan."

"I barely know him."

"How long were you in this writing group?" she demanded.

"Four plus years."

"And did he join before or after you?"

"Before."

"So?"

"So nothing. He's a nice man who called me once to find out what had happened in class the night he was out sick."

"Which probably took every nerve he had in his whole body. And since you were living with Kenny, you never stopped to consider the significance of the phone call."

The fact was, I knew Ferris Porter had had something resembling a crush on me. But I wasn't Isabel and he wasn't Guy VanVleet, so neither of us had said a word or moved a muscle.

"He called you," she persisted. "You should have given him some sign."

"Of what? He was calling for the assignment."

"Where I come from, a phone call is an opening move. You should've conveyed something, sent a return signal."

I told her my life wasn't defined by that kind of drama, by moves and declarations between sexually charged men and women. Ferris was fussy and fiftyish with carefully combed thinning red hair and the look of an ex-priest about him. And

I was, well . . . me. After a while I learned a few facts, like what he did, that he was younger than he looked, that he taught Shakespeare In Context and two sections of freshmen composition—but indirectly, through his comments on my pages.

"How did he act in class?"

"Friendly. Helpful."

"Attentive?"

I considered the one incident I could offer as if I, too, had male-female encounters worth reconstructing. "Once," I began, "after the first writing class, everyone had gathered on the sidewalk outside the Y discussing how many taxis they'd pile into to get to their favorite bar. I had stood there, a little off to one side, like I wasn't assuming anything. They chatted about this place and that place, but nobody asked me what I thought. Ferris finally explained, 'We generally go out for a beer after class.'

" 'I think I'll skip it,' I said, even thought it wasn't exactly an invitation. He looked worried, as if he were going to take it up with the group. I said, 'Don't bother. I know how these things work. I'd probably be intruding. They probably need to gossip about the new member of the workshop.'

" 'I'll feel terrible if it's left this way,' Ferris said. 'I insist that you come.'

"I told him he should catch up with the rest of them and have a good time. Really. I had worked all day and was tired. Even if they *had* invited me, I would have excused myself with regrets.

"That was it," I told her, meaning, No offer to leave the group and go with me. No bracelets, no teddies, no sparks flying in dark bistros. Ships that passed in the night. I had gone home to Kenny feeling sorry for myself. He had said,

"Why would you want to go out drinking with a bunch of assholes who didn't want you along in the first place?"

When Isabel had no comment, I said I knew it wasn't a good story, but whose life is? Most of us stand out on the sidewalk and watch the taxis pull away without us.

"He didn't give you that *look*?" Isabel asked, approximating the male meltdown she drew in place of handshakes.

"Ferris?"

"Sure." She waved her arms dreamily. "Out on the sidewalk, under the stars."

"That doesn't happen to most people."

Isabel thought it over, frowning. "You'll write him tonight," she said.

Postcard of Pamet Harbor

Dear Ferris,

How are you? How are Inspector Shoemaker &
Fanny & the other Haligonians? I identify with
them even more now because I'm living a few
yards from the Atlantic Ocean & because the
subject at hand has more in common with your
themes than mine. How is school? Drop me a line
if you have time: c/o Krug, General Delivery,
Truro, MA 02666.

Best regards,

Harriet

Letter from My Parents

Dear Harriet,

We're not upset. We suspected it might be about us because we never got a straight answer when we asked. We know writers get ideas from their families and we've discussed it and decided if that helps you get published then we can give up a little privacy as an investment in your future. Here are the answers to your questions.

Q1. In the original shop on Harrison Ave. in the South End

Q2. Secretary-Receptionist to Dr. Isadore Polansky at B.C.H., Department of Medicine

Q3. He's not positive, but around 36¢ per doz. for plain

Q4. Can't remember. Uncle Leon might

Q5. I said I was meeting my girlfriends

Q6. "A Bell for Adano" (Boston Pops did come first but that was just an accidental meeting)

Q7. NO! nobody did back then

Q9. A justice of the peace

Q10. Niagara Falls

Now that I think about it, the Boston Pops concert was important because I saw your father for the first time outside of the shop in street clothes as a person who liked music and it was because of that that we talked the following Monday morning and eventually I said I'd go to a show with him. Good luck. Talk to you Sunday.

All our love,

Mother and Daddy

XXXOOO

12

SOME FRIEND

 "PETE," I CALLED to him, a flight below me on the dune steps, "do you think your father ever cheated on your mother?"

"Doubt it," he said over his shoulder. He had offered to keep me company on my daily constitutional, since Isabel had no appropriate outerwear and since Costas seemed out of the question for anyone without a death wish.

"Ever?" I asked. We had reached the beach. The sand was frozen in ripples and the tide was coming in. Immediately he searched for the right rocks for skipping—worn flat and fitting just so in the palm of his hand.

"He was no saint," Pete said, throwing his sidelong pitch into the waves for at least four skips. "He could be a sonovabitch, as mean as they come, but I'm pretty sure he didn't screw around."

"Son of a bitch in the bad sense?" I asked.

Pete laughed. "You mean, did he go around beating up on people? No. He was from the old school—mean, but good. Went to church, loved us kids, his country, his boat, his mutha . . ."

"His wife," I offered.

"What's with the wife stuff?" he asked. "You writin' a book on that, too?"

"Not on purpose," I said. I told him Isabel had just depressed me with the tale of how she had met Guy VanVleet, which hadn't helped my outlook on men as loyal and faithful human beings.

"Are we talkin' about the bagel guy?"

"The bagel guy was one chapter."

"But not the worst?"

"Not the worst," I repeated.

Pete said, "Can I guess?"

I nodded.

"Your fatha?"

I recited my list: My father with my stepmother. Kenny with young Amy. Guy with Isabel. Costas with young Isabel.

"That's not so many," said Pete, "when you consida that there must be a hundred guys you could name who didn't ruin anybody's life."

"Well, don't you do it," I said. "Don't cheat on someone who loves you."

Pete said, "I'll keep that in mind when I meet her."

I said, "Really. You have to think positively; you should

ISABEL'S BED

visualize a lease and a security deposit on a summer rental
flying through the mail this minute."

He smirked and skipped another rock toward the horizon.
"Oh, yeah. These summah women love us townies in pick-up
trucks." After a minute he said, "Women aren't the only ones
who get their hahts broken, you know. You probably even
broke old Kenny's haht a few times."

"Kenny had no heart," I replied.

"Why'd you stay with him so long?"

"Because I thought I was better off with someone than
with no one, and I thought we were at that mature friendship
stage all the magazines talk about which follows the fireworks
stage and the cooling down stage."

"Some friend," said Pete, moving two steps in the direction
of Great Hollow.

"Of course they don't tell you that while you're in the
friendship phase, he's out cruising for someone new in heat."

"You've been bahkin' up the wrong trees," said Pete. "All
these guys you're talking about are from the big cities, right?
Kenny, New Yohk. Your fatha, Boston, right? Costas, New
Yohk. Guy VanVleet, more or less New Yohk. People in those
places get hit on by women who come up to them at pahties
and on the subway and say, 'Would you like to meet me after
work some night for a mahtini?' Then if you say, 'I'm
married,' they say, 'This is strictly business. Here's my
cahd.'"

Demographically I didn't think his theory held water, and I
told him so.

"All I know," he said, "is that none of my friends' parents
got divorced."

"So you think it's opportunity rather than character?"

"Something like that."

115

"You think your father was faithful because no one ever tempted him?"

"Jesus," he said. "If you'd evah seen what he looked like. I'm a movie stah next to him."

"There's thousands of women here every summer, right? Swarming around in their bikinis, looking for a fling. Isn't that enough opportunity?"

He shrugged. "If that's what you want."

"And what about Guy VanVleet? He worked in New York and according to Isabel never fooled around until he met her."

"And she believed him? A guy who didn't even botha to hide his foolin' around?"

I asked how he knew that.

"People said so, the witnesses." He stopped and squinted into the water, then said, "Look."

I looked. Gulls. "Gulls?" I asked.

"Diving," he said.

"For what?"

"Bait fish," said Pete. "Which usually means something bigga's chasin' them. I'm gonna get my rod. Wanna wait?"

I said, sure, why not. He jogged back to the stairs and took them three at a time, five flights to the top. In what seemed liked seconds, he was tap-dancing back down, rod in one hand and tackle box in the other.

"Take it easy," I yelled against the wind.

He bounded to the spot where he'd been and kneeled down to open the latches of the tackle box. First thing he fished out was a navy blue knitted cap, which he patted onto his head as if it were Step One.

"Your fatha," he began without stopping what he was

doing—tying a fake fluorescent fish onto his line—"how'd he meet your stepmutha?"

"Why?"

"'Cause I wanna see if it fits my big-city barracuder theory."

I held the pole while he tied metal things to the line. I said, "She was his teacher. He finally went back to school after years of us nagging him to get his degree, and there she was, first semester: The Novella."

"When was this?"

"When I was sixteen."

"Oh," he said, as if sixteen weren't so bad.

"Sixteen was lousy," I said. "My younger sister couldn't be told the gory details unless the child psychiatrist was there, and my older sister was away at school, so I got the brunt of it."

"Yeah," said Pete, "but at least you had both parents the whole time you were a kid."

I said, "It was lousy because my mother thought I was old enough to hear everything. Every detail, all through high school. And then I couldn't leave her, except to commute to Newton College of the Sacred Heart down the street." I didn't repeat aloud the kinds of tidbits my mother took strange comfort in dissecting with me as her lab partner. Such as:

—The identity of the anonymous caller who said carelessly over the phone, mistaking me for my mother, "Mrs. Mahoney, I think you should know that your husband's teacher is throwing herself at your husband." And how I had to be the one to watch my mother's face as her whole life changed with one phone message, to see her straighten her shoulders and say with false brightness, "Well, it doesn't mean he's throwing himself back at her, does it?";

—The end-of-semester supper, spouses not invited, at which Professor Harris asked my father to stay, at which time she had the unmitigated and transparent gall to consult him about a frayed cord on a lamp on her bedside table;

—The probability that Professor Harris had said something like, "Was I wrong in thinking you felt the same way about me?" And, "I had no idea you were married," to which he probably said, "I lost my wedding ring in a mixer and had to throw out the whole batch. . . .";

—His not knowing, standing by her king-size bed, how to refuse such a dedicated teacher; how he had slipped into a deep sexual black hole unexplored with a wife of nineteen years, and couldn't climb out of it; and how we thought it occurred to him as he drove home from the pot-luck supper, "I'm forty-seven. I might die soon. Other men do it and get away with it";

—Everything she found out from studying the transcript of Professor Harris's divorce from Maury Harris, maker of raincoats, founder of HarrisWear, who had a history of getting blow jobs from women on the payroll—screened and hired for this very talent, Frances asserted in court;

—The Pygmalion thing Professor Harris had for my father, her seeing in him a doughnut maker with a brain and beautiful eyes and a penchant for Jewish women and thinking, Arthur Mahoney is a two-carat diamond in the rough. I'll dress him in HarrisWear and parade him before my friends;

—The two horrible Harris sons who would gain a father figure;

—Either my overhearing or reconstructing his telling my mother that he and Frances were engaged. That this horrible Frances Harris, at forty-three, was pregnant with his child like some kind of miracle, since she'd had one and three-quarters' ovaries removed due to benign cysts;

—The nerve of calling it an engagement, like two children with a secret pact, like two teenagers with a hope chest;

—And his sorrow, his being so deeply ashamed that he left one morning before I woke up, assuming he'd see me soon enough, that I was old enough to drive myself to visit him, and almost old enough to understand.

Pete cast and reeled in nothing; cast and swore. He told me it was too early in the year for blues but that the ocean worked in mysterious ways.

Maybe a cod, though, possibly a pollock. He shook his head at my question: No, it was not a nice way to make a living. This was called surf-casting, and this was a surf-casting rod. This was fun; well, usually it was fun. When you fished commercially you used nets. For a week at a time you're out there, hauling in the fish, gutting these big mothers, scaling them. Eating fish and boiled coffee three times a day. Hard, brutal, freezing work. He studied his hand, palm up, and said, "I applied for my hunting license and found out I didn't have any fingaprints left. You think you miss the kind of work that does that to you?"

"How long did you do it?"

"All my life."

After a while I asked, "How long were your parents married before she lost him?"

"Thirty-four years. Goin' on thirty-five."

I told him that when Frances died last year, my parents remarried. Each other. I could tell he had little aptitude for gossip when he asked only, "How'd she die?"

He winced when I said "breast cancer" as if to say, I'm sorry, but on the other hand I know you hated her.

"She wasn't so bad," I said.

"What about the baby?"

"She miscarried."

"After they got married?"

"Before."

He asked how long they'd been together.

"A long time. A year longer than my parents were the first time. Long enough to be a respectable couple."

Pete jerked the rod up, left, right. Its tip was bent and its line taut as if he had hooked a whale, but his face was grim. "Goddamn it," he muttered. "I don't know why I keep tryin' on this goddamn flotsam beach." He handed me the rod and I took it gingerly, half expecting it to thrash away like a wily fish who felt a difference in our grips. He took a knife from his tackle box and cut the line, still cursing the seaweed.

"Do you lose that fish thing on the end?" I asked.

Pete said, "It's called a poppah. And yes, I lose it unless I go for a swim."

I asked if he was going to try again and he said no. I said, "Then I'll just keep walking up a ways. In New York I got exercise just living there and getting where I had to go."

"Be glad you're not in New Yohk," he said. "Remembah? Land of evil? City of cheating men?"

"At least one or two get punished," I said. It didn't seem to register, so I said, "You know—Guy."

"You're saying it was punishment?"

I nodded.

"Like God punished him for screwing around with Isabel?"

"In effect."

"'Cause my father died in a squall that came outta nowhere, and he had *nothing* to be punished for. He neva hurt

120

anybody even if he was a sonovabitch. God had nothing to do with Guy VanVleet, either, unless God put a thirty-eight into the wife's hand."

I stooped to pick up a big, unbroken quahog shell that I thought would make a perfect spoon rest. "A thirty-eight?" I asked. "Was that the murder weapon?"

"Jesus, Harriet," said Pete.

"It's a gun," I said. "I know that much."

"Where'd she kill him?" he asked.

"Greenwich, Connecticut."

"How?"

"Shot him."

"Where?"

"In bed."

"Where'd she hit him?"

"Chest," I said. "Heart. Some important vessel."

"Christ," he said. "I thought you were gonna be the world's greatest authority on this."

I pointed out that I knew the names of all three VanVleet children and the date of their parents' wedding anniversary; I further pointed out that Isabel, the employer here, was being eminently reasonable and had no unrealistic timetables for my acquainting myself with every aspect of the case.

He pulled me to my feet with one good-natured tug. "Go," he said. "Read what you've gotta read so she won't fya you."

"Well," I said, "in that case, thank you. That's very sweet, in a caveman kind of way."

"Harriet," he said. "In plain English: Go upstairs, sneak into your room, sit at your desk, read your ass off, and don't get up till you're a fuckin' expert on this case."

He pointed resolutely at the stairs. "*Now*. You're outta here. Get up there."

Okay, I said. I'm going. Coffee break's over. You don't have to put a reprimand in my file.

And thanks, Pete, I thought: I really wanted to be reminded that when all of this was peeled away—the house, the beach, the view, the jets of water in my glass bath—I was just somebody's secretary.

I curled my index finger around a perfect specimen of a skipping rock and let it sail. It sank without a trace.

13
THE PEOPLE V. NANCY VANVLEET

 ATTORNEY JEFFERSON BAD-
gett had been imported
from Houston where he'd
become an undefeated champion of the rich temporarily
insane. In court he peered over half-glasses like a kindly
character actor, referred often to his alma mater—that
pointy-headed law school up the road—and called the
prosecutor "my brother Harry." On December 7, 1992, in
his opening statement before Associate Justice E. Susan
Garland, he described his mission in tabloid terms: The state
would never prove beyond a reasonable doubt that Nancy

VanVleet was sane on that tragic April night, stumbling into a wife's worst nightmare—her husband in the arms of a young, glamorous, voluptuous sexpot; rather, the evidence would show that his client sustained an emotional blow of such force that her head spun, her heart broke, and her mind snapped. Tragically, yes, her adulterous but beloved husband died at her hand—not, ladies and gentlemen of the jury, in a rational, cool, deliberate act of murder, but in a flash of insanity that shattered her life, too.

Guy had died from a single gunshot to the chest, which passed through the left ventricle of the heart, causing extensive tissue damage, "exploding the heart muscle," according to Dr. Raymond Sandulli, the medical examiner. In his opinion, Guy had been shot from a distance of two to three feet, had been knocked to the ground by the force of the .38–caliber bullet, which Dr. Sandulli likened to a concussion grenade. "Let me put it this way," the doctor continued, "an adult male wearing a bulletproof vest who gets hit with one of these is left with bruises the size of pancakes. It knocks the wind right out of him."

On cross-examination, Attorney Badgett greeted Dr. Sandulli warmly, then asked the doctor if he would mind doing a bit of freehand drawing on an old man's belly.

"Whatever," said Sandulli.

The record noted that Attorney Badgett took off his suit jacket, bolo tie, and shirt, then handed the doctor a felt-tipped pen.

"Would you please circle the spot on my chest where a bullet would have to enter to hit the left ventricle of the heart."

"I can do without the showmanship," said the judge.

The defense attorney said he was going to put his shirt on in a minute—these Yankee courtrooms were chilly. May he proceed?

"Make it snappy," ordered Judge Garland.

"Dr. Sandulli, wouldn't the average person hearing that Mr. VanVleet died from one gunshot think, 'Boy, whoever did this was a sharpshooter. Bang! One shot and she hits the very spot on a size forty-two chest where the left ventricle was. She must have taken target practice to have killed a full-grown man with one shot?'"

"No," said Dr. Sandulli.

"Because?"

"Because Mr. VanVleet was shot at close range."

"Is it your opinion that someone who had never fired a gun before could—the Lord forgive me—get lucky at this distance?"

"Yes."

"At this distance, could a person even have her eyes closed?"

"Possibly."

"Is it your opinion that someone without control of her faculties could have fired the fatal shot?"

"I'm not a psychiatrist," said the doctor.

"I'm talking forensically, sir: finger on the trigger, not state of mind. Could an hysterical person have fired the fatal shot?"

"Yes."

"An insane person?"

"Yes."

"And the fact that she didn't fire over and over again wildly, screaming and crying like a movie murderess, but pulled the trigger once, does not mean it was a cool, deliberate, rational act? In your opinion?"

"Correct."

"Do you think Mrs. VanVleet pulled the trigger one time and one time only because she coolly assessed the situation and slid her gun back in the holster—figuratively, of course?"

"No."

"What, in your opinion, happened? Based on a reasonable degree of medical probability. Why only once?"

"I think she fired the gun once, that she couldn't tolerate the sound, that the gun jumped in her hand, that Mr. VanVleet was knocked to the bedroom floor, and Mrs. VanVleet did not shoot it again."

"Pretty loud, huh, Doc?"

"Deafening."

"Dr. Sandulli," said the defense attorney, "just for the record, you are an expert witness for the state of Connecticut, correct?"

"Yes."

"Not for the defense. Not for Mrs. Nancy VanVleet."

"Correct."

"Your fee for testifying—as wholly deserved and probably inadequate as it is—is paid by the state of Connecticut?"

"That's right."

"Your salary is paid by the State of Connecticut, which is prosecuting Mrs. VanVleet?"

"Correct."

"A raving lunatic could have killed Mr. VanVleet at this range, in your opinion, based on a reasonable degree of medical probability?"

"Unfortunately."

"I thank you, sir," said Attorney Badgett.

* * *

Where Isabel's testimony began in the typescript, she'd written, "I have this on videotape. It's in the carton."

She was the state's tenth witness, called on December 15: Isabel A. Krug, 115 East 82nd Street, New York, New York. She wore a navy blue man-tailored suit with a white silk, jewel-necked blouse under the jacket. Her white-blonde hair was French-braided and her face had angles she'd since lost; her contact lenses were less electrically blue than her current color; discreet pearl earrings were her only jewelry. She looked ladylike, confident, and gorgeous.

Prosecutor Harry Arnold, Jr., came to videotaped life: young, thirtyish, preppy in tortoiseshell glasses and yellow medallion tie, tall enough so that the fixed camera cut off his head from certain angles. He never smiled.

"Personal shopping consultant," Isabel stated when asked her occupation. She defined it for the jury, speaking slowly as if it were a branch of science that required translation into layman's terms.

The prosecutor asked the nature of her relationship with the deceased.

"Lover," she said matter-of-factly.

No, she didn't see any point in sugar-coating her relationship with Guy VanVleet.

"I take it you're not embarrassed by your relationship with the deceased, or trying to hide your relationship with him?" said the prosecutor.

"That's right."

"You're not denying that you had an on-going affair with Mr. VanVleet because it's not your morality or his on trial—"

"Objection! Leadin' the witness."

"I'm laying the foundation for her testimony."

"Overruled," said Judge Garland.

"Miss Krug, you are here today under subpoena, aren't you?"

"Yes."

"Is it fair to say that you are not reluctant to testify about your relationship with Mr. VanVleet?"

"I told the police the truth right from the beginning—you heard the tape when I called nine-one-one. I said I was in bed with him. I've never denied my relationship with Guy."

"That's very refreshing," said the prosecutor.

"Objection," said Badgett. "We're not innerested in Mr. Arnold's editorializing."

"The jury will disregard Mr. Arnold's comment," said the judge.

"I'd be much obliged if Mr. Arnold stopped tryin' to make Ms. Krug her own character witness," said Badgett. "It offends mah sensibilities and your honor's intelligence."

"Don't worry about me," said the judge.

Attorney Arnold asked Isabel how and when plans were made for their date on April 3.

"He called me Monday," said Isabel, "and he said, 'Guess what? My wife's going up to Colby for the weekend.' I said, 'Great. What'd you have in mind?' What I was thinking was a hotel, a show, a late dinner, the stuff we didn't usually get to do because he'd always take a late train back to Greenwich."

"Had you ever had unrestricted time like this before?"

"Not a whole weekend."

"In how long a relationship?"

"Since the November before. Five months."

"And how did Mr. VanVleet respond?"

"He said, 'How does this sound?—we spend the weekend at my house, every minute together.' I said, 'No offense, but

why would I want to spend the weekend in Greenwich?' "
Laughter from the Stamford spectators. Isabel acknowledged
the joke with a grin but quickly got back to business. "He
said, 'Because I'd be there if anyone tried to call. I wouldn't
have to make up any cover story. Besides, what could be more
sinful than making love to you in my own bed?' He said I
should take the same train he took from Grand Central but we
wouldn't sit together, I'd take a taxi to his house from the
station, he'd pick up dinner. It would be dark by the time I got
dropped off, and once we got there, we'd never have to leave
the house."

"And is that what you did—took Metro North from
Grand Central to Greenwich, and then a taxi to ten-ten
Round Hill Road?"

"That's correct."

"And was Mr. VanVleet there when you arrived?"

"He got there a little later. We had it planned that I'd give
him a fifteen-minute jump on getting a cab, which is what he
figured it would take to get supper, but he stopped by a video
store to get us a movie."

There was a titter in the crowd: newspapers had reported
that *Dicks and Janes* had been in the VCR when police
inventoried the murder scene.

"Do you remember what time it was when you got to the
house?"

"Around seven-fifteen P.M."

"Which you know because . . . ?"

"I was waiting on the back porch and I kept checking my
watch until Guy showed up."

"Where did you wait, vis-à-vis the street?"

"I was on the back porch, which was on the side of the
house where the driveway was."

"Could you see the road from your vantage point on the back porch?"

"Yes, I could, because I was standing on the porch steps so I could watch for Guy's car."

"Ms. Krug—did you notice anything unusual, any signs of life, as you waited for Mr. VanVleet to arrive?"

"Yes," said Isabel firmly.

"Could you tell us what you saw or heard."

"I saw a car drive by, which I noticed because it looked like Guy's, so I stepped a few feet away from the porch to wave—"

"You weren't worried that neighbors would see you?"

"Unh-uh. The houses are far apart, and there's all kinds of trees and bushes between them. Besides, it was dark."

"Were there any lights on?"

"Yes. The driveway was lit up with lights every few yards or so. Low ones, very attractive, set into the lawn on either side."

"Please continue, the car that drove by?"

"It looked like Guy's, a Mercedes, a light color. I stepped out a few feet and waved."

"What happened then?"

"The car didn't stop, so I realized it wasn't his. But then it backed up and drove by more slowly."

"Were you still in full view of the driver?"

"I assume so. I was still thinking it was him, and that he'd missed the turn-off or something. Then I had this moment of thinking, "Damn it! I'm at the wrong house.""

"What did the Mercedes do next?"

"It stopped at the bottom of the driveway, backed up a few yards like it was turning in, but kept going."

"Could you see who was driving?"

"No."

"Could you tell the sex of the driver?"

"No."

"Could you tell the color of the car?"

"It was light, like an ecru or almond, but not any more than that."

"What happened next?"

"I went back up on the porch, and in another minute Guy arrived."

"Did you mention the other Mercedes?"

"Yes, as soon as he got there."

"What was Mr. VanVleet's reaction?"

"He didn't make anything of it."

"Didn't make anything of the fact that a neighbor might have spotted his lover waiting for him? Or, at the very least, a burglar?"

"He wasn't the nervous type. He was a little reckless about us being seen together. I think he liked it."

"Can you tell us in your own words what happened from that time on, when Guy VanVleet arrived home and you two entered ten-ten Round Hill Road?"

Isabel shifted in her seat and took an exaggerated deep breath. "Okay," she began. "We entered the house through a back hall, which led into the kitchen. Guy turned on the lights, went to the refrigerator, got out a bottle of beer and an open bottle of Chardonnay, which he handed to me, then got out two glasses. I put the bottles on the kitchen island, assuming we'd eat there, but he came over and, well, put his hands on me, and said, 'We're eating in bed.' So we took everything upstairs."

"Did you lock up and shut off the lights behind you?"

"Guy did."

"Go on."

"Okay, so we undress, and we get into their bed, and we kind of fool around for a few minutes."

"Did you have sexual intercourse at this time?"

"No."

"Did you engage in sexual activities at this time?"

"Yes."

"Can you describe that activity."

"I was starved," said Isabel, "but he didn't want to wait until after we ate because he hadn't had any sex since the last time we'd been together, which was more than a week." Isabel stopped there. The prosecutor was quiet, as if he wanted the inadequacy of the VanVleets' marital sex to sink in. Finally he asked, "Could you tell the court what you meant by 'he didn't want to wait.'"

"He indicated that he'd like me to go down on him," Isabel murmured.

"Meaning, Mr. VanVleet would be brought to orgasm through oral sex?"

"Thank you for that definition," said the judge. The spectators laughed.

"Yes," said Isabel. "We usually did it that way: we'd take our time and eventually have intercourse, maybe after watching a movie."

"What happened next on this particular night?"

"We ate," said Isabel. More laughter from the spectators. The judge asked for order.

"You ate your take-out dinners?"

"Correct."

"Still in bed?"

"Right."

"Did you watch the movie?"

"Not right away. We watched the end of 'MacNeil-Lehrer' and the beginning of 'Washington Week in Review' while we ate."

"So, with respect to CPTV's programming, we know you finished eating a little after eight P.M."

"Yes. And then we started the movie."

After a pause, the prosecutor said, "And is it safe to assume that the adult movie had its desired effect and that you and Mr. VanVleet subsequently engaged in sexual intercourse?"

"Yes."

"Could you estimate how long into the viewing of the movie that this happened?"

Isabel, not looking up from her lap said, "Ten minutes?"

The prosecutor walked away from Isabel and sat down at the state's table. Offscreen, he said slowly, "Ms. Krug, would you please tell the court what happened next."

Isabel looked up from her lap and fixed her eyes in the direction of the defense table. "We watched some more of the movie. We finished the wine. At eight-thirty, Guy turned off the movie and we watched 'Wall Street Week,' which he loved."

"Did you hear anything?"

"Not anything outside the bedroom."

"No car?"

"No."

"Not the car drive up, or the car door slam, or the key turn in the lock, or the back door open? Wouldn't that suggest that the driver was taking extraordinary measures not to be heard?"

"Objection," Badgett bellowed, offering no grounds.

"Sustained."

133

"I would think so," Isabel volunteered, nodding at the jury.

"Did Nan VanVleet appear to sneak up on you, or did she enter the house in a normally audible fashion?"

"Objection," said Attorney Badgett, "the state is leadin' the witness, who obviously is not buyin' his cat-burglar theory vis-à-vis my client's perfectly normal return to her own home."

"I sustained that objection, Mr. Arnold," said the judge.

The prosecutor tapped his pencil on his legal pad for a few seconds, frowning, then asked, "Was there any noise in the bedroom?"

"The TV was on and I was a little . . . I was giving myself a massage. With an electric massager." She stopped. The prosecutor didn't say anything until the judge prompted him to continue.

"Would that electric massager also be called a vibrator?" he asked.

"Yes."

"Was it noisy?"

Isabel's face changed color. "It buzzed pretty loud." She looked to the prosecutor for encouragement. He nodded. "I was making noises myself. . . . I guess you could say I was climaxing." Isabel nodded, satisfied that she had pronounced a wholly suitable medical term. "Which I only mention because it explains why I couldn't see what was coming." A hoot of laughter from a corner.

"Oh, grow up," grumbled Judge Garland. She told Isabel to proceed.

"Then a lot of things happened at once. Guy jumped toward the door, the door opened. Then—" Isabel's voice caught, and she put her fingertips to her mouth.

"Take your time," said the prosecutor.

She waited a few moments, then signaled she was ready. "I saw this woman come through the door, and I didn't see the gun because Guy was blocking my view of it, but I heard her swearing, then this horrible loud shot, and Guy was knocked backwards—first I saw a spurt of blood coming from his back as he fell."

The prosecutor asked Isabel to identify the woman who had entered the bedroom. Isabel pointed to the defense table.

"Would you please describe something she is wearing."

Isabel tilted her head and pursed her lips. "A merino wool cable knit dress in hunter green."

"Let the record reflect that the witness has identified the defendant, Nancy M. VanVleet." The prosecutor walked over to the jury and, with his back toward Isabel, asked, "What did you do when Mrs. VanVleet burst into the bedroom?"

"First, I pulled the covers up and I scrunched down to keep out of her way, but when Guy fell, she dropped the gun like a hot potato, and I jumped for it. I gave her a big shove because she was crouching over him and whimpering."

"What did you do with the gun?"

"I grabbed it and I ran into the bathroom, which was off the bedroom and I hid it in the Kleenex box, then put that under the sink."

"Did Mrs. VanVleet say anything?"

"Objection," sang out Badgett.

"Overruled," said the judge, without waiting for the grounds, "particularly in view of your contention that Mrs. VanVleet was *non compos mentis*."

"What did Mrs. VanVleet say?" repeated the prosecutor.

"When she came in the door?"

"From the moment she entered the bedroom."

135

"She was swearing—'bitch,' 'whore,' things like that. I think she screamed when the gun went off, then cried hysterically for the whole rest of the time, until the police got there."

"In your opinion, was it quite literally hysteria, or did you say 'crying hysterically' to mean 'crying uncontrollably'?"

"I meant 'crying uncontrollably.'"

"Did Mrs. VanVleet seem to know where she was?"

"Objection! Ms. Krug is not qualified to speak to my client's state of mind."

"Overruled."

"Ms. Krug."

"Would you repeat the question."

The court reporter looked at her tape and said tonelessly, "Mr. Arnold: 'Did Mrs. VanVleet know where she was?'"

"She seemed to."

"And how do you know that?"

"Because I screamed at her to leave him alone—that he was still alive, even though I knew he wasn't. . . ." She covered her mouth again, crying softly. "And she was *shaking* him and leaning on top of him."

"Do you want to take a brief recess?" asked the judge. Isabel shook her head and wiped carefully under her eyes, checking the tissue after each dab.

"When did you call nine-one-one?" asked the prosecutor.

"The second I hid the gun."

"And from the time you called nine-one-one until the time that help arrived, what happened, with respect to your actions and those of the defendant?"

"I tried to get her off Guy so I could see if he was alive."

"Was he?"

"No," she whispered.

"How did you check that?"

Without speaking, Isabel put two fingers to her neck.

"You checked his carotid artery and found no pulse?"

Isabel's lips were trembling and her answer was a hoarse "Yes."

"Did Mrs. VanVleet say anything?"

"She whimpered, and kept saying, 'Guy, Guy, Guy,' and said she was sorry, she didn't mean to do it. I didn't know what to do. I put my clothes on and I kept yelling, 'Don't touch him.' 'Stay off him!' Then I heard sirens and I ran down to let the police in."

"What, if anything, did Mrs. VanVleet say to you?"

"Nothing."

"Did she appear to know who you were?"

"She knew my name," said Isabel.

"How was that expressed, and when?"

"I heard it once, when I was hiding the gun. It came from the bedroom: 'Are you Isabel?' in this creepy voice."

"Was this before your call to nine-eleven?"

"Yes."

"Did you answer her?"

"No! I called nine-one-one and I tried to do what I could for Guy because I wasn't sure, because his eyes were open, and I tried to keep myself between Nan and the bathroom in case she went crazy all over—"

"Your witness," Attorney Arnold snapped, turning on his heels.

Defense Attorney Badgett all but hooked his thumbs in his armpits to play country lawyer meets femme fatale. "Miss

Krug," he boomed, "explain one thang to me: Why did a young, pretty, vivacious, and if ah may say so delicious little thang like yourself want to be hangin' around a middle-aged, married old coot like Guy VanVleet?"

"Lots of reasons," she said coolly.

"Gimme two."

"We were strongly attracted to each other. And there was a lot of chemistry."

"Ah think that's *one* reason," said Badgett wryly.

"Sexual attraction. Sexual compatability."

"It was mutual?"

"Yes."

"Would you say it was true love?"

Isabel said, "He always told me he loved me."

"And what'd you say back to him?"

"He knew I didn't feel exactly the same way on an emotional level, but that was okay with him."

Badgett turned toward the jury. "Because who needs true love when you're gettin' exactly what you want?"

Laughter from the spectators. "It wasn't one-sided," Isabel protested.

"It was an affair between consentin' adults based on glorious sexual relations. Does that state it fairly?"

"Yes."

"But why did Mr. VanVleet call all the shots? Where did he earn the right to plan your weekends for y'all?"

"He suggested things. I said yes or no."

"He didn't schedule his time with you like appointments?"

"He scheduled *dates* with me."

"Not appointments? Not assignations?"

"I don't understand the question."

"Did Mr. VanVleet pay you for these dates?"

"Mr. VanVleet *paid* for what we did—dinner or a show or a movie."

"But he didn't pay you for sex?"

Isabel leaned into the microphone and said primly, "No, he did not."

"Did he pay you in any other fashion, in a way that didn't involve the exchange of cash money?"

"Objection," said the prosecutor. "I've heard enough. Mr. Badgett is badgering the witness, who has testified repeatedly and frankly to the nature of her relationship with Mr. VanVleet."

"Sustained," said the judge.

"It goes directly to the issue of the witness's character," said Badgett. "The state's star witness."

"Maybe the witness's character would be an issue in Texas," said the judge, "but it's not in Connecticut."

Attorney Badgett grinned and held out his yellow legal pad. "See, your honor—I'm turnin' the page. I'm onto somethin' else." He turned back to Isabel, unsmiling. "Ms. Krug, in the transcript of your call to nine-one-one you said, 'Send an ambulance. And bring a straitjacket if you have one.' Is that a fair and accurate transcription?"

"Yes."

"Why did you ask for a straightjacket?"

"I asked because I thought she might kill someone else. Like me."

"You thought she needed to be restrained?"

"Yes."

"Wouldn't handcuffs have restrained an allegedly armed and dangerous suspect?"

"I suppose so."

"Doesn't 'straightjacket' connote the restraint of a crazed or insane or berserk or out-of-control person?"

"Yes," said Isabel, "but I said the first thing that came into my head, which didn't happen to be handcuffs."

"You repeatedly used, in answerin' the state's questions, the words 'high-sterical,' 'whimperin',' 'crazy' in describing Nan VanVleet's behavior on the night of April the third. Is that the condition of the cool, calculated, rational, sane first-degree murderer described by Mr. Arnold?"

"Like I said, I used those words loosely, the way you'd say, 'I went crazy' or 'I was hysterical' but you don't mean that you literally went crazy. They're figures of speech."

"Was it a figure of speech when you testified, 'Ah tried to keep myself between Nan and the bathroom in case she went crazy all over again'?"

"Yes, it was."

"Crazy enough to kill her beloved husband? Is that the kind of crazy you mean when you use a figure of speech, when you say to a friend, 'Ah went crazy over that new French restaurant' or, perhaps, 'I'm crazy over mah new boyfriend'?"

"I didn't mean crazy-insane."

"I think you did," said Attorney Badgett.

Robert Henshaw testified that he had seen Guy VanVleet at Café Des Artistes in New York City with Isabel Krug on February 14, 1992. Sitting next to each other on the banquette, squeezed onto the same side of a small table. His hands were all over her. They kissed, they cooed, they made a spectacle of themselves. He had been shocked and appalled. He'd excused himself—he was having a Valentine's Day dinner with his then fiance—approached Guy, and said he'd

like to have a word with him in private. Guy said, "I think I
know what you're going to say, and you can say it in front of
Isabel." Robert said, "I'd rather not." Guy got up and
followed Robert to the men's room, where Guy slapped
Robert on the back jovially. Could Robert *believe* Isabel? Had
he gotten a load of those tits, that body; guess how old she
was . . . on and on in that fashion as if Robert were an ally. As
if the jig weren't up.

"How did you feel seeing Guy VanVleet with another
woman?"

"Shocked. Sad. Offended. I didn't like his assuming we
were co-conspirators."

"When did you report the incident to your ex-wife?"

"The next evening. I called her."

"To what end?"

"To ask what we should do, if she should tell Nan."

"What did your ex-wife say?"

"She said women in Nan's shoes wanted to know, even if
they thought they didn't."

"Did you discuss the particulars—how, when, what she'd
say?"

"I left it up to Polly. I knew she'd handle it with great
compassion. She'd gone through something like that herself,
and she was Nan's best friend."

The state's final witness was Audrey Shepherd of 1018
Round Hill Road, Greenwich.

Yes, she did consider herself to be a close friend of Nan
VanVleet. No, "confidante" would not be too strong a word
to describe their relationship. Yes, she had known of Guy
VanVleet's infidelity. It was common knowledge within a
small circle of Nanny's friends.

Because one of the husbands, ex-husband actually, in that circle had seen Guy with Isabel Krug in the city at Café Des Artistes, acting in a manner that didn't leave much to the imagination.

Definitely Isabel Krug; Guy introduced her to Robert by name.

From Polly, Robert's ex-wife. Polly, Nan, and Audrey played tennis together.

On the night of April third, she purchased chili and fries at The Chopping Block on Greenwich Avenue for her sons' dinner.

Guy VanVleet, also picking up dinner, two seafood platters.

Yes, she knew Nan was away, en route to Maine.

She did ask him and he said, "For me and Nan."

A Mercedes 300E. Nineteen eighty-nine. Cream. Yes, she did drive by 1010 Round Hill Road on the night of April 3, 1992. She did see a woman in the VanVleet driveway carrying an overnight case who looked like she was the Krug woman. Because Polly's ex-husband had described the woman at the restaurant to Polly, who had described her to Nanny, who had confirmed the description with Guy's secretary.

Yes, she did slow down and back up in her cream-colored Mercedes, but then she drove away.

Yes, she did call Nan VanVleet's car phone.

Yes, she did reach her.

To the best of her recollection: "You'd better come right home."

On Friday, April 3, 1992, Nan VanVleet hung her garment bag in the back of her Lincoln Continental Executive and took the Merritt Parkway to White Plains to catch a 6:29 P.M.

plane for Boston then Bangor, Maine, the closest airport to
Colby College where Heidi, her baby, was a junior. She called
her daughter's dormitory from the car phone at 5:52 P.M., at
which time she told Heidi that she didn't feel well, was
nauseated, and had vomited by the side of the road. She said
she couldn't fly feeling like this, would rest, and turn around.
It was probably a twenty-four-hour bug, because Elaine
Barron, whom she had had lunch with on Wednesday, was
sick as a dog on Thursday.

Nan rested in the car, having pulled over to a rest stop. She
fell asleep. She made no more phone calls. She was too
indisposed to drive, but would have felt foolish calling an
ambulance. "What about your husband?" asked the prosecutor on cross-examination. "Wouldn't it have been the logical
thing to call your husband and say, "Dear, I'm sick. I can't
drive. Could you come get me?"

"He worked in the city," said the defendant.

"Or were you just waiting for the appointed hour when you
could return to Round Hill Road and catch your husband in
bed—"

"Objection," cried the defense attorney.

"Rephrase the question, Mr. Arnold."

The prosecutor asked, "Did you know your husband would
be at home in Greenwich?"

"I most certainly did not," said Nan. "His reason for not
coming up to Colby with me was because he had appointments Friday afternoon and a client dinner Friday night. I had
no reason to doubt his word."

"Didn't you deem this an emergency, your lying sick by the
side of a road? Wouldn't Mr. VanVleet wanted to have known
this?"

"Objection," said Attorney Badgett. "The witness can't

143

speak to what Mr. VanVleet would've wanted or not wanted to know."

"Neither can Mr. VanVleet. Overruled."

"I didn't call him because I felt better after I cleaned out my stomach," Nan testified. "I always do. I thought I should rest and drive when I felt stronger."

"Did you think about driving to a drug store and getting some Pepto-Bismol?" asked the prosecutor.

"I thought of it, but I didn't know where one was."

"What time did you begin your drive back to Greenwich?"

Nan didn't remember exactly. The prosecutor asked how long a drive had she had back to Greenwich once she felt strong enough to drive. Nan said approximately twenty minutes.

"And you didn't call anyone else from your car phone to say you were sick and that you'd had a change of plans?"

"No."

"Did you call the airline to cancel your travel plans?"

"No."

"Did you think of that?"

"Yes—"

"But you didn't call the airline to say you were sick and couldn't make it?"

"No."

"Did you want it to appear that you had, in fact, flown to Boston and on to Bangor?"

"No."

"Just in case there was a murder in your house on Friday, April the third? You'd have the tickets to prove—"

"Objection," said the defense attorney.

"Sustained."

"Mrs. Shepherd testified that she called your car phone,

after seeing a woman in your driveway that she assumed was Isabel Krug, your husband's mistress."

"I don't remember the phone call. I vaguely remember getting wakened up by a call, but I don't remember anything else."

"You don't remember a phone call where someone said, 'Nan, it's Audrey. He's brought her home, your arch enemy, to your marital bed. Turn your car around and surprise them in the act?'"

"I don't believe she said that."

"Do you remember what impulse it was that made you sit up and start the car and turn it toward home?"

"I felt well enough to drive, finally. And it was dark when I woke up, and I was nervous about being parked on the side of the parkway."

"That reminds me—no good Samaritans stopped to see if you were okay?"

"Not that I'm aware of."

"Because anyone looking into a big luxury car and seeing a woman slumped across the front seat would be pretty alarmed, wouldn't he?"

"I suppose so."

"Does it annoy you, as a Connecticut taxpayer, that your state police didn't spot you and come to your assistance?"

"No. I parked in an inconspicuous spot so no one would bother me."

"And where was that spot?"

"I think it was a rest area."

"In Greenwich?"

"I'm not positive."

"How long did it take you to drive home to Round Hill Road?"

"About twenty minutes."

"So you were, by all accounts, on the road, either driving or sick or recovering from approximately five P.M. to eight-forty P.M. on April the third?"

"That's correct."

"And the thing that prompted you to turn around and drive home at approximately eight-twenty P.M. was . . . ?

"I felt better. Less nauseated."

"But not well enough to catch a later plane to Bangor?"

"I had already told Heidi I was sick and couldn't make it. She didn't seem terribly disappointed."

"At this point, you claim no knowledge of your husband and his mistress being at your house."

"I know I was told—"

"But you don't remember speaking with Audrey Shepherd somewhere around seven-thirty P.M. on your car phone?"

"I know there's a record of it, but I don't remember speaking to her."

"Even though your car phone number is on two phone bills, and Mrs. Shepherd herself testified that she called?"

"I don't remember. Do you want me to lie and say I remember when I don't?"

The prosecutor said, No, of course not. Then: "Could you tell me if you know a Costas Dimantopoulos?"

No, she said, I do not.

"Do you recognize the name?"

"Could you say it again?"

"Costas Dimantopoulos."

"No. Definitely not."

"Not even as the name of the artist who took the photographs hanging on the walls of the family room?"

"I think you mean the paintings," said Nan.

"Do you recognize his name as the artist of that work?"

"In that context I do."

"But not in any other context?"

"No," said Nan.

"You've never met Mr. Dimantopoulos?"

"Your Honor," said the defense attorney, "I'm finding this line of questioning exceedingly tedious."

"Overruled," said the judge.

"You've never met Mr. Dimantopoulos?" repeated Attorney Arnold.

"I may have met him socially at some time in my life, but I don't remember doing so."

"Was Mr. Dimantopoulos ever in your home?"

"Not that I recall," said Nan.

"He *never* visited your home to install or to advise in the installation of—"

"Objection! Mrs. VanVleet has answered this question to death and because it's not the answer he wants, my brother is badgering her."

"Sustained. Move on to something else, Mr. Arnold."

The prosecutor turned on Nan: Did she dispute the facts of the shooting, as related under oath by Ms. Krug, by the medical examiner, by the E.M.T.s, by the Greenwich police officers and detectives—did she dispute their testimony under oath that she killed her husband, Guy VanVleet, by a single gunshot to the chest?

"No."

"But you want the court to believe that you're not to be held accountable for his death?"

"I'm not guilty by reason of temporary insanity. I didn't know what I was doing."

"But wait," said Attorney Arnold. "You drove home, you

147

obeyed the rules of the road, you found your house, your house key, you punched in the alarm code, slipped off your shoes, you procured the family gun from the first-floor study, you found the right room, you caught your husband and Isabel Krug *in flagrante delicto* and you shot him dead. Doesn't that sound like the actions of a sane and rational person? Doesn't that sound like premeditated first-degree murder?"

"No!" said the accused. "It wasn't like that."

"You were fine seconds before the shooting, fine enough when the police arrived for them to call your family doctor for only a mild sedative. And you're fine now. Sane as anyone in this courtroom. Yet you weren't fine or criminally responsible when you pulled the trigger?"

"I wasn't! I know I wasn't."

"You've testified that you were traumatized, upset, horrified, heart-broken to find your husband in bed with Isabel Krug. But you weren't surprised, were you? You knew what to expect and you made your plans, loaded gun in hand—"

"You don't have to answer that—" said the judge.

"No," cried Nan VanVleet. "I was insane. I was. I didn't go there to kill Guy. I loved Guy. I wanted him back. I thought he'd get over her. I lost my mind. I never would have killed him if I was in my right mind."

"Enough, please," said her attorney. "I pray your Honor's judgment—"

But Nan couldn't stop. "I wanted *you* dead, not Guy. I didn't know I was shooting him. I came back for you."

The accused collapsed, sobbing, and was led away. The defense rested. The judge said quietly to the stenographer, "Let the record show the witness was addressing Isabel A. Krug."

14
SAME TIME TOMORROW

 AFTER READING ABOUT Perry
VanVleet and catching
glimpses of his whitebread
good looks a row behind the defense table, I watched "If
This Be Joy" as soon as I had the chance. The newspapers
couldn't mention the VanVleet children without noting that
son Perry played perennial high school senior Kerr Greenwood on America's highest-rated daytime soap. By the time
I tuned in, Kerr had been promoted to college in the fictional
town of Rosewell, where all his outerwear had Rosewell U
embroidered on a pocket, no matter what the garment.

Isabel had invited me to watch in her bedroom, and I knew immediately that she was a regular. "Do you know how soap operas work?" she asked, settling back against her gray velvet tufted chaise longue a few minutes before showtime, remote control poised. "There are several stories going at once, so we might not catch him for a week." She was wearing blue jeans with zippers at the ankles and a bulky black sweater dotted with fist-sized pom-poms in pink, red, and orange.

I told her I had watched "The Doctors" in high school, but that it had disappeared when I was in college, leaving me with the feeling that tormented souls Althea, Maggie, Nora, and Brock remained trapped forever in my parent's black and white floor console. I asked if she watched Perry every day and she said, as if she ever left the house, "When I'm here."

"Is he a good actor?"

"He can cry," she said, "and he can kiss."

I laughed and said, "The perfect man."

"You're goddamn right," she said, and laughed back.

I asked if she'd ever met Perry, the real Perry.

"Not outside the courtroom."

Portentous music trilled, introducing a sampler from today's menu. Perry was in the last of the three, backing away from a beauty queen in a lab coat.

"When was the last time you saw a college student who looked like *that*?" I asked.

"She's the instructor. Her father's president of the college."

Kerr was stammering and resisting the beauty queen's advances, but by the time the thirty-second scene was over he had agreed to get tutored at her place. "Don't do it," I warned him.

Isabel shushed me and said she could tell I wasn't going to

be much fun. "Guy used to talk to the TV, too," she said after a pause.

"You watched it together?"

"I taped it if he was coming over on a weeknight. That's what got me started. Guy loved watching Perry—well, you can imagine: Your own son on TV looking like everyone's dream prom date."

I said maybe Guy, now that I understood his proclivities, had gotten a vicarious thrill out of Perry's TV love scenes.

Isabel said no; Perry's sex scenes had come after his dad died. *Because* his dad died. The murder raised his character's profile and gave him—on TV if not in life—new appeal.

On the screen, photographs of handsome men and women drifted through blue sky and turned into leaves on a family tree. A balladeer sang,

> *My heart goes out*
> *To each girl 'n boy*
> *For the days they doubt*
> *If . . . This . . . Be . . . Joy . . .*

Isabel's door opened. Costas tip-toed in without a word, closed the door carefully, and sat down beside me on the sheepskin bedspread. He was wearing white painter's overalls, a yellowed, long-sleeved thermal undershirt, and sandals with no socks. I could tell from the way he slipped into place without drawing a word or a glance from Isabel that this was their daily routine.

The titles dissolved to Kerr/Perry on the screen, with Holly the professor working him out of his letter sweater.

"They didn't waste any time," I said.

"She has a death wish," Isabel explained. "She wants her father to fire her so she can do what she really wants to do instead of teaching chemistry. She's always throwing herself at students and deans and such."

"What does she want to be doing instead?"

"Sing," said Costas.

"She can't sing on the side?"

"She does that already at a club in Bigtown where nobody knows her."

The professor, in a slutty red foundation garment, sat astride Kerr, who was looking liquid yet reluctant. I couldn't resist sneaking a sidelong glance at Costas to see if he was enjoying it more than I thought fitting for a proven dirty old man. He chose the same moment to evaluate my reaction. Our eyes met and snapped back to the show.

"It's an act," Isabel confided. "She's not really a nymphomaniac, but she thinks it'll get her fired, and it'll guarantee nobody will want to hire her at any college, even if her father uses his pull."

"Why can't she just resign like a normal person?"

Isabel shushed me. Holly was slipping her red spaghetti straps off her gleaming shoulders.

Costas said, "He won't go through with it. He's a virgin and they're saving him for Melissa."

"Who's Melissa?"

"A nice girl," said Costas. "An angel."

"I—I—I didn't come prepared," Kerr stuttered in stereo.

"Don't worry about that, baby," moaned Holly.

"You're a scientist!" cried Kerr. "Don't you know there are worse dangers than getting pregnant? I may not have a lot of experience, but I know I wouldn't do anything without protection." He adjusted his voice to that of a public-service voiceover: "Because when I have sex with you, I'm having sex, in effect, with everyone you've ever slept with."

"Redeeming social message?" I murmured.

Costas said, "They have only contempt for their viewers."

Holly dismounted and said petulantly, "If all you want to do is talk about stupid condoms, I'm going to fix us something to eat."

Kerr, who had never taken his chino pants off, raised himself on his elbows. The water bed undulated. "I'd love nothing more than making love to you, but I don't think it's right."

Holly pulled on a silky leopard-print robe and tied it with an angry jerk. "Why'd I have to pick such a nice kid?" she muttered. "Why couldn't I have just picked some insensitive macho creep in his last semester who wouldn't argue and wouldn't look back?"

Kerr maneuvered himself off the bed and slid his hands up and down Holly's arms. "You're too fine a person for that, Professor Townsend."

Costas, Isabel, and I groaned in unison.

Holly whirled around, her back to Kerr, and made caught-on-the-horns-of-a-dilemma faces at the camera.

"Is she good or bad?" I asked them.

"Good," said Isabel, as Costas said blandly, "Bad."

When the next commercial came on, Costas asked me in his goad-Isabel voice if I knew the real-life identity of the young man we were watching.

"Of course," I said.

"The stepson Isabel never had."

"Oh, please," she said.

"Here's my analysis: If Mrs. VanVleet hadn't killed Mr. VanVleet, this young matinee idol's father would have left his

153

mother for my wife. The children would resent her, but would come around after a year or two, especially after she sent them imaginative gifts for Christmas and birthdays. The boy would be first to attempt a rapprochement because he inherited the VanVleet sex drive and therefore would empathize with his father."

Isabel turned up the sound with the remote control to drown out Costas's speech. When his mouth stopped moving, she returned the volume to normal. Costas tried again. "Master VanVleet is just a vapid teenager who has nothing to offer besides his all-American face and his smooth body, but she's smitten just the same."

Isabel sighed as if she'd heard this harangue before.

"Aren't you going to respond?" he asked her.

Isabel snapped off the power.

"Hey," he said.

Isabel stuck the clicker behind a pillow of the chaise and leaned against it. Costas rose and turned on the television manually. Isabel waited until he had sat down again, then killed the power with the remote.

"Don't be childish," he snarled.

I turned to Costas. "And you're not being childish? No matter what she says, you insult her. It's extremely unpleasant for anyone who has to be in the same room with you."

He said, "I'm only teasing her."

"Well, it's obnoxious."

"Don't waste your breath, Harriet," said Isabel.

"Why don't you watch the show in your own room if you're going to make snide comments every time Perry comes on the screen?"

"Because you're here and he's showing off," said Isabel. "Besides, he doesn't have a set."

"Well leave me out of it." I moved to neutral ground in the form of the mauve carpet. We watched the show in silence. When an exterior shot of a tudor mansion appeared, I asked whose house it was.

"The Wheatcombs'," Isabel and Costas answered together.

A man and a woman were drinking from gold-handled tea cups at an enormous table. He had a terrible silver toupé, and she looked thirty years younger than he. They called each other "Hugh, darling" and "Georgina, darling," and spoke with Bette Davis accents.

A handsome man in his late thirties entered the dining room and kissed Georgina's cheek in a lingering and not altogether filial manner.

"Her stepson. They just started an affair yesterday," said Costas.

Georgina wobbled her tea cup and said she felt oddly woozy.

"Pregnant," I said.

"You think so?" asked Isabel.

Costas said she'd have some explaining to do because Hugh was sterile and everyone knew it.

"Where did Franklin come from then?"

"He got the mumps after Franklin, and that was the end of that. He kept divorcing women, thinking it was their fault—"

"Without ever getting a sperm count?"

"I told you," said Costas, "they have great contempt for their viewers' intelligence. It's absolutely maddening how these people act."

So I asked them: Why keep watching? Why so loyal?

Isabel looked at Costas. "A bad habit," he said.

"You get addicted," she added.

"It breaks up the day," he said.

The Wheatcombs' doorbell chimed and a Fifi kind of maid opened the door. In rushed Perry, looking disheveled.

"Kerr, darling," sang Georgina.

"Mother," he said. "Good morning, Stepfather. Frank."

"Darling, you look like an unmade bed. Bettina, set a place for Kerr. Have you had breakfast? Cook could make you a mushroom omelet—"

"Mother, I want to drop chemistry. I can't go to one more lab—"

"But, darling, you need chemistry if you want to go to medical school next term. Isn't that what Professor Townsend told me at parents' night?" She turned to Franklin. "We were so delighted when Kerr was assigned to her lab. All the students love her."

Franklin narrowed his cheating eyes. In flashback we see him dancing close with a mini-skirted Holly Townsend at what must be the country and western bar where she sings. His large hands slide down her back, out of view, so we'll understand that he fucked her, too.

"Franklin?" said his stepmother-lover, jarring him back to the present. "Franklin? Do you think Kerr should drop chemistry? What would you do if you were studying under such a marvelous instructor?"

Franklin, in that soap opera way, stared but never answered.

When the show ended, Costas slithered onto his feet and nodded, "Ladies."

I offered no pleasantry in return but looked to Isabel to see if we were mad at him. "What're you working on?" she asked.

He answered pleasantly enough: hand-coloring a small still life.

"How small?"

"Four by five."

"Inches?" I asked.

"Feet."

"Do I know this one?"

He shrugged and said it was some fruit he arranged in a wooden bowl. A cliché, of course, like everything else, but the light was lovely.

She talked. He talked. Their faces wore looks of mild interest and courtesy, like department heads making small talk at a water cooler. When they finished with art, they argued about the family: How Holly should see a shrink; how Franklin should move out before he broke his father's heart; whether Kerr should screw Melissa or wait until graduation.

When their time was up, Costas said good-bye with a taut, silent salute. It wasn't warm, but it was respectful, as if an hour of other people's messed-up lives had been therapeutic. As if to say, "Same time tomorrow."

"Perry's in love with me," Isabel said, frowning at the blank screen. I sat down at the foot of the chaise like a mother whose daughter had said something sad but essentially true: I'm fat. I'm ugly. I have no friends.

"Perry?" I repeated.

She nodded.

"How do you know that?"

"He calls my service in New York and pleads with them for my number here."

"Since when?"

157

"Since Christmas."

"How often?"

"A dozen times."

"Have you ever spoken with him?"

"No."

"And you think this means he's in love with you?"

"Go ahead, be skeptical," said Isabel. "I don't blame you." She reached behind her for a fuzzy mohair throw of pale ice blue.

I said, giving in to my impulse to tug its corners into place, "You don't?"

"I make it sound like every man who comes within six feet of me finds me irresistible. So you're thinking: Yeah, right. First she tells me about Guy, then I hear about Costas. And now it's Guy's son, who could have any housewife in America."

I hesitated, then said, "The others made a kind of sense—"

"See?" she said. "I knew if I told you about Perry you'd think I was completely full of shit."

"But you told me anyway."

"Because it's on my mind. And because you listen. And *while* you listen, you don't look as if you're judging me, even if I'm saying obnoxious things."

I told her it came from being the middle sister and the daughter who lived at home to keep her mother sane. And from listening to high school girlfriends in the cafeteria. All in all, a pretty steady diet of other people's sexual adventure stories assimilated with a straight face.

Isabel asked if I had dated in high school.

"I went to dances," I offered. "And I worked on the committees that planned them."

"So they'd eat their lunches and brag about their social life knowing you didn't have one? Real good friends," she huffed.

I said it was okay; it put me on the fringes of the popular girls' group, where I otherwise would not have sat. I was flattered to be included; I'd listen and ask questions and try not to let on that inside I was saying, "Holy shit! He *what?* You touched it! On *purpose?*"

"Is that what you're thinking when I tell you about me and Guy? Or when Costas and I told you how we met?"

"Partly. I mean, it's never a case of meeting someone in line at a movie, then two weeks later you invite him to a poetry reading and have coffee afterwards, then wait for his call, which takes a couple of weeks—"

"Which movie?" Isabel asked, "because it sounds like *When Harriet Met Kenny.*"

I considered denying it or embellishing it, but finally just said, *"E.T."*

"And what about the poetry reading? Whose idea was that?"

"Mine. It seemed kind of, I don't know, chic. And literary."

"Because you felt 'chic' and 'literary' were what you needed to impress a baker of bagels?"

"He was a grad student then."

"Was it love at first sight on line at the theater?"

"Not exactly."

"What else? How'd you know his name and number?"

"We had introduced ourselves in line. He said, 'Ken Grossman.' I said, 'Harriet Mahoney.' I saw the little light go out in his eyes with that so I said, 'My mother's maiden name was Goodstein.'"

"Just like that? A wild guess?"

"Just like that."

Isabel threw back her head and laughed.

"He had said he lived on Third Avenue, so I called Information. I knew he wouldn't call me first—"

"How did you know that?" she demanded.

"Experience. It didn't take any great insight. After a certain point, after a couple of weeks went by, I said, 'What do I have to lose? He isn't going to call, so if he turns me down I'll be no worse off than before.'"

"Okay, you called him. You said, 'Remember me, Harriet Sadie Mahoney from *E.T.*? Would you like to go to a poetry reading?'"

"Just about." .

"And he said yes, obviously."

"He said"—I imitated Kenny's whine—"'A poetry reading?' I said, 'It's Erica Jong. You know—*Fear of Flying*? She writes poetry, too.'"

Isabel cut in, "And he said to himself, Hmmm, Erica Jong. Could be better than *E.T.* Could be R-rated."

"Probably."

"So, how was it?"

"The date? Wonderful."

Isabel blinked hard.

"Aren't they usually wonderful at the beginning? We went out for coffee and dessert afterwards—marble cheesecake— and he was charming, for Kenny. We even talked about the poems. He made some comments about the reading and the crowd that I thought were insightful. Plus, it turned out he had taken a course as an undergraduate with Elizabeth Hardwick."

She rolled her eyes, meaning, whoever that is.

"A writer who was married to Robert Lowell."

"Which made old Kenny a little deep and even a little sexy in your eyes?"

"I didn't say he wasn't sexy twelve years ago."

"So then what?"

"He said he'd call, but he didn't. Then about three weeks later, he did. To invite me over."

"Did he say anything about why he didn't call?"

"He said he'd been busy with school."

"Oh, sure. Like he didn't have five minutes to call you. What did you do on your second date?"

"It was an apartment-painting party. He invited a couple of friends over to paint his kitchen and hallway."

Isabel opened and closed her mouth. "I'm speechless," she said finally. "What a cheap son of a bitch."

"Look—you know he turned out to be a shmuck. You should be glad I'm not telling you heartbreakingly romantic details. It would only depress you more, given the outcome."

"I know he's sending you bagels," she said after a pause.

"The only point I was trying to make was that your affairs never grow out of rainy, dateless Friday nights at the movies. You've probably never even *been* to the movies by yourself. And I'm sure you've never waited by the telephone, worrying if there's going to be a second date."

"I certainly have," said Isabel. "I just haven't bothered to tell you about those guys. I tell you the big ones because either I married them or they died in a sensational kind of way."

"And Perry qualifies because he's Guy's son—"

"And he could be a chapter in our book if he keeps it up."

Keeps what up? I asked. Exactly what was Perry saying to her answering service?

" 'Please tell her I have to talk to her.' 'It's not about my

161

father.' 'It's not about my mother.' 'Is there any chance I could see her in person?'"

"Couldn't that be a million other things—"

"Harriet. Sweetheart. I saw him at the trial. I saw the way he looked at me. I saw everything there is to know."

I said I too had seen Perry during Isabel's testimony. And, no offense, but he was glaring at her with unbridled hatred.

"Of course he was! He's an actor. The only son and protector, sitting between his two sisters? Behind his mother, who's in the biggest trouble of her life? With cameras and reporters all over him? What's he going to do? Lick his lips? Ask me to lunch in the courthouse cafeteria?"

"I don't know," I said slowly. "Given your history with his family, it seems to go against some law of nature."

Isabel touched my arm. "I know for a fact that Perry talked to Guy about me, that he went to him man to man to try to get Guy to knock it off, and Guy told him, essentially, that I was too good to give up. In every way. Fun, true-blue, agile, even if I was his mid-life crisis. That Nan was his wife and he loved her but man oh man, now he had won the lottery. This was a drug and he didn't want to be cured of his addiction. Now you tell *me* that his son isn't going to remember that, especially after his poor dad is gone and the woman in question is more or less unspoken for."

"How much did his father tell him?" I asked.

"Everything. I think he even showed him pictures."

"Pictures?" I said as nonchalantly as I could.

"Just a few Polaroids," she said. "Nothing in bad taste. Nothing he could ever be blackmailed with."

I imagined Isabel in Guy's wallet, sharing a glassine window with Nan's college graduation photo. "He carried a picture of you in his wallet?"

"Oh, God no. Not even Guy was that reckless."

I said, "It wasn't nude, was it?"

"Just from here up," she said with a chop to her waist. "You know he had this thing about my upper body."

I asked if she knew what Perry's understanding of her relationship with Guy was. I mean, did he know about the trinkets?

"I know for a fact he knew."

"Guy told him?"

"Guy thought that if Perry saw me as a kept woman, he'd think, Boys will be boys, which was better than, You betrayed our mother."

"Oi," I said.

"Right. So now he's a grown man, twenty-five years old, a TV star with normal drives, a lot of disposable income, his mother's locked up, and his father's endorsement is ringing in his ears."

"Of you."

"Of me."

"So you think he's calling to make a date with you?"

She leaned back against the chaise and smiled. "Some people from Brookline High School might call it a date."

"And you don't think it's because he hates you and is trying to harass you?"

"He's left messages with my lawyer. You don't call someone's lawyer if you're planning to harass his client—"

"Or planning to buy sexual favors from her, either."

"You think I've got it all wrong?"

I stood up and walked over to the wall of clippings. After reading a few leads I said, "Everyone in the family hates you. There isn't one nice or sympathetic word about you anywhere."

"All the more reason for him to feel sorry for me," said Isabel, "and to seek me out. Maybe he thinks I'm destitute and friendless."

I walked back and sat down. "Is there a chance you see this everywhere you go?"

Isabel was shaking her head before I had finished. "I *don't* see it everywhere I go. I never said that my lawyer was in love with me, or all those trial attorneys, or my agent, or those asshole reporters. Or Pete. I know there are women who see it everywhere, but I'm not one of them."

"Have you answered him?"

"Would that be so terrible?"

"What would be the point? Chat with him on the phone? Meet him halfway for a drink?"

"Wouldn't you be intrigued if Kerr Greenwood had left a dozen messages with your service, each sounding more desperate than the last?"

"He might be out to kill you," I said. "Or blackmail you with a compromising photo."

She shook her head primly. "I'd be very surprised."

"You said yourself, he's an actor. He could be acting the part of a suitor or heir to his father's mistress, but that doesn't mean you have to take the bait."

"I know men," she said. "They're much simpler than that."

"Can't you just watch 'If This Be Joy' and let it go at that?"

"And do what about the messages?"

"Ignore them. It's a perfectly reasonable thing to do, considering his mother meant to kill you and shot his father instead."

"She's locked up. She's not going anywhere too fast."

"Maybe she's getting a furlough. Or maybe she's getting

her own bedside phone at the insane asylum and wants to put you on auto-dial."

"I know men," she repeated. "He wants to talk to me. He's not riding shotgun for his mother."

"And you need that—one more complication? The phone ringing and you diving for it, hoping Costas doesn't get to it first?"

"I'm not saying it's a good idea—"

"It's a terrible idea! If the press ever found out that Guy VanVleet's son was trying to date Isabel Krug, or *sleeping* with Isabel Krug, neither of you would have an ally in the world. You'd have to take your lawyers on 'Geraldo.'"

She leaned forward from the waist so her words had a shorter distance to travel. "Harriet," she said, "First of all, I'd die to go on 'Geraldo.' And second of all, how many allies do you think I have in this goddamn world?"

Two Pieces of Mail

Dear Harriet,

How nice to hear from you!

Inspector Shoemaker is on hold while I deal with mid-term foolishness, but I hope to give him my full attention during spring break (March 21–28).

I have a lead on an agent in Somerville, Mass., who used to be an editor at Little, Brown. She specializes in mysteries and has agreed to read two chapters and an outline of the current book.

I'd very much enjoy hearing more about your job, which sounds intriguing, if not idyllic, and a bit Jane Eyre-ish in the very best sense.

My colleagues who summer in Provincetown tell me lovely things about the Truros, that they are still wild and unspoiled. Hope this finds you well, and that you will favor me with more updates.

Yours, as ever,

Ferris

Amy Beth Solomon and Kenneth Sheldon Grossman

joyfully announce that they solemnized

their profound commitment to each other

on February 14, 1993,

and henceforth will share the surname

Solo-Grossman

"Farewell, farewell the heart that lives alone . . ."
—William Wordsworth

15

DIFFICULT HAIR

WE CALLED HIM from Isabel's bedside phone, cross-legged on her deep purple sheepskin, the same night she told me of her romantic suspicions. It was late, after eleven; she had dialed and said to his answering machine, "Perry? It's Isabel Krug. I understand you've been trying to reach me."

Just after ten the next morning, a woman returned the call on his behalf. Isabel didn't catch her name or title, but we took her for a smart-cookie/personal assistant with a little too much self-esteem. As Isabel spoke and by turn listened, her confident smile slid into something more guarded.

"Five-oh-eight *is* Cape Cod," she said. "You can call the operator to verify that."

"Mine," she said sharply after a pause. "I can't see who else's book I'd be writing." Isabel raised her eyebrows to signal this wasn't quite what we'd expected. "Maybe that could be arranged for the chapters in which he's quoted."

I signaled, Be careful; don't give anything away.

"Excuse me." Isabel put her hand over the receiver and said, "This dame wants to know if Perry can see the manuscript before the book comes out."

"Tell her that's not standard procedure."

Isabel repeated what I'd said with attribution: Her ghost-writer, Ms. Mahoney, who had had experience in these matters, handed down the verdict. "I guess so," I heard her say, handing me the phone.

"Don't make me ," I whispered. "Tell her we'll check with our lawyers and get back to them."

Isabel hissed back, waving the receiver, "Are you my office temp or are you my collaborator?"

I took the receiver and said warily, "Hello?"

A pleasantly professional voice said, "Ms. Mahoney?"

"Yes?"

"Ms. Krug tells me you're writing a book about her that relies heavily on the VanVleet family."

I told her that was correct, but we were still in the research and development phase.

"Do you have a commitment from a publisher?"

"Not yet," I said, "but there's plenty of interest."

"Are you a serious writer?"

I said, yes. Extremely serious.

"How were you paired up with Ms. Krug?"

I told her proudly: *"The New York Review of Books."*

Isabel was gesturing: get to the point already.

"We'd very much like to interview Perry," I said crisply.

"About what exactly?"

"His father, of course. His feelings about everything. . . ." I trailed off.

"What if he wants to write his own book someday?" she asked.

I thought for a few moments. Isabel was mouthing, What? What's the matter?

I said into the mouthpiece, my eyes on Isabel, "Is that why he was trying so assiduously to reach Ms. Krug? Was it about his own book?"

Isabel smiled broadly.

"Are you planning a trip to New York any time soon?" this assertive personal assistant wanted to know.

Getting away without Costas was easy because Isabel had always made monthly trips to New York, insisting that only Vidal Jr. at Sassoon's could color and cut her difficult hair. Of course it was a ruse: Isabel's hair was highlighted at her sink and trimmed at whatever walk-in franchise was closest to her shopping and lunching, including M'Lady's Coiffures in Provincetown.

We planned the interview carefully: We were to shake hands all around upon arrival, briefcases at our sides, and sit down at Perry's dining room table or equivalent. Isabel was to sit opposite Perry for maximum eye contact. She would operate the tape recorder and I would take notes, longhand. We were to listen intently to his answers so as to ask penetrating but not confrontational follow-up questions. If he didn't offer us any liquids, we were to ask for boiling water for the herbal tea we'd brought from home. I would excuse myself at regular intervals to use the bathroom, citing the diuretic effect of the tea, allowing Perry multiple opportunities to declare himself. If he did so compellingly, Isabel would remind me of my four or five or six o'clock appointment with the manicurist, at which point I was to leave.

At this time I was to proceed to our hotel and check us in. I'd wait until seven and if she wasn't back, I'd make my own plans, leaving her key at the registration desk. If she wasn't sleeping at the hotel, she'd call me at midnight to let me know she was alive and happy and that she had been right about Perry's motives. If Costas bothered to check on her, I would make something up.

Isabel wore a butterscotch wool jersey dress, a chiffon scarf patterned with tiny valises, and a gold bracelet of chunky links and charms. I wore my charcoal and camel houndstooth check suit of 10 percent cashmere, which Isabel pronounced the first thing she'd seen me wear that didn't look apologetic.

I studied my Perry file on the short flight to New York and reviewed my questions: When and how had you learned of your father's relationship with Isabel? What had your father told you about her? Could you be more explicit? Were you close to your father? Do you understand what led him to act as he did? Did your family actually hire a private investigator, as you told the New Haven *Register*? What word or phrase best describes your attitude today toward Isabel's role in your father's death? Do you feel that you know the real Isabel Krug? Do you blame her? (If "no," ask why not.) Would your family approve of your talking to us? Would they be upset if you were quoted in the book? What is your current relationship with your mother? Do you hate her for shooting your father? When all is said and done, do you feel that Isabel is a victim herself?

I read the questions aloud to Isabel, who said she couldn't wait to hear Perry's answers. I warned, "We could be way off here. He could be spewing venom."

She smiled and propped her little airline pillow between her cheek and the window.

"So you think it's safe?" I pressed.

She leaned toward me. "This could be something of a coup, you know: Guy's son willing to go on the record." She unlatched her tray table as a male flight attendant approached with a metal pitcher in each hand. "Coffee," said Isabel.

"Coffee," I echoed. When it was poured I said, "He could change his mind when we get there. He may have consulted six libel lawyers by now."

Isabel shrugged. "Even if he doesn't go on the record, we can probably get him to talk, and we'll use that as deep background."

"*Deep background?*" I repeated. "Where did you pick that one up?"

"Woodward and Bernstein."

I asked which of their books she had read.

Isabel made a face. "I had a client who dated Bernstein. She came to me two months before his birthday, wanting something intellectual but also a show-stopper. I came up with this inspired idea, leather-bound copies of his books, hand-tooled, gold embossing, gorgeous endpapers. Then the day before the big event—no warning—he broke up with her. She got stuck with his goddamn life's work in deluxe editions! Talk about unreturnable presents." She took a gulp of coffee and shook

ISABEL'S BED

her head. "I learned something from that. It taught me to be a little less creative when it came to birthday presents between uncommitted couples."

A male voice announced that it was thirty-four degrees in New York, that sleet was mixing with rain; the flight attendant would pick up our trash; please return seats and tray tables to their full upright position.

Isabel took a makeup pouch from her tapestry saddlebag and applied her long-wearing Ooh La La Red. She offered me the jeweled tube and the tortoise shell mirror; she said nobody could see that teenage gloss I called a lipstick, while Ooh La La would give me definition and would last.

We were first off the plane and first to the taxi stand. When we crossed the bridge into Manhattan, our smiles matched.

Our first stop was a walk-in hair salon at Madison and Fifty-eighth. Isabel asked for the best French braider, and the receptionist said coolly, "They all do that."

"She wants her hair done, too," said Isabel, pushing me forward, "by someone not too threatening."

I protested. I said every time I asked for an inch off they took six.

"Which wouldn't be the end of the world," said Isabel.

The phone rang and the receptionist answered. She used the eraser end of her pencil to flip the pages of the appointment book.

Isabel said, "My treat. A belated welcome-aboard present."

"I wasn't planning on this," I murmured.

She said, "Harriet, I'm not offering you a surprise pelvic exam. A haircut doesn't take any advance notice."

I reminded her of the plan: Would it be convincing if I

173

arrived smelling like a beauty parlor and *then* announced I was running off to a manicure? I'd look like a pampered house-wife.

The receptionist said, shoulder hunched to the receiver, "No, you won't."

Isabel motioned we should move back from the desk. "What's the real problem here?" she whispered.

I shrugged.

"You can't tell me?"

"I'd tell you but I don't think you'd understand."

"Thanks a lot," she said.

I told her that the reason she wouldn't understand was because hairdressers didn't try to intimidate people like her.

"How do they intimidate you?"

"They're very condescending. They're only nice to people who look a certain way or who have nice jewelry or who don't need a hairdresser in the first place. They're very rude when they think you come in once a year off the farm and don't know enough to dye your hair."

"Then you sit down in the chair," Isabel instructed, "and you say 'I don't want to hear anything about my gray hairs.' That's what I do when they start on me about going short."

"John Michael is free," said the receptionist.

John Michael smiled and waved from his station. He was wearing an apricot polo shirt and tight pressed jeans and was lifting his sandy forelocks with a pick.

"She's afraid you'll cut it all off," yelled the receptionist.

"No way," he answered.

Isabel nudged me toward him. I left her side and sat down uneasily. John Michael swiveled the chair left, right, and said, "Can I say one thing?"

I nodded.

"Your widow's peak."

I waited.

"People with widow's peaks should not part their hair in the middle under any circumstances."

I asked him what he would do if given a free hand.

"What would I *do*?" He chose a brush from his collection and planted himself behind me to appraise my reflection. "Three things," he said finally. "We cut off to here, so it's still long but not ruling your life. We blow it dry so it's less bushy. We pull back from here, no part, but soft, and secure it at the crown subtly—no squishies, just a grown-up accessory—and we create a nice look, half up, half down."

He began brushing from the roots to the ends. I let my head loll back with each stroke. After a hypnotizing minute I said, "Maybe I am due for a change."

"We all get into ruts," he said. "Sometimes it's hair, sometimes it's the frosted lipstick from high school or whatever the popular girl at the next locker wore that was cool."

I confessed under the brush that the man I had lived with preferred long hair.

"Long hair right or wrong, even if you look like a cave woman? I hate those guys."

"I hate those guys, too," I said.

He pulled strands out from my temples at forty-five degree angles and met my eyes in the mirror. "What's the worst that'll happen?" he asked. "He'll get angry and sulk for a few days?"

"He won't see it."

John Michael rested both hands on my shoulders. "Can I ask why not?"

"Because he married someone else on Valentine's Day."

175

"What a cruel bastard," said John Michael. "Who needs to be reminded of that every time you look in the mirror?"

"Can you brush it some more?" I asked.

His bristles were magic. I closed my eyes. He crooned to me that short hair was easier, and advised me that the very brush in his hand—this week only—was on sale.

"It's been long forever," I said.

"How long?"

"Twelve years."

"Did he, like, forbid you to cut it?"

"I just kept letting it grow. A couple of times a year he'd trim it himself."

His fingertips were sweeping my jaw: *here,* he was saying. Let me cut to here.

I said no, too drastic. Longer, to there, so I can still pull it back.

"What's your name?" he asked kindly.

"Harriet."

He pumped the foot pedal and my chair rose in jerks. "We're going up to the shoulders, hon," he said.

He performed a duet with a hair dryer and an oversized cylindrical brush that left me straight, almost sleek. I said, "Do you think it's too preppy?"

"Be serious," said John Michael.

"Think I can do this at home?"

"Like this," he demonstrated, "under, under, twirl, twirl. One section at a time."

I asked if this brush was on sale, too.

He said definitely: under, under, twirl, twirl. Put the time in, use the blower; if I let it air dry I'd be back to bushy. "Some people's gray is ugly," John Michael went on, whipping off my plastic cape with a flourish, "but yours blends nicely." He asked if he should sweep up my clippings and put them in a bag marked "Never again will I let a man tell me how to wear my hair."

I smiled and said that wouldn't be necessary.

"Hey," John Michael called down the line to Isabel, who was chatting with her stylist as if they were reunited college roommates. "Take a look at your friend here."

Isabel blinked hard and declared calmly, "The man's a genius."

Strangers waiting for appointments said nice things about my hair as Isabel paid, new brushes included. "Do you apologize?" she asked when we got outside.

I said yes, I did. I needed a haircut and John Michael was an exception to my rule.

She looked me up and down, from my widow's peak to my houndstooth hem. "You look great, you know. And what's more, I think you feel great."

I said, "Don't go overboard. It's only a trim and a blow dry."

She stepped out from under the awning to hail a taxi, cursing the sleet. I asked, "Wouldn't a bowl of soup feel good right now?"

Isabel said yes, then no, she had a better plan for lunch, a better place to celebrate our gorgeous selves.

"Where is that?" I asked.

"TriBeCa," said Isabel. "Suddenly I crave a decent bagel."

16

LUNCH

 THE CAB DRIVER stayed out of it, his chin sinking to his chest as if his wife and sister-in-law from the old country were arguing in the backseat.

"We're this close," Isabel pleaded. "Can't you give me the satisfaction of buying a few bagels so I can put a face with the name?"

I said I hadn't come all this way to squander our one lunch—

"What does he serve at lunch?" she asked earnestly as Lexington Avenue flew by.

"Bagels! Tuna on bagels. Chopped liver on bagels. Bagels Benedict."

She told me to give the driver the address. I mumbled so she'd have to repeat it, "Chambers Street, between West Broadway and Greenwich. And then he can drop *me* off at the World Trade Center."

"What if I get something to go—anonymously, of course —and you wait for me?"

I said no, what the hell would be the point of *that*?

She asked why I wanted to deny her the small satisfaction of setting eyes on the man with whom I had spent my thirties.

"Because it's not a game," I said. "It's still painful and I didn't come to New York to scratch the scab."

She asked the driver—his license showed a sixtyish-year-old man named Leonard Pincus—if he minded waiting two minutes while she ran into a store on Chambers Street after which he could drive both her and her friend to a second destination.

He shrugged his consent. I told her to run in and run out and do me the favor of not bothering to buy anything.

"How will I know which one is Kenny?"

I told her to look for the shiny gold band.

"Two minutes," she said, and darted into the sleet.

I waited in silence. The driver said, "Must be *some* bagels."

I said, "No, they're not; they're too cakey for my taste. This is purely a social call."

After another silence he said, "I once took a fare from Central Park South down to Essa Bagel on the Lower East Side and back again. All the way down he talked them up, so I said, 'Ya know what? Get me a dozen, mixed, no pumpernickel.'"

179

"Did he?"

"Sure he did."

"How were they?"

"How were they? They were good. Were they worth a twenty-six dollar fare? Probably not."

I asked how many bagels the guy bought for himself. Leonard Pincus said he didn't recall; a few shopping bags full, not including his own dozen.

"Why didn't he call the bagel place and have them sent uptown in a cab?"

The driver turned around to get a better look at me. "That's what you and I would do; that's what a normal person would do. But people with so much money they can't count it don't operate like you and me." He nodded, satisfied, and turned back to face the steering wheel. The meter clicked up another dollar. I asked Mr. Pincus if he'd see what was taking my friend so long.

"Sorry," he said. "Against regulations."

I explained that I'd go myself but that the situation was a little awkward.

"Why's that?" he asked.

"My former fiancé owns the place."

"I get it," said the driver. "She's in there to give him the once-over 'cause she never met him."

I said that was correct. She meant well, but—

"You single?" he asked.

I said yes.

"You live in New York?"

I said not anymore.

"I knew that," he said. "You know how I knew that? You smiled when you got in here and said hello. Only tourists do that. Never the ones who live here."

I said I used to live here, but I didn't take taxis then.

"What about your friend? Is she someone I know? An actress? You know why I ask? She has a very confident air about her. Not that she isn't a nice woman, don't get me wrong, but she knows how to get her way."

"Maybe that's because she's beautiful," I said. "It has the same effect."

He turned around again. "I didn't notice that about her."

Suddenly Isabel was at the door, carrying an umbrella she hadn't gone in with. She pantomimed, Roll down the window, which I did, a crack. "Don't get mad," she began.

"You told him?"

"I did *not* tell him. He recognized me. I swear to God."

"How could he recognize you? He doesn't know you!"

"The only thing I said was 'Are you the owner?' just to be certain I had the right guy. Then he said, 'Sure, who are you?' in a way that was more charming than you led me to expect. So just to be sure I said, 'Kenny?' and he said, 'Yeah,' and asked my name and I said 'Isabel,' and that's *all*. No last name."

"Like 'Isabel' wasn't a major clue?"

"It's my name! What did you expect me to say?"

"Jesus Christ," I said. "Let's get out of here."

"There's one more thing." She switched the umbrella to her other hand and surveyed the crosstown traffic. "He wants to take us to lunch."

"No!"

"Is that so terrible?"

I pressed the heels of my hands against my forehead to keep my brains from falling out. Isabel barked, "Don't mess your hair," then, more gently, "I told him it was okay with me if it was okay with you."

"It's not okay with me!"

"What're you going to do? Avoid him for the rest of your life?"

"Yes!"

Isabel opened the door and nudged me over. "I'll tell you something: You couldn't have avoided him forever. He said one of these weekends he was coming up to the Cape. He could have rung the doorbell and you could have been standing there in your baggy stretch pants and your ripped Boston College sweatshirt with your mouth open. My feeling is this, if you're going to see him, why not on a day when you've just walked out of the beauty parlor and look like a million bucks?"

"Because I don't want to."

She patted my hand. "I really think it'll be fine. I told him you wanted grilled shrimp and maybe a white bean salad and a delicious glass of Chardonnay, and he said he knew just the place. He's on the phone right now making a reservation at a place that we wouldn't be able to get into without his contacts."

"He has no contacts," I said.

"His treat." She reached down and came up with her makeup pouch. "Here," she said, pressing the jeweled tube into my palm. "You lick your lips too much."

Then she was out the door, promising to return with our host. The meter was up to twenty-one dollars and change. After a long silence Leonard Pincus said, "I'd look at it this way: At least he's buying."

"I don't see Bob," Kenny said for the umpteenth time, squinting and craning from our window table at the TriBeCa Grill. De Niro, he meant, his bagel patron, a category Kenny confused with close friend. For the second time he confided that Bob liked a plain bagel with peanut butter even first thing in the morning.

"How fascinating," Isabel said in a voice I recognized from the Old Anchor as completely insincere.

Kenny said, "He's not the only celebrity I get. I get a ton of actors down here: Tom Hanks when they were filming the bonfire movie, which was quite a few years now." He paused, then added coyly, "Black and white bagel with cuke-dill cream cheese. And, what's her name, she won an Oscar."

"Mercedes Ruehl," I said.

"Half a honey oat bran bagel, toasted, with butter on the side."

"Who else?" asked Isabel.

Kenny hitched his chair an inch closer to hers. "Once this guy came in who looked familiar. I couldn't place him and I couldn't place him and after he left I said, 'Kenny, you shmuck; you just waited on Placido Domingo.'"

Isabel held up her hand. "Let me guess: jalapeño corn."

I stared at her: *You conversational slut. What's the next topic, smoked sturgeon?*

Kenny shook his head with pride and incredulity. "You know about my jalapeño corns?"

"You FedEx'ed them—" I began.

"I *know*," said Kenny, "but still. I wouldn't expect them to be on the tip of her tongue."

"I love my breakfast," explained Isabel. "Harriet will testify to that." She opened her menu, humming softly.

"So. Harriet," said Kenny.

I looked up.

"Ghostwriting seems to agree with you."

An unexpected "Fuck you" flew out of my mouth.

He looked to Isabel, his ally and confidante. She passed him the bread basket, murmuring, "I don't think she meant anything by it."

"What could she possibly see in that sentence that could offend her?"

Isabel answered calmly, "You threw her out on the street, Ken. You cheated on her, which is humiliating enough, but then, after all those years of whining about what difference would a piece of paper make, you ran to City Hall to get married as fast as your little legs could carry you. Maybe this is the first chance she's had to say, 'Fuck you.'" She opened her eyes wide and half-shrugged as if to say, Nothing personal.

Kenny looked as if lunch were collapsing around him. "But that's just the point, isn't it: I *wanted* to get married. Amy and I talked about marriage almost from the beginning. I never had one moment of doubt."

"Can I tell you why?" Isabel asked.

Kenny parted his lips to answer, but Isabel got there first. "Because you didn't have the upper hand," she said.

He looked at me and back at Isabel.

"Men propose because they're nervous. Harriet never made you nervous. Amy, on the other hand, was not a sure thing. *You* needed the commitment." She poked his shoulder with an Ooh La La Red fingernail. "*You,* not her."

Kenny was saved by our waiter, Ethan, who arrived to perform a charming at-your-service routine, clicking his heels and poising his pen. "How are *we* today?" he asked, beaming exclusively at Isabel. Kenny noticed and perked up. He was the host of this table and here was a handsome moonlighting actor giving him credit for delivering a trophy customer.

"Is Bob around?" Kenny asked, leaning back in his chair.

"Bob?"

"De Niro."

"His friends call him Bobby," the waiter said softly.

Isabel changed the subject by coyly reading from the menu, "Ask your waitperson for the specials du jour."

"Our fish is grilled snapper with saffron butter," Ethan recited. "Our chicken is roasted with fresh rosemary, lemon, olives, and wild mushrooms; our pasta is tagliatelli with smoked salmon, new peas, dill, and cream; our risotto is with crab, leeks and fennel. Our soup is tomato and eggplant."

"Very nice," Isabel murmured.

I scanned the entrees and decided "Market price" would be the most expensive. I followed it across the page and asked what they stuffed the grilled lobster with.

"Rock shrimp. It's fabulous."

I said I'd have that and the Caesar salad with the fried oysters.

Isabel asked the waiter what he would recommend and he said he personally couldn't resist their free-range rotisserie grilled chicken. See? Over there, turning on a spit. Served with Yukon Gold potatoes.

"Mashed?"

He smiled and said, "We could do mashed."

"Sold!" Isabel cried.

Kenny repeated our choices à la 1950. "For myself," he said, tapping a finger to his gourmet lips, "the *zuppa* and the *riz-o-do*. And a bottle of, let's see . . . ah, you have Sequoia Grove Chardonnay. Very nice. We'll have that now." Ethan collected the menus. Kenny murmured, *"Grazie."*

I thought: how did I ever stand him?

Once, four or five years before, I had broken up with him because of an incident that drove me into creative writing and became the core of my first short story: his crush on a neighbor named Kathy. She lived in our building and had a colicky baby who was soothed by the white noise of the laundry room. Every night after dinner she brought Nicholas to the basement, buckled into his car seat, sat him on the dryer, and let the noise and the vibration lull him to sleep.

Kenny happened across this scene when the baby was six weeks old, and began describing every facet of it with daily updates in feverishly happy terms. I, of course, was not supposed to be detecting a crush or noticing a thing—not his nightly loads of laundry; not his new silk bikini briefs; not his hoarding of quarters as if they were non-negotiable outside the building.

One weeknight I went down to the basement to look for an allegedly lost sock. Kathy was there, cute as a button in her husband's starched white dress shirt over legwarmers and striped socks, reading Newsweek against the same dryer that held Nicholas. We exchanged pleasantries and she explained the white-noise treatment. She asked what I did and I said I worked for a law firm. Kenny arrived at his usual time with his usual small load of all-male clothes. She greeted him warmly and called him Kenny; she introduced him to me as her best friend in the building.

I said, "What a coincidence. He's my best friend, too."

Kathy said too quickly, "Yes, I knew that."

"Has Ken ever mentioned me?" I asked.

He didn't even have the reflexes to put his disloyal arm around my shoulders and say, "Kathy, this is Harriet. *My* Harriet. The one I talk about all the time."

She said, "Of course he's mentioned you."

I asked in what context.

"As his friend in the building. As his *first* friend in the building," she added, looking pleased with that pinch hit.

Kenny finally came to life. "Harriet and I are, uh, room-mates."

"I knew that," she lied. "Did you think I didn't know that? Harriet Mahoney, right?"

For the moment, I was appeased. I looked into the unused machines for stray socks with all the dignity I could manufacture under the circumstances. Kathy pointed out the lost-and-found carton, from which I elected someone else's navy blue cabled kneesock. "You coming or staying?" I asked Kenny.

He pointed to the washer. "I've just started my cycle."

"Really nice to have met you finally," said Kathy. "We should all get together."

"Do you think," I had yelled as I threw my clothes into a suitcase, "that she's going to leave her husband and move in with you and let you adopt that obnoxious baby?" I told him that women like Kathy, small-boned girls from the South, viewed men like him as nice, approachable, safe. As friends. As Jewish people, not sexual prospects. He was making a fool of himself, giving her a shoulder to cry on about sleep deprivation and blocked ducts. So what if her husband didn't get home until the baby had been through the laundry cure and was asleep in his crib? Did that mean she wanted a divorce? Had he seen this husband? Because I had. He was tall and handsome with his camel top coat and his hair wet from the health club. I asked Kenny: Hadn't he realized that Kathy confided in him and breast-fed in front of him precisely because she felt no stirrings?

I moved in with Maureen, a co-worker and paralegal in

training, for two nights. "Are *you* perfect?" she demanded. "I know I'm not. So, he's got a crush. He's human. Can you guarantee you'll never get a crush on a man other than Kenny?"

He called me at work and said, "Kathy and I are only friends, I swear, but if it bothers you that much, I'll cool it."

I said, venting a thought I'd had twenty times, "Don't think I was fooled by her pulling 'Mahoney' out of thin air. My name's been on the buzzer for two years."

He said, "Maybe I've been deeply affected by her mothering. Maybe we should talk about having a baby."

I called him back first thing in the morning and asked, "What did you mean, 'We should talk about having a baby'? Do you mean you and me?"

He said, "Ya know, maybe I'm ready. I could be. At the very least, I'm ready to open discussions."

I stayed away another night. He called again, crying, and said he loved me.

It wasn't the best bargain I ever made. Kenny stopped doing his own laundry. We didn't find out for almost a year that he had sluggish sperm. Even after it was tested the doctors said conception was not unheard of with these numbers. I envisioned trysts with balding, five-foot-seven Semitic strangers for the sake of covert insemination. Married couples would have agreed to any number of low-tech tricks that beefed up sperm, but Kenny wanted it to be natural, without intervention.

He argued that beating the odds on our own would cure his ambivalence about marriage. Artificially getting me pregnant with his or someone else's sperm was, well, not the sign from God he was looking for.

I began typing creative sentences at work that weren't first dictated by attorneys. I found the writing group through a flyer on a health food store bulletin board. It said, "If you think you have something to say but you're not sure how to say it, we provide the emotional pen and ink."

For the first six Wednesday nights, I just listened. On the seventh Wednesday I brought my story, "White Noise." In it, my narrator found her boyfriend kissing a pretty young woman in a laundromat while a baby named Nicole nodded off to the slosh of washing machine suds.

The members of the workshop listened respectfully, the way writers do when the work under discussion has clearly sprung from personal tragedy. In the silence that followed my first reading, Ferris Porter delicately raised the idea of the objective correlative. He explained that I could render some different set of events from these now-familiar ones, which would stand for such a betrayal and would evoke the same emotion in the reader. T. S. Eliot, he explained modestly, not his own theory. The workshop teacher said Ferris's idea was a damn good one. For the next class I was to take the same set of events and render an objective correlative. In fact, why didn't everyone try their hands at objective correlatives for next week? Questions?

In my next few drafts, New York became London, the laundromat became a series of small businesses, and my narrators became housekeepers or unhappy wives or plucky shopkeepers. Still, my writing group detected too much autobiography in my fiction and too little drama.

No matter how I turned my sentences around, they wanted to discuss the person behind the story. The men in the class asked, "Is a kiss such a betrayal? The narrator and the guy weren't married, right?"

The teacher said, "Here's a good exercise: How would you have rendered her discovering the boyfriend and the new mother, her breasts engorged, her womb still tender, copulating on the folding table?"

And the women of the group wanted to know what kind of low self-esteem a person needed to back out of the laundromat as if she'd never seen a thing.

Isabel had the nerve to disappear for ten minutes, leaving Kenny and me alone at the table. I waited for him to speak first, to say something insensitive or pretentious that I could memorize and hold against him in the years ahead. Instead he smiled shyly as if we were alone for the first time on a double date.

"Go ahead," I said. "Say what you were going to say."

"Nooo," he said. "I don't think so. I tried that once."

"I won't say 'fuck you' again."

He said, after what looked like a silent rehearsal, "Are you okay? Because you seem happy with the way things turned out. I mean, you've left the city and you're doing what you've always wanted to do." He grinned and gave me a friendly cuff to the shoulder. "I mean, here you are, heading off with a tape recorder and a briefcase to interview a famous actor about a famous murder trial. That's what I call the big-time."

"I still have to write the thing."

"You know what I think? You'll get this book done and they'll want another one, a novel. And you'll be in the big-time permanently." He lifted his glass and with the last swallow of Chardonnay toasted my future.

I said thanks; I also said, knowing that someone with a future would act magnanimously, "Hope your marriage is happy."

Kenny clinked my glass and stared moistly. "I hope——" he began, but his voice cracked.

"Oh, c'mon," I said.

"To your work," he managed. "May it bring you success of every kind. And happiness. Especially happiness."

I leaned closer across the table and asked, trusting the lump in his throat, "How do I know I can write a book if I've never written one before?"

"She picked you, didn't she, of all the people she had at her disposal to write her book? Why would she have done that if you weren't the best writer for the job?"

"Because she liked me," I said. "She needed a friend. And mostly because she doesn't know anything about writing."

"You needed a friend, too—is it all right to say that?—and a place to live. And a job. You've written a ton of stuff. All those stories and, what?—two, three novels?" He swept the room with his arm. "And you hit the jackpot, everything rolled into one."

I looked up to make sure Isabel wasn't on her way back to the table. I said, "Except for the fact that I'm completely alone."

"Nah," said Kenny. "That's because you're new to the place. It's like going to sleep-away camp: You feel lonely and homesick until you make friends, and then you don't want to leave."

I shook my head. "I'm not talking about friends. I'm talking about having no one next to you, inside your skin, no partner."

"You mean in the——"

"I mean unloved. Unwanted."

"That's crazy! You have parents, sisters, brothers-in-law; and there's Isabel and your friends from the writing group. And you know," he said—precisely the quote I would harvest for future ridicule—"you *know* you always have me and Amy."

I must have looked like I was benefiting from his counsel because he drove the point home almost cheerfully: I didn't want to turn back the clock, did I? Because, in all honesty —and Amy had taught him a lot about honesty—could I say I had felt loved and wanted, really, when we had been together?

I said sometimes.

"But overall, don't you think I was holding you back, fulfillmentwise?"

"Yes," I said rotely, wondering what ever had possessed me to confide in Kenny Solo-Grossman. So I told him I had exaggerated the loneliness part. Winter was desolate on Cape Cod but summer was coming and we were expecting a houseful of people every weekend. Had he ever heard of Wellfleet? In August it was jammed with vacationing psychiatrists and professionals.

"Single people?" he asked. "Eligible men you might see a movie or have dinner with?"

"Sure," I said. "And sleep with. Definitely. I only hope it doesn't slow progress on the book."

He asked when I thought it would be finished.

I said I had a one-year contract with Isabel.

"And then what?"

"And then I'll revise my novel," I said.

"Where?"

I named the places people name—Seattle, Santa Fe, the Bay

Area. As if chic relocation was one of the advantages of being all alone in the world.

"Any chance you'd stay on in Truro?"

"Who knows?"

He winked. He gave my sagging shoulder another fraternal punch. I had no idea why.

17
PERRY

 THE DOORMAN ACTED both
weary and contemptuous as if
we were the ninety-eighth
and ninety-ninth autograph hounds to appear before his
marble rostrum and say, "Mr. VanVleet, please. He's expecting us."

"Names?" he asked, slapping a piece of the management's
stationery into place.

"Ms. Krug and Ms. Mahoney," I said.

He studied his list and looked up with his old bulldog-
bachelor's face. "Whaddya know: must be three P.M."

Isabel and I affected our own looks of weary contempt.

"We're a few minutes late for our appointment," she said, "so I'd appreciate your letting him know we're here."

He frowned at a laminated telephone list, shielding it from our view as if we were well-known for cheating on exams. He moved the red telephone to a precise spot before him and jabbed the numbers, checking the list after every digit. "Ladies here to see you," he said. "Misses . . . ?"

"Krug and Mahoney," I repeated.

"Misses Krug and Mahoney." He hung up and asked to see identification. I fished out my license; Isabel said she didn't have one—who drove in New York?—but Ms. Mahoney would vouch for her.

Happy to be crossed, he met Isabel's stare for a stand-off. I said, "What about a credit card?"

She took a Bloomingdale's credit card from her spangled wallet and tossed it onto his rostrum. He studied the slivers of plastic, then nodded curtly. "Elevators to the left. Mr. V. is on seven."

"Which apartment?" I asked.

"Seventh floor is all you need," he said, refusing to look up.

Isabel barely waited until we had rounded the corner to the elevators before spitting out, "Passive-aggressive asshole."

I lit the *Up* button and we waited. Isabel smoothed her hair in a gilt-frame mirror that was partially obscured by a mammoth Chinese urn on a rococo chest of drawers.

"He must get a lot of fans trying to sneak upstairs," I said.

"I don't give a good goddamn how many fans try to sneak upstairs," she said, raising her voice so it could double back around the corner. "It's his job to be civil to people who have legitimate business here."

The doors opened to reveal an elevator with dark green velour walls and crystal buttons; "7" was already lit. Once aboard, I pointed to a discreet video camera above our heads.

Isabel gave it the finger and enunciated into its lens, "I'm sure it's necessary with all the riff-raff slipping past security."

The elevator stopped with a gentle whir; the doors opened and we were inside a black lacquered foyer. Double doors faced us. Isabel and I stopped and checked with each other. "Let's knock," I said.

The inner door opened and there stood, for all intents and purposes, Kerr Greenwood, the clean-cut student body president of Rosewell U. His face was thinner than it appeared on television, and his curly blond hair was wetter. He extended his right hand, which Isabel took in both of hers.

"Oh, my God," she whispered. "You look so much like Guy in this light."

I didn't think so, but I admired her directness, since my own philosophy was to avoid topics that reminded people of unpleasant episodes in their lives.

"You're the first one to say *that*."

"Maybe the coloring is your mother's, but the features are his."

I stopped her by extending my right hand. "I'm Harriet Mahoney."

"Please come in," said Perry.

We crossed the threshold into a living room with white adobe walls decorated with what looked like papier maché fertility gods painted in electric colors. The rug was black with white cacti designs. The sectional sofa was upholstered in white and black cowhide.

"Who did you use?" asked Isabel.

"The Fowlers."

"Senior or Junior?"

"Junior."

"I wouldn't have guessed the Fowlers," said Isabel, "but

that's to their credit." She said to me, assuming correctly that I had no knowledge of interior design firms, "They're a little conservative and a little stuffy." She asked Perry who had made the referral.

"Two friends," he said vaguely.

Isabel became the tour guide, leading us into the next room, a combination dining room and large-screen TV theater, where the Southwestern theme had gone desert. There were sandy browns and grays and an animal carcass motif. The surface of the dining room table was apricot-tinted glass that rested on an antler base.

"Stunning," said Isabel. "Did you just have it done?"

"Just."

I asked what it had been like before.

"Bor-ing. Beige walls, no window treatments, a little tweedy. *Plaid* wallpaper in the kitchen."

"You didn't live here when I was seeing your father, did you?" Isabel asked, running her palm along the fringe of the rough-cut suede couch, "because I remember him talking about a place in the East Village. With a roommate? David? Dan?"

"Dana. That was two places ago. He and I stopped being roommates and then I moved into a sublet. I bought this place when the market began to fall."

"Good for you," said Isabel.

"He was a college friend," Perry added. Then for good measure: "He left to get married."

Too late; *we stopped being roommates and then I moved* had only one connotation as far as I was concerned. I checked with Isabel, whose lips moved silently as if testing the right compliment. "There's something very virile about your choices," she said finally. "Yet they're warm and—what's the right word?—whimsical." She led us into the kitchen where the junior Fowler had chosen unglazed terra cotta tiles with accents of yellow and pale aqua.

"Just great," sighed Isabel.

I asked, since the butcher block counter had no scars and the hanging copper pots looked newly minted, if he liked to cook.

"Why do you ask?"

"It looks so perfect."

"I cook a little." He thought it over and said, "Although I don't really like to." He smiled as if he suddenly remembered he was playing a gracious host. "You know how bachelors are about cooking: We do steaks, pizzas, the occasional veal parmigiana."

"Do you have a roommate now?" I asked.

His dark blue eyes narrowed slightly. "Did someone tell you that?"

I said no. I put my briefcase down on the terra cotta island and said, "I should probably be asking you these questions on the record."

"I think the factory whistle just blew," Isabel said dryly.

Perry pulled out one of the two Old West bar stools and sat down.

"Could we impose on you for a drink?" Isabel asked.

He said sure, not moving.

Keeping faith with Plan A, I asked if he had tea. No, he had seltzer, soda, wine.

"Seltzer."

"Diet soda for me," Isabel said. "And I think Harriet and I would like to spread out on your dining room table if that's okay."

Perry nodded. Isabel and I returned to the dining room and

sat down at the apricot glass table. As soon as I heard ice tinkling against glass I mouthed, "Gay?"

"Definitely," she mouthed back. She shook her head in a prim way that said, Be careful; he's coming, we'll discuss it later. As Perry came into view, Isabel pasted on a wide-open smile. On anyone else I would have seen it as artificial, but on Isabel, for this occasion, it seemed kind, even nursery-school-teacherish, as if his first impression crossing the threshold would determine his lifelong attitude toward strangers.

He handed us cobalt-blue glasses that looked as if they had been hand-blown somewhere in the Mountain time zone.

"Lovely," said Isabel.

I set up the tape recorder and put my assortment of felt-tip pens, sharpened pencils, and a package of tissues on a new yellow legal pad. Perry turned a chair around and straddled it, cowboy style. I pushed the red record button and said, "Perry VanVleet, March 19, New York City."

Isabel, as choreographed, read the first question from her crib sheet. "Perry, we want to know about you today, your work, your life, what drives you, what makes you happy." She looked up and blinked.

He held up his right index finger: *Wait. I've got just the ticket.* He disappeared into the kitchen and beyond. Isabel and I waited, our features in neutral. After a minute she whispered, "Did you ever meet a gay man with less personality?"

I thought maybe it was shyness; maybe he'd warm up.

She smiled dreamily. "It could have been so great—having a charming, intelligent, young, gay actor to pal around with when I came into the city."

Perry returned carrying a tabloid newspaper. *SoapSpeak* said the masthead. He leafed ahead to a double spread, opened it proudly, and sat down. There were three color photos: one of

Kerr, lips pursed uninvitingly, kissing a coed; a wide horizontal shot of Perry in black jeans and black T-shirt stretched out on his Holstein couch; and one of the whole family in tennis whites behind a trophy in happier days. "Perry VanVleet," blared the headline, "ITBJ's B.M.O.C."

Isabel pointed to the first block of initials and murmured for my benefit, " 'If This Be Joy.' " I angled the pages so we could both read the copy: "A year ago last Christmas Eve Perry VanVleet, flanked by his teenaged sisters, sat in the first row of spectators in a Stamford, Conn., courtroom. The last rays of a distant December sun were forcing themselves through dusty blinds. Except for the muffled coughs of the spectators and the scratchings of reporters' pencils, the room was silent and tense. The two people standing had the weight of the world on their shoulders: the jury foreman and the defendant, Greenwich socialite Nancy VanVleet, charged with murder in the first degree of her husband, Guy.

"Justice E. Susan Garland's voice rang out: 'Mr. Foreman, have you reached a verdict?'

" 'We have, your honor,' he said.

" 'How say you?'

" 'We find the defendant Nancy VanVleet not guilty by reason of temporary insanity.' "

"The courtroom erupted. The defendant sagged against her counsel. Spectators gasped. Reporters scrambled for phone booths. The handsome young man in the front row drew his younger sisters to him. Tears spilled from their eyes, not tears of happiness or relief, but of far more complex emotions. Yes, the defense had prevailed and had won hospitalization over incarceration. Yes, it was the best possible verdict the jury could have reached. But that didn't change the fact that a murder had been committed, or the fact that tomorrow was

Christmas, and no amount of tears or prayers would bring their beloved father back."

I looked up from the text to check on poor fatherless Perry. He was rerolling the left cuff of his blue-oxford button-down with great concentration, as if measuring a perfect length of exposed wrist.

I skimmed the remaining text, which covered the swelling of Kerr Greenwood's role and the director's memories of Perry's audition and call-back. To one side was a box head-lined I.D. Card. In boldface it revealed that Perry had no nickname, that his birthday was December 26, that he had no pets, that his favorite food was buttered noodles, his favorite color was gray, any shade of it, his most prized possession his father's cuff links. His pet peeve was people who didn't shut off lights when they left a room; his hero was his maternal grandfather, once a lieutenant governor of Connecticut.

Isabel was reading more slowly. I fixed my eyes on hers so that we might swap silent assessments as soon as she looked up.

"I think it's pretty accurate," Perry offered, "except for her saying that my sisters were both teenagers."

"Do you mind them discussing your private life?" I asked.

"Where?" he asked sharply.

"Here," I said, "and here—your parents, the trial . . ."

"Oh, that. We planted that. This reporter wasn't even at the trial." He explained that his publicist considered it necessary. And, yes, it was hard on the girls, but they understood.

"Understood what?" I asked.

"That I have to put my name out there."

"Out there where?"

"In the public eye and in the newspapers. Not just in the

trade papers. So I can break out. Right now I'm labeled 'daytime,' which can keep you from other stuff. Like feature films. Even prime time."

"Who's your publicist?" Isabel asked.

"Dorothea Woo."

"Any good?"

"I don't know," said Perry. "What was your impression?"

Isabel said, "My impression?"

"She said she talked to you to set up this interview."

Isabel took a sip from her glass before answering. "Of course I remember," she said tightly.

I asked Perry if Dorothea had set up the *SoapSpeak* profile as well.

"I'm pretty sure she did."

"She must be pleased with it."

Perry rubbed away a smudge on the glass tabletop with his elbow. "She wasn't real happy with my answers. Now she coaches me before an interview because she says I have to be consistent and say things that build an image."

"Like what?" I asked.

He turned the *SoapSpeak* pages toward him. "Like in the I.D. Card. She thought I could have named Robert Kennedy or Clint Eastwood as my hero, someone with sex appeal. She thinks it was a lost opportunity."

I asked if gray was really his favorite color.

He looked lost and teenaged, like Kerr puzzling over a hussy's demands. "Do you think that was such a bad answer?" he asked.

"I think you did the right thing," said Isabel, "because if you let someone else put words in your mouth you'll sound coached."

"Did Dorothea coach you before this interview?" I asked.

He shrugged and said, "Not really."

"You can tell us," said Isabel. "We're on your side."

"She wrote me a memo about it."

"Can you tell us what it said?" asked Isabel. "Or maybe it would be easier to show it to us."

"I remember what it said. It said, basically, there was no such thing as bad publicity."

"So she doesn't mind your cooperating with us?" I asked.

Perry said no, she liked it a lot. And she had said the book might become a best-seller, which could really increase his audience.

"I'm surprised she hasn't suggested you write your own book," I said.

"She did at first, but she stopped talking about it after a while."

Isabel drained her glass and asked Perry if she might have a refill before we got down to serious Q and A. He said sure, be back in a jiff. As soon as he was out of sight, Isabel said matter-of-factly, "He has no personality. None. He's a flat line."

I asked if she still wanted me to excuse myself for trips to the bathroom.

She ignored my question and sat there stonily. Finally she said, "Do you believe how far off I was?" She shook her head. "I've seen this in actors before: they come alive on stage or in front of a camera but in real life, forget it. Dumb as dirt."

Perry returned with Isabel's glass. She consulted our list of questions and asked him, before he even sat down, "Perry, do you despise me for committing adultery with your father, and do you blame me for his death?"

"Gee," he said. "I never really thought of it like that, like if you hadn't come along my mother wouldn't have freaked and he'd still be alive?" He thought that over for a few seconds, then announced, "Nah. It wasn't your fault."

I looked at my list. "How come?" I asked.

He pushed a drop of water around the table with his index finger. "My mother pulled the trigger. And because my Dad loved Mrs. Krug—he told me that—and he wouldn't have blamed her for anything. Even if he could see into the future, I think he would've kept seeing her."

I looked at Isabel, knowing how goodness and mercy made her unsteady.

"Would Heidi and Sara agree with that?" she asked after a pause.

"They're kind of bummed out. They're like, 'We're orphans, we're all alone in the world,' because they're living at the Greenwich house, which they find totally creepy, and even though we're allowed to visit my mother at the hospital, it makes them really depressed."

"Do you go?" Isabel asked.

"Where?"

"To visit your mother at the hospital."

"Sure."

"What's that like?" I asked.

"I bring her tapes of the show and we talk about the hospital food which she thinks is way too starchy, and I tell her what I'm doing to the apartment, and she complains about her roommate and the nurses. She thinks the only reason they're nice to her is because of me."

"They're fans, you mean?"

"Yeah. They have me sign weird stuff, like their shoes. And the shell of a hard-boiled egg once."

"Do you mind that kind of attention?" I asked.

I could see his brain cells scanning for a deeply masculine

answer. "It comes with the territory," he said. "Women want you when you're on Daytime."

"That can't be so bad," Isabel murmured.

"Except," said Perry, "I never date fans."

I asked if he was in a relationship and he said yes. With an actress.

"Who is she?"

He said he didn't give out that information, and for good reason: The guys his sisters went out with during the trial who got their names in the paper couldn't handle it and walked.

"Because they got their names in the paper?" Isabel demanded.

"I think it was more like when a guy you're dating—not engaged to or anything?—goes with you to a family wedding or funeral, everyone assumes you're serious even if he's, like, a casual date. With the trial, any guy who was photographed with Heidi or Sara became The Boyfriend, quote unquote."

Isabel said Heidi and Sara shouldn't worry. They were young and pretty; besides, a well-publicized tragedy can place people in demand socially. And Nan herself would probably be back in Greenwich's good graces soon after she was sprung.

"How is your mother doing?" I asked.

"She's fine," he said, sounding pleasantly surprised.

"I mean, is she coping, or is she angry or miserable or—?"

"Crazed with revenge?" Isabel asked.

"She's kind of bored. And putting on weight because they don't have tennis courts or even a pool. She'd much rather be at home."

"No kidding," said Isabel.

"I mean, how's her mental state?" I asked.

"Harriet means, is she cured of her insanity?"

"That was just temporary at the time she fired the gun," said Perry.

I asked how much longer she'd have to stay in the hospital.

"That's up to the psychiatrists. And I guess the judge has something to say about it."

"How do you think she'd feel about your talking with me?"

"I wasn't planning to tell her."

"You don't think she'll read the book?"

"No."

"Why not?"

He hesitated and asked if we could go off the record. I put my pencil down—by this time I had stopped worrying about making a good intellectual impression and had slipped into shorthand.

He said, "She doesn't read books."

Isabel laughed.

"You don't think she'd make an exception for The Isabel Krug Story?" I asked.

Perry thought it over. "Not really."

Isabel held up her hand to signal Important Question; go back on the record: "Does your publicist view me as someone who's good for your image or bad for your image?"

"I think good."

"How did she think I could help?"

Perry answered as if repeating concepts that had been carefully explained to him in the most basic terms. "If we were seen together, say at a club or a restaurant, she would phone the gossip columnists at the papers and they'd print it like they'd actually *been* at the restaurant."

"Wouldn't it look staged?" I asked. "If you two were really

an item, you'd be sneaking around, hiding from the public, wouldn't you?"

Perry said, "I really think I should call her."

"I'm available tonight," said Isabel. "If it would help, I could speak with Dorothea directly."

He left the room, nodding gratefully as if he'd been granted a hall pass and wouldn't dream of abusing the privilege.

"You could find something to do tonight, I assume?" Isabel asked me.

I said yes; this was New York City, but why in the world would she—

"At least he asked me. He doesn't hate me and I owe him something."

"Do you think if the tables were turned, the VanVleets would ever do you a favor?"

"I don't care," said Isabel. "That's not why I'm saying yes."

We waited. "He must have reached her if it's taking this long," said Isabel.

After another minute I said, "You're a very kind person."

She took a tissue from my packet and blew her nose. "Poor guy," she murmured. Or maybe it was "Poor Guy."

18
FERRIS

IT WASN'T A case of having
no friends in New York; it
was that 5:30 on a Friday
night was impossibly short notice for dinner. I tried Maureen,
who said she was attending law school nights and was on her
way out the door. I tried Lucy from my last job, who would
have loved to have seen me but had been ordered by her
obstetrician to lie on her left side; I tried Ginny from my
desktop publishing seminar and Athena from my Dukakis
days; I tried Nayla from my sourdough workshop, whose
answering machine thanked me for the good energy, then
failed to beep.

So at 5:45, with my last quarter, as I was making peace with the notion that room service and a pay-per-view movie wasn't the worst way to spend a rainy night, I called Ferris Porter, who answered out of breath on the tenth ring.

He said he was tickled. I said I knew it was short notice, but I had just arrived in the city today, a last-minute business trip—

"I'm free," said Ferris. "And I'm simply astonished that you would choose today to call me."

I asked what he meant and he said he'd rather tell me in person.

I sagged involuntarily. I had a history with that phrase. Even coming from a person with no power to jilt me, it sounded like bad news.

"I hate surprises," I told him. "Couldn't you tell me now?"

"One hint, but that's all: A letter."

"A rejection letter?"

"Not another word until I see you."

"What's good for you?" I asked. "And where?"

"What does someone who's been living on New England's blustering shore, communing with Neptune's empire, want to do when she comes to this great hive?" he bubbled.

"Eat good Chinese," I said.

So we did, in Chinatown, at a storefront restaurant where Ferris pointed to wall signs in Mandarin and asked the waiter if he might translate the specials. He opened a menu and pointed to Chef's Delights. "Same thing," he said.

We followed a pink mountain of lobster meat and jumbo shrimp on its way to an all-Chinese table.

"What was that?" I asked.

The waiter said, "Shrimp with black beans."

"You sure?" I asked.

He pointed to the #12 Delight. "Same thing. Maybe they get extra seafood because it's a big party. Special occasion."

Ferris said solemnly, "This is a special occasion, too."

From the inside pocket of his black watch plaid jacket he brought forth an envelope and handed it to me. The return address read in wedding-invitation script The Priscilla Miller Agency.

I withdrew the letter: one thin, nerve-wracking piece of stationery with Ferris's future forecast in a single paragraph. "Dear Professor Porter," it began. "I would be most interested in reading the remaining chapters of Malice Emeritus. I do not charge a reading fee, but I do require temporary exclusivity for as long as a manuscript is in my office for evaluation purposes. The novel should be submitted as loose, double-spaced typewritten pages placed in a manila folder. Please include return postage and I will get it back to you as soon as possible. Yours sincerely, Priscilla Miller."

I let out the yelp that we writers save for momentous news that usually never comes. I leaned forward with the intention of planting a congratulatory kiss on his freckled cheek, approaching slowly so I wouldn't startle him. At exactly the right moment he turned his face—no flinching, no blushing —to receive my kiss squarely and easily on the lips.

I smelled soap. I felt firm, warm flesh. I blinked and saw a new caption at the bottom of my viewfinder: Ferris Porter possesses sexual reflexes and exquisite timing, replacing one that said, Ferris Porter is not good with women.

"What's the matter?" he asked, smiling.

Nothing, I said. Nothing at all.

"Well," he said. "I know it's not an outright yes, but at least she wants to see the rest of it."

I shook my head. "I'm sorry," I said, meaning, I'm lost; start over.

"She's seen fewer than forty pages."

"I bet she'll take you on," I said.

Ferris said the odds were against things working out: look how many people had passed on the novel. Still, it was more encouragement than he'd had from anyone else.

I pointed out that Ms. Miller wouldn't have asked for more if she hadn't liked the opening.

"Openings are easy for me," he said. "You know that. I start something new and the class says, 'Excellent.' And maybe after the second chapter they still say, 'Excellent,' but how long do I sustain it?"

"This one's different," I said. *"Something's different, obviously."*

He caught the attention of our waiter and asked for a Tsing Tao beer. I said, no, I'd had wine at lunch; then, "Oh, what the hell."

He told me the draft in Ms. Miller's possession had new scenes added since I had left, scenes the group had insisted on. Sexual in nature. Quite.

"Between whom?"

"Can you guess?"

"Between the Inspector and Fanny?"

He said he was flattered by my careful attention to his text. He hoped I wouldn't be offended by his pandering to popular tastes.

I said, "Don't apologize. Plenty of very literary authors use sex all the time."

"I don't want to jinx anything by saying it made the difference," he confided, "but it might have been what was missing in Thornton's personality—a sexual context."

I asked how old he was in *Malice Emeritus*.

"Fifty."

"Fifty's good," I said. "Look at all those fifty-year-old actors who still play leading men."

"Do you know what one agent told me? He wrote, 'To be blunt, who cares about a fifty-year-old police inspector from Nova Scotia with no sex life?'"

I said I didn't know what offended me more: the fifty-year-old part or the no-sex-life part. How do you answer something like that?

Ferris said, "One doesn't, although one falls asleep many a night fashioning an imaginary riposte in which every famous celibate in the English language testifies to his or her literary merit."

"First of all," I said, "that agent was a lousy reader. He completely missed the subtext of the scenes in Fanny's pantry. And secondly, I never said this in class, but I found there was something sensual about Inspector Shoemaker, something latent, which I always thought you could explore."

"You should have spoken up," said Ferris. "Your approval would have meant a good deal."

"I couldn't, especially since I didn't know how to make it happen in my own pages. I could hardly raise my hand and say, 'I think you need to develop the sexual side of your protagonist, Ferris.'"

He leaned closer. "Well, I did it. I put a clean sheet of paper in my typewriter and I sat there and wrote until Thornton and Fanny made love."

"And how was it?"

The waiter set down our shrimp—embellished with one fried soft-shell crab—and our garlic chicken. "I surprised myself," Ferris began, pausing for plate-passing and serving.

I nodded yes to rice and yes to the mathematical division of the single crab. "Go on," I said. "I want to hear how."

He hesitated, his chopsticks poised in mid-air.

I said, "Look, it'll be out in the world eventually. Thousands of people will read it: me, your mother, your old teachers from grade school. . . ."

He rolled his eyes. "What a thought." He put the shrimp down without tasting it. "Okay: Fanny goes to the station house because Thornton forgets his lunch pail. After she leaves, his colleagues tease him about having such a splendid-looking landlady. When everybody else goes out to lunch, he rings her at home and thanks her warmly for coming by. Something unexplained but magical flows through the telephone wires. To his own astonishment, he invites her to dinner that evening at a restaurant in downtown Halifax."

I interrupted to ask what chapter this happened in.

"Not too early," said Ferris, "and I know why you're asking: This has to build over time so that the reader is rooting for them and saying, 'Thornton, you goose. Can't you see that Fanny is waiting for your overture?'"

"When do they finally do it?" I ask.

"I had hoped not prematurely," said Ferris, "and then only behind closed doors. But Becca of all people said something in class that stayed with me; something very crude that I won't repeat here, but a phrase I couldn't get out of my head once I'd heard it."

"You can say it."

"Even if I wouldn't say it in my own classroom?"

"I'm not as delicate as you think," I said. "And even if I

were, I've been living with Isabel Krug, famous adulterer, for a month, so I doubt Becca could say anything that would shock me."

"In that case," said Ferris. He coughed into his fist. "Becca used the term 'fucking accident.' She thought Fanny and Thornton should have a fucking accident. Which I took to mean they would tumble into bed without thinking through its ramifications."

The chicken was spicier than I expected. I gulped some water. Ferris said plain rice would help. When I could talk and breath normally again I asked, "So? *Do* they have a fucking accident?"

He smiled. "They do. A very nice one. After returning from their evening at the restaurant."

"Did you render it explicitly?"

"I had to. They wouldn't let me stop at the various junctures I originally stopped at. They kept saying, 'Go for it.'" He smiled sheepishly. "It became something of a chant, "Go for it.' Each week I'd take the chapter back and go a little further for the next class."

"Until?"

"Until they go right from the restaurant back to the boardinghouse and make passionate overdue love for the rest of the night."

"Wow."

"I think it works," he said.

I said I'd love to read it; he said he'd run me off a copy. And mail it. Or, for that matter, drop it off should an editorial summons from Ms. Miller, God willing, bring him north to Somerville.

I asked if Thornton was divorced—I'd gotten that impression from an early draft of an earlier Inspector Shoemaker effort.

"He never married," said Ferris, "although he had opportunities. And normal drives."

"Married to his work, probably."

"Although that's about to change."

I said that was the great thing about fiction—playing God. Giving Thornton the life he really wanted. I raised my glass and said before I could check the sentiment, "To Thornton, who was probably great."

Ferris clinked my glass. "And to Fanny, who was even better than he had dreamed of."

There was an awkward pause—people like us don't say glib things without feeling self-conscious afterward. So Ferris asked, "Did I tell you that your new hairdo is very becoming?"

I looked across at his freckled head, face, ears, and eyelids and saw very clearly that once Ferris Porter had been a red-headed boy who was smart and shy and most likely greatly loved by his mother. Staring helped me notice his new look: he had stopped combing the thin auburn strands across his scalp to disguise his baldness.

"Speaking of hairdos," I said, "I really like your new effect."

He rubbed his head apologetically. "I read too many descriptions of pathetic old men who part their hair lower and lower until it starts at their ears. I don't want to be bald, but I don't want to be pathetic, either."

I heard Isabellike protests and coy phrases—"the honesty of the bald scalp," "the half-halo of hair"—flow from me to him and back again.

In our joint self-consciousness, we argued about the check. I said, "I called *you*, didn't I?"

He said, "But it's my celebration."

I said, "Then the guest of honor shouldn't be paying."

He said, "I've wanted to take you to dinner for a long time."

"How long?" I asked.

"Since you first joined the group."

"Why didn't you?"

"I couldn't very well ask you for a date when I knew from your narrators that you were living with a man."

"Didn't you assume if I was moving away that meant I was breaking up with Kenny?"

"I didn't assume anything. Except the worst."

"Which was what?"

"That you'd say, 'As a matter of fact, I did break up with my boyfriend, but I don't see how that concerns you.'"

The waiter walked by and Ferris managed to slip him the check along with his credit card, fencing with me to avoid my grasp. "I insist," he said. "Here, have a fortune cookie."

I broke one in half and unfolded the fortune. "He should at least let you pay the tip," I bluffed, "especially if you called him up in the first place."

"Thank God for that," he said quietly.

We waited in silence for his credit card. I counted—for no clear reason—to thirty, then put my hand on top of his.

"Harriet," he asked, his pupils huge, "do you have to get back right away?"

I said too easily, "I should. It's late," not imagining how the light in his eyes would fade. A second later to bring it back I said, No, I was wrong: the night was young.

216

19
LATER

 WE SAT ON a loveseat in his living room, which was completely lined with nineteenth-century novels and twentieth-century English mysteries; it practically glowed orange from the spines of the Penguin classics. We sipped Sombreros as we listened to Tony Bennett sing Frank Sinatra's torch songs. Ferris returned his highball glass and compact disc remote control to the coffee table, applied a clandestine swipe of Chapstick, and took me in his arms.

Feeling the need to make conversation, I said, "Nice cologne."

"Kipling," he whispered, nuzzling my hair.

It wasn't that long a journey from kissing my hair to kissing me. Which was perfectly nice, perfectly competent.

But the restaurant mood was gone. Neither the Kahlua nor the Kipling was helping me melt into the moment or shake the strange idea that the mentholated lips heading for my neck belonged to Ferris Porter, the nice older man in jackets of various plaids who had buffered me from the class's criticism, who, in all honesty, hadn't merely combed hair across his bald spot, but had grown it from behind his left lobe into a scrawny wreath.

"Is there something wrong?" he asked after a few minutes. "Do you like the music? I can change it if you'd like something else: jazz, classical, chamber music, show tunes—"

"No, keep this on."

We sat quietly, holding hands through another song. I put my Sombrero down on a "Moulin Rouge" coaster and asked if he danced.

"You mean do I go dancing?"

"I mean in the privacy of your living room. To Tony Bennett."

"I could," said Ferris.

We stood up and faced each other. Tony was singing "I Thought About You." I put my left hand on Ferris's shoulder and said dancing could be very pleasant, didn't he think so? Not that I did it often—at the occasional formal function— but I always enjoyed it when the opportunity arose.

I rattled on. Ferris said he had fewer and fewer occasions at which he took to the floor. I knew that: He danced with his shoulders rounded and our hands pressed to his sternum like the teachers who chaperoned my high school dances. Worse, he hummed in my hair and referred to Tony as "Mr. B."

So there I was, dancing with Ferris Porter, stripped of his jacket down to his shirt, tie and yellow V-necked sweater. I thought, I'll use this in my fiction if I need a symbol of dying romance: a couple dances lifelessly to hits of the 1950s; a gust of wind blows through the window, no, the French doors, and extinguishes a candle they had lit—no, *kindled*—over dinner. The candle flickers, then dies. The end.

As I was working on my metaphors, he nudged my chin into kissing position with a crooked finger. I stopped his hand and said, "Ferris."

"What?"

I said what you say in these situations: "Dancing is nice. Could we just dance?"

"There *is* something wrong," he said.

I took a falsely tormented deep breath and said, "I had lunch with Kenny today."

"I'm so sorry."

"I guess it left me feeling more alone than usual. Confused. Vulnerable." On and on I went, deeper into the convenient subject of the man who had spurned me, not sure where I was going with it except to reinforce the idea that I was a mixed-up woman. "He's married now," I continued. "Did I tell you that?"

"Already?"

"On Valentine's Day. To the woman he left me for. You can imagine how that felt: He couldn't bring himself to marry me in the twelve years we were together, yet he ran off and married Amy in three months." ("Thank *God*," I had told Isabel in the taxi after lunch. "Thank God it was her and not me.")

"How old is Kenny?" Ferris asked,

"Forty-two."

"He probably felt that if he didn't get married now life would slip by him and it would be too late to marry anyone."

We continued to sway back and forth in an unconvincing manner to "Night and Day." I said, "Is that how you feel?"

Ferris said, "Some days I feel more hopeful than others."

"It could happen tomorrow," I said. "You could walk out the front door and bump into her on the street. You don't know what's in store for you. None of us does." Except me: I was devoting the second half of my manless life to work.

"Do *you* believe that?" he asked. "Do you wake up and say, 'Today could be the day?'"

I said, "No, but in my case it's because there are no people outside my front door in Truro. And I don't dwell on things personal or romantic anymore because I need to concentrate on getting published."

"I used to meet more women—colleagues, staff," he mused. "But somewhere along the line, they found husbands. Years went by, and then the new colleagues coming in seemed younger and younger. I learned I had to accelerate the courtship rituals. But at a certain age, and if you do it more than once, you're viewed as peculiar."

Tony began "The Lady Is a Tramp," which we couldn't manage tempowise. Ferris led me to the loveseat, like a true gentleman escorting the wallflower back to her girlfriends. He asked if he could refresh my drink. I said no thanks.

"Coffee? Tea? Postum?"

I shook my head. Ferris snapped his fingers to the beat.

"Seeing Kenny this afternoon wasn't a good idea," I lied. "It made me susceptible."

"I'm always susceptible," said Ferris. "I think we writers are a susceptible breed."

"Not that it hasn't been a lovely evening. And I absolutely

meant every word I said about the inspector being a very appealing character. Very attractive."

He leaned back against the loveseat in a discursive, even relaxed fashion, as if he were analyzing the compliment. After a few moments he asked if I could be confusing author with character. Conflating personalities. Perhaps in discussing the new scenes, I had ascribed qualities to him that were uniquely Thornton's.

"But they came from you. If Thornton's a certain way—"

"I made him the way I'd like to be," said Ferris.

I noticed one of my dark hairs on his yellow sweater, but resisted the impulse to pick it off. I said I was sorry. Whatever it was that I had done to disappoint him, I was sorry.

He held up a hand and jiggled it in front of me as if to say, "No need."

I said I felt foolish; I'd never done anything like this before.

He smiled what for Ferris would be a cynical smile and said, "Isn't that what people usually say when they wake up in the bed of someone of relatively short acquaintance? But I don't think you have to apologize for feeling like kissing me and then . . . not feeling like it. It seems I'm the one who's fallen far short."

No, I said. Not at all. Please don't think that. What I had done was unforgivable. At least, thank God—and I nudged him with my elbow—we hadn't had a fucking accident.

He smiled like the philosophical injured party that he was. He said perhaps both of us had been swept up in the excitement of his good news, the glamour of his practically gaining literary representation.

"And I look better than usual tonight," I offered.

That made his sad eyes send out one last admiring glance, one final appeal.

I said briskly that I'd still like to read *Malice Emeritus* and discuss the manuscript, same as ever.

"When will we do that?"

"As soon as I've read it."

"How?"

"You mean how will we discuss it? I'll call you. Or you'll visit us in Truro."

"As what?" he asked kindly.

"Classmates? Colleagues? . . . Friends?"

Tony was winding up with, "I'll Be Seeing You," which I filed away as too obvious and flat-footed for a fictional parting. At the door we exchanged one apologetic kiss—my lips, his cheek.

Isabel was waiting up, pacing our room in her stockinged feet, taking angry bites from a half-peeled banana. She greeted me, her eyes darting—"Hello, Harriet; so nice of you to return. Hope *you* had a nice relaxing evening out on the town"—sarcasm that didn't match the panic in her eyes. She motioned towards the closed bathroom door, mouthing a word I couldn't get. Again, banana-mouthed and wild-eyed, she repeated whatever it was she was trying to tell me.

The bathroom door opened. A woman walked out, blonde, pudgy, tall, smiling serenely. She was rubbing her hands together, as if she had helped herself to our complimentary lotion and liked it. When she saw me, she said, "Well! Hello!" holding up her hands if to say, How thoughtless of me to have greased myself up before our introduction.

I got it—what was wrong with Isabel tonight and who this invader was: Her dinner date's mother. Her lover's wife. Isabel's stalker: Nan.

20

NAN AT THE CRANLEY

SHE HAD COME with a letter
signed by two psychiatrists
and an Ed.D. attesting to her
authorized discharge from Wisteria Lodge, A Residential
Treatment Center for Addictive and Remissible Behaviors. I
read it slowly, mindful of the lunging distance between Nan
and me, calculating the force and the moves it would take to
overcome her or save myself. I wondered about Isabel's
reflexes. Would she respond like a buddy cop if I lunged first? I
looked up. She was yawning. Nan was smiling warmly and
offering me a piece of fruit.

"Nan brought us a fruit basket," Isabel explained.

I said no thank you, I'd just come from a big Chinese dinner.

"What'd you have?" Isabel asked.

She's at the breaking point, I thought. She's identifying with her captor and denying the big picture. "Mrs. VanVleet," I said, handing back the discharge letter, "I hope you know that Isabel never meant for you to get hurt. She tells me all the time that she only wants the best for you."

Nan said, "You keep it. It's your copy."

I asked her permission to take my coat off. I wasn't trying anything, I vowed, but the room was hot and we should all keep cool. I let my coat slip off my shoulders and down my arms passively and nonthreateningly as if I were the SWAT psychiatrist negotiating with the hostage-taker. Smiling in robotic fashion I asked, "So, what have you two been up to?"

Isabel said, "Well, Harriet, it seems that while you were having a Chinese banquet and I was back at the hotel watching The Home Shopping Club, Mrs. VanVleet was being honorably discharged, having paid her debt to society."

Nan nodded in earnest agreement.

"And how did you happen to come here?" I asked her.

"It was the funniest thing," said Nan. "I called my house—of *course* I would after being discharged today, to arrange for Heidi to pick me up—and neither of my girls was home. So I called Perry and his roommate said he was out and I said it was an emergency, so Dana promised to track him down at the restaurant, which he did." Her voice tightened. "And apparently my son said, 'Tell her I can't come get her until tomorrow because I'm in the middle of an important business dinner.' So I called the front desk at his coop and said there was a family emergency and who was Mr. VanVleet's last appointment of the day, and he said very obligingly, 'A Miss Krug.' He also remembered that Ms. Krug had given her local address as, 'The Cranley.'"

"Quite the little detective," Isabel said.

I turned back to Nan and tried to think of something to say that was both chipper and therapeutic. "How are you feeling and everything?" I asked.

"Grand," said Nan. She sat down on the nearest twin bed and gestured with a gracious sweep of her arm that Isabel and I should make ourselves comfortable. "I went straight to Lutèce: Dover sole—first a salad of roasted peppers with a delicious little flan of goat cheese—and a tarte tatin for dessert. But no alcohol of any kind, not even a glass of wine."

"Nan's doctor thought it would be a nice treat for her to spend her first night in New York—"

"No one wanted me to return to the Greenwich house by myself. For obvious reasons." She turned to Isabel and asked brightly, "Where did you and Perry have dinner?"

"In the Village."

"Were you noticed?"

"He signed several autographs at the restaurant but no one recognized me."

"He's a superstar now, you know," she explained. "There are more than eighty thousand people of all ages in his fan club." She frowned. "Or is it eight thousand? Some enormous number."

I looked at my watch and faked surprise at the hour. "We've had a long day and we have to get up early to catch our flight," I said.

She turned to Isabel and asked, "Did you get my notes?"
"Which notes?"
"I wrote you three notes as part of my therapy."

Isabel said, "Um, I think I must have."

"They said they'd find out your address and put stamps on them, but I bet they didn't mail them."

I asked Nan what the notes had said.

She looked at her hands and massaged the last traces of lotion into her cuticles. "I wanted to tell Isabel how I felt," she said.

Isabel touched the back of her head, patting her French braid. She murmured, "Which we've now discussed at length."

I said she must have done very well at the facility to have been discharged this fast.

Nan said she was, in fact, sane and sober and having few side effects from the medication. But *fast?* How could I possibly use the word "fast"? She hated every minute of Wisteria. So would anyone. So would we.

Isabel and I said yes, of course we would. Who wouldn't?

"The facility wasn't exactly state of the art. But the work they do is the best. I came through a twelve-step program that was very victim-oriented." She smiled and smoothed her skirt over her kneecaps. "Dear Lord," she intoned, "let me see through the eyes of others what footsteps I have left in the sand. May the tide wash away the false impressions. May the sun preserve the true ones. May the lives I've hurt grow strong as I get stronger. May they find peace in my surrender to wellness and self-respect." She returned her voice to its normal gossipy pitch. "That's how we opened and closed every group session."

"Sounds great," said Isabel, "but we've made so much progress tonight that my brain has hit overload. Maybe we could talk on the phone tomorrow."

Nan leaned back to rest on both elbows. "So?" she asked. "What did you gals do for fun today?"

I looked at Isabel. "We got haircuts," I said.

Nan said, "That is so amazing. One of the main reasons I came here first instead of to Greenwich was so I could get a great haircut from someone who didn't know me." She looked perplexed for a long few seconds as if picturing the alternative—herself under a dryer between judgmental neighbors. She brought her smile back after a struggle and felt for the ends of her hair. "I didn't get around to it today, but I'm sure I will soon."

Isabel stood up and said she was going to get ready for bed, if Nan would excuse her. She hoisted her overnight bag onto the bed with a thud, unzipped it, and rummaged through it, naming each item in lieu of conversing: "Nightgown, robe, hairbrush, toothbrush, toothpaste, face junk . . ."

"What's that?" asked Nan.

"Rip-off night cream," said Isabel. "My cleaning lady sold it to me."

Nan held out her hand, and Isabel gave her the small jar after first tightening the cap. Nan read the label—front, back, and expiration date—then unscrewed the lid to sniff the contents. She looked up, evaluated Isabel's skin, and asked, "Do you think your cleaning lady could get me a few jars?"

Isabel said carefully, "I'm not sure if she sells it anymore, Nan. She went back to school and I don't see her on a regular basis."

"I could write you a check."

"Let me find out and I'll let you know." Isabel took the jar away from Nan, handed it to me, and went into the bathroom. I heard the lock turn and the shower head gush.

Nan smiled a fresh smile for me. "Do you think she'll be long? Should I wait?"

I went to the front door and opened it. Finally Nan stood up and put on her raincoat, buttoning it with great care. She picked up her purse as if leaving were her idea and yelled, "Isabel! Thanks for listening!"

I said, "I'll tell her you had to go."

Nan thanked me with the kind of absent-minded smile a mistress bestows on a passing servant. I closed the door and moaned, *"Oi vey iz mir."*

"Call me for breakfast," I heard gaily from the other side. "Or I'll call *you*."

According to Isabel, Nan had arrived in the form of a phone call identifying herself as a reporter for the *New York Times* saying, "We're following soap opera stars around for a week, and we know you had dinner with Perry VanVleet tonight. Would you mind answering a few questions? I'm in the lobby."

Isabel had said, "No, not at all," assuming Dorothea had arranged it. The woman had asked, in a totally sane and professional manner, "Would you like to come down for a drink or should I come up?"

Isabel said she had refreshed her lipstick, shut off the television, removed her glasses, and had answered the door faking the smile of a woman who had just returned from a date worthy of newspaper coverage.

It hadn't immediately registered that the caller was either an impostor or Nan VanVleet. The hairdo, raincoat, suit, cream-colored silk blouse, triple strand of faux pearls, and facial expression, Isabel said, could have belonged to any middle-aged reporter who had gone to finishing school. The caller had said, "I don't know if you remember me."

I interrupted Isabel to ask how in the world she could have failed to recognize Nan VanVleet.

"Because I didn't," she said calmly. "She was fatter and grayer than she had been at the trial. And she had this serene look about her"—Isabel imitated her vacantly moony expression—"compared to the psychopath's face I remembered. Plus I didn't have my contacts in. Plus who the hell expected to find Nan VanVleet knocking at my hotel door with a basket of fruit? It didn't make sense."

The two women had stared at each other, Isabel waiting for an introduction and Nan waiting for Isabel to recoil. Finally Nan said, like an old Army buddy whose voiceover goes unrecognized on "This Is Your Life," "Isabel, it's me, Nan."

Isabel said she had felt the kind of dizzy terror you feel when your worst nightmare is standing in front of you and your death is going to happen in a dim hallway in a cruel city. "I screamed," she said. "I figured Nan had a gun and the gun had a silencer and I was a goner anyway. I thought to myself, Harriet will find me dead without a clue. It'll be an unsolved mystery and after a certain number of years they'll close the file."

I said, "Hardly. She'd be the first one they'd suspect. She's on record as having tried to kill you."

Isabel said, "Whatever. I could barely get a word out. I asked if she had a gun. She squeezed the outside of her purse—did you see it? A royal blue glove leather clutch with a plastic tortoise clasp?—so I could see there were no suspicious lumps. She said, 'I have no gun. I'll never touch another one as long as I live. I came here because I never had a chance to tell you things I always wanted to tell you because my lawyers wouldn't let me."

I asked Isabel where all this had taken place.

"Out in the hallway! A hotel security guy showed up because of my screaming. Nan turns to him, all of a sudden very cool, and says, 'I'm a guest of The Cranley Hotel, room such-and-such,' and shows him the key. Then she says, 'Ms. Krug was frightened when she realized it was I because I had been institutionalized in the past. I can assure you that I wouldn't harm a flea, but maybe you could stay with her while we talk.'

"So I say to Nan, 'Puh-leeze. I don't think the judge would like your being here. She might think it's a bad sign and send you back to the hospital.' She starts to cry; well, not cry, but her voice is shaky. Her eyes well up and she says, 'Do you think it was easy for me to come here and face you? After everything? And do you think they would have discharged me if they thought I was dangerous?' I look at the hotel cop and he shrugs. Nan puts the fruit basket down on the carpet and opens her purse—I jump a mile—and takes out the letter from her shrink that claims she's been discharged for real. The security guy reads it. I read it. He says, 'Ma'am, it's up to you.'"

"So you let her in?" I asked.

Isabel closed her eyes, then opened them, looking repentant. "What could I do? I said, 'Okay. Come in. It's okay.'"

I knocked on the bathroom door to tell Isabel the coast was clear. She charged out with a towel not seriously wrapped around her sputtering, "I'm calling that little shit Perry."

She picked up the phone, snapping her fingers for his number. Frisking herself with the towel she said, "Perry, if you're there pick up. This is Isabel." After a pause she said, "Your mother showed up here tonight and scared the shit out of me. I never told you but my lawyer wanted me to get a restraining order because of her meaning to kill me. But I said, 'No, she's locked up. She can't hurt me.' And now she's at my hotel, and she wants to be my best friend. I suggest you come here and take her home with you." She slammed down the receiver, then picked it up and hit the numbers from memory. "And furthermore, your mother thinks you and I have a little romance going, so I suggest you enlighten her on that subject. And watch out, because she slips bribes to everyone in her path, including your doorman. Call me." About to slam the receiver, she jerked it back to her mouth and added, "I thought you were going home for the night."

Isabel threw her towel in the direction of the bathroom and pulled on her teal satin nightgown. "Do you think it's safe to go to sleep?" she asked.

I said I'd like to take a bath, if that wouldn't keep her up. And I hadn't had the chance to tell her but I had spent the evening with Ferris Porter. She followed me into the bathroom and asked if I wanted one of these little bottles of hotel bubble bath.

"If Nan didn't take them," I said.

She dumped the contents under the running water and said, "What a family, huh? I sure know how to pick 'em." She closed the toilet lid and made herself at home.

"Aren't you going to bed?" I asked, not undressing.

"I need to talk," she said.

She meant I should strip, get in the tub, and chat in the manner of an utterly unself-conscious Isabel Krug. I undressed quickly, facing away, and slipped into the bubbles even though the tub hadn't filled to my waist.

"I'm a wreck," she was saying. "Now that she's gone, I'm a complete wreck. I don't even want to be alone in the bedroom. I'm going to have to sleep with the lights on."

I said Nan had struck me as essentially harmless: sad and harmless.

Isabel said, "I talked to her longer than you did."

"You'd have to be a little crazy to want to sleep in the bed where your husband died."

"So it's a good sign that she came here instead of Greenwich, is that what you're saying?"

I said more or less.

"She told me things I didn't know," said Isabel, shutting her eyes, shaking off whatever visions Nan had supplied.

I asked if she could tell me.

"Guy's mother is still living. And has all her marbles, so she knows everything that happened." She opened her eyes: "Then there were the two miscarriages after Perry. She wanted to stop trying, but Guy wouldn't let her give up. She also told me she and Guy had separated for a couple of weeks when the kids were teenagers, but they couldn't stand it so they sneaked off to Bermuda without pajamas and things were wonderful after that for a long time." She paused. "And still would have been wonderful."

I said, "It doesn't mean she's telling the truth."

"She kept saying, 'What you gave him was only sexual. Men can separate sex from love. He never loved you.'"

I asked if she had refuted that.

"No way! I told her what she needed to hear: 'I know Guy loved you. He made it clear at all times that what we had was just physical. And temporary. Just because he enjoyed sex with me didn't mean he loved me.'"

I said, "Even Perry knew Guy loved you."

Isabel raised her voice. "So what was I supposed to say? 'Your husband was nuts about me. He fantasized about us living as man and wife, which sheds a little light on why he wanted to play house in Greenwich and screw me in your bed, doesn't it?' But I didn't because all she wants now is to be a respectable widow who can say, 'I had a long, happy marriage. I lost my husband in a random act of violence one horrible April night, but other than that, things were grand.'"

I said, "Maybe she should've thought of that before she killed him."

Isabel said, "If it gives her some kind of peace to call me a slut, then why should I care? I know how he felt about me." She stared at her bare feet, heels planted on the white chicken wire tile floor. "I'm sure he did love her," she said, "even if he couldn't stand her most of the time."

"I don't see why you have to be her new psychiatrist."

When she didn't answer I said, "You think it's going to end with one visit?"

Isabel said, "Maybe she'll make some new friends when she gets back into a routine."

"What about her old friends, all those women who played tennis with her and who testified and called her on the car phone."

"Is that what you think? Those Round Hill Road types like to hang around with murderers? One carload of them had a jolly little outing to visit her—they brought a picnic lunch and presents in shiny gift bags with ribbon curling off the handles like they were going to a birthday party—and that was it: one visit. And now that she's out, she'll be a pariah. It's hard enough to get dinner invitations when you're divorced and widowed for the usual reasons."

I said, "She's a little off, don't you think?"

"Who wouldn't be?" Isabel huffed.

I said, "I have no desire to dine with Nan, and—let's be honest—you weren't exactly thrilled to find her at the door."

"Because she was after me when she shot Guy! None of her so-called friends were ever in any danger. They could have stuck by her and said, 'Don't worry, you'll always have a place to stay; you'll always have a friend to lunch with and to shop with.'"

I said, "She'll find a way back to her old life in Greenwich. She's got three children on her side, even if they didn't give her a welcome home party. Even if Perry lies to her."

"Perry," she spat. "Don't even get me started on the subject of that little asswipe."

She left the bathroom and returned munching a giant Golden Delicious apple and wearing her glasses. "Did I mention what he wore? Black leather pants, black washable silk turtleneck. I could tell Dorothea had taken him shopping, and I could just hear her saying, 'Very now, very chic, very this, very that.' But she forgot to tell him not to wear it under his Aquascutum chino jacket and his Burberry scarf."

"Is that so bad?"

"He's young," said Isabel, "and he lived a sheltered life until the accident."

I hadn't heard her call Guy's death "the accident" before that moment. I thought it represented a shift in sympathies toward the surviving VanVleets, away from Nan the villain to sad, repentant, friendless Nan.

I asked about dinner; she said they had eaten at some trendy bistro in the Village (wood-oven wild mushroom pizza for her; spaghetti Bolognese, sauce on the side, and a small Caesar for him). Isabel said the only reason she got through dinner at all mildly entertained was Perry's flair for gossip—who hated whose guts on the show and who was sleeping with whom. The actor who played the hired hand, Sage, at the ranch? In real life he was married to Danielle/Holly but was sleeping with the actress who played Tess, the vet.

The bathwater had reached a level that allowed me some privacy. I turned off the faucet, rolled soap around my washcloth, and washed my arms, shoulders, neck, and face—any place that was impersonal. I said, "Do you think Nan really tried to reach Heidi and Sara?"

"She says she did. And when she couldn't reach them, and Perry blew her off, she called her doctor and he pulled some strings and they arranged for a driver to bring her home. The driver comes—he's no prize citizen, just some guy in a uniform—and she offers him a C-note to forget Greenwich and drive her to Manhattan."

"You know this for a fact?"

"She told me! She bribed Perry's doorman to tell her which hotel I was at, and she bribed the driver to head for the city. She was here for at least an hour before you sashayed in from wherever the hell you were."

"Ferris Porter's."

"Ferris," she repeated.

I asked if she remembered who that was.

"Sure I do. You called him?"

235

"I called a bunch of people and he was the first one who was home."

"Was he thrilled?"

"Not because of me. Mostly because he heard from a literary agent today who'd read the first two chapters of his novel and wanted to see more. I called just at the moment he was in a mood to celebrate."

She thought it over. "Is that something a person celebrates?"

"Are you kidding? An agent asks to see the rest of your manuscript?"

"So you went out for Chinese food. Then what?"

"Then we kissed in the restaurant and I enjoyed it and somewhere between Chinatown and his couch I fell out of the mood."

She squinted at me as if she had never experienced such a thing. "What do you mean, you fell out of the mood?"

"You know," I said. "I liked the kiss—he was quite a good kisser—and I hadn't expected it. But after a while, I realized I didn't feel anything for him, and it would be a mistake to lead him on."

Isabel tossed her apple core into the wastebasket and wiped her hands on her nightgown. "I hope you explained it better than that to him," she said.

We locked and chained our door, and for good measure, pushed a wingback chair up against it to stop both Nan's illegal entry and her .38 caliber bullets. At regular intervals, just as I was falling asleep, Isabel would whisper, "Harriet? Are you awake? What if she never left and is actually hiding in the closet?" And a half hour later: "Harriet? Could there be an explosive device in the fruit? I think I hear a ticking sound." Finally she fell asleep and I did too, uneasily; when the phone rang at 7:30 A.M. I felt as if I hadn't slept at all. Isabel murmured from somewhere under her pillow, "Oh, shit." I said I'd answer and tell Nan we had to catch the shuttle in—what sounded good? An hour?

I picked up the receiver and said in as starched a voice as I could manage, "Harriet Mahoney."

"Oh, good, you're still there," said a male voice.

"Perry?"

"No. It's Ferris. Did I wake you?"

Isabel was on her stomach, squinting, her hair electrified and her face greasy from last night's cream. *Ferris,* I mouthed.

He was saying, "I want to put aside the events of last evening and declare it a new day. Could I treat you to breakfast and could we talk about fiction and, why, even nonfiction the way we always have?"

Isabel by this time was quizzing me in a thick voice, and finally got my attention with a swat from her pillow. I turned around and said, "He wants to have breakfast with me. Shhh."

"Tell him to come here," she whispered. "I want to meet him."

Ferris was saying that he had slept poorly, worrying that he had sacrificed our friendship to a coarse-fibered impulse.

I said, "Forget about it. Let me tell you what was going on here last night when I got back to the room."

That cheered him up, a friendly confidence.

"Is it okay if Isabel joins us?" I asked.

"Why, a writers' brunch," he said happily.

* * *

Isabel, Ferris, and I were on our first cup of coffee when Nan, dressed in widow's black, entered the hotel's cute, café-curtained breakfast room and joined us without being invited.

After sketchy introductions, Ferris repeated "Nan VanVleet" as if rolling a snip of delicious but mysterious herb on his tongue. "Why do I know that name?"

Isabel, probably kicking him under the table, said, "The trial?"

"You know, the Mr. VanVleet who lost his life?" I said.

"I'm his wife," said Nan. "I shot him."

"You did?"

"I was found not guilty for being momentarily insane."

Neither Isabel nor I corrected her semantic error. Isabel said, "Nan was discharged yesterday and came to New York to be near her son."

"The actor," said Nan.

"Well," said Ferris. "I can only imagine it's been a very painful few years for you."

Nan asked, "Who are you again?"

"Ferris Porter. I'm a professor of English at LaGuardia Community College."

"Tenured?" she asked.

"Tenured."

"And you're a friend of Miss Krug's?"

Ferris smiled politely. "Now I am. We met for the first time this morning. I'm a much older friend of Harriet."

Nan's head swiveled from me back to him. *"How* old?" she asked.

"We know each other from our writing group."

"About four years," I said.

"I meant, how old are you?" Nan asked.

"Fifty-four," he said.

"Are you seeing each other?"

"We're very good friends," said Ferris.

Nan smiled a private smile and flicked two packets of Equal simultaneously into her black coffee. "Today is my first full day of freedom," she announced. "Also the first day of my diet."

Ferris asked Nan how one marks such a momentous beginning.

"See my son first. Figure out where I'll be living." She flung one arm out to the left, Ethel Merman style, saying, "See a movie"; then flung the other one to the right and said, "See a play."

"Activities you've missed the most?" he asked.

"Absolutely," said Nan. "And as soon as it can be arranged, I want to visit my husband's grave. I want to do that by myself. I haven't done anything all alone for the last fifteen months, and that should be the first thing."

"I would imagine that will be very difficult," said Ferris. "I hope you'll accept my sincere condolences."

Isabel and I stared at him. Nan, however, seemed to be finding inspiration in Ferris's excessive good manners. "Isn't it funny how we need to go to a loved one's grave to talk or to leave a present?" she asked. "Because if you believe in an afterlife, then the person who's passed on is everywhere, isn't he? In your house, in your garden, in your breakfast room."

"Where is your late husband buried?" asked Ferris.

"In Greenwich."

"Which is what?" asked Ferris. "An hour, hour and a half?"

Nan turned to Isabel. "What would you say: Manhattan to Greenwich on a weekend?"

"How would I know?"

"I didn't mean I was going there today," said Nan. "I meant as soon as I saw Perry and got New York out of my system." She smiled at Isabel. "Do you know last night was the first uninterrupted night's sleep I've had in years."

"Years?" said Isabel.

Nan counted on her fingers: "Fifteen months at Wisteria. The eight months between the accident and the trial. The months before that of . . . well, our troubles. But last night was delicious."

"They didn't knock you out at the sanitarium?" asked Isabel.

Ferris answered for her: " 'Sleep that knits up the raveled sleave of care, the death of each day's life, sore labor's bath, balm of hurt minds, great nature's second course, chief nourisher in life's feast,' " he recited, adding modestly, *"Macbeth."*

Nan clasped her hands together. "Poetry! At breakfast!"

Ferris smiled and pointed one index finger in the air. "Ink runs from the corners of my mouth. There is no happiness like mine. I have been eating poetry . . . Mark Strand."

Nan pressed her hand to her chest. "Did you make that up?" she breathed.

"If only I had," he said.

I volunteered that Ferris was by no means lacking in creativity: He wrote mysteries, excellent mysteries. Recently we had celebrated what could turn into very good news.

"And what is that?" asked Nan cautiously as if she was used to derailments masquerading as good news.

"You're going to jinx it," Ferris murmured.

I said, "Don't be superstitious. The news is that an agent has read a part of his novel and wants to read the rest."

"What do you mean, 'an agent?'" asked Nan.

"A literary agent," said Isabel. "A person who takes your book and sells it to the highest bidder."

"I guess I don't understand," said Nan. "You don't just hire this person the way one hires a lawyer?"

"We're being wildly premature," said Ferris.

"They choose you, in effect," I said. "They have to believe in your work sincerely enough to call up editors and say, 'I adore this book and so will you.'"

"How interesting," said Nan, "and what an odd position to put a writer in." She reached across the table to touch Ferris's forearm. "Tell me: Have you been turned down by agents in the past?"

"Several."

"How awful."

"I have an agent," said Isabel quietly.

Nan, still staring at Ferris, asked, "What for?"

"Because I'm writing a book. With Harriet."

"I'm her ghost," I said.

Ferris leaned a few inches forward and confided to Nan that that phrase meant Harriet was the ghostwriter on the project. "As told to" Harriet Mahoney. Harriet would be doing the actual writing.

"About what?"

Isabel was patting lox and onion onto her bagel without benefit of utensils. "I'll let Harriet explain the project," she said.

I recited the one-sentence summary we had prepared for

such a query: "We see it as a study of the social, sexual, legal, public, and private pressures of a woman who was in the wrong place at the wrong time."

"Ghost *and* mouthpiece," announced Isabel through her food.

"It's about Guy, you mean," said Nan.

"It's about me mostly," said Isabel. "I'm only going to mention your family where I really have to."

"Is it written yet?"

"Not every last word," I said.

"You're going to write a book and make money by dragging us through the mud all over again."

"No way," said Isabel.

"It's not going to be a sensational book," I said.

Ferris replaced his cup gingerly into his saucer. "Nan, Harriet is not that kind of writer. She is a writer of quality, literary fiction. This book will have her name on it. She won't write anything that would embarrass you because that would embarrass her. She wants to be proud of this book. She wants to build a career on this book. Isn't that right, Harriet?"

"That's right," I said.

"Besides," said Isabel, "you could write your own book from the perpetrator's point of view and say anything you want to about me."

"Or," said Ferris, "you could view your new beginning as a rebirth, and look to the future instead of reliving the tragedy. You might say, 'There's a wall between yesterday and today, and there's a door in that wall, and I have found it and passed through it and I'm going to lock it behind me.'"

Nan closed her eyes as if she were hearing both Shakespeare and religion. "Oh, Harris," she whispered.

No one said a word. I turned to Nan, after a stage-mother's

nod of encouragement from Isabel. "How nice for you that your children are grown and you're free to come and go as you please," I said.

Nan nodded. "Sara called here this morning. They want to come get me."

"That's excellent," said Isabel.

"They're furious with Perry for letting me wander around the city without a chaperon."

"Is Sara your daughter?" Ferris asked.

"My older daughter. Heidi would drive—my baby. She's absolutely fearless about driving in the city."

We each murmured our admiration for Heidi.

"Even on a weekday," Nan added. "Even during rush hour."

I said, "It'll be nice to get back home, don't you think?"

Nan said, "Not really."

"Will there be family members living with you?" Ferris asked.

"The girls. Heidi has twin beds in her room." She rotated her fruit plate a quarter-turn and stared at it.

"So?" Isabel prompted.

Nan picked up her fork and put it down. "I get to share a room with Heidi. Sara has a double bed so she'll stay where she is." Her voice faded. "Right down the hall. A shout away."

"So you have the best of both worlds," I said heartily. "You have children who are clearly devoted to you to be your housemates and at the same time, if you feel like seeing a play, you can hop on a train and be here in an hour."

Nan said that was true, wasn't it? Her children were adults. Wasn't she smart to have started so young and to have raised daughters who put their mother ahead of their friends and their own grief. She smiled too brightly. "Harris, do you have any children?"

"Regrettably, I've never married, Nan."

I checked with Isabel. Her eyebrows were telegraphing the same thing as mine: Harris, Ferris. Close enough.

We flew home in the late afternoon after Isabel had had a chance to shop for her spring wardrobe. She invited me along, but I said I wanted to write. My novel was only six pages longer than it had been when I moved to Truro, and Ferris's nibble from the agent had inspired me. I went to the 42nd Street branch of the public library and sat at a table in the main reading room. My modest goal was to render in flashback the scene in which my parents had gone separately to Jerome Kern Night at The Boston Pops in 1946 and recognized each other from Mahoney's Donuts. I tried to do something with Helen Morgan vowing in song to love one man till she dies as if she were sending my mother a message from the stage in a magical-realism kind of way, but it was a very difficult effect to achieve.

I watched a college-age student at the next table flogging the keys of his laptop as if whole paragraphs were bleeding from his fingertips. I thought, So what? He's probably writing a long letter to his girlfriend. No novel would drive his fingers like that; even if it did, surely he wasn't simultaneously producing a full-scale work of nonfiction like The Isabel Krug Story.

Then I remembered: What Isabel Krug Story? What work?

All I had done in a month was read newspaper clippings, share countless meals with my collaborator, interview her dead lover's dull celebrity son, and practice psychotherapy without a license on the dead lover's wayward widow.

I sneaked another look at the busy college student and his hardware. At second glance he looked older, like a graduate student, an M.F.A. candidate; maybe like a twenty-five-year-old author awaiting publication of his debut collection from Alfred A. Knopf.

I said to myself, Harriet, tomorrow you have to apply yourself: transcribe Isabel's tapes, fill in the gaps, make an outline, start a chapter, price a laptop.

Stop saying you're a writer and write.

21
UPON RETURN

THE HOUSE WAS dark when
we got back to Truro. Isabel
said she hated that—Costas
shutting off all the lights no matter how early he went to
sleep, as if to say the hell with everyone else.

I went right to bed, happily comparing the toast and
marmalade hues of my well-lit room to the greens and grays
of the dark hotel. I read a few pages of *The Baked Bean Supper
Murders* before falling asleep with the paperback resting on my
chest.

Sometime after midnight, I was startled awake by a
high-pitched yelp, either a floor above me or a floor below,

which hiccupped into the sounds of lovemaking, then stopped.

I listened hard, gripping my bedclothes. Nothing.

With the lamp on, I decided it had been a dream, an auditory hallucination. Or the wind, or the bell buoys, or the wolves everyone talked about, or me.

After my heartbeat had receded to normal, I heard it again, a crescendo of unmistakable sounds, male and female. It was Isabel and a man having what was definitely sex. And, God, were they enjoying it.

22

JUST BLACK COFFEE

I DECIDED TO skip breakfast and bring coffee back to my room without further social intercourse. If Isabel asked why the change in my morning routine, I'd say, "Deadline pressure. We have to get serious."

I found them at the kitchen table, she in her hooded orange caftan with the ball fringe, and he fully dressed in his usual jeans and chamois shirt. Isabel was barefooted. Her lips were carrot orange and her green contacts were already in.

"Isabel's telling me about your trip," Pete said. "Wild, huh? Mrs. VanVleet showing up at your hotel? Isabel said you saved the day."

I said coolly, "I wouldn't go that far."

"Well, if you hadn't returned when you did, Nan would've curled up in the second bed," said Isabel. She turned to Pete. "I tried for a good hour to get rid of her, but she wouldn't take a hint."

I walked over to the granite counter and said, "I wish you'd put the coffee into the vacuum bottle after it's dripped." I asked how long it had been sitting.

"Not long," said Isabel carefully, and after a pause, "There's sourdough English muffins if you want one."

I said, "Maybe later."

She said, "Your hair still looks good."

"Thanks.

"You notice a difference?" she asked Pete.

He said, "Let me look."

I stayed where I was against the kitchen sink, sipping burned coffee without my usual milk and sugar, my bad mood worse now that the male groans from Isabel's bed had an owner, and the owner had been my ally, and I was now, by definition, an outsider and third wheel. I said, "I've slept on it for two nights. It's starting to frizz again."

"I like it," said Pete.

"She promised to keep on top of it," said Isabel. "Regular trims and no more air-drying."

"Not that there was anything wrong with it before," he said.

I kept my distance, drinking my bitter coffee by the sink. "We'll see how much time I have for my hair," I grumbled.

Pete asked what I thought of Perry the actor.

"Brain dead," I answered.

"Heard he has quite the snazzy apahtment."

Isabel took her feet down from the third kitchen chair and said, "Wanna sit?"

I said, no, the work. Whatever I ate would be at my desk. As I walked to the refrigerator for a nonchalant survey, the phone rang and I answered it.

"Itsy?" asked a woman's voice.

"Who?"

"This isn't Itsy?"

"Do you mean Isabel?"

"I want Isabel. Who's this?"

Isabel strode over and took it from me. "Hello," she said cheerfully. Her expression changed at once to annoyance. She leaned against the sink, anchoring the phone cord to her elbow. "Yeah," she said sourly. Then, after a pause, "How would I have seen it? . . . Okay, so read it to me." She listened for a minute and said, "I was, but it was staged."

The phone emitted muffled crabbing from the voice on the other end. "So what?" said Isabel. "Ma—"

Ma?

"Ma—" she tried again. "It's show biz. If fans are talking about it over breakfast it's good for his career. He hired a publicist to plant these things in gossip columns so your friends will read them and think Perry's a big star."

After another irritated pause she said, "Tell them the truth! Tell them I was cooperating with his publicist as a favor to the family and we weren't on any date. He's only twenty-five years old. . . ."

She half-turned away and murmured, "Harriet Mahoney . . . *Mahoney.* She's helping me with my book."

More muffled sniping from the other end. "I can't help that now, can I?" Isabel said. "Yeah, fine. . . . The same. Okay. 'Bye. . . ."

I had slipped into her seat at the half-moon table, the demands of eavesdropping taking the edge off my guard. Isabel came back and said, "My mother the media scout."

I said, "I guess this means Dorothea got an item in the paper."

"In the *Daily News*." She reached for a piece of Pete's toast. "I'll kill Dorothea if it's her wording."

"What did it say?"

"I expected they would say the usual—'Who was that blonde with soap star Perry VanVleet last night at Penelope's, blah blah blah—but then she goes on to say something like, 'Followers of the trial will remember a certain electrical appliance figuring heavily in her testimony.'"

"Jesus," said Pete. "They said that in the papah?"

"My mother read it to me."

"What did she call you?" I asked.

Isabel said, "Itsy," matter-of-factly, no embarrassment, the way a Joseph might say "Joe."

"Itsy," said Pete. "I like that."

I bet you do. I said to Isabel, "You never talk about your mother."

"Neither do you," she said.

"I talk to them once a week, don't I? I hear what movies they see and how their friends are feeling and if they've gotten flu shots. And you know their whole story: how they got divorced and remarried and how my mother got a skull fracture at my stepmother's funeral."

"Say that again?" said Pete.

"It's all in her novel," said Isabel. "Ask her if she'll let you read it some time."

I said, "You can read it when it's published." Never, in other words.

Isabel said, "Maybe he can give you a male reader's point of view."

"I think Pete has better things to do."

Pete said, "You may not think so, but I read books."

"He does," said Isabel. "He has built-in bookshelves in his room."

"Just 'cause I read books doesn't make me a judge of anyone's writing," he said to Isabel.

"I just meant it was a way to hear about Harriet's family."

"It's fiction," I said. "I made a lot of it up."

Isabel said, "I wish I could do that." With her hands in her caftan pockets, she pulled the fabric one way then the other across her lap and said dreamily, "Maybe my book should be a novel. We could change whatever facts we didn't like and make the story do whatever we wanted it to. And if you spell a name wrong, who cares? It's all made up."

I didn't respond immediately because it was a moment of truth that I didn't want to be observing: Isabel was dreaming. Her biography was so unformed that she could see it as something else—if not a biography, a novel. Or a skit. Or a poem.

"You can't change hawses in midstream," said Pete. "You brought Harriet here to write a true story. You can't just say, 'A novel sounds like more fun. Let's write a novel.'"

I said, "Your agent wants nonfiction, right?"

Isabel shrugged. "He wants a bestseller."

Pete tried, "You couldn't call it The Isabel Krug Story if it was fiction."

"I'm trying to be spontaneous and flexible," she said. "It's like a chef who goes to the market at five a.m. and plans his menu around what looks freshest that day."

Pete said, "How are you going to top the real story? Make the wife crazier? Make the guy a U.S. senita? Put more sex in?"

"I'd have Guy survive the shooting and give it a happy ending. He and his wife would have an amicable divorce—she'd find someone around town—and their children wouldn't take sides."

"Then what? What would happen to the Isabel character?" I asked.

She closed her eyes. "The Isabel character could be living in New York, expanding her business—maybe she'd have an associate by now—and wouldn't have had to go through a trial and be tailed by 'Hard Copy' or 'A Current Affair.' She'd have gotten just enough attention to make her business take off, but not enough to force her into hiding. She'd see Guy once or twice a week, but she wouldn't marry him, because she likes being on her own. She'd go out a lot. She'd have kids from a previous marriage who were smart and funny and enjoyed their mother's company. Maybe fourteen and sixteen, two girls." She smoothed her hair back with both hands and groaned at the ceiling, elbows akimbo.

When she seemed to be back with us, I said, remembering my new resolve, "You'll give me your tapes today?"

"Tapes?"

"Your tapes," I repeated. "The autobiographical tapes."

"Fine."

"I don't think there's any reason why I can't get started on what you have."

"It's fine," she said firmly, meaning, It's not fine but I'm indulging your mood.

Pete pushed his chair back and said he was going to pick up

lumber for the wine racks. "See ya," he said to me, not including Isabel in his good-bye so I'd forget why she had knowledge of bookshelves by his bed.

As soon as we were alone Isabel said, "Something's been bothering you from the second you came into the kitchen."

I said, "No, it hasn't."

"You're acting funny. Everything I've said, starting with 'Good morning,' has annoyed you."

I waited a few seconds before saying, "I didn't sleep well last night."

"Probably the excitement of the trip."

I said no, I was quite relaxed and happy to be back in my own bed—

She closed her eyes. "Harriet. Just say it."

I raised my cup to my lips and put it down again. "I'm not absolutely sure."

"But?"

"But it sounded like a man and woman making love in the middle of the night."

She said easily, "Is that right?"

"As far as I could tell."

She said, "And you figured the woman was me?"

"Was it?"

She smiled and asked, "What if it was?"

"Then I guess you had a good time."

Isabel asked, faking a wince for delicacy's sake, "How loud was it?"

"You woke me up."

She looked around the kitchen and over the railing down to the atrium. "It isn't what you think," she said.

I said that she didn't have to explain anything. Besides,

hadn't I assured her in my job interview that I wasn't squeamish about male visitors?

She put her feet back up on the empty chair and said, "You think it's Pete, don't you? That's why you're pissed off."

I said okay, maybe Pete had occurred to me when I came upstairs and found them feeding each other breakfast. But that was no business of mine.

"It wasn't anyone," she confided. "It was just me, alone. No man."

"I heard a male voice."

"You couldn't have," said Isabel. "Unless it was the TV. I turned it up to drown out the sound of my voice."

I said, "I see."

"You know how loud I can be," said Isabel.

I said, no, I didn't. How would I know that?

"From the trial! That horrible moment when I had to talk in front of the whole world about using a vibrator?"

I said I hadn't realized until today that people dwelled on that particular snippet of testimony.

She said she'd take it up with the builder: The noise was disgraceful; Costas had paid for soundproofing in every wall.

She delivered two cassette tapes to my room. Two. I smiled absently at the labels, assuming she was bringing me music to work by. "Me, the early years," said one. "Me, part two," said the other. I turned them over, rereading her titles, hoping they'd multiply in my hands.

"I'm working on a third one," she said. " 'Me, part three,' which will be my thirties, and then I'm in the homestretch."

"Isabel," I said, opening my door wider. "Why don't you come in and we'll talk."

255

She walked across the threshold and stopped for an inspection of the room. It had a writer's clutter, which was no accident: my dictionary, my thesaurus, my *Elements of Style*, my *Writer's Marketplace*, my autographed copy of *How to Get Happily Published*, my clutter of rough drafts that I had a hard time throwing out in case the *Paris Review*'s "Writers at Work" series came calling. She picked up the framed photograph I had of my parents, the 1946 wedding portrait from the first time around, and said, "Handsome."

I sat down on my bed, a tape in each hand, feeling the first signs of physical anxiety in my digestive tract. "Do we have a timetable?" I asked.

"For what?"

"A deadline?"

Isabel plopped happily into my desk chair as if visiting Daddy's office and trying out where Daddy sat all day. She swiveled one way, then another, and executed two complete rotations with her feet hovering an inch above the carpet. I pronounced her name sharply and she stopped. "You worry too much," she said.

"Will I find everything I need squeezed onto these tapes, so that after I listen I'll relax?"

"I certainly hope so."

"What's on them—I mean roughly?"

"You know," said Isabel. "My childhood—school and all that. Some memorable birthday parties and toys. Stepfather problems; problems I had being so shy."

I said, "Shy?"

"Very."

"If you're shy, what am I?"

"I might not appear shy because I do a pretty good job of hiding behind my gregariousness."

Let me remember this sentence so I can repeat it to Pete and we can laugh, I prayed. Then I remembered with a pang: My days of confiding in Pete were over.

"We all hide behind something," she continued. "Even the worst arrogant asshole is hiding behind something."

I asked what she thought I was hiding behind.

She hesitated for a few seconds then spoke. "Most of the time? You really want to know? Kenny."

I said that wasn't fair. Kenny! I had no use for Kenny, no respect for Kenny, no feelings for Kenny—

"Because of Kenny, you wasted your thirties. Because of Kenny, you had no confidence in yourself or your writing. Because of Kenny, you can't trust any man. You can't get involved with anyone unless he signs a piece of paper promising he won't leave you for a twenty-six-year-old."

I said, "That's not true."

"Then how come you won't let a guy within six feet of you?"

I said, "I'm forty-one. I've got different priorities now."

"I'm forty-two! Do you see me discouraging male attention?"

I asked if she was asking that question in all seriousness. She hadn't noticed that I was Harriet Mahoney, oversized Campfire Girl, and she was Isabel Krug, femme fatale?

She frowned and pronounced my attitude very bad. The worst.

I said, "It's a fact. I see what happens when men get in the same room with you."

"You think it would happen if I had your hang-dog view of my own sex appeal?"

I said, "Isabel. Give me a break. You put me in a room with

257

some men and you in the same room and tell me how many men would punch my ticket."

"More than you think."

"Because your line would be too long."

"No! Because I wasn't their type. Or because you were."

I said we should change the subject. We were getting into areas that were highly personal and sensitive.

"In this very house there are men who like your type more than mine."

I said, "I don't want to hear about it." What a thought: Costas and his misguided affection for my shower and my fruity soap.

I asked for my chair back—it was time to hear the tapes and assess our progress. Isabel rose and gave the chair a playful spin before I could sit down. At the door she said softly, "Think it over. I'll be in my room."

I said, "I'm much too busy."

Before I Start

Monday 3/22

Dear Ferris,

I'm back at my desk in Truro, about to plunge
into the serious research. Just wanted to drop
you a line to say I appreciate your having dinner
with me on such short notice and I hope that our
evening and conversations sit well with you.
Glad, too, that you got to meet Isabel and to
experience Nan VanVleet firsthand. You certainly were a help and a good sport in that department.

I've got my fingers crossed that things work
out for you with this new agent and that I'll be
welcome at the party that your (powerful New
York) publisher throws to launch MALICE
EMERITUS. Not to mention the premiere of "Malice Emeritus, The Movie"!

Please keep me posted and I'll do the same.
Assuming that's okay.

All best,

Harriet M.

23
SOME FINE POINTS

 I MUST HAVE been concentrating more on her actressy Books-on-Tape tone than on her content, because it wasn't until a second playing of the tapes that I heard the new facts.

Such as: She had been born with a rudimentary sixth finger on her left hand. It had been tied off and snipped away leaving only the slightest bump of a knuckle, which no one noticed unless it was called to his or her attention.

Also new: Her godfather had been the fly-weight champion of the world for ninety-eight days in 1951.

Similarly: She had willed her body to Columbia College of Physicians and Surgeons.

And: Before Costas was a big-name photo realist, before he met Isabel at his sham wedding to Margaret, before he built this house and rescued her from public scrutiny and got debunked, Costas had been married to Annette Suchecki Krug, Isabel's mother.

"I *did* tell you," Isabel said in her bedroom doorway. "I distinctly remember telling you I went to his wedding because he'd been married to my mother briefly and his relatives were boycotting it so I was there as whaddyacallit—as someone to sit on the groom's side." Isabel paused, glanced down at her big transparent plastic watch, and asked if I was sure. Because she would have sworn—

"Not a clue. Not until I heard it on tape."

She touched the face of her watch again. I asked if she had an appointment. "Only 'Joy,'" she said, "but we have a few minutes." She left me in the doorway as she took her accustomed place on the tufted gray chaise. Seeing me standing there, still perplexed after a minute, she asked, "Is it that important that Costas was my stepfather?"

I didn't scream yes or say that the news had shocked me and turned my stomach. I did say, "It's important if it makes me feel like a fool. And even more important if I can't trust you to tell me the truth."

Isabel phfffed and batted away my charge. "Look—I thought I told you. But if you say I didn't, I didn't." She pulled her ice-blue mohair throw onto her shoulders.

I stood there feeling graceless and helpless, wondering if this was where a highly principled ghostwriter would tender her resignation.

261

"Besides," Isabel added, "if I wanted to keep it a secret, why would I put it on my tape?"

In lieu of resigning I asked grudgingly, "When was he your stepfather?"

"When I was a little girl," she said, "and not for long."

With my eyes on the carpet I said that I had been repulsed enough by his seduction of a perfect stranger at his own wedding, but now this: his own stepdaughter.

Isabel looked up, puzzled. "Incest you mean?"

I nodded.

"Except," said Isabel, "I hadn't seen him for all those years. Almost ten. I was a fully grown woman. He had been stepfather to a whole other person." She leaned forward and spoke with as thoughtful an expression as I'd ever seen on her face. "Look, you might think I take the father question too lightly. But we talked about it plenty and here's what we said: In dirt-ball families, stepfathers sleep with their stepdaughters and vice versa—you see this all the time on talk shows. But this was different. He was never out of line until he was well past being my stepfather. I mean, look at psychiatrists: They get disbarred for having sex with patients, but not if they stop treating them first and then wait for some time—a year or two maybe?—to sleep with them. If there was such a thing as a grace period for this kind of relationship, I think ten years would be more than plenty." She sat back and looked at the television. As if her speech had been timed to come up to the hour, the VCR clicked then whirred. "It tapes automatically Monday through Friday," she explained.

After a long pause she said, "I might have crashed the wedding, now that I think of it."

"How?"

"Easy." She smiled proudly. "You do your research. You

call the bride's house and say to a maid, 'I'm so sorry but I lost the invitation and I can't remember the exact time of the ceremony,' and when she tells you, you say, 'And the address again of the church? Thanks awfully much. Please give my love to Margaret.'"

"At what point," I asked, "did the bridegroom realize it was you?"

"I announced it in the receiving line. I said, 'I'm Isabel,' and he knew exactly who I was."

"What did he say?"

"Say? He didn't say anything. He got tears in his eyes and he put his arms around me until I wiggled away."

"Not, 'Look, everybody, here's my stepdaughter Itsy all grown up. Isn't she beautiful?'"

Her lips pursed, she shook her head.

"Why wouldn't he have said something?"

Isabel blinked as if to say, Harriet, most women know these things. "He wouldn't have *said* anything because he took one look at me and knew there'd be some funny business between us before the night was over so why call attention to his stepdaughter Itsy."

I moved into the room and sat on her sheepskin comforter. I said, "I guess I don't understand why you'd want to be at his wedding in the first place."

Isabel left the chaise to close her door. She joined me on her bed. "All I wanted," she said in a hoarse whisper, "all I was looking for was a moment of revenge: I wanted to say, 'See what you missed by never calling me or visiting me?' I didn't mean to seduce him. I wasn't even thinking *Gigi*. I just wanted his eyes to pop out."

"But if you were so angry at him and wanted revenge—"

Isabel shook her head. "When none of your fathers have

stuck around, you say you hate them, but then when one of them comes back, no matter in what form, and says, 'I want you,' then you think, 'He wants me. I'm lovable. He loves me. Of course I'll go with him. He wants me.'"

"I don't get it. You come to a wedding reception looking for a reunion with your stepfather, maybe *some* kind of long-lost affection, but you end up going home with the groom?"

Isabel closed her eyes. "I adored him. I had had a crush on him when my mother brought him home. He was tall . . . cool . . . mysterious. And very kind."

I asked how her mother had taken the news of their engagement.

Isabel said, "We kept it a secret."

"Till when?"

"As long as we could," said Isabel.

I said, "You never told her?"

"Not really," said Isabel. "It would have been different if she had been interested in anyone but herself. That's probably what makes it hard for you to picture the whole scenario. Your parents are normal."

"Normal how?"

"Normal," said Isabel. "You love them. You keep their picture on your desk, for crissakes. Do you see any pictures of my mother around here?"

"She calls you," I pointed out. "She sees your name in a gossip column and she picks up the telephone."

"That's only lately," said Isabel. "Since I've become notorious."

I asked how she explained Costas's taking her in after the trial.

Isabel reached inside her caftan to scratch one armpit absent-mindedly. "I think we said—let me get this straight—that Costas was taking care of me in a stepfather kind of way because he had the money and I was in trouble. We said the newspapers were wrong—we weren't married and never had been."

"And she believed you?"

"She's stupid," said Isabel. "I tell her Costas is old and feels sorry for me and has no other children. It also helps that I send her a check every month."

I heard footsteps outside, then an insincere knock, then the door opening. It was Costas in his denim painter's pants and a new flannel shirt that still had its packaging creases. "Aren't you watching?" he asked.

"We're talking," Isabel said. "I'm taping it."

He sat down on the chaise and held his hand out for the remote control.

She looked at me.

I said, "Go ahead."

"We can finish this later," she said.

The show was in mid-scene. Characters I didn't know were talking in a hospital waiting room about a car accident. Costas watched intently, his jaw slack and his eyes fixed on the screen.

I stared at him when I thought I could discreetly. Isabel's disclosure, I realized, had softened my view of his wedding behavior. He knew Isabel, I found myself thinking. He knew her and presumably had been fond of her at one time. Perhaps he hadn't been the world's most despicable groom if he had turned his attention from a bride of convenience to a long-lost stepdaughter.

A string of commercials interrupted the program. Next to me Isabel confided that she had told Costas about Perry's lifestyle choice.

"It adds a whole other layer to my viewing," said Costas. "I had my suspicions, of course."

"He's thrilled," murmured Isabel, "as you can imagine."

I sat up straight to say that Perry's lifestyle was his private business and his constitutional right. Unfortunately, because nothing of substance came out of our meeting, his sexual orientation—

"You thought there would be substance there?"

Three theme notes sounded to signal "If This Be Joy" was back. Kerr's mother and stepfather were hosting a black-tie affair. All the women wore rustling gowns in beautifully coordinated deep jewel tones. The town doctor congratulated the sterile Hugh on his wife's pregnancy, and the music trilled.

"If he's the only doctor in town, how come he doesn't know that Hugh is sterile?" I asked.

"Georgina covered her tracks," said Costas. "She saw a specialist in Bigtown who lied for her and said he had live sperm in his sample."

I said I didn't think a doctor would do that.

"You think the best of people," said Costas. "Which is an admirable way to be." He looked squarely at me. "Admirable but not very realistic."

I watched a little more, and noticed that Georgina's belly was swollen. I said she looked pretty far along for someone so recently inseminated.

"They do it at their own convenience," said Costas. "They have no regard for the passage of time. They think viewers accept whatever they put before us."

"I think Hugh is going to die before the baby's born," said Isabel.

"Hugh is not going to die," Costas countered.

"I know the signs," she said. "He's gonna die. I'd put money on it."

Costas harrumphed that he'd like to watch the show if we didn't mind. Isabel mouthed a grumpy few words in imitation.

I nudged Isabel and patted my stomach. She nodded enthusiastically. I pointed my chin toward Costas. "Sure," Isabel whispered. "Sandwiches and Juicy Juice? And chips if we have any. And those Canadian biscuits?"

I slipped away to the kitchen. When I returned with the tray, Costas and Isabel were fixed on a new development—stepson Franklin stealing kisses from a woman wearing a stethoscope. The chaise was empty, the only sign that either had moved a muscle in ten minutes. They continued to stare unblinking at the television, side by side, holding hands on Isabel's bed.

24
THE OLD ANCHOR

IT WOULDN'T HAVE been my
first choice of restaurants, but
I had ten dollars to spend and
knew I could afford the price of an Old Anchor linguiça sub.
Money was beginning to be a problem, since none was
coming in and I hadn't found the right moment in my six
weeks of quasi-employment to broach the subject. I had
arrived with my savings and with the cash from liquidating
my spices and potted plants, about two thousand dollars,
which seemed enough pocket money for someone getting
room and board in a house with laundry privileges in a town
with no winter commerce. Our one-page letter of agreement

said we'd split future royalties according to a formula that at the time seemed consistent with the fact that I was a nobody and Isabel was a tabloid celebrity. Accordingly, I budgeted forty dollars per week for incidentals. More and more frequently I was imagining the letter I might write to my parents asking for cash for my April birthday.

I had scribbled a note to Isabel—"Taking the night off. There's tuna and frozen pizza. See you later"—but then buzzed her on the intercom instead. I said, "I'm thinking of running to Provincetown for dinner." I heard her repeat my words, presumably to Costas.

"Where are you thinking of going?"

I said, "Just to the Old Anchor."

"What about Angie's? I'd rather have Italian than Portuguese."

I said, "I was thinking of a night off. By myself."

"Oh," said Isabel. She was silent for a few moments, then said, "Still, I don't know who you're going to meet at a place like that."

I told her not to worry. I was bringing a book and would take a quiet table in the corner. How crowded could it be on a Monday night?

I heard an exchange of murmurs in the background. "Could you bring us back something? Like a fisherman's platter and maybe some chowder." Another murmured consultation. "Two. One fried and one broiled."

It was my own fault, asking her permission to leave the house. I said I'd need money. Should I come to her room and get it?

"No," said Isabel sharply. "I'll bring it to you."

* * *

I put on my black stretch pants with the stirrup feet and my oversized Peruvian sweater. Isabel had come to the kitchen barefoot in Costas's white terrycloth robe with the Ritz-Carlton crest over her teal satin nightgown, waving a hundred-dollar bill. She said I should treat myself from that, too, maybe at a place a little classier than that bar.

I said, "I appreciate that because I'm using my savings for pocket money and I can't really afford to eat out very often."

Isabel blinked hard as if I'd said something unintelligible. "You're just telling me this now, that you're strapped? How come we never discussed this before?"

I said, "It's not a crisis. I have some money."

"But still," she said.

"And we have the agreement about future royalties, right?"

"But Harriet—I don't come from money. I don't assume a person has money when they don't have a paying job." She took back the hundred-dollar bill and folded it into my palm anew, squeezing my fingers around it. "Buy yourself dinner and wine. Buy a new book, too. And after you get our food, keep the change."

"That's very kind," I said. "Especially after my haircut and my new brushes."

"Do I owe you money for anything? Groceries? Or gas? What about the supplies you bought for Perry's interview?"

I said I had kept receipts—maybe twenty-five bucks total.

"I'll get you that. First thing tomorrow." She bit her lower lip. "Now I'm wondering how much Pete's put out for groceries that I haven't reimbursed him for. And the supplies."

"Ask him," I said. "He'll tell you. He's not shy."

She walked to the wall intercom and buzzed the lowest

button, once, twice, but got no answer. She turned back to me and asked how much I had, total, in savings.

"Enough to get by."

"Thousands? Hundreds?"

I said after a pause, "Forty bucks a week."

She sat down and splayed her left hand across her bosom. "What did I think you were living on? You were a secretary, living in the most expensive city in the country, and I assume you come here with—what? What was I thinking? A trust fund? Alimony?"

I laughed and said, "Palimony?"

She still looked worried, but allowed herself the beginning of a nervous smile. "You're not mad?" she asked.

I said I wasn't.

"Not about anything?" she asked.

"Like what?"

"You know—things. You were pissed off this morning." She waited, then prompted, "About getting wakened?"

"We went over that," I said. "Remember? It was none of my business?"

Isabel put a hand firmly on my shoulder. "The situation has changed somewhat."

"Yours and Costas's, you mean?"

Isabel's eyes widened. "You know?"

I laughed, fingering the collar of the borrowed robe. "I picked up a few signals."

"Wow. I am really impressed. I didn't know myself till last night, when we got back."

I asked her why she felt she had to make up a story about a vibrator, especially after I had distinctly heard him.

"Isn't he the *worst*?" she asked, "bellowing like a wild animal. And of course there's no shushing him."

I asked her again—why did she feel she had to make up a story and say she was alone in her bedroom?

Isabel said, "I guess my gut reaction is to protect my privacy."

I smiled and said, "Your being so shy and all."

"Costas is even worse. He wouldn't want you drawing conclusions where sex is concerned. It's happened before where we've gotten back together in bed, but the relationship doesn't change."

"Do you want it to?"

She leaned forward and confided, "Life is a hell of a lot easier when he's happy. And don't get me wrong—he's great in bed. I'm not making any big sacrifice."

"Are you happy?"

Isabel held her hands apart as if describing a foot-long hot dog. "He's got a dick this big," she said.

I said, I know, I had seen it. Remember?

She looked surprised in a mildly amused, indulgent kind of way.

"Not like that," I said. "The night I found him in my shower."

"Oh, right. He's sorry about that. He thinks he was rude."

I wanted to ask if she loved Costas, but I knew the question would sound quaint, and she would think that after all her lessons in the way the world worked, I had failed to grasp the principles.

I said I was happy for her, and for Costas, too. He was the lucky one. Now I was going to slip away. Okay to take the car?

"Of course! Is Monday going to be your regular night off?"

I said I'd let her know after I saw what Monday nights in P-town looked like. I took the keys off a Plexiglas hook by the door and picked up my purse. "Hey," she said. "You're going without a coat?"

"This is as heavy as a coat. Plus I'm layered." I plucked at the neck of my cotton turtleneck as proof.

Isabel looked doubtful.

I said, "Have fun."

"You, too," she said. "And watch out for those Province-town artist types. Most of them don't make a cent from their work so they're out to prove they're real men."

I laughed. I said I'd buzz her when I got back with the fishermen's platters.

She said, "If you meet someone and you want to go back to his place—and I'm dead serious about this—then forget the take-out. Just give me a call so I can defrost something here."

I said, heading toward the ground floor via the circular stairs, "I think you can count on dinner from Provincetown."

"Then get extra tartar sauce," she called after me.

I didn't see him because I walked straight to a table, my eyes on the blue and white checked oilcloth of my destination. He came and stood at my elbow while I pretended to be too engrossed in *The Baked Bean Supper Murders* to notice the filled blue jeans in my personal space.

"Quite the bahfly," he said. "You walked right by me." Pete's Massachusetts accent. I looked up: Pete.

The sight of him—Pete who had not slept with Isabel, the friend I hadn't missed until the second he materialized—caused my throat to constrict from something unnameable. "You know how it is," I managed, "alone in a strange town. I was trying not to make eye contact."

He pulled out the extra chair and sat down. "No Isabel?"

I said no Isabel. It was my night off.

"Did you know I'd be here?"

I said not really.

"I didn't think you liked this place after your first visit."

I reminded him it was Monday night in the middle of winter; my options were limited.

He looked at his big-faced diver's watch. "Mahch twenty-second is spring. I guess you've been too busy writing to notice."

"Too busy traveling with Isabel and brunching with Nan VanVleet."

Pete laughed. "I gotta hear this. Somethin' tells me your version isn't gonna be quite the same as hers." He asked if I'd like to go somewhere else—Italian? Better Portuguese?

I said I'd had good Italian in New York. Was there a place I could get a good fisherman's platter in the middle of the winter, broiled and fried?

Pete said, "This is Cape Cod—the best fish money can buy."

A waitress finally came over, not the Stephie of my last visit, but someone who could be Stephie's less gracious older sister. "Anything here?" she grunted.

Pete said, "Not tonight, Sandy. Thanks. We're headin' out."

When she had gone I said, "I want to apologize for this morning."

"Fa what?"

"The way I acted at breakfast."

He closed one eye and grimaced for comic effect. "Yeah. I wondered what all that was about."

I said, "I heard noises during the night—male and female noises."

"And you thought it was me and Isabel?"

274

"Sort of. But she set me straight."

"Did she?" he asked. "Completely?"

"It was Costas," I said. "I know that now."

"I heard them, too," he confided. "You'd have to be deaf to miss that racket."

"Did you know who it was all along?" I asked, "or did you think it might have been someone else besides Costas and Isabel?"

"Like who for instance?"

"Like Costas with a guest?"

"I was pretty sure it was the two of them," he said, then more quietly, "Maybe I didn't want to think about other combinations." He stood up and waited until I followed suit. He worked a dollar out of his pocket and left it for the do-nothing Sandy, guiding me toward the door so I wouldn't argue about his generosity.

We ordered through a screened window. The guy asked for a name and said he'd call us when our order was ready. Pete pointed out that we were the only ones there.

"Name?" the guy insisted.

"Harriet Mahoney," said Pete.

We waited in the cold. I asked who lived in Provincetown at this time of year and he said same as any artsy town—some shopowners, some rich people, a couple of lawyers, the teachers, a big contingent of gay guys and lesbians, even more on weekends: painters, writers, lost souls. Fishermen, but not here in the high-rent district. I asked where he lived and he said, "My mutha's house is in Noth Truro when I'm not at the big place. Ever been to Dutra's Mahket?"

I said sure, a hundred times.

"Not fah from there. Up the hill on 6A toward here."

The take-out window was a one-man operation—the guy who took our order was now manning the Fryolater. I watched him jiggle the handle of the basket for a few minutes and wondered silently how often they changed the oil.

"It's good," Pete said. "They get fresh stuff every day and they turn around a lotta meals."

The cook-cashier strained great lumps of big-bellied clams and shrimps that glowed pink through the batter. My taste buds strained in their direction. "I could go for one of those dinners myself," I said.

"We can deliver theirs and eat at the big house, in the dining room. Evah eaten in the dining room?" I said no.

"Two more of those plattahs to go," he called through the screen, adding wryly, "That goes with the Harriet Mahoney orda." He turned back to me and said, "You can pay for theirs, but I'm buyin' the rest." For the second time that night, someone folded my fingers back around the hundred-dollar bill and told me to spend it on myself. He said it was his town and I was new and that should be enough reason for me to give up the fight. "Besides," said Pete. "I get paid a salary. And I get the feelin you're something between a boarda and a roommate and no cash flows between you and Isabel."

I shrugged as if I hadn't neglected to negotiate myself a living.

"I get seventeen an owa plus insurance," he said. "Just so you'll know what they can pay."

I said, "I'm jealous."

"I wasn't bragging. It's not like I'm writing a book where you could find a pot of gold at the end."

I said, "Who knows if I'm writing a book, either?"

The guy behind the screen asked, "Fries and cole slaw with those ordas?"

We nodded to each other and both said yeah. Pete asked if I liked calamari, because this place was one of the few that had it on their fisherman's platter.

I thought of saying, "I'm getting too old to eat fried food at eight o'clock at night," but didn't. I said, "I love it."

We waited, shoulder to shoulder, watching the guy dart between his stations. Pete said, "If you thought it was the middle of winta, how come you didn't wear a coat?"

I said this was a heavy wool sweater made by indigenous South Americans.

He laughed and said, "Who really know what to wear in freezing weatha."

I said I found winter on the Cape milder than I had expected.

"I guess that's why you're shivering." He put his arm around me. Not for long. A few seconds maybe. I could only think, I'm so much older than he is. He smiled his trustworthy smile and put his hands back in his pockets.

The cashier-cook stepped up to the desk mike and called out, "Harriet Mahoney?" Pete and I looked at each other and laughed. "Three plattahs," said the cashier-cook. "One mackerel dinna. Two medium chowdas. Extra tahta."

"Cocktail sauce?" I asked.

"Ketchup," said the guy.

I asked him if he could change a hundred dollar bill. After looking in his cash drawer he said yuh, if that was all I had. Pete handed me his money and reached across to receive the horizontal brown bags of take-out from the window. His gallantry reminded me of Kenny in reverse: how no one had taught Kenny to hold doors open or carry bundles; how he had no let-me-get-that-for-you impulse; how in the name of women's liberation he had been a lazy slob.

"I've got this," said Pete. "You grab the change and some extra napkins."

He asked where I was parked and I said in the public lot. "Should we go in one cah or two?" he asked, "'cause I can leave mine where it is ovanight." In the normal context of male-female transportation arrangements, it was a loaded question, but in this case, I reminded myself, we both had the same home.

I said I'd drive him back to his car in the morning, or whenever.

"Good," said Pete. "It'll give us a chance to talk, just us, in case we get stuck with Mr. and Ms. Dimantopoulos as a double date."

Double date, I thought. He's so charitable.

"I think they're back tagetha," he said. "Not that it's permanent or anything. He'll get pissed at her tomorrow and staht his routine all ova again."

I opened the driver's door and unlocked his side. Not that I was making comparisons, but Kenny, who couldn't lift a finger outside A Decent Bagel, always had to drive.

I depressed the clutch and put the gear shift in reverse.

"How come you drive and they don't?" he asked.

I said I was a Bostonian—and here's where I made a joke—where all the best drivers came from. Isabel and Costas were—who knew? From the planet of famous, beautiful people where they only hailed taxis.

Pete laughed. "You can say that again. And it was a lucky day for me when anotha person from Earth moved in."

I nosed the car out of the lot and up a narrow storybook residential street that looked like every other one in Province-town. "Tell me where I'm going," I said at the next stop sign, and Pete said, "So fah you're doin' great."

25
JUNE

WHEREAS I WOULD have
buzzed Isabel and waited
proudly by the Styrofoam to
elicit positive reinforcement over my excellent choices, Pete
didn't need that kind of thing. At his suggestion, I buzzed her
room and said, "Food's in the kitchen. I'll see you tomorrow."

Isabel said, "Harriet?"

I said, trying to sound as if I were on the run, "Yes?"

"Did you have a good time?"

I said, yes, I did.

"I'm glad," she said.

"Don't let it get cold."

"Do we need cutlery?"

Pete signaled, let her worry about that.

"There's plastic forks and knives in the bag."

"Harriet?"

"Hmm?"

"Thanks a lot."

"No problem."

Pete drew his finger across his throat: end of conversation, and I realized that in fact it was. I released the button and twirled the air with my newly liberated finger.

"Let's get outta here," said Pete.

"Beer," I said.

He backtracked to the refrigerator for a six-pack and said, "Thirty seconds, tops, after you ring the dinnah bell."

We made it down the steps before we heard Isabel's door open.

"Not the dining room?" I whispered.

"They'd join us," said Pete.

I followed him down the long hall, past the living room in the opposite direction of my room, down a half-flight of stairs to a large room that was empty except for a card table and two metal folding chairs. It showcased the bay from its picture window, like every north-facing room, but the view was one story lower. It was carpeted and fireplaced—the children's playroom for the next owners. An unframed bed-sized painting hung on the wall.

"Is it?" I asked Pete.

"Costas's? You bet."

I walked up to it and touched the thickly textured surface. I said, "It's beautiful."

"It used to be in a museum."

I said it looked vaguely familiar. Or maybe it was the men. They all looked like Costas.

"His uncles and their wives. All Dimantopouloses. It's a family wake."

I asked which museum had sent it back.

"A big one. Boston, I think."

I said, "No wonder he's so bitter."

Pete led me into a short, no-nonsense hallway with two doors off it and a linoleum floor. "Another wing?" I asked.

"My wing," he said. Then I heard barking.

"Easy, girl," Pete cooed to the front door. "I'm back." Still holding the brown bags, he maneuvered a key out of his pocket. "Hold on, hold on," he said. The barking changed to muted whimpers. The door opened into the ecstatic leap of a brown and gold mutt, beagle-sized, with beagle ears and a German shepherd's coat.

"Pretty ugly?" Pete said happily, already on his knees, the take-out raised above his head, where I took it from him.

"Pretty cute," I said.

"Her name's June." He rubbed the dog's belly and wrestled with her forelegs. "June bug," he crooned. "Junie girl."

I said I couldn't believe there was a dog under my roof. I loved dogs. I would take this dog for a walk every day on the beach. I heard my speech evolve into baby talk. June stared from her back, paws limp-wristed, tail twitching, as if "walk" had registered.

"Junie loves walks on the beach," he said in his doggie voice. "She likes it even more if you throw sticks and you don't mind if she gets wet and yucky." He stood up and said, "Here it is, my room. The famous janita's quahters at the otha end of the buzza."

It was like a new dorm room in a well-endowed college, not

large but efficient and architectural: bed, desk, built-in bureau and bookshelves of blond wood, one window, no view, beige walls, rubber tile floor in red and tan squares. A huge tidal chart of Cape Cod Bay on the longest wall and a poster clamped behind Plexiglas of the original *Jaws*. June's paraphernalia cluttered the floor: a beanbag bed, some knots of chewed rawhide, a disgusting tennis ball, water and food bowls on a hound-dog placemat, a security blanket that at one time must have been a gray sweatshirt.

I said, "How come Isabel never mentioned June?"

"Because," said Pete, "Isabel doesn't like the idea of June. I almost didn't get the job because of June." He beamed at the mutt, who shivered with joy. "I figured she'd stay at my mutha's most of the time except when my mutha was up at school but Isabel kind of forgot about her."

Crouching again, he scratched June's ears with both hands. "Big bad Itsy lives way up on the second floor, right? She can't hear the nasty bahks of this big ferocious dog, right? And when it's nice, Junie stays outside chasin' those very interesting seagulls and hermit crabs. Isn't that right? Gettin' those burrs in her fur? And those bad ticks? Pantin' up those big steps?" June bared her teeth in a doggie grin.

"Harriet and I a gonna eat now," said Pete. "This is Harriet." He held out a cautionary forefinger. "You can come with us if you lie down and don't beg." He asked me if that was okay, out in the rec room on the table and chairs?

The fried food was barely warm, but was still as good as any I'd ever had. We both said no, we'd be crazy to go back to the kitchen to microwave it.

Pete said, "Tell me about this novel you're writing."

I said I was stuck and felt like I wasn't ever going to get unstuck.

"How come?"

"Because I've started to hate it."

"How fah did you get before you got stuck?"

"Fifty or so pages."

He asked what came first, getting stuck or hating it?

"I never loved it, but since I got here I haven't been able to write a sentence that doesn't stink."

"You've got a lot on your mind," said Pete. "How's a person supposed to write two books at once?"

I said what worried me was that I wasn't writing two books at once. I was writing no books at once. The Isabel Krug Story was still in the note-taking stage while "A Room in the Cantor's House" was in a coma.

"That's the title?" he asked, piercing a big clam with his fork and clamping his mouth around it.

"The working title," I said. "My main character is a Jewish cantor and he makes a home for his ex-wife in his guest room after he's widowed from his second wife and the first wife gets a skull fracture while he's sitting *shiva*, which is when people come to pay their respects."

Pete smiled and coughed, waving his hand as if to say, It's nothing, I'm all right.

I continued: Isabel had filled him in, right? How my novel was based on the true story of my parents' two courtships? And he already knew how my father had left my mother for his professor at the community college who seduced him after a pot-luck supper in her house?

Still coughing, he took a swallow from his beer, then put his napkin to his mouth. I could tell from his eyes that his coughing was disguised laughter.

I said, "Do you think it's funny?"

Pete said, "Harriet—it *is* funny."

"Funny that my mother was almost killed by two punks who read the funeral announcement in the Brookline *Chronicle* and broke into the house at the exact moment my stepmother was being buried? Two punks who spent less than eighteen months total in jail for robbery and assault with a deadly weapon?"

Pete was getting red in the face trying not to let his laughter burst out beyond the napkin. He nodded, his eyes bulging.

I said, "Maybe I'm not telling it right."

Pete couldn't hold it any longer. He laughed like a mob was tickling him. "The deadly VCR," he managed between convulsions. I continued to eat as if this would pass. Maybe I had said something witty, even if it wasn't deliberate on my part. Pete slapped his chest in several places as if a firm touch to the lungs might stem the hysteria.

June raised herself up on her forelegs and barked.

Pete squeaked, "It's okay, girl," and lost it again.

Why had no one else ever laughed at my concept, I wondered. Maybe if someone had had this reaction in the workshop, I might have approached it differently. Might have reworked my premise. Might have explored the comedic opportunities.

Pete waved his hand again: Forgive me, I can't help myself. I smiled politely, waiting for him to finish. In a minute, shaking his head, still grinning, he stood up, walked around the table, and took my face in his hands. He kissed me once, twice. He sat down again and picked up his fork, saying, "The look on your face. Trying so hahd to be polite." He shook his head and inhaled a ragged breath. "Talk about rude," he said. "I'm really sorry."

I said, "Don't be sorry."

"I didn't plan that. You looked so brave I suddenly wanted to kiss you."

He drank some beer. "Okay," he said. "That's a lie. It wasn't sudden."

Of all the appropriate things I might have uttered, I broke my own silence with, "How come you don't have a girlfriend?"

Pete said, "How come you don't have a boyfriend?"

"I asked you first."

He folded his arms and slid his elbows half-way across the table causing our Styrofoam containers to collide. "I don't have a girlfriend because I haven't met anyone lately who I wanted to be with."

Rationally, I knew his face was red and his eyes were tearing from his laughing spell, but the overall picture was one of great tenderness. I said, "I don't have a boyfriend because I'm not good at having boyfriends."

That was all. I think he smiled first. He said June needed to go out. Did I want to come?

We sat on the top landing of the stairs to the beach, shoulder to shoulder, a crocheted throw from his bed across both our backs. I could hear and smell the water, but there was no moon to light the beach below us. June rustled the blueberry bushes and maniacally dug holes. At regular intervals Pete yelled behind us, "Cut it out. I mean it." June would check in with us, sniff us, lick Pete's face, and return to the brush. Pete said, "She thinks if she digs unda the bushes instead of next to the foundation, I'm not gonna notice."

He couldn't have known the effect all this was having on me—Pete doting on his dog. And if that weren't enough, he

285

knew the constellations. He observed, assuming I saw what he saw in the night sky, that Leo was directly overhead tonight and Orion was especially beautiful. In his June voice he said, "And you know Junie's favorite, right? Canis Major? See, girl"—he pointed the dog's head straight up, palms holding her velvet ears—"there's Sirius."

June looked skyward obediently, then lay down and let me pat her. I said, "I wonder if they liked the seafood?"

"Rest assured they ate every bite."

I said, "Hope they can digest it."

"Why shouldn't they be able to digest it?"

"You know," I said. "It gets harder to digest fried food as you get older."

"Costas didn't have the fried fish."

"I meant Isabel."

After a long pause he said, "Ahn't you and Isabel around the same age?"

I said, yes, I'd be forty-two next month.

"I know that. You keep telling me that."

"Do I?"

"And I know why you keep telling me." He stopped. "You can't believe I'd want to be with someone olda than me."

I said, "Six years is a lot when one person is in the prime of his life and the other one is going to be middle-aged tomorrow."

He took my hand and held on to it. June barked from the bushes. Pete yelled over his shoulder, "Get outta there, you mutt. You're gonna get Lyme Disease." When he turned back around he squeezed my hand and rubbed it for warmth with his free one.

Of course I had to make one more apology, had to initial

one more contingency clause. "So you don't think this is a May-December, maybe a June-November sort of thing?"

He didn't answer for a minute. When he did, his voice was low and careful. "Are you sure it's that? Or are you worried your friends would say, 'A handyman? Did you lose your mahbles?'"

"If this is losing my mahbles," I said slowly, "I'll give them a going-away pahty."

I could count the seconds it took until my answer slipped past his guard and sunk in. He smiled. I couldn't see it in the dark but I knew it was there.

26

MANICURES

 ISABEL, IN PINK and gray spandex, her raccoon coat thrown over her shoulders, was holding her final layer of nail polish up to the sun. "I could almost use sunscreen today," she said. "Almost."

My eyes were closed. On the warm pine of the steps, we were ignoring the fact that beyond the reach of the tide, the beach was covered with snow. "I can't believe you don't think this is heaven," I murmured.

"I'm bored. There's nothing to do here except work."

I said, "We have to."

She asked what was left.

"Everything. A whole book's worth."

"You *know* everything," she said. "You know about my childhood, my adolescence, my mother, my various stepfathers, my meeting Guy, our affair, the trial." She lowered her fingernails for an appraisal and put them back onto the mysterious shelf of air.

I said, "But Isabel—you've read biographies: They go into a lot of detail."

Her big white-framed sunglasses were hanging around her neck on a turquoise cord. She raised them, using only palms and no fingers, onto her nose. "Here's how I see it: There's Guy's death. And there's the events that led up to that"—she paired two fingers and made them scurry through the air—"and there's the events that grew out of that." Another scurry in the opposite direction. "Stuff I told you on tape might interest a couple of people, but the majority of them are going to buy my book to read about my fucking someone else's husband in their bed and being a witness to the murder."

I said, "Okay. Maybe you're right. But biographers have to throw that other stuff in."

"No one cares where I went to school." She thought about that. "Or where I didn't go to school. Or what my favorite flavor ice cream is."

She took one of my hands and placed it flat on her right palm. "Can I do you?"

I said no thanks.

"Why not?"

I said the red wasn't me. I'd look down at my hands on the keyboard and be startled.

"How do you know? If you don't like it, you can take it

right off. I'll do one coat." She tugged my left hand out of my parka pocket, then uncurled the ball I had squeezed it into. "C'mon," she wheedled. "I'll talk while I do you. I'll tell all."

I said if that was the deal, okay. I flipped my steno pad open to my questions, written in shorthand so Isabel wouldn't see them coming. "One of the things I don't get is, where was Costas in all this?"

"When?"

"When you met Guy."

"He knew about Guy."

"Because you told him?"

"Because he made it his business to know."

"But you were separated?"

"He had his own definition of 'separated.'"

I asked what that was. Isabel hunched over my hand with greater attention. "Well," she said, "it was pretty much the same definition he had for 'married.'"

I said, pencil poised, "Could you please explain that?"

"He always had his studio. In Chelsea, not that close. I had the apartment. We didn't spend every night together even when we were getting along fine. Not because we were cheating but because that's the way it was: He painted, he traveled, he had to do his European husband thing. And I liked it that way."

I asked what she was doing then. Working? Going to school?

Isabel looked up from my nails and into the horizon. I could see her squinting behind her dark glasses. "Let me see. When we were first married? I worked."

"Where?"

"B. Altman and Company."

"What department?"

"The beauty salon."

"Doing what?"

Isabel stopped filing for two beats. "This."

"Nails?"

She smiled and said, "This is an exclusive. Nobody ever asked what I did before I became a personal shopper."

I confirmed for the record: "You were a manicurist at B. Altman's?"

"B. Altman and Company. Correct." She pushed back my cuticles with her longest nail. When I said, "Ow," she said, "Stop being a baby. They have no nerve-endings. I'm almost done. Ask me another question."

"Is this what you were doing when you met Costas, or re-met Costas?"

"I think so. Altman's wasn't my first job but it was right around then."

I said, "Did you enjoy it?"

She said, "I did Arlene Dahl's nails once and Gloria Swanson's."

I wrote down those names; asked who else's.

"Happy Rockefeller. Kitty Carlisle. Sometimes I didn't recognize people, then after they left the receptionist would tell me who I'd just done. But the store was very hush-hush. They didn't want us gossiping about the clients."

I said, "Not to sound like a snob, but your husband was this big-time photo realist and you were a manicurist. Isn't that unusual?"

"He painted and I worked. It gave me an employee discount and I liked the girls I worked with. And it wasn't the worst thing in the world: I'd be at an art opening or a party and

291

someone would ask what I did and I'd say I worked at B. Altman and Company and the person would say, 'That was my mother's favorite store,' and we'd go on from there, the same as if I had said I worked at IBM or Columbia or some other highbrow place." She shook the bottle of polish lazily and smiled. 'Once in a while, when I knew the person was an asshole and a snob, I'd say, 'I paint, too.' Which wasn't so far from the truth when you think about it."

I reminded her that I was no snob: Mahoney's Donuts and all those secretarial jobs?

"I know you're no snob," said Isabel. "I picked you because you were no snob."

She painted each nail with confident strokes. I asked what this color was called. She held the bottle above her eyes and said, "Arrest Me Red." She told me to hold my fingers up to the sun as she had done—this formula was made to dry in a sec under light. I flipped back in my steno pad as best as I could one-handed and asked what caused their separation.

She was touching up her own perfect nails absentmindedly, sunglasses atop her head. "I didn't tell you that, either? The big scandal about his work?"

"Oh that," I said. "You did tell me about that."

"Well, that happened. He was furious, depressed, angry, wouldn't sleep, he ranted and raved about the reporter who wrote the article that said he was misrepresenting himself as a super realist." Isabel yawned and said loudly, mid-yawn, "No fun."

I asked if she had considered sticking by Costas in his career crisis.

"Sure I did."

"But?"

"You can't stick by Costas, because he's the one who runs away. He took off for a long trip to Greece, painted some relatives and some houses he'd lived in, and stayed there more than a year."

I asked what had happened when he'd returned to New York.

"The main thing was that no one wanted his new paintings. Not his old gallery, not the private collectors who owned his Polaroids. It was like he proved what they were saying: You may have developed an interesting technique that you called photo realism, but you ain't no painter."

I asked why they had never divorced.

Isabel said, "Why bother? I didn't want to get married again."

"So you could lead your own life."

"Harriet—it doesn't work that way. Divorce doesn't solve anything when it's from a man like Costas. In his own disturbed way he takes the marriage vows very seriously—till death do we part."

"He divorced your mother, though. And Margaret."

"He wasn't obsessed with them." Isabel readjusted her coat over her shoulders and said, "Look: he was over forty when we met and I was twenty. I had these boobs and no belly and a waistline and a tanned butt. I had long legs and long blonde hair." She sighed and shook her head.

"Excuse me," I said. "Like you've lost it? Like you're not still knockin' 'em dead."

Isabel touched one of my newly red fingernails lightly. Dry. She put her arms around me and hugged me to her as much as the raccoon coat's precarious perch allowed. After a few moments I pulled back and asked, "What was that for?"

293

She said, "Do you know how many girlfriends I've had who would pay me a compliment like that?"

I said, "Not many?"

"None! Nada. Nic."

"Maybe they're jealous."

"See! They wouldn't even say that, wouldn't even admit that much, that there might be a reason for jealousy. I haven't had good friends in my life. Like these people who keep in touch with their best friend from high school and their college roommate? Not me. I don't collect friends like that. I don't stay in touch with people I knew from twenty years ago."

I said, "I hope I know you in twenty years."

She touched the sleeve of my parka. "Really? You're not just saying that?"

I said, "Want to make a date for lunch right now, twenty years from today?"

"Where?" she cried.

"Here. Corn Hill Beach."

"What if it's washed away?"

"We'll talk first," I said. "We'll pick a restaurant."

"Really? Do you think we'll both be alive?"

I said, "Alive and in print. Working on a sequel."

"This is so great," she said. "I don't think you know what it means to me to know that no matter what happens, I have a lunch date in my sixties. Maybe we could make it a weekly thing."

She carried her smile back to my fingers. "You have nice moons on your nails."

"I do?"

"There was a time when the style was to leave the moons unpainted." She demonstrated on my right thumb, painting most of it but leaving a half-circle of plain nail at the cuticle. "When our children are grown up they'll be saying, 'Remember when we were little and people used to paint their fingernails bright colors like red and orange? And carve them into strange shapes and put racing stripes on them?'"

I laughed. "What children?"

"A figure of speech," said Isabel. "I meant the next generation."

"Maybe you have six children in New Jersey and you forgot to mention it."

"I don't have any children hidden away," said Isabel, "although it's not the horrible thought it once would have been."

I said, "I know what you mean." I told her about trying to get pregnant for years with Kenny, who didn't want any medical help with his low sperm count.

"Why the hell not?"

"Because he didn't want to get married. Not to me anyway."

We made the same face: *men.*

Isabel reached for the thermos of coffee, which sat one step below us. She unscrewed the stopper and filled the plastic cup, offering me the first sip.

I said, "But then again, we'd be divorced by now and the children would be from a broken home."

"I never would've hired you for this job if you were moving in with kids." She smiled and nudged my elbow, causing the coffee to slosh. "Especially short, whiny kids with receding hairlines."

I didn't mind the insult. Back when we were trying, I had worried that our baby would be the unlovely fruit of the most aggressive sperm in Kenny's arsenal.

So I joined in. "Yeah, whiny, pouting—"

"Can't make a commitment."

"Fingers sticky from cream cheese."

"And riz-otto," Isabel yelped.

We laughed and leaned into each other's shoulders. Suddenly I straightened up and pretended to search the beach like a hunting dog on alert. "Bob?" I called. "Is Bob around? Has anyone seen my bagel customer and best friend Bobby de Niro? And could someone bring me some excellent Chardonnay that isn't too oaky?"

Isabel laughed and handed me the cup. I swirled it first, sniffed deeply, and said, "Ahh. Very nice."

She nodded, satisfied, then stood up to stretch. "You're over him," she said.

A Reply

March 26

Dear Harriet,

Yours of March 22 in hand. Thank you for the concerns expressed. I am quite well, better than ever. Although there has been no further word from Ms. Miller about representation, I hardly expected a decision on her part so soon after I mailed the full manuscript.

I have had a busy and diverting spring break: two plays in three days, (Guys and Dolls and Les Miserables) which is something of a weekday record for me, and a Connie Francis concert tomorrow night.

Could you please send me your telephone number in Truro? There is no listing under I. Krug.

Regards,

Ferris P.

27
NEWS OF A LITERARY NATURE

 I SENT FERRIS my Truro phone number with a note saying I expected to be the first person called when he received good news of a literary nature. He telephoned immediately. Isabel took the call and buzzed my room saying, "It's Ferris Porter for you. He sounds funny."

I answered with a friendly wariness I had perfected in law-firm reception. He said without small talk that he was calling with respect to Nan VanVleet and an idea she had for a book. My brain supplied a picture: breakfast at The Cranley, Ferris reciting Shakespeare, Nan clasping her bosom.

"A book?" I repeated, instinctively reaching for a pen. "What kind of book?"

"Nonfiction."

"About what?"

"About a sheltered woman whose innocence is shattered by public and private tragedies and the tools she employs to mend the fabric of her life."

I knew everything with that. I knew that Ferris's spring break had been spent in Nan's breakfast nook, outlining The Nan VanVleet Story, crafting a one-sentence summary and undermining me. "You don't even know her," I said.

"Well," said Ferris, "that isn't strictly the case anymore." He asked if I had a spare copy of Isabel's book proposal.

I said, "No." As if Isabel had ever written a proposal. "Her agent must have it."

"What's his name?"

I said, "Do you think he's going to send you a copy of a client's confidential proposal?"

"I'd like to talk to him," said Ferris.

"Why?"

"Because he's obviously interested in a certain kind of confessional celebrity book."

"What about Priscilla Miller? Hadn't she asked for exclusivity?"

"I hardly think she would handle a big commercial book."

I said, "I don't even know the guy. You'd have to talk to Isabel."

"Would you put her on?"

"Who gave Nan the idea to write a book?"

"She's always intended to write a book about her experience. She kept a journal while she was hospitalized and it's quite compelling."

"You've read it?"

Ferris said, "Most of it. The legible parts."

I said, "A journal's a pretty personal thing to show a total stranger."

Silence. Then: "May I please speak to Isabel?"

"Why do you want to help Nan with her book?"

"Why do you want to help Isabel with hers?"

I said, "Because it's my job."

"I'm doing it," said Ferris, "because she can't do it herself. And I'd like to help."

"As what?"

"As her friend. As a professor of English and as a writer."

"You mean correct her spelling or write it for her?"

Ferris said, "Nan very much liked the notion of a ghost-writer when you explained it to her. She hadn't realized that that kind of collaboration was an accepted practice. She thought if someone ghosted a book it was like buying a term paper."

"So you're going to write the other side of The Isabel Krug Story and put it out there so there's two books in the stores competing against each other?"

To his credit, Ferris remained calm. He said, with a kind of teasing lilt to the phrase, "Not necessarily."

Isabel called Jay, the agent. Jay the agent said, "Where do we stand pagewise?"

Isabel said, "I'm putting on my collaborator, Harriet Mahoney." Passing me the receiver she said formally, "Harriet, Jay."

I heard him at a distance speaking into another phone. "Send him a bottle of scotch, single malt, and beg for one more week and make nice. Bill me for the booze."

I said, "Hello?"

"Gotta take this." His voice came closer. "Harriet?"

I said, "Hi."

"What the fuck's going on?"

I said, "Well, Guy VanVleet's widow wants to write her own book—"

"From prison?"

"She didn't go to prison. She was found temporarily insane. She's back home—"

"Where's home again?"

"Greenwich, Connecticut. And she has a ghostwriter picked out—"

"Porter. He called here."

"He figures if you're interested in Isabel's story, you'll be interested in hers."

"I don't do mercy fucks," said Jay.

I said, "I don't want to help them. Isabel and I thought we should tell you what the competition is up to."

"She's old, right?"

I said, "Excuse me?"

"The widow. She's what—a dumpy Joanne Woodward?"

I said, "I don't understand."

"Do you think there's a movie in it?"

"In what? Nothing's been written."

Jay said, "Never mind. When can I see some pages?"

"How many do you want?"

"I want enough to sell: a drop-dead chapter and an outline."

"I can have a chapter soon."

"This widow, the one who wants in? Is she still crazy?"

I said, "She was discharged by a panel of psychiatrists."

Jay said, "That could work—a sanity hearing? With

shabby lawyers, but noble? Like *Splendor in the Grass* meets *Inherit the Wind*"?

I said, "She can't write."

"So? She's got some shmuck to write it for her."

"He's a professor of English at LaGuardia Community College."

"What are you?" he asked.

I said, "I'm a novelist."

"Right right right. Iz said you had stories in *The New Yorker.*"

I looked at Isabel. "Actually, not in *The New Yorker.*"

"Whatever. She said you were the best of the bunch. Now I remember—New York–based, ran a writing group, wanted to transition?"

I said that was true; I had wanted to transition.

"Busy," he yelled to a buzz from another phone, then back to me. "Pages. When do I get them?"

"A month?"

"Harriet. Honey. Don't say 'a month.'"

"A.S.A.P.?"

"Tell me again—what does he want from me?"

"Nan VanVleet's ghostwriter, the shmuck, is going to ask you for Isabel's book proposal."

"You know him how?"

I said we had been in the same writing group for years.

"How fast can he write?" Jay asked.

I said, "He's only done detective novels before this, so I couldn't say."

"Do you know who did them?"

I said, "Huh?"

"Who made them? What director?"

I said, "They haven't been published as books yet."

He said, "We'll look into it. Do you know who his people are?"

I said Ferris didn't have people. I heard scratchings that sounded like fountain pen on paper. I waited, then said, "Jay?"

He said, "I'm faxing something to you in two minutes."

"We don't have a fax machine."

"Where are you again?"

"Cape Cod."

"Somebody must have one, some lawyer. Do they have businesses there? I have a client with a fax on Martha's Vineyard. Isn't that Cape Cod?"

I said I'd find one and call the number in. I asked, "Is the thing you're sending bad news?"

"Don't get crazy," said Jay. "It's an idea. Which hit me while you were talking and I think it's huge."

I asked if he wanted to speak to Isabel again. "Gotta run," said Jay.

"Isn't he great?" Isabel enthused when I put down the phone. "I always feel as if I'm talking to this entertainment genius who has his finger on the pulse of—I don't know— power."

"He wants us to write with Nan," I said.

An accountant-cousin of Pete shared office space with an insurance agent in Truro Center who had a fax. Pete arranged its transmission with one phone call and picked it up for us, saying that the 90210 zip code on the letterhead had caused some excitement in the office.

My guess had been right: Jay's huge idea was a book with two points of view and two front covers. You'd pick it up and read The Isabel Krug Story from say, the pink side, then turn it over and upside down and read The Nan VanVleet

Story from the back, now the front, in, say, a pale green. Pages, too—half pink and half green, or a nice taupe, whatever. Two books for the price of one. Enemies working from each end toward the middle. And maybe there could be a third color, say a cool gray chapter, or white type reversed on black, where the voices come together and the reader gets wife and mistress face to face, eyeball to eyeball! Or feels their forgiveness! Forgiveness could work, too.

I said to Isabel, "Have you ever seen those rag dolls where one side is white, then you turn her upside down and her skirt inside-out and you have a black doll?"

Isabel stared distastefully at his crude sketch.

Pete, who had stayed to listen, asked, "Can he make you do this?"

I said, "I don't think so."

"But what if he says he won't do The Isabel Krug Story without The Nan VanVleet Story?" Isabel asked.

"Then you get anotha agent," said Pete.

Isabel said, "Easy for you to say."

I took the fax from her. "The Isabel Krug and Nan VanVleet stories as told to Harriet Mahoney and Ferris Porter."

Pete said, "I thought this Ferris guy was a good friend of yours."

Isabel answered without even looking up from her address book, "Harriet spurned him."

Pete said, "She did?"

"When we were in New York, right after her haircut? They had dinner together and went back to his apartment. Which wasn't the brightest idea she ever had."

"What happened?" he asked.

"What do you *think* happened?" said Isabel. "He took it as a green light, so of course he was disappointed when Harriet told him to put it away."

I said, "Not only is she telling it wrong, she's neglecting to say how Ferris joined us for breakfast the next morning—his idea—and there were no hard feelings. We came away from it friends."

Isabel said, "That's bullshit. Men can't stay friends."

"You and I are friends," Pete said to her.

"Because we never fucked!"

I said, "I barely even kissed Ferris."

"Same thing," said Isabel. "He wanted you and you didn't want him. Now you're paying for it."

I asked if she considered this crisis my fault.

"It's Ferris Porter's fault. He's punishing you." She handed me her telephone book, one squared-off fingernail pointing to Jay's three numbers.

I said, "You call him. He barely knows me."

We called from the sitting room, from the long flesh-colored satin couch where I had first spotted her the day I arrived. She took the phone onto her lap and hit the numbers slowly with a clenched knuckle.

Jay, naturally, was on another call. No, it wasn't advisable to hold. He had meetings all afternoon. He'd get back to us.

He did get back to us eventually, at nine-thirty P.M. our time from his car. With Isabel on the phone and me next to her on a portable extension, we said that we'd prefer to write our own book and not split the profits with Nan VanVleet or add two more names to the byline.

"Besides," I asked, "which cover would face out on the shelf?"

"Not an issue," said Jay.

I said, "How can that not be an issue—a book with two front covers and two authors?"

"Four authors," amended Isabel.

"We'll get you that in the contract—cover dominance."

"Yeah," said Isabel, "like every bookstore in the country will know which end goes up."

"You bet they will," said Jay, "because we'll get twenty-four copy dumps and four-color print ads with you above the title."

"Dumps?" I repeated.

"Floor displays. Maybe T-shirts."

I said, "Isn't it kind of gimmicky?"

Jay said, "Not even close."

"I want my own book," Isabel repeated.

"Iz?" said Jay. "Can I say what's on my mind here? You need this. Guy VanVleet died—I wrote this down somewhere—twenty-three months ago. The American public doesn't wake up in the morning and wonder, 'What happened to that cunt'—their word, not mine—'who was in his bed? Is she writing a book?' This angle is the difference between a sweet little kiss-and-tell book and a major crime study. This is big. I'm being honest with you."

"You used to say mine was big," Isabel said after a moment.

"This is bigger."

Isabel and I looked at each other. I said, "How do we know something else won't come along tomorrow that you'll like even better?"

"How do I know? Because this will be sold tomorrow."

Isabel said, "You mean to a publisher?"

"No question."

"Without a sample chapter and an outline?" I asked.

"Hey," he said, "this is Jay you're talkin' to."

Isabel tried once more for the record. "No chance you'd sell it with just my story?"

"I didn't say that."

"Meaning for a hell of a lot less?"

"The publicity alone—you and VanVleet side by side in armchairs. There isn't a talk show in the country that wouldn't soil its pants for you."

I said, "I'm not so sure VanVleet will like this idea any more than we do. I'm sure she wants her own book."

"The widow? She loves it. And she loves you two."

Isabel, her face more flushed than usual, said, "Of course she loves it! She never had a pencil in her hand and suddenly an agent calls out of the blue and offers her God knows what to write a book."

"No more than half," said Jay.

"Half," Isabel repeated. "Half of everything?"

"Look," said Jay, "We're getting you top billing and cover approval. We can't do anything less than half for her without her questioning our loyalty."

"I started it," Isabel yelled. "There wouldn't be any goddamn two-faced book if I hadn't been in every headline and in *People* magazine."

Jay said quietly, *"I started it."*

"I don't think you'll find Nan's ghostwriter too crazy about the idea. He's an academic," I said. "He won't want to be attached to anything commercial."

"I talked to him, too. He said sure he'd rather write his own book but it was my call."

Isabel and I looked at each other. She said into the phone, "Do we have a choice?"

"Look," said Jay, "Gotta run. I'm having drinks with

307

Barbra's people and the valet's here. You guys are the best. You're number one, so remember that. I'll call you tomorrow."

The line clicked. Isabel said, "No, you won't."

She and I rationalized late into the night, sitting on the kitchen floor, leaning against the refrigerator: Even with Nan's version bound onto ours, it would be two separate works. And let's be frank, we said, sipping Spanish champagne: Only one of the voices belonged to a headline-grabber, to a woman the *New York Post* called "a human magnet," to the only witness whose testimony was broadcast live on Court TV. Better than that, we'd make our half livelier, more colorful, more explicit.

And the surprises, I noted, were all in our half of the book: Costas was her stepfather! Guy paid for sex with trinkets!

Good. Let the wife/mistress juxtaposition get it published, but let our side of the story sell the books. We'd blow Nan out of the water. And you know what? we said, refilling our glasses: It made our job easier. Fewer pages to write to fill a book; twice as good in half the pages. Quality rather than quantity. And poor Nan. She needs something to live for. Imagine the humiliation of the trial: that terrible wire-service photo of her looking even more washed out than she was in person. And now with her twelve-step view of life, her empty house, her guilt.

And, I admitted, confiding in Isabel over the jars of peanut butter and jelly we'd broken out around midnight, Ferris wasn't that good a writer. I had wanted to like his work because he was nice and so constructive about mine, but really, to be utterly candid—something was missing.

"And now that he's Ferris the shmuck, why pretend you're a fan?"

I said, "He'll do a decent enough job with Nan's story, but I don't think he has a great future as a novelist."

"I wondered about that," said Isabel, "why someone with his own books to write would get involved with a dope like Nan."

I leaned into my answer, knowing how much she'd like it: "So he can fuck her."

Isabel beamed. "We know *that*. We knew she was interested from the moment she came to the table in her widow's weeds and asked if he had tenure."

"It seemed kind of sweet, two lost souls."

Isabel made another lumpy sandwich, cut it on the diagonal, and gave me half. "More like two sweet lost souls with the heart of Donald Trump."

I said, "Isn't it amazing what one little rejection does to a guy?"

Isabel widened her eyes above her full cheeks, chewing and swallowing strenuously until she could shout, "Are you kidding? Some men shoot perfect strangers and later they tell the cops, 'She gave me dis' funny look so I goes home and gets my piece and goes back to da' party ta' wipe that snooty look offa her face.' So why should it be any surprise that he wants to ruin your career?"

I said we couldn't blame Ferris for everything. Nan got the book idea into her head, then the ghostwriting idea, and where else would she turn but to Ferris?

"She could've called me and said, 'Mind if I throw in my two cents? I'd like to be interviewed for your book.'"

I said I disagreed. She'd be just the person to undertake a

book so blithely because she didn't live in the real world and didn't understand what it takes.

Isabel laughed and said, "Not like us."

I said, "You know, if it weren't coming out of our pockets, I'd be happy for him. Here he is fifty-four and all alone and suddenly he becomes the answer to a lonely woman's prayers."

"I know. I saw it happening and I thought, Good, this will give Nan something to do besides trailing after me reciting prayers. She'll get a respectable companion, someone who won't cheat on her and bring women home to her own bed. And *he* gets a girlfriend who thinks he's Will Shakespeare."

I wondered aloud if Ferris would write himself into Nan's half of the book as the happy ending.

"Step thirteen," said Isabel, licking jelly off the inside of her arm.

28

WE CELEBRATE

JAY HAD EXAGGERATED slightly. *GUY AND I* didn't sell the next day—he needed time to write his one-page proposal—but seventy-two hours later for 1.2 million dollars to Argonaut Books, which wasn't even the highest bidder. Barbra Streisand gobbled up the movie rights sight unseen. Her people said she'd wait until she had a finished screenplay before announcing whether she'd play the wife or the mistress.

I didn't participate in the negotiations. Isabel fielded the calls in her bedroom, talking to Jay after every round, reassuring me that the ghostwriter-credential thing was working itself out. At 750 thousand dollars Jay started slipping other demands onto the bargaining table: a six-figure advertising budget, best-seller bonuses, first-class airline tickets to tour destinations; author photos by Annie Leibovitz; video coaching; group therapy.

Ultimately, Argonaut was Isabel's choice for reasons that seemed a little high-minded for her, especially since Condor Publishing was willing to pay more. After the bids reached 1 million dollars, Isabel said it was no longer an issue of money; as long as they were eating out of her hand, she wanted something else. She insisted on talking privately to the dueling editors. What it came down to, she said publicly, was simply liking the woman at Argonaut more. Privately, she assured me that the ghostwriter question was locked in firm, that not everybody had been totally comfortable with her choice of me, but not to worry.

Jay argued that the editor's personality, character, whatever, was worth squat when it came to pushing the book, but, hey, he was only the agent with a thousand home runs to his name. Finally he said, "It's your call, Krug," because it was; Nan didn't know she had a voice in any of it. Jay called Greenwich after every round, but rushed off the phone while Ferris crunched the numbers.

The Costas who heard "1.2 million dollars" was no one I had seen before. He crossed himself; he threw his fists into the air; he let out a sound that would have pierced twice the soundproofing. He danced himself around in a circle, then pirouetted Isabel, then me. He led us in a line dance, stomping and prancing like a father of the bride.

She said, "What? I never had a payday before?"

"One point two million," he yelled. "For a fucking *book!*"

He threw himself face-up onto Isabel's bed, where he bicycled his legs then jumped back to his feet with the spring of a Russian acrobat.

I said, "I guess he doesn't think it's such a terrible idea now."

"Why so much? I never dreamed of so much for a book by Isabel."

"You didn't dream of it because you're cynical. You had no faith in me," said Isabel, "and you certainly had no feel for what the American public wants to read."

"Five publishers wanted it," I said. "There was a bidding war."

"Un-be-liev-able!" he bellowed.

"Kiss my ass," said Isabel. "You thought it was a pipe dream. Good thing I didn't listen to you."

He called for a celebration—for ouzo and *mizethes* and *patriotes* to dance with. It was Friday, almost Friday night! Let's drive to a town and find a Greek restaurant!

I said, "Can we invite Pete?"

"Anyone!" he yelled. "The whole town. Do we have food for a party? And champagne?"

Isabel asked who we'd invite. We didn't know anyone except Pete and his mother and his cousin the mechanic.

I said, "Wouldn't it be a party with just the four of us?"

Costas flung his arms ceilingward again. "Four is enough! Four can dance and drink and celebrate."

"Harriet's not cooking tonight," said Isabel. "We'll get food delivered. Pete will know where to call."

I said I'd get on that. You guys get dressed. Chill the champagne! Polish the crystal! Sort the C.D.s! Pete and I would be back with the closest thing P-town had to grape leaves.

Costas said, "No! I get the food. How would you know
what to get?"

Isabel said, "You'll tell them. What's the big deal?"

"He's not your errand boy! You dispatch him for every little
whim like he was a messenger with a bicycle."

Isabel said, "Then go! Shut up and go. I don't want to
argue."

Costas announced that he would buy the ingredients at the
A&P and would drive himself there for road practice. He
knew they had feta and bottled grape leaves, eggplant and
chicken livers, phyllo dough in the freezer, fresh spinach in
bags, pita and calamata olives.

Isabel said, "It's our celebration. I don't see why you're
dictating the food. I'd get pizza if it was up to me. Or fried
clams. Why should you decide what the food will be at our
celebration? And forget driving. Harriet's taking you." Her
voice changed so the next word was not a challenge but a
decision: "Oysters! We'll get a couple of hundred oysters and
have Pete open them and we'll slurp them down with
champagne and cocktail sauce until we can't eat any more.
What time does the fish market stay open till?"

"Six?" I guessed.

"I'll call them. What'll we get? Two dozen apiece? Four?"

I didn't have the heart to tell her I had never eaten a raw
oyster. I was about to say, "Lobsters are festive," when Isabel
added, "Pete knows how to shuck them, so make sure he's
around." She walked over to her bedroom intercom and
hesitated.

I said, "Try the cellar. He's sanding."

He answered her buzz with his usual, "Yup?"

"Petie, can you come to an oyster party tonight?"

ISABEL'S BED

"Where?"

"Here. Upstairs. It's a celebration for the book."

"Who's coming?"

"Everyone," said Isabel. "You, me, Costas, Harriet."

"Is everything settled?" he asked.

"With the book? You bet. They're paying us a fortune. It just happened. Like ten minutes ago."

"Good," he said. "I was gettin' worried. I hadn't heard anything since a couple of the biddas dropped out."

"We're having oysters."

"You told me."

"Can you come?"

He laughed. "You mean can I come and bring my oysta knife and my glove?"

"Can you?"

"What time?"

"As soon as Harriet and Costas come back from the fish market."

Pete said, "I could've gone with Harriet."

I knew Isabel would have pursued the topic of Harriet and Pete on an outing with gusto if I weren't standing there listening.

"Oh," she said, "Well, Costas wants some fresh air, and he wants to help out. Besides you've got the hardest job ahead of you."

She looked at me and said to Pete, "Don't think we're inviting you because you can open an oyster in three seconds. You were first on our guest list when we were talking about moussaka."

"I'm touched," said Pete.

"Grab a couple of bottles of champagne while you're

there," said Isabel. "And could you check the fluted glasses? I think they're clean enough."

"That's great news about your book," said Pete. "Is Harriet happy?"

Isabel turned to inspect me for a few seconds before answering. "Something's doing it," she finally said.

As we drove toward Wellfleet on Route 6, Costas said, "Don't you find it peculiar that someone whose job it was to shop for other people sends everyone else to do her bidding, especially when it comes to food?" We had a twelve-minute drive to Wellfleet, where the fishmonger had agreed after Isabel had cajoled—she'd autograph a book for him as soon as it came out—to stick around until her people got there.

I said, "You volunteered. Besides, you can't shop around here if you don't drive."

"I'm going to change that," said Costas. "I used to drive. I still know how to. I just don't have my license. I think I'd enjoy driving when the weather is warm on a more consistent basis."

I said, "I'm looking forward to the warm weather, too."

He filled up the car and smelled faintly of turpentine and wet wool. I had had to reach around his ankles to find the lever that made the seat slide back, and I had to give his seat belt the final click into its holster. His gray wool cap grazed the ceiling. "Does that mean you expect to be here when the weather turns warm?" he asked blandly, as if he were only mildly interested in the question of my tenure.

I said, "It's spring now. I hope it'll be warm in a month or so."

"How long does it take to write a book like this?"

"A year. Just like Isabel arranged." *As if you didn't know.*

We passed Moby Dick's, which Costas noted had a broiled fisherman's platter that he missed when the season ended. He also said, "You must be very happy for Isabel."

I said, "I'm happy for me, too."

"Of course you would be." He waited another minute before he asked, "How much will she be paying you for the actual ghostwriting?"

I said, "Have you discussed this with Isabel?"

"I'm asking you," he said. "I don't think it's out of line to ask you when I'm working out the terms of your stipend and your insurance."

I said, "I don't get paid for the writing—not like an hourly wage. I get a percentage of whatever the book makes."

"Which is?"

I hadn't typed contracts for Rittenberg, Egan & Galazka's copyright division for nothing. "Forty percent." I checked sideways to see his reaction. It wasn't dark yet, so I could see him flinch. He asked, "Is there a written agreement between you and Isabel?"

"A letter."

"Is this letter signed by all parties?"

"I'd have to look it up."

"Was it notarized?"

I repeated that I'd have to look it up.

"I'd like to see it," he said. He paused. "To verify your employment for the insurance carrier."

I said, "I'll check my files."

"I don't think Isabel knew how much money she'd be dividing up when she calculated your share."

ELINOR LIPMAN

I asked lightly if he had volunteered to accompany me so he could grill me about the financial arrangement.

He said, with an intensity that sprang from nothing except his acting ability, "No, Harriet. I wanted to be alone with you."

I said, "I don't think so."

He smiled. "You're right."

Drops of freezing rain had begun to fall. I switched on the wipers and counted six long seconds between intermittent wipes. I said, "What's the point of saying something like that?"

He shrugged. "To get a reaction. To see if you're as easy to tease as you were when you arrived or if Isabel has toughened you."

When I didn't answer he said, "Isabel brought you here and took you under her wing." He looked out the passenger window. "Against my wishes. I don't like living with strangers."

I said, "You hired Pete."

"Pete is different. Pete is a necessity here. We couldn't take care of this house ourselves, and we couldn't function without a car. Besides, he lives downstairs and isn't part of the family." He turned toward me, then reached over to pat my cheek. "Don't look so stricken. I like you now."

I jerked my face out of reach. Costas looked out the passenger window again. After a silence he said, "Servants are one thing. They don't think that what passes between a husband and wife is their business."

I stopped at the red light and put on my blinker.

"You'll find me that letter of agreement between you and Isabel?" he asked.

318

I didn't answer, pretending that driving through sleet took all my attention.

"Will you?"

I said, "Look. This is getting very boring. If you don't like it, take it up with Isabel. It's her book. Hers and Nan's. She must've kept a copy of the letter."

"Nan?" said Costas.

"VanVleet."

Costas closed his eyes and said, "I have no idea what you're talking about."

"The book. Nan's going to write half of it. That was the new angle that got us so much money."

Costas spit out, *"Putana!"*

I said, "I thought you knew. We've been talking about it for days. Our agent is licking his chops over signing both sides of the story."

"How can she write a book?"

"Same way Isabel can—with a ghostwriter."

"Idiot," he muttered. "Husband-killer."

Before reaching Main Street he yelled, "Here. Pull over." I swerved into the parking lot of a red clapboard mini-mall.

I asked, "What for?"

He said, "We're here. You go around back behind the stores. Ring the bell."

I craned my neck and could see signs over doors for ice cream, needlepoint, and travel. I said, squinting into the sleet, "I thought the Wellfleet Lobster Company was behind Town Hall, off the municipal lot."

"Lobster Company?" Costas repeated as if he'd never pronounced those syllables within my earshot. "I meant the bakery."

I turned on my high beams and repeated, "Bakery?"

"Not the actual bakery. The apartment of the bakery owner, a Mrs. Betses. She does special orders in the off-season."

I said, pulling the emergency brake a tad higher, "How stupid do you think I am?"

Costas tsked, then said sadly, "I don't know why you mistrust me so."

I put the car in gear and inched past the closed storefronts. "What apartment?" I demanded. "There's no apartment here."

"It's around the back."

I said, "For some reason, you're trying to get me out of the car, which leads me to believe you're going to dump me here and take off."

"Without a valid driver's license?"

"Probably."

"Okay," he said. "I'll confess. I was arranging for some Greek food without getting it approved for the party menu. That's why I insisted I accompany you to town. So I could indulge myself. Just ask for Mrs. Betses. I called her and she's selling me a pan of *spanikopita* for the party. Tell her you're with me. You have money, right?"

I said, "You get it. I don't know any Mrs. Betses and I don't see any bakery."

"I'm an old man," said Costas, "and you're my employee. I believe it's your duty to save me a walk across an icy parking lot."

"No."

Costas replied, after a long but surprisingly meek stare into the windshield wipers, "Well, in that case, I'd better go myself."

"Hurry up. The fish market guy is staying open for us."

Costas said, "Could you drive over and get the oysters? I'll be here waiting when you finish." He looked at his watch. "Say, fifteen minutes?" He stepped out of the car and closed his door respectfully, like a man who had lost an argument with someone holding a gun.

I pulled away, watching him in the rearview mirror. He saw me and waved solemnly. I followed Pete's directions to the Wellfleet Lobster Company, where the owner told me he knew of no apartments behind the Briar Lane shops and no baker named Mrs. Betses. I bought a bushel of local oysters, four lemons, and a bottle of cocktail sauce. I got back into the car and asked myself, Now what?

I decided I could turn left out of the parking lot and go home solo, or turn right to keep an appointment with a liar who had probably spent these fifteen minutes hatching a new plot to overpower me at the wheel or, at the very least, strand me in Wellfleet.

I buckled my seat belt and placed my hands squarely on the steering wheel at ten and at two o'clock. I put on my left blinker, and after a minute's debate with the internal spokespersons for the new and old Harriets, followed through—a hard left turn away from Costas, his bogus bakery, and a grudge I found to be wearing thin.

The lumpy bag of oysters was upright on the passenger seat, friendly and benign, smelling like the air in Truro. I turned on the radio and heard that Chelsea Clinton liked her school and was having both new friends and old ones to a sleepover at the White House. I pressed the *seek* button and found music. I followed Main Street until stores and galleries ended and I could hear the highway. In a minute, I was on Route 6,

familiar ground after the locked-up streets of Wellfleet. As I
approached the turn-off that could lead back to where I'd
abandoned Costas, my foot came off the accelerator for a
second, but I put it back and shifted into fifth. I scolded myself
for feeling guilty—for the nice-girl apology rehearsing in my
brain—and drove the oysters home.

29

THE PARTY

 I HEARD MUSIC in every
room, which I didn't even
know was possible in the big
house. A woman singing, then a man, both vaguely familiar
tunes with full orchestral back-up and intermittent guttural
purrs: the Broadway cast album of *Cats*. I struggled the oysters
up the circular stairs to the kitchen, where Pete was drying
champagne glasses with a paper towel. Transferring the bags
to him I said, "I may be in deep trouble."

"You pushed him out of the car?" Isabel squealed when I
explained why I had returned alone. She had come to the

kitchen, first one in her party clothes, a bronze sequined sleeveless shell over cheetah-print chiffon palazzo pants.

I said no I didn't push him; how would I have pushed Costas out of the front seat unless he was unconscious and child-size? I said he exited of his own free will—well, at my suggestion that he perform this counterfeit errand himself—then I burned some rubber.

Isabel wasn't clear. "How did you get the oysters then?"

"I bought them. I left him at the closed shops and came home without him."

"What was she supposed to do?" Pete asked, "Chauffeur him around like he was hahmless?"

"He'll call," said Isabel, who suggested I set just three places at the half-moon table, no, the dining room.

"You don't think he'll be back?" I asked.

Isabel was digging in a drawer for silverware, but stopped the clanking to answer. "Not in any big hurry. He has to punish us. A couple of hours. Just as we're about to go look for him, he'll show up in a taxi. If they have taxis around here." She walked to the table and handed me the object of her search, cocktail forks. "He'll get dropped off at the bottom of the road in a couple of hours so he can trudge up the hill himself and make it look like he walked back from Wellfleet."

I said, "He wasn't wearing a winter jacket."

"Oh, excuse me," said Isabel. "Do you also worry what prisoners are wearing when they break out of jail?" She dumped half the oysters with a loud clatter into the sink and told me to relax. She ran water over them and pronounced them pretty clean. Pete said we had to scrub them anyway.

I said I'd like to take a quick shower and change if they could spare me. Isabel followed me out of the kitchen and down two steps to whisper that I should dress up—did I need to borrow anything?—and put some makeup on. And not to worry. Costas would sulk but she'd make him apologize. And what the hell happened in the car that made him want to get rid of me?

"Nothing! He was grilling me about the book, about how much I'd get in the deal after you and Nan got yours."

"Nan?" Isabel repeated sharply. "I never said anything about Nan."

"Well, I did."

Isabel sat down on the top step and smoothed the cheetah chiffon around her knees. "You know how he is about Nan," she said.

I said, "No, I guess I don't know."

"He hates her guts."

"Because she was trying to kill you when she shot Guy?"

Isabel shook her head. "That's not the kind of thing that fazes Costas."

Pete yelled from the kitchen, "I got a dozen open if you want to staht. They're beauties."

Isabel yelled back, "Be right there. You start."

"He hates her guts for another reason?" I asked.

Isabel said, "She humiliated him! Here he is this big-name artist—people don't forget so fast—and she gets on the witness stand and whines, 'Costas who? I don't know anyone by that name.' Like she hadn't paid him twenty-five grand for the two pieces and thrown a party to show them off."

Pete came out of the kitchen, wearing a glove on one hand and offering a shucked oyster. Isabel parted her lips like a baby bird in the nest, and he tipped the shell into her waiting mouth. She closed her eyes and grunted. "The best."

"What're you guys whispering about out here?"

"Costas," I said.

Pete looked at his watch and said, "He'll probably hitch home."

"Pity the good Samaritan who picks him up," I said.

Pete said, "I have to say, I don't like driving with him eitha."

I gestured, palm up, in his direction and said to Isabel, "Even Pete doesn't trust him; even Pete who's his lifeline to the supermarket and the art supply store. He told me himself tonight that Pete was a necessity, not like a ghostwriter."

Isabel said, "He's a little jealous of you. Men don't have friendships like women do."

"I have lots of friends," said Pete.

"We're a different generation," Isabel said. "We have friends."

"My fatha had friends."

"Sure he did. He was a fisherman. They hang around together. People write books about men going off in boats."

Pete and I traded smiles over Isabel's literary insight. She said, "Are we going to sit here all night or are we going to open the champagne and eat oysters?"

I said I was going to get into my party clothes. Pete said he had what looked like a thousand oysters to open. How many people had I thought we were feeding?

At the bottom of the stairs, I turned around. Isabel was sitting on the top step, staring into space, one hand holding each instep. I wanted to say, "Even if the book falls through and it means moving to a one-room apartment in New Jersey and working as a manicurist again I'd get out of here." I called up, "Are you worried?"

She came to and said, "Not about him."

"About you?"

"About you," she said.

I locked my bedroom door and my bathroom door. Before undressing I adjusted the shower jets and extinguished my bathroom lights so any vengeful peeper skulking in the bushes would not see me naked. I showered in the dark and dried myself back in a room with solid walls. My closet offered one choice, one best dress, bought three years ago for the fifth anniversary party of A Decent Bagel. It was black velvet, long-sleeved and scoop-necked, a party dress from Blooming-dale's with a waist and a full skirt. I said nah; I'd never pull this off, couldn't wear this unself-consciously to a three-person party.

The intercom buzzed: Isabel asking what was taking me so long. I said I had blown-dry my hair correctly and was deciding what to wear.

"Do you have something attractive?"

I said, "I was thinking of a skirt and sweater."

"No," she said. "You dress up, and if you don't have something dressy, I'll bring you something of mine."

I said, "I do have something dressy, but it seems too much."

"I'm all dressed up," she said, "and Pete went to put on a tie and jacket now that he's got the oysters opened. You should see them. He cracked some ice and it looks like a raw bar in here." She paused then said, "Hear that? I changed discs. It's Luther Vandross."

I said okay. I'd be up in a few minutes.

"Do you have shoes, too?" she asked.

I said yes. Black suede pumps.

She said, newly animated, "I have some clip-ons for shoes—floppy black flowers or rhinestone buckles."

I said, "No thanks."

She said, "Need a real lipstick?"

I said again, "No, thanks. Any calls?"

"Forget about Costas," she said. "He's laying low so you'll worry. He's probably drinking wine and eating rack of lamb somewhere, hoping he's ruining our party."

I said okay, I'd make it snappy; I'd be up as soon as I got into my dress. I repeated after her: Costas wouldn't have hesitated to leave *me* stranded in a strange town. He got what he deserved, a long walk home in the freezing rain. Didn't he?

At 10 we sent Pete out in his truck to cover the route between the mini-mall and Corn Hill. At 10:45, after he'd returned without a sighting, we called Truro Police.

I explained: I had left him at the shops on Briar Lane at approximately 6 P.M. and no one had heard from him since.

I agreed: it was hardly a long time for a grown man to be away from home—

No, he wasn't ill or disabled. A painter. No, an artist.

Usually one or two glasses of wine with dinner.

Not his wife. I was an employee of his household.

No, he doesn't have a girlfriend to the best of my knowledge.

No, he never left the house except to walk on the beach. Yes, we checked his room and every other one in the house, too.

The officer said, "I'll tell you what. I'll put out a broadcast: sixty-five-year-old man, six feet tall, wearing a corduroy sports jacket over painter's overalls, answers to the name— could you spell that, please—may be disoriented, lost in Wellfleet Center."

I said, "Thanks a lot." I also said, "He can be a little nasty."

"Dangerous?" he asked. "Armed?"

"Not armed," I said, "but he can be unbelievably rude."

The officer sighed as if "rude" had been one silly adjective too far; as if I didn't appreciate that only in the off-season could he humor the family of a guy who's run off to pout.

"Anything else we should know about him?"

"Like what?"

"What's his wife's name?"

"Isabel."

"Kids?"

I said no kids.

"And your name?"

I hesitated and said, "He's going to be furious with me. I'm the one who dropped him off there. I wouldn't mention my name."

"Which is?" he asked impatiently.

"Harriet Mahoney."

"Your position, Ms. Mahoney, at Mr. Diamond Topless's house?"

"His wife's collaborator," I said without thinking how that sounded to a guy in law enforcement.

30

SLEEPLESS NIGHT

 ISABEL WAS THE least concerned. She said Costas was capable of disappearing for a month if he thought it would make a point. Happily, Officer Medeiros had gone to high school with Pete's middle sister, so he didn't ask questions that implied he viewed us as a love triangle of strange New Yorkers.

We showed him Costas's studio/bedroom—my first view of it ever. It was huge and dark. We turned on his battalion of floodlights, and I saw that for all his talk about northern light, he had hung sheeting across his windows. By the number of canvases set on easels it might have been the workplace of six artists. There were canvases hung on nails from stretchers; canvases set on cinderblocks leaning on walls. Several cans from the brand of coffee I had introduced held brushes. The tubes of paint were as big as midget salamis.

"Is this guy busy or what?" said Officer Medeiros. He picked up the corner of a shroud that covered a refrigerator-sized object—Costas's large-format, custom Polaroid. "He takes pictures of his paintings when he's done?" the officer asked.

Isabel said, "Actually, he used to paint on top of Polaroids, but he doesn't anymore except by special request."

"You can do that?"

"It depends what you call it," said Isabel. "He got into hot water over it, so now he doesn't do it anymore."

Officer Medeiros flipped open his notebook. It seemed to be the first fact he wanted to record. "What kind of hot water?" he asked.

"Not that kind of trouble. Artistic trouble. Museums took his paintings down."

"So what's he doing now?" asked the officer, taking in the paintings with a sweep of his hand. "How come they still look like photographs."

Isabel said, "See the slide projector? He projects a slide onto a canvas and paints what he sees."

The officer made a long notation. I said, "I don't think his paintings have anything to do with his being missing."

"He's late," said Isabel, "not missing."

"Does he make a living at this?" asked the officer.

Isabel said, "He built this house."

"When did he get into trouble with his painting?"

331

"Not recently," said Isabel. "Maybe ten years? He was considered one of the founders of the movement before they made the stink."

"Who's 'they'?"

"Some big art critic—MacDonald? MacDonnell? O'Connell?—in *Artforum,* a magazine. Then it got picked up by the newspapers."

"Was it true?"

"Sure it was true."

"Was he ruined by it?"

"People still buy his paintings. They like the finished product so they're not finicky about how he gets there."

Pete said, "He doesn't sell to collectors anymore."

Isabel said, "Well, not to real collectors."

The paintings were all of vegetables, one variety per canvas. I recognized kohlrabi, oyster mushrooms, tomatillos, radicchio, fennel, bok choy. Each looked like a different close-up of the produce department at an upscale supermarket.

Officer Medeiros asked, "How come they're all alike?"

Isabel said they weren't. See? In this one the vegetables were a purplish-red, in this one the fennel had these feathery wisps that looked like dill, in this one, they were small green balls with papery skin like Japanese lanterns.

"Was he working on all of them at once?" I asked Isabel.

"Sure," she said. "Nothing wrong with that."

Pete surveyed all the paintings and said quietly, "They're signed and dated."

"They still look like photographs," said the policeman.

"Of course, they do," said Isabel. "That's his genius."

I said, "It's called photo realism."

"He's not using that term anymore because people have

made fun of the 'photo' part since the trouble. With this new series he's going to call himself a New Precisionist."

I said, "They're pretty darn good."

"What's he gonna to do with them now?" asked the policeman.

"Have a show," said Isabel.

I said, "I didn't know that."

"In Wellfleet."

"Which gallery?" asked Officer Medeiros, writing.

Isabel thought hard. "It's two last names," she said finally. "Two guys own it."

"Stern-Appel?" asked the officer.

"That's it," said Isabel. "They've been selling his stuff since he's been here. They don't care what the New York art mafia says."

"Maybe he's with them now," I said.

"Not open," said Officer Medeiros. "They come down Memorial Day weekend."

"Nothing's open!" said Isabel. "You can't even go out for a meal around here unless it's June the first."

"So where could he be?" I asked the group at large.

"With friends?" said the officer.

Isabel said, "I wish."

Pete said, "My guess is he hitched somewhere, maybe P-town, then he'll hitch back here when he thinks we're all asleep."

The officer made another tour of the studio, taking notes, glancing at the magazine clippings push-pinned everywhere, tapping smears of paint on a glass-topped table. "How long did it take him to paint all of these?" he asked.

Isabel said, "I have no idea."

I said, "Yes, you do. The first time I watched 'Joy' with you he said he was doing fruit in a bowl, so this had to come after that."

"Oh, right," she said. "That was about a month ago."

"Isn't that kinda fast?" asked the officer.

Isabel said, "You can be good and fast at the same time."

"Whew," he said, and wrote something down.

"Well, look," said Isabel, "he used to get a fortune for a painting before he was disgraced, and now he gets five figures tops. You have to sell a lot to make a go of it. Besides, there's nothing wrong with painting fast."

Officer Medeiros closed his notebook and slipped it into his shirt pocket. "I'm gonna drive around," he said, "check out the open places. Put in a call to Provincetown. Nothing official."

I said, "Will you call the hospitals?"

"Hospi*tal*," said Isabel.

"Dispatch already did," he answered.

The officer asked if Costas had identification on him. Isabel said yes—his wallet and credit cards; he had been on his way to buy oysters.

We walked him out through the garage. He asked why we were all dressed up. Isabel said, "I sold my life's story today for a good chunk of money and we were celebrating."

"Mind if I ask how much money?"

Isabel asked, "Is that an official question or are you being nosy?"

"Official," said Medeiros.

"Seven figures," said Isabel.

He reached inside his jacket and took out his notebook again. "Who else knows about this?"

"Just us," said Isabel, "and the publisher."

Pete said, "What are you thinkin'? Someone knew Isabel got a windfall today and kidnapped her husband for ransom?"

"It's been done," he said.

Isabel patted the officer's arm. "Don't you worry your hunky head about that. Anyone who knew us would know I'd never pay a penny to get him back." She leaned into him to confide, "Most of the time, we can't stand each other."

I said, shivering in the cold, not hiding my exasperation, "I drove him to Wellfleet. I left him in the parking lot because he was making up lies about a bakery being there. He was trying to get me out of the car so he could drive off with it. This can't be anything like a kidnapping. He's just lost. Or maybe he fell on the ice and broke his hip."

"I didn't even want them to call you," said Isabel.

"Tell me again why he was threatening to drive off and leave you there."

I repeated for the third time that night, "He wasn't threatening. He was lying about there being a bakery and I figured, why would he be trying to send me around to the back of the building for a bogus reason if he wasn't trying to pull a fast one. I refused to get out, so *he* did and I drove away."

"Okay," said the officer, climbing into his front seat. "I'm sure we've got a family squabble here and there's been no foul play. My guess is he's fine, nursing a beer somewhere and taking his time because he's angry."

"Sulking," Isabel supplied.

"That's what I think," said Pete. With two hands he closed the patrol car door carefully and offered a starched salute. Medeiros rolled down his window a few inches and beckoned to him. They whispered back and forth. Pete shook his head

ELINOR LIPMAN

with some emphasis, the cop nodded a thank-you and rolled up the window.

When he backed out of the driveway, we asked Pete what that last exchange was all about.

"He asked if I have relations with Isabel."

Isabel laughed. "I love that word *relations*." She slipped an arm through each of ours and said, "He was cute but he watches too many cop shows."

At my door Pete said, "This may be outta line but I don't think you should sleep in your room tonight."

I said, "You think he's coming back for me?"

"No way," he said—too quickly to be convincing.

"You think it's out of the question?"

"I think it's possible that if he came back in the middle of the night he'd try to scare you."

"The good news being you don't think he's unconscious by the side of the road?"

"No chance," said Pete.

"Even in this weather?"

"Look: You left him in the middle of town. He said, 'Screw them. I'm gonna spend the night at a motel.'"

"Except for the few minutes when he pops in on me?"

"I'm playing it safe, that's all."

I said, "So where did you have in mind?"

"My room. There's no way he'd pull any stunt down there."

I asked if there was enough room.

"I'll sleep on the floor and you can have my bed."

I said, "I wouldn't take your bed. I have a sleeping bag."

He said, "If you're my guest, you get the bed."

* * *
336

He was waiting for me outside his door, holding two glasses of champagne. June's beanbag had been moved into the hallway. He said, "You changed."

I said, "Just into something comfortable." I didn't confess I had done the kind of primping a woman does when she thinks a man might be seeing her body sometime in the course of the night: a quick shave here and there, hand cream to the legs, a swipe of nail polish remover to the toes which hadn't had a touch-up since Kenny told me about Amy. I had brushed my teeth, packed my toothbrush, remembered my hair brush, dabbed a dot of eau de toilette behind each earlobe. After changing into my most presentable underwear and most flattering jeans, I had studied the effect of one, two, then three unbuttoned buttons on my cardigan.

Pete asked if I was still worried; did I think the sleeping arrangement was overkill? Was he acting paranoid about Costas? Because he hadn't meant to scare me. Costas was all bluff, a lot of noise, a big baby.

I said no, spending the night in his room felt like the right decision.

He checked his watch. He asked what I'd like to do now. Unless midnight wasn't too early to turn in.

"Want to dance?"

Pete looked down and said, "Juno, you keep Harriet company while I put on some music." June followed him to the bottom of the stairs, where I heard him say, "Stay. I'll be right back." In a minute I heard the applause of a live concert, then guitar music, then the opening phrase of "Sweet Baby James."

He jogged back downstairs. I said, "I love James Taylor." We moved the card table to a corner, and the chairs in front of the ocean-facing window. Pete slid the dimmer switch to low.

The first song ended before we had time to settle against one another. We sat out the next one—too fast for the dance we were counting on—sipping champagne and looking out at the water and Provincetown. Before the next song began, he smiled slyly. He took me in his arms, in position, waiting for the first notes as if we were contestants in a ballroom competition. The guitar played a few chords and the audience cheered in recognition: "Handy Man." We moved slowly to the music. I said, "I bet you play this for all the girls."

He pulled his arm tighter around me and said, "It would only make sense to someone who knew my job description."

"Like Isabel?"

"I don't dance with Isabel."

James was singing in his clear voice about one man causing heartbreak that a better man would repair.

I moved my left hand up to hold the back of his neck.

"I saw him once at the A&P," said Pete.

"Who?"

"James Tayla. He was in the regula line with just a newspapa and a bag of dry dog food. I told him to go ahead of me."

"What did he say?"

"He said thanks."

"When was this?"

He murmured some year or season into my hair.

"Did he look sad?" I asked. "He always struck me as a sad man."

"I hear he's fine now," Pete said in a hoarse whisper. He moved his lips to my forehead, my cheeks, my jawbone. "Nice of you," I whispered back, unsure if I meant his courtesy at the A&P, or his body against mine, or every deed he'd ever done. We danced in a clench, barely moving, until the music stopped. June stirred and went back to sleep. Pete murmured that it was a two-disc album. Should he . . . ?

His eyes had that blurry, anxious look of hormones crashing over him. I said, "Later."

Before the fact, I had imagined I would request darkness for undressing, and explain that a woman's body after a certain age, unless she is an exercise fanatic, does not conform to the Hollywood/*Sports Illustrated*/teenage firm-flesh ideal that American men hold all women to. A younger partner such as Pete could slip in beside me, dressed or undressed, and we would proceed under the covers with the emphasis on the sense of touch rather than sight.

But then it happened, the meltdown. We fell onto his bed and I forgot my guidelines and my self-consciousness. Pete didn't recoil at the sight of anything. He didn't run his hands down my sides and frown at my hips, didn't make disparaging remarks or trace any blue veins with a reluctant finger. If anything, he stopped for a few seconds when I was out of my clothes and took the kind of breath that could only be interpreted as appreciation. We weren't quiet or still. When he murmured about condoms and dragged himself into the bathroom, I turned on his reading lamp for extra brightness so I could see his body coming and going—thirty-six years old with muscles in his tush and fine lines around his eyes from squinting into sun. He returned with the little foil package and said, his hands shaky as he tore it open, "I bought these special. They're brand-new."

ELINOR LIPMAN

I laughed. "As opposed to used?" I put my hands on his waist and pulled him toward me.

He breathed from above, "You used to be so quiet and well-behaved."

The old Harriet from a great distance wondered who this woman was in Pete's bed and where her aptitude came from. The new Harriet asked, "How many did you buy?"

31
MONDAY MORNING

COSTAS CALLED ISABEL the next day from Worcester, Mass. Except for saying he'd arrived there by bus, he remained vague and almost inarticulate. She knocked on my door—I had told her I was writing our introduction today and couldn't be disturbed for anything short of police matters—and announced in passing, "We can call off the dogs. He turned up in Worcester."

I jumped up from my blank page to bring her inside for questioning. "Did he say he was hurt or furious or anything?"

Isabel said, heading straight for my typewriter, "He thinks I don't remember he has cousins there."

"What did he say exactly?"

"This is how he sounded: 'Who is this?' So I said, 'It's Isabel!' and he repeated my name like it didn't register. I said, 'Where are you?' and he hesitated as if he were looking around for a street sign and said, 'Worcester?'—pronouncing it like he'd never heard of it and like his cousins didn't own half the city. I said, 'Are you all right?' and he said, 'I think so.' I asked how he got there and he said, 'I don't know—'"

I interrupted, annoyed, to ask why she wasn't worried. I said, "Maybe he *is* hurt. Maybe he had a stroke and he's aphasic."

Isabel fixed me with her disappointed-mentor's stare. "You don't see what he's doing?"

Before I could think she yelled, "He's pretending to have amnesia!"

"How do you know he's pretending?"

"People in real life don't get amnesia! Did you ever know anyone with amnesia who wasn't on a soap opera? And always in bus terminals. He's fine! He's staying at Nicky's house, eating their imported feta and thinking I fell for this."

"Maybe you should call there and talk to these cousins and find out if he's really okay."

Isabel said, "If you think they're going to tell me anything, then you don't know Greek men."

"If he was pretending to have amnesia, how did he explain knowing the number here?"

"I didn't ask. My reaction was, fine, you've got amnesia. Maybe someone will hit you over the head with a two-by-four and you'll get your memory back."

I said, "Did you laugh?"

"I was so cool. I said calmly, 'Your name is Costas Dimantopoulos. You're sixty-five years old and a Greek-

American. You're an artist and I'm your wife.' Y'know what he said? 'What kind of artist?' I said, 'A New Precisionist. And I think your new series is dynamite.'

"He said—trying to sound out of it—'You can give it to my gallery to sell. If I have a gallery.' I said, 'Of course you do. You're a big name. They'll be thrilled.' He asked, 'What are you going to tell them?' I said, 'About what?' He said, 'My condition. Maybe you shouldn't tell them I have amnesia'— notice how he knows his own diagnosis—'Maybe you should tell them I'm missing.' I said, 'That's fine. Or dead? How about dead? Dead painters' prices usually skyrocket.' I was sure he'd give up the act then but he said, 'They're calling my bus. I have to go.' I said, 'Have a nice trip. Should I call you Costas or do you have a new identity?' He said, 'I'll phone this number in a couple of days." I said, 'Ask for Isabel. I'm your wife. Oh, and you better not lose the number; it's unlisted.' Then he throws in, 'There are slides of the new paintings in a manila envelope on my desk.'"

I said, "And you went along with it?"

"With a straight face!" Again she imitated his slack-jawed monotone: "'I woke up on a bus and I had to buy a newspaper to find out what year it was.' That came directly from 'Joy' when Dean Townsend had amnesia for a couple of months. He couldn't just turn to the guy in the next seat and say, 'Hey buddy, can you tell me today's date?', couldn't just take himself to a police station and say, 'I lost my memory. Has anyone reported me missing?' He had to travel around for six months with all the other hobos. I wouldn't be surprised if Costas stuck to the story line and told me he had stowed away on a Merchant Marine vessel." She shook her head sadly. "Doesn't say much for his creativity."

"Do you think he really was getting back on a bus?"

"I doubt it. His cousins have plenty of room—there's three of them, three brothers; they own a supermarket chain. He'll move around. They all have spare beds and wives who don't say boo." She went into my bathroom and didn't shut the door. I could hear her peeing and over it yelling, "It's always his first stop, Worcester. If he was faking amnesia you'd think he'd at least say, 'My bus got into a place called Port Authority. It seems to be in a very large city.'"

I said, "Shouldn't we call Officer Medeiros and tell him Costas turned up in Worcester?"

"Don't say anything about the amnesia. Just say we heard from him. Or that he was sighted in Worcester."

"Like Elvis."

I didn't hear her laugh. She flushed, ran the water, and reappeared. I said, "You *are* a little worried."

"Not worried—goddamn furious."

I said, "He'll be back soon."

"No, he won't. He does this sort of thing when things are going good. Not when we're fighting—when we're fighting he has to stay underfoot and annoy me—but when things are going good."

"That doesn't make sense."

"To you it doesn't make sense because you're from a normal family. Leaving to you means Curtains, The End. He thinks it's safer to leave when things are good between us, like I won't run off with anyone else or sell the house out from under him."

I said, "He was so happy when he heard about the book and the big windfall."

"You're damn right—because he was off the hook. What do you think all that dancing around was for? Because I was getting all this money and the project wasn't just a figment of my imagination. I'd get money and I'd be busy. He was celebrating because he could answer his call of the wild."

"I thought he was genuinely happy for you."

Isabel went over to my unmade bed and started making it. "Right: Mr. Feminist Husband. If he was happy for anyone, it was himself."

"Did you realize this at the time?"

"I should have, shouldn't I?"

I said, "It leads one to the conclusion that you'd rather have him around."

She swiveled her head to look at me over her shoulder. "Like you don't prefer having a man around the house?"

I waited a beat and asked what she meant.

She fluffed my pillows and threw them into place. She said, "Harriet, don't be an ass. I know what's going on."

I didn't say anything. I typed, GUY AND I: ISABEEL'S SIDE a third of the way down the page, cursed the typo, and said I was going to get a word processor as soon as my ship came in.

Isabel said, "Did you hear what I said: *I know what's going on.*"

I ripped the paper out of the roller and twisted it into a cruller. I sat there for a while and finally asked, "Do you mind?"

She grinned. "Mind what?"

I weighed the possible euphemisms and grinned back. "The help screwing around?"

"Was I right?" she demanded.

I said, "About what?"

"About him being adorable and fabulous?"

I said, "Isabel, please don't ask me about our private—you know—stuff."

345

She tilted her head like June might do when begging. I gave in and smiled. "Okay. You were right."

She crossed her heart with one finger. "I promise you, I won't pump you for any details."

"Thanks."

"Who made the first move?—I don't mean who asked who to dinner; I mean, who made the first real move?"

I stared hard. With icy professionalism, I put a fresh piece of paper into my roller, returned my hands to the keys and my eyes to the shorthand.

After a while she said, "You're right. I'm crossing the line. I withdraw the question."

I said good.

"Is he adorable naked?"

I said, "My last answer. *Yes, he is.* Don't ask me anything else."

"Boy," she said, "and you must've been way overdue."

I ignored her comment. Staring at page Roman numeral *i*, I asked, "Do you want to call it 'prologue' or 'preface' or 'introduction' or 'author's note'?"

"I like 'prologue.'" She looked around my room for another household chore. "I also like 'epilogue.'"

I said, "We can do an epilogue."

"That would be, like, what's going on now?"

I said correct.

"It's gonna go like this: 'I used to be a woman who got mixed up with crazy men who had a little too much money to throw at me, but not anymore. I'm on my own. Life is simpler this way. I recommend it.' It would serve the bastard right, saying, 'The very day I got my life back on track, on the very day I got validated by the publishing world, my husband of nineteen years took off for the open road. After doubting me every step of the way—'Who cares about Isabel Krug and her affair with a Greenwich, Connecticut, blue suit?'—he didn't even stick around for the celebration."

I said, "That could be my fault. If I hadn't driven off, he'd have come back for oysters and champagne."

"That's what he hopes you're thinking. It was exactly what he wanted to happen. You pushed him out of the car, and one thing led to another, but he asked for it."

I said, "I didn't push him. I said, 'There's no bakery here. If you want spinach pie, you go get it yourself.'"

"Whatever. He wanted it this way. You drive away and leave him stranded and he says, 'Fantastic coincidence. I've been itching to leave and I get left by Harriet Mahoney, who will spend the rest of her life apologizing for it. I'm on my way.'"

I said, "I'm not apologizing for it. I might have had some normal concerns about whether he died because of it, but I'm not apologizing."

"Good."

"If I had been upset, I hardly would've spent the night drinking champagne and enjoying myself."

Isabel said, "So you admit you enjoyed yourself. Are you going to be sleeping together every night now or is this more of a date thing?"

I said, "That's a personal question."

"So? I tell you everything."

I said, "I'm your ghostwriter." I turned back to the keyboard and said, "As far as Costas goes, I'm feeling even less apologetic now that I know his penchant for skipping town."

"And never like a normal person! He never calls up his cousins and asks if he can visit, then packs his suitcase and tells the post office to hold his mail. He walks out in some dramatic fashion and calls a day or a week later and says, 'I'm in San Francisco.' Or 'I'm in Crete.' I should have seen it coming: He paints night and day, gets ready for a show, then leaves. That's the real indicator: six finished paintings, signed and titled. Time to walk."

I said, "But he always come back, right?"

"No, he does not always come back."

"He's already called and the amnesia thing is perfect for him because the minute he gets homesick he can call back and say, 'I'm cured. I'm coming home.'"

Isabel said, "You always expect people to act normal. But they don't."

I said, "His work is here. Doesn't he like to be at his own openings?"

"Not since the trouble." She took a tissue from my bureau and worked on mirror smudges with her saliva. "Fistfights," she said between licks. "With the art critics."

I asked what he did for money when he was on the road.

"Are you kidding, in this day and age? He goes to automated tellers and he uses plastic."

I said, "Well, now *you* have money. You can go wherever you want to go, too. You can answer the call of the wild."

The rubbing stopped.

"I meant, after we finish our half of the book."

She returned to my perfectly made bed and smoothed my leather comforter all over again. She smiled unconvincingly and said, "I have responsibilities here." She noted that some tapestry or Kilim throw pillows would look great against the glove leather.

"What responsibilities?"

"Well, the house isn't completely finished. After the wine cellar, we're going to talk about one of those indoor lap pools.

And don't forget with Costas gone I act as the broker for the paintings. I make sure they get hung the way he'd like, and when they get sold, I take care of the money."

I said, "Why can't the guys who represent him put the money into his checking account?"

"They could," she said after a pause.

"You don't even like it here."

"I like certain things."

I got up from my chair and sat down next to her on my bed. "Do you think you have to stay here so I'll have a place to live?"

The whites around the bright blue of her contacts turned a watery red. "Of course not."

I said, "I knew this wasn't a job for life."

She examined the tissue she was still holding from buffing my mirror and wiped the tip of her nose with it. "Where would you go?" she asked.

I said, "I'd probably get a place here with my share of the royalties. Or I could house-sit for a family who only spends summers here and I could work part-time and write."

"Where would you go in the summer?"

I said, "Isabel—I've supported myself my entire adult life. You make it sound as if I'd end up in a shelter if I moved out."

"But you love it here," she said. "You don't mind the quiet and the wind howling and the fact that there's nothing to do for nine months out of the year. You didn't even mind the quiet when there was nothing going on between you and Pete."

I said, "You have to do what's best for you, not what's best for me. Or what you think is best for me."

"I like it here," she said weakly.

"You miss New York."

"Not really." She wiped her eyes in a manner that was disguised to look like lens difficulty. "There's Pete, too," she said. "There's hardly any construction down here. And he sure as hell isn't going to start living on boats again."

I said, "Maybe this isn't a good time to decide, the day Costas disappears."

"He can rot in Worcester," she said. "He always comes back from those visits with a Greek accent and with ideas about how a good Greek wife should act."

I said, "How long do you think it'll be? A week? A month?"

"He can go fuck himself. And he can forget about finding himself on the Acknowledgments page."

I put my arm around her shoulder. "You know what we'll do soon? We'll go back to New York and do some research. Have a holiday. We won't think about Costas."

"And spend some money?"

"Definitely. Maybe we can meet with our editor or go to a play."

She said, "What about Pete?"

"Pete could come."

"We'd get two rooms."

"Good."

"My treat."

I said, "We'll see."

"I'm going to set myself up with a date, some fabulous guy."

I spread my hands apart. "With a dick this big?"

She nodded bravely as if I had made a sober suggestion.

I said, "So? Are you going to let me get any work done today?"

She said definitely. The sooner we get it done the sooner we get a holiday.

I asked what she was doing this morning.

She said, "Tracking down the goddamn gallery owners. They live in Key West but they're not answering." She said she'd have Pete bring Officer Medeiros a couple of bottles of wine from Costas's collection with her apologies. Did I think cops accepted thank-you presents?

I said, "I bet he'll want proof that Costas is alive."

Isabel made a face—*I told you not to bring in the police.* "I'll tell Pete to have him call me. I'll explain how my husband abandons me every so often and how we have an open marriage, which can cause all kinds of embarrassing misunderstandings."

I said, "Do you think you should say that? It kind of sounds like an invitation."

"You get going on my prologue," said Isabel. "I'll handle Officer Michael Medeiros."

Even with Costas out of the immediate picture, I looked for my letter from Isabel delineating our 40–60 split. I found it in my current-year file of rejection letters. It was on her scalloped stationery in aqua felt-tip, the first correspondence sent after our gentlemen's agreement by telephone. Thankfully, it was dated and signed. I called my favorite former boss at Rittenberg, Egan & Galazka, faxed her the letter from Truro Center, and received an answer while I waited. In her judgment, this document would stand up in a court of law. Neither the fact that the employer's husband disputed the terms, nor the employer's chatty paragraphs about the shitty shopping on the outer Cape would diminish the contract's validity. Accordingly, I made a copy of the original—the scalloped edge was barely noticeable when reproduced on 8½-by-11-inch 20-pound paper—with a note saying the original document was on file in my lawyer's Manhattan office. I felt compelled to post it above my typewriter as if it were a permit at a construction site, as if inspectors would be checking my credentials.

Postcard of Eugene O'Neill in Provincetown

Dear Kenny,

My belated thanks for lunch last month and for the new shipment. I'll let you know what the consensus here is on the pesto bialys, but my gut feeling is that pesto's time has come and gone.

Thought you might like to know our agent sold Isabel's story to Argonaut Books (16th St. & 5th Ave.) for a fortune. Things could not be better.

Yours in haste,

H. H.

353

32
CHAPTER ONE

 I DID MY best. I started with
Isabel's birth: July 7, 1952, in
Jersey City, New Jersey, at
Margaret Hague Hospital at 7:20 A.M. by Caesarian section.
Mother (Annette Sucheki Krug, age 26) had been told by her
obstetrician that she had too small a pelvis to deliver a child
normally, and her only hope was to be on a strict diet so the
fetus wouldn't get too big. Defying her doctor's orders, she
had sneaked coffee milk shakes, egg creams, and hot fudge
sundaes during her pregnancy. Isabel weighed seven pounds,
eight ounces; was healthy; was pronounced beautiful by O.R.
personnel; was born with a full head of black hair (it fell out

by four months and came in white-blonde). Mrs. Krug stayed in the hospital in a triple room for fifteen days. One roommate had been a first-prize winner—tap—in the "Ted Mack Original Amateur Hour"; the other was a home ec teacher at West Orange High School. Mr. Krug (Frederick S., age twenty-seven), an assistant manager of a package store, visited whenever he could.

For lack of any direct quotes, I created some dialogue that I thought new parents might exchange standing beside a crib, gazing at their adorable new baby girl, nicknaming her Itsy. I wove in whatever else I had from the pre- and post-natal period, studying the black and white snapshots to report that baby Isabel slept in a bassinet, was bathed in a white porcelain sink, was bottle-fed, didn't like being in the wooden playpen, and, even as an infant, looked happiest naked.

It was a short first chapter, but to the point. Successive chapters would be layered with more emotion and more elaborate detail. Scenes where Costas is exposed as her stepfather and Guy buys his way into Isabel's bed would be rendered novelistically. I wasn't too worried about volume, since the trial alone could expand to fit whatever pages I needed. In a pinch, even though she wanted to respect Guy's privacy, I could excerpt conversations from the videotape they had filmed from a tripod once their inhibitions vaporized.

Chapter one took eighteen days to write. I rapped on Isabel's door and yelled, "Fini!" She yelled back that she was in the bathtub, please come in. I crossed through the mauve room into the bathroom and ascended the throne steps leading up to her deep black tub. Isabel took the pages with a squeal of excitement. I sat down on the wrought-iron stool. She was wearing a pink eyelet shower cap that matched the flush of her face. One hand was rolling a bar of vegetal-green soap in her armpit. The mirrors were fogged. She was smiling with the promise of being entertained and moved, of seeing herself on the page as the whole world would see her. I watched her eyes move from left to right with less and less speed, then back up the page to reread paragraphs just finished. Her smile faded slowly and her features reset themselves into a diplomatic question mark.

I said, "What's wrong?"

She said, "Nothing. I'm still reading."

"You don't look happy."

She arched one eyebrow as if to say, Shut up, Harriet.

I said, "You hate it."

"I don't hate it."

I said, "You look like you just lost your best friend."

She read the rest without comment and put the five pages back in order. She uncorked the drain and sat there as the water level fell. "Maybe it's not what I expected," she said, finally meeting my eyes.

I asked with difficulty, "How so?

"I expected it would sound like . . . me."

I said this was a first draft—it wasn't; I'd rewritten every sentence ten times—so there was ample opportunity to work on the voice until it was utterly her.

"What do you mean 'voice'?"

"Your voice—how it's being said. The way you sound."

She turned back to the first page and reread it slowly, looking pained, trying to name the problem. Through the 20-pound paper, I spotted the mirror images of my dull proper nouns: *Annette Suchecki Krug, Margaret Hague Hospital, Bergenfield, Beechnut.* Even backward they looked like the work of someone trying to turn a homegrown story into a term paper. Some big literary achievement: a date and time of birth, ages, occupations; nothing there was sexy enough or good enough; nothing in my pica type was what Argonaut Books was paying us 1.2 million dollars for. A few hopeful brain cells made me ask aloud, "What if I capture the reader's attention with something explosive and thread the biographical stuff throughout the book? Isabel?"

She said, like a mother distracting a child too young to climb onto the school bus, "You know what I might do? Now that I've seen a professional first chapter, I might talk into my tape recorder for a while. Wouldn't that be fun?"

I said, "You've already done that."

"Except this time I have a better idea of what they want."

Perspiring from every pore, I said, "Sure. That's fine. I'll start chapter two."

"Why don't you hold off, take some time for yourself. You and Pete could have a day together."

I said, "Please. I know I can do much better than this."

Isabel stood up and exchanged my pages for a towel. After a few moments, her face brightened, as if the brisk toweling had revived her. "You know what? I'll talk into the tape recorder and you could type that up and I'll send both to Argonaut and say, 'Here's two different ways of starting the story. Which one should we go with?'"

"What if they choose yours?"

"If that happens," she said, "maybe we can alternate. I'll write some and you write some. It'll take no time at all."

I said, "If they choose yours they won't want any of it touched by me."

Isabel pulled off her shower cap and wiped it dry with far too much care. "If they choose me," she said, not looking up, "then you'll be my assistant. You'll transcribe the tapes and fix it, which is extremely important. You're so good at that, and so fast."

Pete, June, and I walked all the way to Great Hollow and back. He said, "Why are you expecting the worst? Isabel can't write well enough to do the job herself."

I said, "It's so embarrassing."

He skipped rocks, which sent June splashing into the water, and made Pete yell at her that she'd catch pneumonia. When he turned back he said, "Not everybody is suited to this kind of tell-all stuff. Just because you can't write this book doesn't mean you're not a good writa."

I said, "It means that to me."

"Do you think Isabel is going to send you packing?"

"She should."

Pete said, "June, do you think Harriet should stay if Isabel decides to write her own book?"

June jangled up to him and shook herself like a cartoon wet dog.

I said, "That looked like a *no* to me."

Pete said, "She's jealous."

Isabel surprised everyone but me with her opening chapter, a riveting description of a Caesarian section, which she had assimilated on The Learning Channel. The first sentence of her version began, "Big deal, so I was breached, feetfirst. Was that any reason to slash a foot-long scar on my twenty-six-year-old bombshell of a mother, who'd taken the trouble to rub cocoa butter on her stomach for nine months and now, thanks to me, would never again wear a two-piece bathing suit in public?"

Given both chapters anonymously for consideration, our editor pronounced sample chapter "B" honest, colloquial, unpretentious, unconstrained. The other writing, she noted, had its moments, but nothing incandescent.

Five days later, Isabel received a formal letter of agreement. Below Argonaut's beautiful golden ram logo, the editorial director put his company's official preference into words: that Isabel Krug (herein called "the Author") will write her yet untitled section (herein called "the Work") of *GUY AND I* (herein called "The Book") alone.

Costas called again from alleged parts unknown, although Isabel suspected he was still at Nicky's duplex in Worcester. He said, still feigning amnesia, "Is this the person I spoke with last time?"

"That's right, your wife. Do you remember my name?"

"I'm sorry, but I don't."

She said, "Is there a hospital anywhere around where you are? You should get a CAT-scan of your brain. You should have a card in your wallet with our policy number on it."

He said, "I don't need a CAT-scan. I have to go now."

"Are they announcing your bus?" she asked.

"I'm calling from a ship," said Costas. "They let me stow away in exchange for being their cook."

"That's nice," she said. "What are you cooking?"

"I can't remember."

"How long will you be gone?"

"I won't know that for a while." He asked if she had received the monies from her new publisher.

Isabel thought of saying, Hallelujah, you must be getting your memory back, but didn't. She dropped the sarcasm, she told me later, because her answer had the potential for creating an honest moment between them. She said, "I get the first payment as soon as the contract's signed. By the way, Blaise and Paul love the series. They want the opening to be Saturday of the July fourth weekend."

He said, "Did you tell them ten apiece after their commission?"

She said, "They think they can get ten apiece."

"Net."

"Net," said Isabel. "Someone's already interested in 'Kohlrabi.'"

"Good. You'll take care of that?"

"Sure."

"And I hope you'll take care of yourself."

She asked if he was catching any episodes of "Joy." Did he need an update?

He said no, he didn't, then asked quietly, "Are you sure you're okay?"

Isabel said, yes, wasn't she always?

"Your friends are staying?"

Yes, said Isabel, her friends were staying.

Argonaut's enthusiasm over chapter one supplied all the motivation Isabel needed. She wrote "the Work" in fourteen days, joyfully labeling herself a compulsive writer if not a workaholic. Newly empowered, she talked and talked into a Dictaphone purchased for the task ahead. I transcribed, matching her hour for hour, acting the role of the perfect secretary. The chapters did require punctuating and some transitional sentences, but, truthfully, they were Isabel's.

She got better, braver, looser. I laughed and I sniffled over the voice coming through my earphones, and reported at dinner which passages affected me most. After I typed up her trial testimony verbatim, she returned those pages with rude remarks in the margins—a device Argonaut found charming: They too would incorporate Isabel's handwritten comments in her finished pale salmon pages. She explained to me, and later in interviews, "Once I got the hang of it, I just saw whole scenes in front of me. I figured out what would look good on paper, what to tell and what to leave out. People like descriptions of clothes, body parts, sex, and food, but they couldn't care less about what color the sky is on any given day. You can *have* that shit as far as I'm concerned."

She wrote both movingly and pornographically about Guy in the chapter titled "Skip This One if You're a Prude." Costas drifted in and out of the story in a way I found to be a metaphor for their marriage. She did a great job describing the fireworks between them at his wedding to Margaret, and an even better job describing their first night together at the Plaza honeymoon suite while the straw bride slept across town in her own bed. The epilogue was personal in an entirely different way: Isabel observed that life would have been richer with children, easier with a formal education, stabler with two parents, more manageable with smaller breasts. She also noted that grafting certain parts of big, gruff Costas onto sweet, eager Guy and subtracting twenty man-years would have given her the perfect lover.

She said, "Just because your name's not on the cover doesn't mean you weren't my collaborator."

I resisted, saying but not believing I didn't deserve any more remuneration than she would pay a clerical assistant.

"That's crap," said Isabel. "You're feeling sorry for yourself. Meanwhile, if you hadn't started off with the C-section and steered me in the right direction, I'd never have discovered I had real writing talent. You earned every penny."

I said, "It would make me the best-paid typist in America."

"It's like my neighbor, the busybody who saw Costas in spattered overalls and assumed he painted walls for a living? You didn't call your fiction *typing* just because you were sitting at the typewriter."

I said, "That was my mistake."

"Look," said Isabel. "You're getting your money whether you like it or not, and, frankly, the next work you do should bring you some satisfaction."

I said, "The money's one thing, but what do I put on my résumé? It still comes down to having typed and filed for someone else."

"I didn't hire you because of your résumé! I hired you because I liked you. And believe me, so will your next boss."

I said, "If you want to be a writer, you need to have written something."

She said, "Look around you. Reread my epilogue. I mean it, Harriet. You need to be reminded there's more to life than having your name on a book."

33

CLIPPING FROM *NEWSDAY*

Dear Harriet,
    Thought you'd be interested in the enclosed.

K

New in Vitro Technique Aids Men

In vitro fertilization programs across the United States are beginning to use a new technique that some specialists believe could provide hope for thousands of men who are unable to father a child because of extremely low or abnormal sperm counts.

The technique, first developed in Belgium by Dr.

ELINOR LIPMAN

Gianpierro Palermo and Dr. Andre C. Van Steirteghem at
the Brussels Free University, involves removing an egg
and directly injecting a single sperm into it using micro-
scopic glass needles called pipettes.

Specialists in Brussels have reported 100 live births, the
only ones so far with the technique, said Dr. Michael
Obasajur of IVF America in Mineola, N.Y., which is
starting to use the procedure but has not yet had a
pregnancy with it.

Intracytoplasmic injection, or ICI, is an extension of
current in vitro fertilization techniques. Currently, in
most cases, the sperm and egg are both placed in a
laboratory dish and the sperm penetrates the egg on its
own. But in difficult cases, a slit is made in the membrane
to assist the process or the sperm is placed under the
membrane, or zonal, a process called sub-zonal insertion.

"This (new technique) is very important in terms of
helping people whom we call severe, male-factor patients
—so bad that the sperm count is so minimal, we can't do
any other procedures. Before the advent of ICI, we were
limited," Obasajur said. "Now their chances are greatly
improved, increased."

Isabel found it hilarious in a pathetic and distinctly Solo-
Grossman kind of way, but I was outraged. I pounded the
numbers of A Decent Bagel; Ramon said the boss was taking
the day off; try him at home.

Amy answered. I said, "May I speak with your husband?"
She must have mouthed my name, guessing that anyone
sounding this bellicose had to be the long-term girlfriend
scorned. Kenny's fake-chipper "How ya doin', Hare?" drove
me over the edge.

I said, "Are you in touch with reality? You actually thought
I'd give a flying fuck about in vitro fertilization for men with
no sperm?"

364

I heard his hand smothering the mouthpiece, then a muted explanation to Amy, then a reopening of our soundway. "I know you like to keep up with things that once interested you."

" 'Once' is right. Once upon a time when it was fine with you that you were shooting blanks."

He said, "I was not."

"Is this some kind of crackpot invitation to get inseminated, like you're offering me a big retroactive favor?"

He said evenly, pleasantly—Amy was obviously glued to every word—"I'm taking the day off and we're going shopping together."

"Good for you. Have a nice life and keep your stupid clippings to yourself. I don't need your help."

"We got a lot of checks as wedding gifts and instead of letting them sit around in a money market account we agreed to buy some stuff we need."

I said, "Must be hard to shop with someone you hardly know."

I heard Amy complain, "I thought you wanted to leave by nine-thirty." His hand muffled the receiver while he soothed her, and I had the urge to bite it.

Back again, Kenny earnestly explained that they were going to look at futons and VCRs.

I said, "I get it: You're fighting. You want to put the money into the business and she wants to spend it."

He said, "Yeah, work is good. It could be better."

I said, "What do you do? Send me bagels as an S.O.S. whenever you have a fight with her?"

He said, "No, but I could talk to Isabel about franchising. Can I call her later when I have some figures in front of me?"

I said, "Did you think the clipping was a peace offering?"

Kenny said, "Around three this afternoon? I'll be happy to toss some ideas around with her."

I said, "I'm not interested in being your friend, and I'm less interested in giving you a shoulder to cry on."

Kenny said, "Sure it could work. Everybody likes good bagels better than frozen bagels. With the right location, it could be a license to print money."

I said, "I thought she was the greatest thing that ever happened to you."

"We can talk about that later."

"Too bad you rushed into marriage. But I guess you had to prove that you wouldn't treat her like you treated me."

Kenny said, "Great. Around three? Nice to catch up with you, Hare."

He called from his closet of an office at A Decent Bagel. He was sorry for having given me the wrong impression earlier: Things were more than fine. Like a business, marriage required hard work and long hours, but from what he'd read, that was true of everyone. They had found a futon and a VCR, VCR Plus actually, where you program in codes from *TV Guide*. They had lots of new friends and belonged to a gourmet club with five other couples. Sure, Amy worked long hours and had to do a fair amount of business entertaining during nonbusiness hours, but hey—who was he to talk, out the door at 4 A.M. and already had half a day's work under his belt when most husbands were home eating breakfast with their wives. She didn't want children yet, but that was fine; lots of guys have kids in their late forties. Besides, they were considering a bichon frisé, which are nonshedding and nonallergenic. He was going to delegate more, let Ramon open one or two days a week and see how that went. For her part, Amy was going to take more clients to lunches than to dinners. As a couple, they were good negotiators—today, in fact, they had both taken the whole day off: breakfast, lunch, shopping, and now some private time. And Amy was going to come by for a sesame bagel before work whenever she could, just like she used to in the early days when they fell in love.

I said, "I couldn't care less."

He said, "Y'know what? It's the craziest thing how the franchise idea just flew out of my mouth when I was talking to you this morning. Now all I've been saying to myself is, Are there really no decent bagels on Cape Cod? What if that's true? How many of those psychiatrists who spend August in Wellfleet schlep bagels from New York and don't even have freezer space?"

I said, "People like a change when they're on vacation. Everyone eats blueberry muffins in the summer. And cranberry muffins. Cranberry's the official muffin of Massachusetts."

"Bagel eaters are not muffin eaters," he said. "Believe me, I know."

I tried, "I can't imagine Amy would like the idea of you opening a branch up here."

"Amy's a businesswoman. She thinks in terms of square feet, light, location, zoning, foot traffic, parking, that stuff. She wouldn't worry about the fact that my old girlfriend is in the neighborhood. Besides, you have what? Another nine-ten months on your contract?"

I told him I couldn't say. Things were fluid.

He said, "I'm thinking seasonal: June first through Labor Day. And frankly, Hare, I know you mean well, but you never had a head for business."

I said, "Fine. Open up a fleet of bagel stores. I hope it gives you what you're searching for."

"The thought of a summer at the beach, especially when we have kids, really appeals to me." He paused—probably remembering Amy's silent biological clock—then amended, "I'd probably be up there by myself for the first few summers. Amy likes the art of the deal but she's not real interested in the hands-on part of it."

I said, "You have a sorry history of rushing into decisions."

"I have to rush if I want to open this summer."

I said, "It's a big commitment. Just because it seems like a summer vacation to you doesn't mean customers would want any less from you. You'll have twice the headaches."

He said, "It wasn't a fully formed plan. I haven't dotted the i's and crossed the t's. It was only an idea I was tossing around with Amy. She has the same entrepreneurial way of looking at things that I have."

I said, "Do you want to go even deeper into debt to open up a seasonal bagel store?"

Kenny said, "Maybe it just takes a little faith and a little confidence in my talents. Which you never had." I could hear him sniffing and exhaling angrily. He continued his litany: "It's good for me to be reminded of this, how you hate change, how you never take risks and keep beating the same dead horses—"

"Which doesn't concern you anymore, does it?"

"Would a little support kill you? If you're sick of pesto does that mean no one else can eat it? A little positive reinforcement and, and, you know what I've been through—a little cheerleading. Is that too much to ask? When I've always been there for you?"

I said, "Don't call me, don't write me, don't FedEx me bagels."

34

NAN'S GIFT

 WHENEVER ISABEL BEGGED
to see Nan's side of *GUY
AND I*, the Argonaut editor
resisted. "We're not sending her your chapters," she'd argue.
"We want there to be a certain freshness and spontaneity
between the two of you when the situation is being discussed
on the air."

Isabel said, "I mean, is it junk? Is it crazy stuff? Is it
brilliant? What's the big secret? I'm the first author. I didn't
need a ghostwriter. I need to know if Porter can cut it."

Jay negotiated an understanding: Isabel could read Nan's

pages, could register opinions, but had to confine her changes to factual errors. Isabel said, "Fine. I want it here tomorrow."

We read Nan's pages together at our various speeds, Isabel passing me a page at a time. Ferris's narrative started off slowly, but it wasn't bad. Some parts were even compelling, like Guy and Nan's long-distance college courtship, their fraternity and sorority rites. Ferris evoked a certain romantic nostalgia for their early days, for Nan's hearty, field-hockey brand of blonde good looks and for Guy's courting etiquette. We learned how Guy had conspired with a sorority sister to measure the third finger of Nan's left hand with thread while she slept, then enlisted her parents to plant the velvet jeweler's box in the same felt stocking that had hung from the McKenny mantel for twenty-one Christmases. We read, translating euphemisms, that Nan and Guy had experimented sexually once they were formally engaged but not horizontally in a bed until their wedding night. The loveliness of that winter night—of the whole honeymoon actually—stayed with the Guy VanVleets forever, in the words of Professor Porter, "informing their connubial relations, sustaining them when, inevitably, crevasses yawned in their matrimonial bed."

Every few pages Isabel would read me a few lines of Ferris's ventriloquism: Shakespeare or Emily Dickinson employed to describe shrubs on the Greenwich property and squabbles with in-laws. "Who's gonna believe this shit?" she'd ask, reminding me how every word of the Isabel Krug story was from her own hand and her own brain.

On page eighty-two of the manuscript, there was a blue Post-it note from Isabel's editor. It said, "Isabel, Nan reveals this fact for the first time here, and I think it's very powerful. Let's talk. Judith." Nan's revelation followed under the heading, *Step Four: Moral Inventory.* The gist of it was this—and it had a fluttery, run-on Nan quality that sounded authentic: She had never strayed, had never thought of straying, until her best friends took her to lunch one excruiating day and said, "We think you should know and we're telling you this because we care so deeply: Guy has been seen with a woman in New York and it doesn't look good."

She ran out without her coat, she miraculously made it home alive, she threw up, she drank glasses of sweet cordial that she shouldn't have drunk. And by the light of the moon, or was it the glow of halogen from a streetlight, she vowed, like Kunta Kinte holding his infant son to the night sky in *Roots,* to sleep with the next man who crossed her path who acted the slightest bit interested.

She hadn't meant anything by it, certainly hadn't meant to seek out the husband of the woman screwing Guy. But whose fault was that? A woman so arrogant that she slept with one man while pushing another man's artwork on the family. Always the personal shopper, urging Guy to buy one of her husband's paintings. And he did, and it was so big and so hard to hang that the artist personally made a house call to supervise its installation and flattered her into something like a date with him—she had majored in art history—and then a second evening, and a tour of his studio, and ultimately relations on a daybed, not that she didn't like his work, but she was very sorry now to have a blemish on her matrimonial record.

I looked up from the page. "Costas slept with Nan VanVleet?"

Isabel, now on her feet, was opening kitchen cupboards just so she could slam them shut. "That prick," she said. "No wonder he took off now. He thought she was going to show up here and have write-a-thons on the dining room table, and he'd better be out of town when she came calling."

I said, "I can't imagine Costas afraid to face Nan VanVleet."

"Not Nan—me. He knew I'd find this out eventually."

I said, "No offense, but if you were cheating on him with Guy, how big a crime is it for them to sleep together?"

She smiled then, a victory grin. "Not a crime," she said. "It's a gift. He wanted me to think he had affairs with hippy heiresses he met in cafés in Athens." She rubbed her hands together; she did a little mamba on her toes. "This is so great. He's gonna come back from his trip, dropping hints about the models and the spies he slept with, and I'm gonna say, 'Unh-uh, no way, pal. The whole world knows that Costas Dimantopoulos makes it with housewives who buy big canvases because their interior decorator tells them to.'"

I said, "Nan seems a little worried. Maybe you should let her know you don't hold it against her."

Isabel said, "That hypocrite. She had some nerve coming after me with a gun after what she did."

Jay said in one of his speedier callbacks, "Don't gloat, especially on camera. It makes Nan look bad. I mean, on one side we have a woman so agitated over her husband's screwing around that she has a psychotic break and kills him in cold blood. And when you flip the book over, there's you saying, 'Fabulous, I love it, what could be better?' Couldn't you act a little devastated? For me? For the tour. I mean, there's great symmetry here—you and Nan invested in the same man and then it loops back on itself and it's vice-versa time. God, I only wish I had known about this before the auction."

Isabel sent Nan's manuscript back to their editor with her

own, larger Post-it note stuck to page eighty-two. "Dear Judith," she wrote with a little guidance from me, "Nan's so-called matrimonial blemish with Costas was common knowledge in my house well before she confessed here (and you can tell her that). Guy knew, of course, but wasn't in much of a position to gripe. *Entre nous,* I think he even got off on it, which I hope doesn't pop out of my mouth on national television. Otherwise I find her writing a little breathy and immature, but I suppose readers will appreciate the contrast in our styles."

To both my astonishment and hers, Isabel was invited to a memorial service for Guy in Greenwich on the anniversary of his death. The engraved invitation—from Tiffany, Isabel certified, showing me the embossing on the envelope— amounted to a note from Guy's children. "None of us really remembers Dad's funeral," it said simply, "so we want another chance to say good-bye. Please join us."

Isabel called Nan and said, "I hope you're not inviting me solely because of our business association."

Nan, sounding graciously vacant, said, "Of *course* you must come. We only invited people Guy would have wanted to be there. Oh, and please tell Henriette she's more than welcome."

After the rector of Saint Bartholomew's Episcopal Church read from *The Book of Common Prayer* and the choir sang "In the Garden," Perry welcomed the standing-room-only crowd on behalf of the family. On the altar he was transformed into Kerr Greenwood, eyes shining; wearing Kerr's navy blue blazer and charcoal gray slacks; speaking and projecting from the bottom of Kerr's all-American heart: "We thought to ourselves, gosh, not everybody who will be honoring Dad today knew him when he was alive. So we wanted to bring you the private Guy VanVleet, to show you there was more to his life than his passing."

The lights went out. Perry's shadowy figure moved to one side. A white screen worthy of a Democratic National Convention glided down from the ceiling. Suddenly we had Guy on a tennis court with a disembodied instructor's voice offering encouragement and tips. Yellow tennis balls kept coming at him. The memorial audience applauded Guy's best returns.

The next thing we saw was Nan and Guy doing a foxtrot, waving to the camera. Seconds later, at a round table over plates of what looked like Cornish game hens, a woman asked, "Any advice for Scott and Betsy?" Guy took the big mike and said, "Scott, my man, here's what I say to you: Be as nice to your wife as you are to your friends." He passed the microphone to Nan, whose lips moved but whose advice we didn't hear.

The tape cut to a reporter, a portly bald man in aviator glasses, sitting behind a desk of what looked like a TV news set. "We asked broker Guy VanVleet of Truesdale Hunt, sitting in for his colleague J. Anthony Truesdale, who's got a touch of the Hong Kong flu, if he was worried." The reporter turned to speak to a monitor filled with Guy, looking pink and freshly combed. Guy answered, "Bill, it's not as bad as it looks. It's just a simple correction as people were taking profits." The mourners sent up scattered, well-bred cheers.

And so the tribute continued: glances culled from other people's videotape archives by a family who obviously owned no camcorder. The final visit was Guy in what must be the front yard of 1010 Round Hill Road, looking thrilled, saying to a woman in a red winter coat, "You know, he's got a small part. Don't get me wrong, we think he's the best, but you have to have a bigger role to be nominated." Guy beamed into the camera, ducking slightly as if to fit himself into our sets. "Of course, there's always next year. My son tells me the writers are going to send him to the college there in Rosewell, so he might get a bigger story line and a couple of love affairs." The reporter turns back to the camera and said, "You heard it here first, folks: Greenwich's own Perry VanVleet may soon be a leading man on CBS's top-rated soap 'If This Be Joy.' That from the actor's father, Guy VanVleet. Back to you, Virginia."

The film ended as abruptly as it started. The lights went back on. The organ struck the opening chords of something familiar, something not quite hymnlike. It proved to be "A Bridge Over Troubled Waters," a self-conscious choice, I thought, for a family trying to forget its headlines.

I felt a premonition of embarrassment when the rector took back the pulpit and announced, "The family invites its guests to stand and share a remembrance of Guy. We hope you will feel free to share light-hearted moments, because we think Guy would want to hear us laughing. Please identify yourself and speak loudly enough for the microphone to pick you up."

Perry, now seated in the front row next to his mother, shot up in a way that made me doubt the spontaneity of the program. "Father Dave? Every Christmas when we were little? Dad used to dress up as Santa and make a lot of noise out on the lawn, calling the names of reindeers, which would wake us up, and then he'd climb up a ladder and make noise above us and then we'd go back to sleep." He sat down, chuckling. Father Dave chuckled back.

Sara, who was taller than both her brother and sister, stood up dutifully and said, "My father used to take Heidi and me to story hour at the library on Saturday afternoons and he was the only dad there. You could leave your kids and come back for them forty-five minutes later, but he always stayed and once in a while the librarian let him read a story." Sara sat down and nodded to Heidi, who stood up even more reluctantly. "Dad could be really silly with us," she began. "And some of the things he used to do embarrassed us in front of our friends, but looking back"—her voice broke—"it showed that he was really a child at heart." She paused. "He used to take me to Playland and he'd get on his own horse on the merry-go-round and make a big show, pretending that his horse was running away with him, flailing his arms and pretty much making a scene. I was always mortified. But now I see he really loved the rides . . . and taking me there. Even when I got kind of old for it, he'd talk me into going." She sagged back into the pew. Sara put an arm around her sister.

Heidi was followed by a tall man who looked like a banker: "Once I was with Guy and there was a homeless family on the sidewalk outside our building with a cardboard sign that said something like, 'Out of work and hungry.' Guy had just bought a sandwich to eat at his desk. He stopped in front of the mother and said, 'Here, I haven't touched this. It's a turkey club on toasted white.'"

The man sitting next to him rose and said, "No one's mentioned this about Guy, but he loved to sing. Sometimes I'd be standing waiting for the elevators on our floor and from the elevator shaft a couple of floors below me I'd hear some song, like 'Hey, there, Georgie Girl,' or 'See you in September,' and I knew it was Guy serenading himself. We all teased him about it—his voice was nothing special—but we all thought it was nice." He coughed into his fist and said, "It's been a terrible loss."

Suddenly Nan was on her feet. From the expressions on her children's profiles, I sensed she was speaking out of turn. "I visit Guy's grave every Monday," she said, plucking at the white lily that identified members of the immediate family, "and I tell him how sorry I am. And I think he forgives me. And I *am* sorry. . . . I'm very, very sorry and remorseful. It's the God's honest truth that I didn't know what I was doing. But I'm cured now, and I miss him so much, and I just wanted to apologize and I hope you accept it."

She sat down. From ten rows away I could see her shoulders shaking. I waited for a chorus of affirmations, for one of her children to put an arm around her, or for Ferris—assigned with three handsome young men to what was obviously the boyfriends' pew—to make his way to her. But no one did; no one moved other than to sneak nervous glances at their neighbors. I could feel Isabel shifting in her seat, clearing her throat, working up to something, but I didn't want her to have to be the one to call attention to herself in her new houndstooth coatdress and her little black fez of a widow's hat with its fishnet veil. If mourners could cheer Guy's backhand at a memorial service, I reasoned, they might be moved to boo his mistress. I passed her my *Book of Common Prayer* and pulled myself up by the pew in front of me. "I didn't know Guy personally," I heard myself say, "so I can only speak for myself, but I think you have to put the past behind you and let your new life begin. Which is to say, I accept your apology." I sat down then half-rose to add, "I'm Harriet Mahoney."

After more stirrings and more silence, the rector said sternly, "Does anyone else have a story about Guy they'd like to share with us? Rob Lewis? How about that funny business you mentioned to me this morning? I enjoyed that vignette very much."

Rob Lewis rose obediently to describe Guy's show-stopping entrance in a red wig at the country club talent show. Rob, in turn, invited the remarks of Annalee Nelson, Guy's co-star, who had penned their lyrics to the tune of "Sixteen Tons"; Annalee turned the floor over to Phil Shepherd, who had roomed with Guy at fly-fishing school and had on tape—if anyone cared to borrow it—a lovely few hours on the Mettawee.

The testimonials continued without further outbursts. I stared straight ahead, my cheeks burning and my mouth dry. Apropos of nothing that was being orated, Isabel reached over and squeezed my hand. In a little while, soothed by the choir, my breathing returned to normal. Eventually I joined in the communal singing of "How Great Thou Art," unsure if it belonged to either of my religions, but liking the sound of my own voice.

35

MY SPECTACULAR SELF/
MY EPILOGUE

 I DIDN'T MEAN to steal anyone's intellectual property or appropriate someone else's dream, but I needed a new career. And, once I thought about it, if there was anything I knew besides shorthand and typing, it was industrial ovens.

In the beginning, I had ethical concerns.

Rittenberg, Egan & Galazka said, "Are you kidding? There's no decent bagels where you live, and because someone points that out to you you think it's actionable?"

I said, "I talked him out of it when he told me he was thinking of it."

The attorney said, "Because you had the idea first and you didn't want him in your territory. You've been contemplating such an initiative for months."

I said, "You know, maybe I have."

Pete said, "Kenny should've known in the world of commerce you keep your ideas to yourself."

Isabel nudged me. "Now who has no head for business?"

"I know what's botherin' Harriet," said Pete. "She doesn't want to staht a business with any kind of uneasy feeling that it wasn't honorable from the get-go."

Isabel said, "What's the big deal? Kenny didn't invent bagels. It's not like you're stealing his stupid recipe."

I said, "I want mine chewier. His are cakey. We never agreed on the texture."

"He's a hack!" she squawked.

"I'd say it's a stretch to call them 'decent,'" added Pete.

To Isabel I confided, "If I think of my time with Kenny as some sort of apprenticeship, I don't feel so bad about throwing away twelve years of my life."

"The women of this house don't look back," she said firmly. "Well, occasionally we do, but only to get even." Still the day I signed the lease on my 500 square feet on Briar Lane, Isabel took me aside to ask, "You're sure you want to do this? I mean, do you know how to make a bagel?"

I said I'd experiment until I got it right. After all, I had spent my childhood at Mahoney's Donuts, on the sidelines of the search for the perfect glazed, raised, filled. Also, I said, my Dad will help.

"So will I," said Isabel.

"You know I will," said Pete.

* * *

I set up big caldrons of boiling water in Isabel's kitchen to try the only bagel recipe the Truro Public Library could get me on interlibrary loan: Bagels Jake from *The Molly Goldberg Cookbook,* copyright 1955. There it sat, an unintimidating half page, seven household ingredients, between Cherry Verenikas and Challah à la Molly. "Form into doughnuts," the directions told me comfortingly, "and press the edges together securely."

The results didn't resemble any bagel I'd ever eaten. I called my father and said, "I'm losing my nerve."

"Why exactly?" he asked.

I read him the recipe. He said, "Too much handling and too much time in the oven."

I said I couldn't picture pinching dough and doing this shaping-boiling-baking thing to thousands of bagels a day.

"You're thinking small," he said. "You have to think big. You have to think, 'I'll have machines to do this for me and automation and bakers. I'm not going to be afraid of success. I'm not going to be kneading the dough by hand or standing by the oven wearing potholder mitts like a housewife.'"

I said, "Say some more. I need to hear this."

"It's hard work. You'll never be able to get out of bed in daylight or drink your coffee sitting down, but it's very satisfying to create something that makes people happy first thing in the morning."

He put my mother on the phone. "Want me to look through my cookbooks? I have a Jenny Grossinger and a couple from temple sisterhoods."

I said, "It can't hurt."

She called back within a half hour. She said she'd found two recipes in the books and one in her accordion file, a stained scrap of paper passed down by her mother, written in quaint English that must have been her grandmother's because she had no memory of homemade bagels. Should she mail them to me?

"Can you get to a fax machine?" I asked.

Eventually, I sent for the original and framed it for display on the wall behind the register. It wasn't of any practical use ("two bowls of flour use blue bowl"; "2 glasses water"; "1 egg or 2 if pullet") but customers always asked if they might step behind the counter for a closer look.

Pete and Isabel were the official tasters during my bagel trials. She was dieting for her thirty-nine-city book tour, so she claimed to welcome the endless parade of complex carbohydrates. For weeks I baked all day and served experimental bagels without cream cheese for dinner. The winner (high-gluten flour, no Redi-Sponge, baked at a higher temperature for a shorter time) emerged chewy but not tough, dense but not doughy, with a delicious flavor and fabulous texture inside and out. My trade secret, I announced at our celebration lobster dinner, was the malt syrup added to the water during the boiling stage that gave them their gorgeous patina.

Pete oversaw the crew that built Mahoney's Bagels, which was located in the bakeryless mini-mall where I had given Costas his walking papers. My mixer, my dough divider, my retarder, and my oven were shipped from Cleveland, but all the labor was performed by Cape Codders. Inside it was a snappy white and deep forest green, like a modern Mahoney's Donuts, with hot bagels in wire baskets and an optimistic Pik-a-number dispenser. I went deliberately untrendy in the flavor department: plain, onion, egg, poppy, sesame, cinnamon raisin, pumpernickel, garlic, black and white, salt. I ordered cream cheese in bulk; the chive was real, not macerated scallions; my salmon, smoked over maple locally, would bring in summering gourmets for that alone.

I hadn't meant to be cute with the name, but the two words, "Mahoney's Bagels," turned out to be a public relations bonanza. Inside my head, it had seemed plain, without sex appeal. I worried that it had no resonance, suggested no graphics; that my Jewish customers would mistrust the juxtaposition of an Irish surname with such a sacred product. But I was wrong.

Ironically, after my dead-end jobs and my creative difficulties, I could do no wrong in print. I made good copy. When I opened my mouth to the writers of columns covering developments in chic food, quotable quotes came out. These writers sensed I hadn't named my shop with an eye toward a melting-pot angle or cheap laughs. They found me sincere. MAHONEY'S BAGELS, said the *New York Times* Style section one Sunday in early June: **A Daughter Comes Full Circle.** I informed the few who challenged my credentials that I was Jewish on my mother's side—named after my grandfather Harry, in fact—but had wanted my own surname above the door because I had always worked for other people.

"Why bagels?" they asked. "Why not a branch of Mahoney's Donuts? Surely some of your father's customers vacation on Cape Cod." I said, "There are decent doughnuts on the Outer Cape but only supermarket bagels." To the Jerusalem *Post*'s Washington correspondent I changed "supermarket" to *goyishe*. He loved it. He visited and wrote a feature. When asked what made me think I could make a go of bagels I said, "A former acquaintance was in bagels and I learned by his mistakes." Measured against Isabel's library of clippings, the coverage was minor—paragraphs here and there in product round-ups and boutique reviews—but it eased my bagels' way into the world.

My parents drove down from Brookline a week ahead of the Sunday opening and stayed in the round gray room with the aquamarine tile bath. Midweek, Pete took them fishing, hoping for stripers, while Isabel and I worked on one last collaboration. "Grand opening Sunday of Mahoney's Bagels," I read from my rough draft. "Free T-shirt with the purchase of a dozen bagels and our six-ounce package of locally smoked hand-sliced Atlantic salmon."

Isabel looked out the picture window and wondered aloud what my parents were discussing with Pete out on the boat.

I smiled and said, "Me."

She said, "When they leave, I might move into the gray room and give you and Pete the master suite."

"You'd miss your view," I said, "and your bathtub. How can you give those up?"

"It doesn't do anything for my big butt to be right next to the kitchen," she said. "Besides, I want someone using the tub while I'm on the road so the jets of the Jacuzzi don't get plugged."

I said, "But you love your room."

"It's meant for two people," said Isabel. "I'm not saying forever. Maybe we can rotate if Costas returns and I feel hospitable."

"Why him?" I asked. "You're going to make all kinds of new friends when you're on the road."

She pointed out that the gray room had a queen-sized bed; she wouldn't exactly be out of action, would she? One favor, though—no dog hairs on the aubergine sheepskin, please.

We moved on to stock for the flyers. I held up samples of hot pink, lime, and marigold paper, advising her to choose a color that would work for T-shirts, too. Isabel said, "I'm going to surprise you and recommend they be subtle: white, with a golden brown bagel over the heart"—she demonstrated on her chest—"*Mahoney's Bagels* here, and underneath: *Wellfleet, Mass.* That's it. Less is more. No fuzzy lettering, no Scratch 'n Sniff."

It was a good decision except for quantity. We were mobbed on opening day, an unseasonably chilly Sunday that was bad for sunbathing but excellent for the purchase of warm bagels and hot coffee. My dad was the first guest to grab an apron and join the bakers in the basement, followed by my mom, and finally Pete's mom, who bragged that she'd never even tasted a bagel until her son fell for a girl who made them. Pete stayed upstairs, slicing and filleting next to me, better and more efficient than Kenny, who'd always insisted there was only one way—his—to do things.

Customers were backed out the door to the parking lot, where a green banner hung across Briar Lane declaring that Mahoney's Bagels, "Better than your bagels from home," was officially open. When things calmed down, I circulated among the tables of eat-in customers, introducing myself as the Mahoney of the title. They congratulated me and asked me questions. Where was I from? Would I stay open past Labor Day? Ship out of state? A favorite was, "Have you always been in bagels?" which I answered truthfully: "I came from a long line of bakers, but I was professionally sidetracked for a few decades."

"Doing what?"

I answered, "Fiction" or "Ghostwriting" or "Typing and

filing," depending on the customer. With some I elaborated: "I changed directions after suffering a number of professional and personal setbacks, or so they seemed at the time."

"Never mind that," they said. "The important thing is, you saw what was missing and did something about it. You must be thrilled"—they gestured with a sweep of their arm—"by all of this."

I looked around the gleaming home of Mahoney's Bagels, at hungry guests being helped by Pete and charmed by Isabel. I said, yes, I was elated—who wouldn't be?—but at the same time feeling foolish: I'd never understood the void until I filled it.

Postcard of the Crookedest Street in the World

Dear Harriet & Pete,
   Nan is homesick already and generally a pain in the ass. Won't drink, won't shop, signs books with drippy poems sent along by you-know-who. She gets the angry women in her line, I get the serious male readers (ha ha). She plugs Perry's show (WHICH YOU'RE TAPING, RIGHT?) every time she opens her mouth. Getting tons of wear out of the black velvet jumpsuit. Sacramento tomorrow.

                                        Love you both,

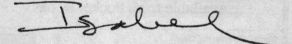